MY NEW ORLEANS,
GONE AWAY

ALSO BY PETER M. WOLF

Land Use and Abuse in America: A Call to Action

Hot Towns: The Future of the Fastest Growing Communities in America

Land in America: Its Value, Use and Control

The Future of the City: New Directions in Urban Planning

The Evolving City: Urban Design Proposals by Ulrich Franzen and Paul Rudolph

Eugène Hénard and the Beginning of Urbanism in Paris 1900–1914

MY NEW ORLEANS, GONE AWAY

A Memoir of Loss and Renewal

PETER M. WOLF

DELPHINIUM BOOKS
Harrison, New York • Encino, California

For Phelan, Alexis, Austin, India, Emory, and Elias

". . . to leave some tracks in the sand . . ."

Author's Note

Some of the details in this book are refracted through the imperfections of memory. Research, letters, diaries, and interviews with people acknowledged herein have helped with authentication and contributed in countless ways. Nevertheless, various conversations and events have been reconstructed as approximations. In some cases I have changed the names of individuals, and disguised aspects of their lives, to protect their privacy.

The end of this memoir presents the dark moods and uncertain prospects that inundated New Orleans in Hurricane Katrina's immediate aftermath. Happily, much has changed in a few years. My New Orleans is again a place of hope and revival.

Contents

Foreword

By Calvin Trillin

Peter Wolf was born a day after I was. Naturally, he has always been like a son to me. That's why I was surprised to discover that the first mention of me in this book has Peter in the role of Henry Higgins and me as Eliza Doolittle—fetching, sure, but essentially clueless. The scene is a New Haven haberdashery, where Peter is helping transform me from an untutored public high school boy who had just arrived from Kansas City—let's not be afraid of the word *rube* here—into someone who appeared to be enrolled at Yale, if you didn't look too closely. It is a measure of his discretion that he manages to discuss my pre–New Haven wardrobe without any mention of bib overalls.

What became known as the Ivy League Style of clothing didn't reach the hinterlands until a couple of years after we had arrived at Yale. Peter owned the appropriate garments because his own secondary education had been at Exeter, a boarding school that prepared its student sartorially as well as academically for the Ivy League. He was not, however, one of the snooty ur-preppies that my high school friend Growler Ed Williams, who went to Princeton, used to refer to as "tweedy shitballs." Peter went to Exeter from New Orleans, and when he graduated he was still pure New Orleans. Aside from giving him a familiarity with sack suits and plain-front trousers, the years he put in at an eastern boarding school seemed to have had no more impact on his cultural core than living for a decade in Midland, Texas, had on George H. W. Bush, of Greenwich, Connecticut.

In some passages of this book, I appear as a witness, and I am prepared to attest that, in most cases, Peter's recollections of long-ago events square with my own. For instance, when during freshman year I showed up in his room to finish the geology project we had to hand in the next morning—we had been paired to do a report on the geology of West Rock (the seven-mile-long, sometimes 700 feet-high mountain ridge west of New Haven) for the course that many mush-head liberal arts majors took to satisfy the science requirement—he was at least as drunk as he says he was. When he spent a week in Paris while I was living there, just after college, he did indeed visit museums while I spent most of my time playing pinball in grubby Left Bank cafés. Of course, he could have mentioned how adroitly I manipulated the flippers on those pinball machines or how authentically I would mutter, if one of my best flips sent the ball into the wrong slot, *"Quelle ironie."* But I don't mention that as a complaint: This is Peter's story, not mine.

Preface

*S*unday evening, *August 28, 2005, East Hampton, New York.* Hurricane Katrina moves steadily across the Gulf of Mexico toward New Orleans, pushing an eighteen-foot storm surge.

"Peter, we're scared."

It's Gail calling again. "Our house is locked; no one is there. Do you think we should try to get back to New Orleans? We're in North Carolina."

"Don't," I caution. "The governor has issued evacuation orders."

I'd been watching news and on the phone all day, talking to relatives and friends in and out of the city about the approaching storm. It had swerved decisively toward New Orleans. More than a hundred thousand people were fleeing. Roads were jammed. Shelters were being hastily prepared. More than a quarter of the population had no means of escape.

"We want to go back," my sister continued. "Maybe we could save our house."

"You have to stay away, Gail," I said. "It's too dangerous. You couldn't even get through the National Guard security cordon."

"I'll check with you in the morning," she said, sad and distraught.

That afternoon I'd hosted croquet and a barbecue for my two children, their spouses, and my four young grandchildren. Afterward I'd hoped to enjoy the magical light cast by a long summer sunset. Instead, I was on edge. What would become of the city I'd left forty-two years before, had returned to so often, and still called home?

Early Monday morning. Katrina slams New Orleans. With sustained winds of seventy-five miles per hour, she's a serious but not ferocious hurricane. The levees appear to hold: water, wind, and rain damage is relatively light.

Monday night. Everything changes. Due to catastrophic structural failure, weak sections of the 350-mile-long levee system cave along the Industrial Canal, the Seventeenth Street Canal, and the London Avenue Canal. Water pours into the 80 percent of the city below sea level. The city's pumps, inundated, fail. "The bowl" fills up. First two feet, then higher and higher—in some areas water reaches above mantelpieces; in extreme cases it rises as high as fourteen feet. Fetid water mixed with oil, trash, and sewage stagnates; the air above turns rancid.

Tuesday. The rank, water-filled city is isolated: electricity, phone, and cable lines are out. No medical service is available. People die, at least a thousand. Others chop through roofs and await rescue. Entire parts of town are now destroyed. Mold begins to flourish. A third of the population becomes homeless. The storm's aftermath will be recognized as the worst civil engineering disaster in U.S. history.

Days pass. Along with people all over the world, I am ever more saddened by the area-wide human hardship, the physical chaos, the manifest government ineptitude. For six generations my family has been at home in New Orleans. At peril suddenly are relatives, friends, cherished neighborhoods, a unique blend of cultures, a landscape that I love, and a long family history in one place. Parts of New Orleans and the Gulf Coast that shaped my early drives, as well as my talents and tastes and habits, are vanishing.

Once I become aware of the scale of human tragedy and physical devastation, a wake-up call on the fragility of life, I decide that in my own way I will try to preserve what I can, and understand what I have not, by writing this memoir.

Peter M. Wolf
New York City, Spring 2013

Part I

MY NEW ORLEANS

1

Swinging

Dad didn't know I was afraid to try the swing. I hoped he'd never find out. When no one was looking, I'd lie across the wooden seat on my belly. I was sure Dad would be ashamed of my timidity.

Even late in the afternoon, when I'd been out of school for two hours, it was still hot. I hadn't told Mom or Georgie, our housekeeper and cook, that I was going to walk down our street, Brockenbraugh Court, to the empty lot at the corner of Metairie Road, the principal street leading into the city. They might have said it was too close to dinnertime. Dad had never been in the lot, but he drove past it every day on his way to work. So did Mom, on her way to play canasta or golf. There was no other way into town. My parents didn't know that the neighborhood boys met there every Saturday morning. When I looked down my street from the lot, I could see our one-story, light yellow ranch house two blocks away.

Metairie, where we lived, was a growing suburb in Jefferson Parish, adjacent to the city of New Orleans, which was in Orleans Parish. Our house was about four miles from the Seventeenth Street Canal, the parish line. So technically we did not live in the city of New Orleans, but Metairie was so close to the parish line that everyone considered it part of New Orleans.

Now I was at the swing. No one was around. No one was walking down the sidewalk. I was alone. The swing hung empty and motionless. Its long, fat ropes seemed to fall out of the gloomy moss and dark overhead branches of the oak tree; they smelled like old hay. The dry dirt beneath looked like a tan-and-brown finger painting stamped into the earth by the soles of our sneakers.

I approached, looked around again to see if anyone was watching, and listened closely for footsteps. Still no sound; no one was coming. I felt the worn-smooth board and tested its strength by pushing down hard on its center. It looked dangerously high off the ground. I examined the coarse hemp ropes. They seemed okay. I could see no signs of fraying where they rubbed against the holes that had been drilled into the seat.

As I had before, I doubled myself over the skinny wooden plank, my belly flat against it. My toes almost touched the ground and my arms dangled in the air. When I stretched my legs and extended my fingers, I could touch the dirt on both sides. There I hung: everything held steady. I lifted my head once again; no one was watching. Very gently I pushed with my toes. The swing started to sway and lift. I was losing control and was scared to do more.

That day I decided I had to sit on it. I wanted to know how it felt to be up there off the ground, like the other kids. After a few more minutes of lying across the board, I stood up and stepped back to my usual place at the edge of the clearing. I could picture my father's stern face, the way he would look if I got home late. I could see my mother recoil at the sight of my dusty shoes and hands. I knew that when I got home I needed to remember to take off my shoes and clean up before going inside.

I sidled up to the seat again and turned it upside down to check for cracks. I reexamined the two big rope holes and the knots. They were so tight that I couldn't begin to pry my fingers inside. So far, so good.

The giant oak was special, even in New Orleans, which had so many old ones. Its massive branches spread through the air in every direction, some arching over Brockenbraugh Court. Silvery Spanish moss mingled with shiny green leaves, filling the spaces between the massive, elongated limbs like knotted, curly beards.

Always, while the other kids were swinging, I only observed. None of them asked me why or when I was going to try. They ignored me as I stood out on the edge of the lot. I knew they called me a "pipsqueak" or "chicken" behind my back when they thought I couldn't hear.

The older guys did amazing tricks. Some of them would swing hard and then, once in the air, twist their bodies until the ropes intertwined one way, then unwound the other—all as they continued swinging, back and forth, back and forth. This was "the spin." The younger guys had their own, easier version, winding up the seat with both hands, squeezing through the ropes to sit, before twirling in all directions.

Thinking about their fun, how they looked at me and called me "chicken," and how Dad would be ashamed if he knew I only stood around watching, I ventured to touch the swing again. It felt as if I were approaching a dangerous, sleeping animal. I stood next to the motionless wooden plank, judging its height above both the ground and my knees. I glanced at the scooped-out dirt below and at the fresh sneaker patterns there. They looked like the flounder impressions I saw at low tide on the shallow edge of the Gulf of Mexico when I was at Gram's house in Pass Christian, Mississippi. Someone must have been here yesterday.

I looked around the clearing again. There was still no one coming, so, with my backside pressed against the hard wooden seat, I grasped the ropes as high up as I could reach. I rose onto my tiptoes and jumped up and backward. When my butt hit the board, it wobbled much more than I expected. I tightened my grip. My palms were sweating.

But I'd made it—I was on, sitting. My feet were off the ground. I squirmed to get balanced on the seat while the board swayed every which way. I was nervous and tense sitting way up there.

My legs, however, knew what to do. They bent backward at the knee. My body remained rigid, hands tight, knuckles white. As my lower legs swung backward, the board moved slightly. Thrusting my legs forward, I glided out into space; the horizon moved. I looked down. The earth flowed beneath me. I was under way!

As the swing rose and fell, the ground came up so fast I felt paralyzed. Then my grandmother's smiling face crossed into my mind's eye. Her steady gaze seemed to hang in front of me, her eyes sparkling with approval and applause. My stomach stopped trembling and my legs began to feel light, almost separate from my body.

I kicked out hard and pulled back with my arms. I leaned into the void. I let my body go. As the ground zoomed away I was propelled into space. Moments later, the earth raced up to meet me, then was gone again. I did it again and again, went higher and higher, farther up and faster down.

At the peak of my trajectory, the overhanging boughs and mossy shadows disappeared, giving way to deep, boundless, late-afternoon blue. The ropes shrieked in time with my motion. Wind rushed against my face in the warm southern light. I opened my mouth and let the air fly inside. The breeze filled my chest and the wind washed my face. With my mouth open wide, I arched my neck and looked up at the sky. The whole universe rocked and spun to my rhythm. I was not afraid.

I thought about jumping but didn't dare just yet. Instead, I stopped pumping, and let the swing glide slower and slower until it came to rest.

Back on the ground, I realized that it was nearly dark and I might be late for dinner. I jumped off the swing, which was now at a standstill. As I hit the solid earth, I felt dizzy, as if I were still in motion. The land felt hard and unsteady, as it did when I got out of Grandpa's skiff after fishing all morning with him in the Gulf.

I ran home, thrilled with my triumph, racing down the block and hopscotching over each crack in the sidewalk. In the fading light, all of the bushes seemed in bloom, a path of gardenias and azaleas lining my triumphal route. I imagined the other kids smiling.

At the back door, I washed my hands under the hose bib and unlaced my sand-filled shoes. Georgie was at her regular place at the stove, stirring a steaming pot with a long wooden spoon. Probably shrimp stew with rice, I thought, because the kitchen smelled of Tabasco and bay leaves.

Georgie smiled at me, her light Creole skin crinkling around her mouth. The cloudy, scratched lenses in her yellowing plastic eyeglass frames made her hazel eyes look so dim that I could barely see their outer rim of amber. "Dinner will be ready in a few minutes," she said. "Better wash your hands. Your mom and dad will be going out tonight."

I walked down the narrow hallway past my parents' bedroom. Their door was closed as usual. They liked to have a drink when Dad came home, without my younger sister, Gail, and me around. I walked through the living room, past the dining room, and back into the kitchen. When they were home, my parents always had supper in the dining room after Gail and I had finished our meal in the kitchen.

The radio was playing gospel music, Georgie's favorite. I liked the sound of the passionate, syncopated singing, but the words seemed strange to me, all about Jesus and punctuated with shouts of "Oh, yeah, Lord!" After filling our plates, Georgie sat down with us in her usual spot at the end of the brown, speckled, Formica counter, near the stove.

As we started to eat, Georgie flashed an amused smile my way and asked, "How come you were out of breath when you came in?"

"Well," I said, "I . . . uh . . . got on the swing in the lot near your bus stop. You know, where the big tree is?"

Georgie's eyes lit up. "You got on that high swing down there?"

As casually as I could I said, "Yeah, but it got late, so I ran all the way home."

We'd nearly finished eating when Mom and Dad walked in, all dressed up. Dad had on a tuxedo and Mom looked dressed for fancy cocktails. Even before they stepped into the room, I could hear Mom's raspy smoker's cough and smell her thick Joy perfume. It always smelled sour to me, since it was mixed with the cloud of cigarette smoke that accompanied her.

My parents stood behind us and off to the side near the sink. From my chair at the counter, it was hard to see them without twisting my head all the way around in an awkward and uncomfortable way. It was even harder to report my big news with them standing behind us, all dressed up and so obviously eager to leave. This is what they both lived for: to go out to restaurants, to gamble at Beverly (the casino along the river), and to visit late-night jazz joints in the French Quarter.

My father took a deep puff on his cigarette, exhaled, turned on the tap, flooded the ash, and then threw the butt into the garbage can. The smoke from Mom's unfiltered Camel spiraled near my face. That night their smoke seemed especially strong. My mother jotted down a telephone number. "We should be home by midnight," she said. "That's where to reach us, Georgie. Good night, kids."

I wanted to tell my father all about the swing and my victory but couldn't manage to say one word about it. He paused with his hand on the doorknob and, looking down at us, said, "Mind Georgie, and go to bed when she says it's time."

I wanted to shout, Wait a minute, Dad—I did it! I imagined his face lighting up with that big smile of his, the one I saw mostly when company was over. I'm proud of you, son, he'd answer beaming.

Dad glanced over. "Peter, how did your neck get so dirty?"

Without making eye contact, I replied, "I was down at the empty lot playing."

"What were you doing down there so late in the day?"

"Oh . . . nothing much," I mumbled.

2

Separate and Unequal

When I was seven years old, I got hooked on fishing "across the lake" with my grandfather, my father's dad, Albert J. Wolf, as he was known downtown. Spending time alone with my grandparents at their weekend house in Pass Christian was the happiest time of my childhood. In 1942, the war was raging abroad, but you wouldn't know it in Pass Christian, which was situated sixty-five miles east of New Orleans, beyond Lake Pontchartrain, past the swampy Rigolets passageway connection to Lake Borgne, then over the state line into Mississippi.

During the war years, while my father was overseas, my mother and sister never went with us to "the Pass," and my mother never went there with friends, either. She needed her allotment of rationed gas just to get to and from work, first at the Higgins P.T. boat factory and then at Godchaux's store. Years later I learned from my mother that she was always bitter that my grandparents somehow had enough gas to continue their routine right through the war, and didn't invite her and Gail to share their weekend house. I also came to understand in later years that she resented my grandparents' interest in me, their lack of admiration for her, and their meager attention to my sister.

When my father got back into a postwar working routine, my parents still never went across the lake with his parents. My mother and Gram did not get along. Mom considered her selfish, and Gram thought of my mother as superficial. Dad was not interested in being with his parents over an entire weekend. Before the war, Mom and Dad did sometimes take friends to the Pass for the weekend when my grandparents were traveling in Europe to visit cotton mills, as they did every summer while Grandpa was in the cotton business, before he became a stockbroker.

My grandmother, Carrie Godchaux, became Carrie Godchaux Wolf when she married Grandpa. She was my link to the huge New Orleans Godchaux-Weis family. It was she who introduced me to her family members by telling me stories long before I met any of them. I got to know the characters in the drama of her life from their modest beginnings. She told me about two penniless young boys, unknown to each other, named Leon Godchaux (born 1824) from Herbeville in Alsace, France, and Julius Weis (born 1826) from Klingen, a small village near Landau in the Palatinate, Germany; about how they scraped together the fare, and crossed the Atlantic in steerage to New Orleans, arriving in 1837 (Godchaux) and 1845 (Weis); about how their separate families thrived, as these onetime peddlers became prominent businessmen, and eventually intertwined when my grandmother's mother, Henrietta Weis, married Paul Godchaux in 1884. These founders, I learned, became large-scale business successes in sugar plantations, cotton brokerage, and retail. They were also charitable icons involved in the founding of Temple Sinai, the first Reform Jewish congregation in the city; a home for orphans; and the principal hospital in town, Touro Infirmary, so named because its first location was on property originally donated by Judah Touro. But she told me so much at once about people I'd heard nothing about ever before that a lot of it didn't sink in.

Grandpa, on the other hand, was from out of town. He was born in Bayou Sara, a tiny warehouse and trading community that clung perilously to the east bank of the Mississippi River sixty miles upriver from New Orleans. He never talked much about his family or his childhood, so what I learned about him came from Gram. My grandparents, Carrie and Albert, married in 1906. At the time, Gram was twenty-one and Grandpa twenty-five.

When I began to go "across the lake" (as we put it in those days) alone with my grandparents, they were in their fifties. They'd pick me up at four o'clock on Friday, after the stock market closed. As my grandfather was by then a partner of the nationally prominent Merrill Lynch, Pierce, Fenner & Beane brokerage firm (his firm, Fenner & Beane, in New Orleans, had merged in 1941 with a New York brokerage to form the new company), he had earned the freedom to come and go as he pleased. However, he always stayed at his desk until the close, even on Fridays.

Going "across the lake" didn't mean crossing any particular lake. It meant driving U.S. Route 90, the old Chef Menteur Highway, east out of town. We traveled in my grandparents' ultrasleek cream-colored, four-door Packard Clipper. Before we started out, its curved sides had been polished and its windows shined by their New Orleans–based driver and houseman, Herbert. Once beyond the plants and factories around the Industrial Canal, we'd loop the southeastern edge of Lake Pontchartrain—the forty-five-mile-long, twenty-five-mile-wide watery northern boundary of New Orleans. For a couple of miles we were so close to its shore that it felt as if I could see the entire length of the lake. But in fact it was so immense that the far shore wasn't visible in any direction, even in the clearest weather. It made me think of the ocean, which I'd never seen, and of New Orleans as a sort of colorful seaside town, like the ones shown in magazines featuring the French Riviera.

The road then moved through the swampy Rigolets passage between Lake Pontchartrain and Lake Catherine and Lake Borgne, at times on a raised roadbed and at others on a causeway. In the water, just a few feet beneath us, were virgin stands of cypress, tupelo gum, and water oak. I saw lily pads, rustling grasses, immobile turtles, an occasional alligator, and lots of swimming water moccasins, their beady black heads visible in the sluggish current at the apex of their V-shaped wake. Those little triangular heads, just visible above the turgid water, made me shiver.

After crossing the Pearl River Bridge, we'd be on higher ground, where overgrown pine, beech, magnolia, gum, and oak trees flourished and wild turkey grazed along the roadside.

Once past the villages of Waveland and Henderson Point, we'd hum across the metal treads of the Bay St. Louis Bridge. "There's the water tower," Grandpa would say. "Ten minutes and we'll be there." One more sharp turn southward and there it was: the open sky and the Gulf, a vast, watery expanse extending to Mexico. We'd arrived at our destination: Pass Christian, Mississippi.

Charlie was always there waiting to help unload the car. "How're you doing, Mr. Charlie?" I'd ask through the backseat window.

From the day we met, I felt happy to be near Charlie Johnson and curious about his life. Bent over from the middle of his back, he appeared unbelievably tiny, thin, and old. His nearly black eyes were yellow-rimmed with age and as dark as his skin. When he spoke to me, his wizened face filled with a smile so broad, the curved wrinkles ran up into his short, curly gray hair. His hands were dried out, leathery and arthritic.

Charlie seemed so old that I thought maybe he'd been a slave before the Civil War. Surely his parents had been. But I could never ask him; I felt ashamed to talk about slavery with Charlie. He was older than my grandparents and could have been born before 1865, which was only seventy-seven years earlier. I didn't ask my grandparents, either. They weren't especially interested in Charlie's personal life or that of any of their servants—or, for that matter, the lives of any black people. In this way, they were distinctly old-fashioned, conservative southerners. Indeed, I rarely heard them discuss blacks in an inquisitive way.

We were living in the segregated South, at a time when the legal foundations of segregation had not yet been challenged. One day, walking with my grandfather in the commercial center of Pass Christian, I heard him refer to a cluster of young black kids playing in a vacant lot off Second Street as "pickaninnies." My grandparents were, after all, products of the post–Civil War New Orleans resurgence, part of what became a mercantile elite with strong connections to the upper-middle-class Victorian customs that endured in the South.

Charlie always called me "Partner" and I called him "Mr. Charlie," innocent of the convention in those days that white people did not address black men as mister. To me it was a term of affection rather than an honorific. (I was certainly unaware that "Mr. Charlie" was a black expression for an oppressive white man.) I never heard Charlie complain. He also never shared much about his family. The only person he ever mentioned was his daughter, Rose, who had several children, was a secretary, and lived in Atlanta. I never saw his house. He had no car or truck. He walked the two miles along the Gulf seawall to and from the village to work.

Charlie's job encompassed every chore that involved the outdoors, although sometimes he fixed breakfast if the cook had not yet arrived. Before we set out to fish, he got the outboard motor working, testing it in a water-filled, cut-down oil drum. He cleaned the fish we caught. He washed the car. He raked the fallen pinecones and set up the hammock under the two big pines just beyond the screen porch. Charlie also kept the green, slatted wooden blinds on the porch in repair, and "DDT'd" the house if mosquitoes got through doors and window screens. He set the fire in the living room on winter nights, and he rolled up the rugs and changed the slipcovers come summer.

My grandparents called their modest weekend cottage, built in 1932, "Shackling." At that time, my grandfather was in the export cotton business. *Shackling* was an industry code word used in transatlantic cable negotiations that meant "the best we can do."

Shackling and the rest of Pass Christian were protected from the brownish waters of the Gulf by a seawall comprising nine descending, rough concrete steps, which hurt my bare feet until they toughened up during the summer. This wall, whose flat top was about fifteen feet above the average tide, extended a long way, beginning at Henderson Point and following the shore east to the Alabama border.

Behind the seawall, land had been filled and built up to contain the two lanes of U.S. 90. The narrow macadam lanes were separated by a grassy terrain twenty yards wide and filled with native azalea, clumps of grasses, and tall pine trees that looked as if they'd long ago migrated from the nearby woods. Over the years, paths had been scoured through this terrain from each house along "the Front," as the coastal strip was called, to the entrance to each house's individual pier, which jutted into the Gulf.

Because of the highway's narrow lanes and its verdant median, the visual impact of U.S. 90 from Shackling was nominal. It seemed to me as if my grandparents' house fronted directly on the Gulf, visible through a maze of tall evergreens growing luxuriantly through the sandy soil in their front yard and through the highway "neutral ground," as we called it.

Once inside Shackling, I felt as if I were safely perched on the edge of the earth, with mysterious, boundless water in front and deep, primal woods behind. A wide, screened-in porch faced the Gulf and extended the length of the house. It caught the breeze, which might be the only air moving for hundreds of miles inland. This was the reason that anyone who could afford to live on the Front would do so in those years before air-conditioning.

One end of the porch was furnished like a living room. There were two bamboo couches and chairs covered in a canvas with broad white and green stripes, and a card table set up permanently near the outer corner.

Friday and Saturday nights, Gram and Grandpa and I talked on the porch. Unlike my parents, they didn't go out. They had no interest in leaving home, or me. Sometimes, on long summer evenings, instead of talking we'd read or work on a puzzle spread on the card table or listen to the sea pound at the seawall. We'd watch the fireflies light up the sand beneath the pines. You could hear the occasional car pass on the highway, but the sound seemed far away and was muffled by the rhythmic crash of waves and the chatting racket of the cicadas, intermingled with the deep bass croaks of a family of bullfrogs that lived in a nearby marsh.

The weekends with my grandparents were so peaceful that they sometimes made me wonder about my parents' contrasting restlessness, their desire always to be going out on the town. I knew from Gram's stories about taking "the children" to Europe on Grandpa's business trips that when Dad was growing up he hadn't been interested in contemplative activities like visiting museums or sitting quietly in parks with his family. He had always wanted to be independent. I would later come to understand that Dad felt driven to distinguish himself from his own successful father and from the generations of cultured and entrepreneurial men and women in the Godchaux-Weis clan, who were still prominent in New Orleans during his lifetime. I would also come to see that when he was younger, Grandpa had been just as restless and ambitious as my father was, and that the two were far more similar than I could see as a child. But that understanding came to me much later. For now, I found balm in the peacefulness of being with my tranquil grandparents.

Pass Christian was nothing more than a tiny dot on the map of Mississippi. City people from New Orleans with adequate means had built informal weekend houses along the Front to escape the debilitating summer heat and the still-lurking danger of yellow fever. The lots were wide enough and the houses built far enough apart and landscaped so densely, with bamboo along each property line, that neighboring buildings were invisible. Pine forest fanned out at the back of each deep lot, blending into undisturbed woodlands nourished by shallow, slow-moving, sandy-bottomed streams that meandered to the Gulf.

Pass Christian was predominantly a commercial fishing community. Its major commerce and landmark was the jumbled assembly of docks, concrete ramps, and tin Quonset huts set atop a rocky breakwater promontory leading straight into the Gulf and which we called the shrimp factory. I could see the shrimp factory from my grandparents' pier. On mornings when Grandpa took me there to buy shrimp, I loved to hang around and watch the fishing boats return with their catch. The huge Gulf shrimp were still snapping and their pale shells translucent as the captain scooped out a bucketful from his holding tank.

Protecting the whole conglomeration of factory buildings and sheltered fishing port was a sturdy barrier of curved jetty walls made of boulders, broken concrete, and enormous piles. In constant need of repair, these creosote-soaked timbers were driven deep into the Gulf bed by a steam-driven pile driver mounted on a barge; it always seemed to be pounding and chugging and sending up smoke and a clamor. The small harbor provided safe haven to the home fleet of shrimpers and fishing draggers that worked as far east as Destin, Florida, and west to Bay St. Louis.

On Saturday mornings, Grandpa usually took me fishing, my favorite weekend activity. The three of us would sit down for a breakfast that Charlie had prepared. Before we shoved off, Gram would say, "Bring me back some croakers for lunch." Croakers—small, sturdy fish with yellow-and-brown-striped tops and small scales that didn't cut your hand—sounded like a frog croaking when you held them by the gills to remove the hook. Other than catfish, they were the most prevalent fish at what was known as first reef. When breakfast was over, we'd head for the pier. Charlie accompanied us, pushing the wheelbarrow that held the outboard, tackle, poles, and oars. He had lived all his life at Pass Christian, but he never went fishing with us. Having never learned to swim, he was afraid of the water.

Grandpa's skiff had been built in the Pass Christian boatyard, which consisted of two beat-up metal sheds next to the shrimp factory. Painted battleship gray, it was seaworthy enough to make it past first reef, even out to second reef—another half mile—in moderately rough weather. It wasn't advisable to venture as far as Cat Island, about five miles offshore.

With a check of our gear and a wave to Charlie to cast us off, we were ready to set out for first reef. Everyone at the Pass—fishermen and city people alike—referred to the long line of oyster shells that ran in front of Pass Christian about a mile offshore as "first reef." All the fishermen said it had once been one of the greatest oyster beds in the Gulf. Now it was still a distinct deposit of oyster shells, about four miles long and two hundred yards wide, where the fish congregated to feed.

"What do you see out there, Grandpa?" I sometimes asked.

"Nothing you don't," he answered. "But when I get out here, I see things inside my head more clearly. It's a place I can think."

I knew he liked the peace and quiet, so I didn't try to interrupt it by talking too much, the way Gram sometimes did. But when I had a question or wanted to tell him about something that had happened at school or had a problem with my fishing equipment, he always listened and tried his best to help. Grandpa taught me more by showing than by telling—about fishing and about a lot of things—out there on the Gulf.

I never asked Grandpa about my father, about his childhood and whether he and his grandpa ever fished together. I would have had to ask, because Grandpa rarely volunteered anything. He was not a storyteller. Gram would tell me stories about Dad and his brother, Jimmy, and his sister, Caroline. She told me how, as a boy, Dad beat up on Jimmy, his inquisitive, quiet, and creative younger brother; how he fought with Caroline, his older sister, and sought to terrorize her friends when they visited. But Grandpa did not talk spontaneously as Gram did about his children, his own relatives, or even his childhood upriver. He would have told me about Dad if I had asked. But it never once occurred to me. By the time Shackling was built, Dad had just graduated from Yale. In the years that I went to Pass Christian, I thought of Grandpa and Dad as being completely separate.

At the Pass we kept our live bait, usually shrimp, inside the starboard half of the skiff's well. Frank Trone, a young black man who lived in town and worked for my grandparents in the afternoon as Charlie's assistant, caught our bait shrimp alongside the pier in a net at low tide. On the falling tide, he'd wade into the water in boots and cast the seine. The net was made of thin cotton twine and had small lead sinkers tied all the way around its edge. When folded and hung to dry, it was only two yards long. But when Frank tossed the net with a magical flip of his wrist, it fanned into the air as a swirling, shimmering circle with a diameter of six feet, before falling quietly upon the Gulf. The oblong sinkers dropped quickly to the bottom, pulling the big ring of tightly woven twine straight down.

Even on a cloudless night, we never could see the stars clearly from the porch, because of the pine tree branches. Gram would suggest: "Let's go out to the pier. My star chart shows an interesting configuration for tonight." We'd start down the driveway. At the highway, Gram and Grandpa would take my hand. They would stand at the edge of the road for a long time, looking in both directions. If we could see headlights, we had to wait. Sometimes, with the continuous roar of the waves and the insects, we wouldn't hear a car until it was nearly upon us.

Once we reached the pier we'd walk out over the water, with the starlit night all around us. The moon would illuminate a silhouetted view of neighboring piers and nearby pilings and skiffs at rest, and cast its own bright streak across the water. A fresh breeze often blew away the hot air. We'd sit down on the bench at the end of the pier and use the pier rail as our backrest. Gram would check her chart with the flashlight, lighting it just long enough to get her bearings. Grandpa and I would stare upward into the darkness until we were sure we had seen what Gram wanted us to. As I listened to the water lap at the pilings and gazed at the stars, I always felt lulled by the sound of their soft voices and totally protected in their presence, enveloped in their love.

The weekend at Shackling always ended right after Sunday lunch. We would pull out of the driveway in time to hear Milton Cross introduce the weekly rebroadcast of the Metropolitan Opera from New York on the car's Philco. We were quiet. I liked hearing the music fill the space of the car, but I couldn't understand a word of the singing.

3

The War and Wounded

Soon after the Japanese bombed Pearl Harbor, on December 7, 1941 (the day after my sixth birthday), and the United States declared war, my father joined the U.S. Army Air Forces. He spent the war years in the Pacific as a communications and intelligence officer, moving from island to island as land was secured for air bases. For all those years, I couldn't get the opening line of the Air Force Song—"Off we go into the wild blue yonder"—out of my head. It still pops up all the time. We didn't see my father or speak to him for more than three years, from the time I was six until I was nearly ten, but we did receive heavily censored thin blue airmail envelopes full of blacked-out lines. My grandmother kept a wall map at her house with pushpins stuck in every war-torn island where we thought he might be.

In August 1945 the United States devastated Hiroshima and Nagasaki and terrified the rest of the civilized world. Shortly after the celebration of V-J Day in September, we got word that Dad was headed for Seattle, where he would be discharged. My mother made hasty plans to meet him. I can still see the taxi leaving Brockenbraugh Court that Saturday morning, bound for the railroad station, where she would begin her long trip from New Orleans to Seattle. She would be bringing him home in a week.

For the first time ever, my sister and I were going to be staying at the house in Metairie alone with Georgie.

I couldn't remember what Dad looked like. I walked into Mom's room to examine the photograph of him in his military uniform that she kept on her dressing table. He looked beautiful. Georgie made us a special weekend breakfast of pancakes with butter, maple syrup, and lots of crispy bacon, our favorite. Right after breakfast I said to Georgie, "Bye. See you at lunchtime. I'm going to meet the guys at the lot on the corner."

"Okay," she said, "but don't leave the neighborhood without letting me know. You know the rules. You're not allowed to cross Metairie Road, don't forget."

"I know, I know," I replied.

On my way, I noticed that the old swing was gone, the largest limb free of those thick, rough ropes. Gray-green Spanish moss still filled the spaces between the dark branches, many of which were as thick as a normal tree trunk. One enormous limb that we were now old enough to climb arched thirty feet above the street. Another emerged high up on the trunk and then curved down nearly to the ground. That was our staircase.

When I got to our usual place at the base of our big oak, one of my gang asked, speaking to no one in particular, "So what are we gonna do?"

No one bothered to answer; we knew the choices. We could ride our bikes around Brockenbraugh, Homestead, and Elmeer, the streets in our immediate neighborhood, to check out what was going on. Or we could work on the fort in the vacant lot between Malcolm Cressy's house and mine. We could go down to the murky canal toward the lake with some bread and string to catch crawfish, and maybe also hunt frogs. Or we could spend the morning climbing our tree. But we knew what we'd be doing come evening. We were going to the movies.

After supper I made a final stop in my room before leaving to meet the guys again. I opened my top desk drawer and pulled out a special instrument that I was going to use in place of a flashlight. Instead of being shaped like a cylinder, it was broad and flat and made of brown plastic, with a keypad on top twice the size of my hand. Inside were four flashlight batteries. Protruding from the flat front of the gadget was a cone-shaped flash lightbulb. The light could be turned on two ways. I could press an ON switch and the bulb would stay illuminated, or I could depress the key and each time it struck the contact plate the bulb would blink on. The bulb remained lit as long as you held down the key.

The gadget came with a guide. It was made especially for kids to learn to send signals in flashes of light in Morse code—a long light for dashes, a short light for dots—the way secret silent messages were transmitted between ships at sea and troops in the field. Malcolm had one, too. We'd signal to each other across the vacant lot from our bedroom windows after dark.

In front of the Metry, our local movie house, the ticket line moved fast. This is where on weekends I met my friends from Metairie Park Country Day, the private day school I attended. Most of them lived nearer school in larger houses than mine. They were all there. At the ticket booth, I was ready with two nickels and two pennies, just like every other kid. We never saw dimes during the war because silver was at a premium.

And just like every other kid in line, I was white. Very few black people lived in Metairie. But those who did would not have been permitted to enter the Metry by the front door; and in that small suburban theater there was no side door, no back door, and no black-only balcony. In the big movie theaters downtown, where I was sometimes taken by my mother on a Saturday morning to see a children's special, the water fountain had a sign mounted above it that said WHITE ONLY. Black patrons were required to buy their tickets at a side door around the corner, then climb a stairway and sit on benches in a restricted balcony. To the white patrons, they were invisible.

Inside the Metry, no one asked to see our tickets. I think the guy at the door knew each one of us; after all, we were there every week. We'd stop at the neon-lit candy counter for a hot batch of popcorn. It cost one nickel for a small bag.

Then we walked single-file down the aisle to the thirteenth row on the left, our regular spot. No one else sat there on Saturdays for the seven o'clock show. Every group of kids had its own seats, and no one would dare challenge another's turf. The entire theater was filled with kids from various schools, almost all boys, from neighborhoods all the way out to the end of Metairie Road. I didn't know most of them, but I knew where they sat at the movies, and I could guess which neighborhoods they lived in. The kids closer to the lake had longer hair, spoke louder, and drawled more. We were there to see new releases or reruns of westerns or war films, which were all that was ever shown at the seven o'clock Saturday night feature. I got to see John Wayne in *Tall in the Saddle*. And none of us cared how many times they replayed *Guadalcanal Diary* or *Thirty Seconds over Tokyo*. Buffalo Bill was okay, but not anyone's favorite.

By 8:30 p.m. we were out. Claren's Drug Store, known as "the Drug," was a half block away at the end of the Metry Shopping Center. We walked past the darkened windows of Algie Hailey's Barber Shop, where we all had our hair cut; past Metairie Hardware, owned by the Schexsnayders, where our families bought household stuff; and Metry Bakery, where our birthday cakes were made. Finally we marched through the recessed glass entry into Claren's, the only store that stayed open that late.

Inside, the pinball machine was on the right, its back wedged into the display window. A round table where no one ever sat was on the left. The floor was made of small, white hexagonal tiles; where the walls met the floor there was a four-inch-high black tile border. At the back of the store, wooden cabinets filled with pills, bandages, and other medicinal items were stacked to the ceiling. We crowded up against the Drug's main fixture: its long, white marble-topped soda fountain. Mr. Claren, who knew each of us by name, mixed our cherry Cokes and scooped out ice cream for the milk-shake orders.

We took our drinks to the second wooden booth in the back. "Man, I'd like to see another Roy Rogers next week," Ken Newburger said, once we were settled. Almost everyone agreed.

Herb Schneidau, the smartest guy in the class, protested: "Not me. He's too much like Hopalong Cassidy. I'd rather see Cassidy than some copy."

At nine o'clock sharp we headed home in various directions. I walked with the kids from Brockenbraugh, my immediate neighbors. At that time of night, Metairie Road was filled with headlights, so we didn't need to switch on our flashlights. Fifteen minutes later, we turned into Brockenbraugh Court. As we walked past the big oak, lights from the intermittent stream of cars lit up its lower branches and cast a wavering pattern of lines and shadows across our path. The farther we walked from the highway, the darker it became. We gradually quit talking and began to walk closer to one another.

As the darkness deepened, the shadows disappeared—even our own. I unhitched the transmitter from my belt as the other guys fired up their flashlights. Beams of light swung here and there, lighting up weeping willow branches, bamboo stands, dense bougainvillea, and scaly roots that had cracked the sidewalk.

"Single file," Bill Wells, who lived across the street from us, commanded in a whisper as the sidewalk narrowed into a broken path—part concrete, part shells, part dirt. We were a slow-moving column of tired ten- and eleven-year-old boys groping their way home. Our thin light beams landed on the ground just ahead of our footsteps. Beyond lay the pitch-black Louisiana night.

I was in front, the point man. We were within a block of my

house. My eyes had become accustomed to the dark, but I was still nervous. My bulb cast just enough light for me to move forward with assurance, one step at a time. I pointed my dim beam at the trunk of an ebony tree. In my imagination, we were now troops prowling through a dangerous jungle, all sounds deliberately extinguished to elude the canny Japanese who were lying in wait to ambush our detail. I clutched my Morse code transmitter and patted the outside of my pants pocket with my left hand to be sure my pocketknife was still there.

Suddenly, my reverie was shattered. I heard the very real thudding gait of an animal racing toward us. The muffled gallop grew louder and approached faster. I aimed my Morse code flashlight at it. As I thrust my hand up and outward, the dim beam of my light framed an immense black throat lined by dark red gums with white fangs, all hurtling through space toward my head. I had no chance to duck.

* * *

The next thing I knew, I woke up alone and my whole body hurt. I was groggy and scared. I felt bandages around my head, across my left eye, and down my back.

Where was I? What had happened? I was not in the street but in a bed. Where were my friends, I wondered? I fell back into a stupor. When I woke up again, I was able to recall being picked up off the sidewalk and put into a car for a very long ride. I touched my bandaged face. Pain flickered in my head, shot down my neck, and moved across my back. My left eye inside the bulky bandage burned like an ember. I could tell from the light coming through the window that it was now daytime.

Then a nurse entered. She approached my bed looking, I thought, extremely sad. "You're in Charity Hospital," she said. "A big dog attacked you. You've been here all night. How do you feel? Are you awake?"

I mumbled, "I guess so."

She looked at me hard, as if to determine how I felt, and touched my head lightly. "You sho' lucky that dog's tooth just missed yo' eye," she said.

When I didn't respond, she continued, "He dug his claws into yo' back, too, but that'll heal up okay." She stopped talking for a minute and examined the bandages on my face and eye, then turned me sideways to inspect the ones on my back.

Exhausted and confused, I had to stop her. "What happened to me?"

"After that dog attacked you," she said, "you collapsed on the sidewalk. You fainted. Then he raced down the street and attacked two other people. He bit one woman on the arm, then bit the leg of a man getting into his car. He had rabies. The sheriff's posse shot him down a few hours later."

"Where are they?" I asked. "And what about my friends?"

"Don't know nothin' 'bout your friends," she said. "The man picked you and the lady up, then brought you all here. They're in rooms down the hall."

"Oh," I said. "What day is this and what time is it?"

"It's Sunday morning," she said. "You're in Charity Hospital. Do you understand?"

"Yes," I said.

"Now, who are you?" the nurse asked. "And how do I reach your folks?"

I had been lying unidentified in the biggest public hospital in New Orleans for more than twelve hours. At that point I didn't realize that I'd gone into shock after the attack and that I might lose my left eye. Also, I was hearing about rabies for the first time.

I told the nurse, "My mother is on a train to the West Coast. She's gone to meet my father. You could call Georgie or my grandmother."

"Who's Georgie?"

"Our housekeeper."

"I'm gonna call your grandmother," she said.

I gave her Gram's name, but I was too groggy and upset to recall her phone number.

A few minutes later, the telephone rang. It was Gram. The nurse talked to her; then it was my turn. As I struggled to stay conscious through the haze of painkillers and sleeping pills, I heard her say, "Petie, we'll be there in a few minutes, as fast as we can." On hearing her voice, I felt safe and saved. I would be going to my grandmother's house. Going to her house was so much better than going home.

When Gram walked into my hospital room, her hair was not up on top of her head in a neat twist the way she usually wore it—she'd clearly rushed out the door. Her arms stretched out toward me, seemingly yards long. Though her mouth was smiling, her eyes were wet. She touched my wrist, then leaned over and patted my shoulder. She ran her hand along the bandages wrapping my head. She held me in her arms. I could feel my body relax and my pain ease. I pushed the good side of my head into her chest and took a deep breath to keep from crying.

Before we left the hospital, Gram went down the hall to thank the man who'd brought me there and took his address. She wanted to send him a present.

My convalescence began at Gram and Grandpa's house. The first evening, their cook, Myria, brought supper on a dark wooden tray. I had no appetite. I couldn't taste the oyster soup, much less the toast or scrambled eggs Gram had asked her to prepare for me. Gram sat in a chair beside the bed as I tried to nibble at the food. "You're going to be fine," she assured me. "Try to eat a little something."

"I'm not hungry."

"Try some soup or a few bites of egg," she said. "You need to eat to regain your strength and get better."

"I'm not hungry and I hurt."

Then she told me, "We decided not to call your mother and father. It would spoil their reunion. They've not seen each other for more than three years."

"That's okay, Gram," I said. "I'm sure you know the right thing to do. Do you think they'll be mad at me?"

"How could you think that?"

"Because I might spoil their vacation if they do find out, or when they get home."

"We're not going to let this spoil their vacation, so don't worry. Try to be quiet, and eat and sleep."

"I'm glad you're not going to try to reach them," I said. But a part of me felt lonely and abandoned by my parents.

"As a special treat," Gram said, "since you're not supposed to use either eye, before you go to sleep I'll read you a story."

"I'd like that."

"How about a story by my favorite Louisiana writer when I was a young girl? It's about New Orleans in the old days. His name is Lyle Saxon."

Before I left her house six days later, Gram gave me her first edition of Saxon's *Fabulous New Orleans*. It was full of illustrations by E. H. Suydam of all the important buildings and sites in the French Quarter.

The next morning my grandmother had finished a new crochet project. She must have worked far into the night. It was a very large heart made with yarn so purple that it practically glowed in the dark. She had sewn a large safety pin into its back, and after breakfast she pinned the handmade Purple Heart to my pajama pocket, over my own heart.

"This is your decoration for valor," she said.

"Thanks, Gram. I'll tell you something strange. Just before the attack, I imagined I was in the war and in danger. Now I've actually been wounded and won a decoration."

Two days later, the rabies vaccine arrived from Atlanta by emergency air shipment; there had been none available in New Orleans. My grandmother took me to the doctor for my first shot. On the stairs, just before we got to Dr. Graubarth's door, I was so apprehensive that I fainted.

Inside the office, I watched Dr. Graubarth take a flat, greenish box, about one inch high and eight inches square, out of his refrigerator. He unsealed the lid. Inside I saw a compact kit with many compartments holding shiny hypodermic needles and a small syringe. Below them were two rows of small glass vials, each filled with a viscous, milky fluid and sealed with a red rubber cap.

Dr. Graubarth removed the syringe and one needle. I started to feel sweaty. He talked to me while he inserted the needle into the syringe, but he kept his eyes on what he was doing. He raised the bottle, holding it upside down, then drew back on the plunger and pulled in the serum.

"This may hurt or burn," he said. "You choose which arm we'll start with. Tomorrow it will be the other one."

"The left," I said. "I'm right-handed."

"Are you ready?" he asked. Gram held my hand. Dr. Graubarth pinched the skin of my upper arm, wiping it with alcohol before giving me what would be the first of twenty-one daily injections. The serum burned all the way to the bone. Afterward, I threw up.

Seven days after the attack, my mother and father returned to New Orleans, expectant and excited. They arrived home, knowing nothing of what had happened to me. Georgie simply told them that I was at my grandparents' house and that my sister was there, too.

When they walked into Gram's living room, my head was still bandaged to protect my eye, which had not yet been examined. My back was slathered in medicated gauze held firmly with adhesive tape. My left eye had been closed since the injury; whether or not I would lose sight in it was still uncertain. Jagged scars had begun to grow the length of my upper back and across my shoulder. The question of whether the rabies would reach my brain was still unanswered. My parents didn't know any of this. They were expecting to celebrate with all of us Dad's momentous, heroic return from the war.

My mother and father stood at the arched entrance to Gram's big living room. Across the room, facing them, I lay on my side on the couch, wearing pajamas and a robe. The taupe velvet drapes had been closed to protect my eye, so the room was almost dark. By the light coming from the hall, I could see my father at a distance in his uniform, now decorated with captain's bars on his shoulders and a band of colorful service ribbons on his chest. My mother stood next to him. They stared at me. Neither spoke. Neither crossed the room. Mom looked stunned and guilty all at once. Dad looked bewildered. They both seemed to be scowling.

No one spoke except Gram, who said, "Petie's been in trouble, bitten by a rabid dog last week."

I wondered if Dad and Mom would rush over to me, to pat me on the arm and tell me I'd been brave. I wanted them to. Instead, I lay there staring at them across the room as they stared back. We stayed like that for what seemed like hours before anyone moved. I thought, They're angry because I've spoiled Dad's homecoming.

I barely recognized Dad, even though he still resembled the man in the photograph on Mom's dressing table. His hero's uniform sagged a bit on his thinner frame. Knowing he'd been promoted over the years to first lieutenant and then to captain, I tried to focus my good eye on his shoulder so I could see his silver double bars. He had earned them by facing down danger, sometimes even behind enemy lines. I tried to identify each of his tour-of-duty ribbons. While he'd been gone I'd studied all the air forces insignia, ribbons, and medals, but in the dimmed light I couldn't distinguish what his were.

Finally Dad walked slowly toward me, an unfamiliar, unsmiling soldier. I looked closely at his eyes, hoping to catch a smile and some sign that he recognized me. I'd forgotten that his eyes were blue. His face was unmarked and tan. I wondered if my own face would be scarred forever, and if I'd be able to see again out of both my eyes, which in contrast to his, were brown, like my mother's.

He got close, and stood above me looking down. My small body was covered in a wrinkled, red plaid robe. I felt wounded, and insignificant. He stared intently. It took me a moment to realize that he was staring not at my injured face or into my one good eye, but at my own service decoration, the immense and vivid Purple Heart shining on my chest.

"Hello, son," he said very quietly. He bent down toward me, his head near mine, and extended his hand to my shoulder. I reached to touch my hero's hand. "I'm glad you're finally home, Dad." I didn't know what else to say.

4

Being Jewish

My younger sister, Gail, and I were the only kids living on Brockenbraugh Court who went to a private school. We were also the only Jewish kids in our neighborhood. At Country Day, Judy Schwarz and I were the only Jewish kids in my class. But Judy lived in town, not in Metairie. Most of my friends, like Merrick, Ken, and Horty, went to Country Day, too, but weren't Jewish, and they lived nearer Country Day in big houses, in the neighborhood around Metairie Country Club, called Metairie Club Gardens.

When I was thirteen, my parents decided I should be confirmed.

Sunday school was at Temple Sinai, which I knew a little about from my aunt Ida, who was actually Gram's aunt, my great-great-aunt. My parents belonged to Temple Sinai, but they did not attend. Nor would they—or any other member of the congregation—ever call it a synagogue, and certainly not a shul, a word I'd never heard at the time. It was a temple, as in ancient Egypt, Greece, or Cambodia, or maybe the first temple in Jerusalem. Temple Sinai was situated in uptown New Orleans. There were almost no Jews in Metairie, where I lived, on the fringe of the city, and certainly no temple.

"Confirmed" is what kids—boys and girls alike—got at Temple Sinai, unlike at the more conservative synagogues in town, where boys got bar mitzvahed and girls got bat mitzvahed. Sunday school at Temple Sinai culminated in a year of confirmation class, which was held on Sunday mornings, just like the religious classes for Catholic and Protestant kids. For a number of years, while Jewish kids from in town had been going to Sunday school, I'd been doing other things—activities I enjoyed, like fishing with Grandpa at the Pass and playing war games with Ken and Merrick in suburban Metairie.

If Temple Sinai's rabbi, Julian Feibelman, and his wife, Mary Anna, hadn't been close social friends of my grandparents, I doubt that I would have been admitted into the confirmation class, as I was in the fall of 1948, without any previous study preparation. All I knew was what I'd picked up at a couple of large family seders. It was the equivalent of being admitted to the eighth grade without knowing how to write a complete sentence. I was accustomed to seeing silver-haired Rabbi Feibelman and his vivacious wife, with her perfectly coiffed, blue-tinged tresses, visiting in my grandparents' parlor, or visiting at our house on Christmas Day. Yes, on Christmas Day!

* * *

My family made a big deal over Christmas. Preparations started early in the fall. The Christmas season, and especially Christmas Day, was the most joyous time of the year. Our annual Christmas party was the only event that we planned and participated in together as a nuclear family and at which our friends and our parents' friends came together in one happy assembly.

The morning after Thanksgiving, my mother would remove from the garage the ten storage cartons marked CHRISTMAS DECO-RATIONS. Over the next three weeks, Santa Clauses in many shapes and sizes, reindeers dragging miniature sleighs, odd feathered birds, and tiny wreaths of baby pinecones seemed to sprout from every table, as well as the fireplace mantel and the dining room sideboard; the dining room table was the centerpiece. Two weeks before Christmas, Mom would raid our garden for fresh banana leaves, holly branches, and pine boughs, which she arranged as accents to our cherished holiday paraphernalia. Of the pervasive iconography of the season, only crèches and the baby Jesus were missing.

On Christmas Eve, preparing for our Christmas Day party, Mother would spend hours in the garden gathering clippings and then hours more arranging flowers, changing vases, rearranging the assortments, and placing each vase just so—standing back, turning it slightly, walking through the house one last time.

The food all came from either Garsaud's, which delivered, or Piggly Wiggly, which didn't, but was much less expensive. Both were nearby on Metairie Road. Gail and I helped wheel the many Piggly Wiggly grocery carts full of food and supplies that Mother selected. Of course, the shopping included: limes; lemons; hollow olives, and maraschino cherries (for the old-fashioneds and martinis); and a variety of scotch , bourbon, gin and vodka, along with masses of club soda and tonic water. All of the cooking was done at home by Willie-Mae, who was our cook and housekeeper. Before the preparations were over and the buffet set out, Willie-Mae miraculously created a huge steamed round of beef, roasted turkeys surrounded by oyster-based stuffing, glazed hams with cinnamon accents, abundant dressings, and as side dishes, cranberry relish served warm in a chafing dish, tomato aspic, fruit ring, creamed spinach, molded shrimp and crabmeat aspic, puréed sweet potatoes with marshmallow topping, sautéed green beans, and mixed green salad garnished with hearts of palm. The dessert was always homemade cheesecake, even better than the ones sometimes sent to us from Reuben's in New York. The only hors d'oeuvre was buttered and salted pecan halves, kept warm in small chafing dishes strewn about the living room, dining room, and bar area, with pots of Sterno glowing beneath them.

The trunk of our Christmas tree always had to be sliced down with a saw to fit under the ceiling in the corner of the living room. Dad or I would cut it just low enough to leave room for the spiky glass ornament that fit onto the highest stem. Then came "tying her fast," as Dad called it. Dad, who must have had visions of the tree toppling over, had anchored permanent hooks into the abutting corner walls. Once the stand was set and the tree rotated to everyone's satisfaction, he and I would climb ladders on each side and adjust the tree's position until it was perfectly straight. Then we'd tie off our guidelines, looped around the trunk in a slip knot. Once I was old enough, wearing gloves to protect my hands from the sharp needles and spikes on the branches, I'd string the lights in circular rows from top to bottom, plugging in female-to-male links between strands deep inside the foliage. We concealed the cord under the round red skirt that circled the base of the tree.

Mother unwrapped the tissue paper from around each ornament and handed them alternately to Gail and to me. Dad was in charge of repairs and rejiggering, refitting, and bending damaged hooks. His "shop" was next to Mom. Gail and I moved back and forth, stopping with each placement to gain approval. Then came tinsel. In the beginning, Gail and I threw great globs of it at the tree, hoping it would stick wherever it landed. Each time one of us did that, our parents would cry out, "No, no! That's not how it's done. Here, watch." Soon we learned to separate out one or two strands of the silvery, shimmering foil to drape delicately across the tips of the branches.

As we decorated, one of us would switch on the phonograph. The rest of the year, our collection of Christmas 78s was stored in a high cabinet above the stereo; now we stacked them on the Victrola's upright metal rod. Billy Eckstine, Bing Crosby, and Frank Sinatra kept us company while we worked, crooning our Christmas favorites over and over, all day long. We were dreaming of a white Christmas, sometimes in eighty-degree weather. That little town of Bethlehem was in our living room. "O Come All Ye Faithful" had a certain invitational connotation, though the word *faithful* lent a touch of otherness that we easily ignored.

All done with the tree, I got to stoop down and plug in the extension cord. We'd turn off all the other lights in the room. Then, magic! The multicolored lights came on deep inside the green branches. The ornaments glistened; the tinsel turned pale blue and green and yellow and red; Santa and his reindeer, scattered all throughout the house, came to life. I could hear him call out to Dancer and Prancer and all the others. From the bottom of one ornament storage box, Mom pulled out our worn illustrated edition of *The Night Before Christmas* and made space for it on a table beside the couch.

Christmas morning was always a rush. Around seven thirty, over coffee and juice and the Christmas hot-cross sticky buns sold all over our predominantly Catholic city, while still in our robes, we rapidly opened stockings and stacks of presents, then cleaned up the living room. We all dressed hurriedly to be ready before the "help" arrived around nine, usually in two cars, one of them driven by Everette, a former Pullman porter now turned freelance waiter, whose voice still resounded as if he were calling out the upcoming station and whose last name, I'm sorry to say, I've forgotten, if I ever knew it.

Before the dining room buffet was completely set up, Uncle Leon and Aunt Hortense Godchaux, Gram's brother and sister-in-law, would ring the front doorbell. Their arrival meant it was now ten thirty. The party was, by common understanding in the early years, expected to start about eleven for brunch. Uncle Leon and Aunt Hortense were always the first to arrive. Uncle Leon, the president of both Godchaux's, our family clothing store downtown, and the New Orleans Symphony, was the grandson of Leon Godchaux, the family founder who had left France as an impoverished adolescent and started life in America as a peddler. The next arrivals were Gram and Grandpa. They came early, and they stayed all day. The big night at their house was New Year's Eve, when their bountiful Christmas tree would be the principal light source in their living room.

About the same time as most of the family arrived, a perennial guest always appeared: Rabbi Feibelman, in a finely tailored, double-breasted gray suit, accompanied by his wife, Mary Anna, who usually wore a dark floral-patterned dress. I didn't think it notable in any way that our rabbi and his wife were celebrating Christmas Day with us. After all, we'd known them for years, and half the members of Temple Sinai were present at our house that day. As far as I knew, everyone at our house—Jewish and Christian alike—was indifferent to the presence on that particular holiday of our family friend, who happened to be a well-known Jewish cleric. Looking back I find his presence a vivid hallmark of the curious time and customs that pervaded our group's particular brand of liberal Judaism, all the way up to the rabbi's own practice. Julian Feibelman was a courageous ecumenical community and civil rights leader dedicated to close relationships between all religions and among all races. He hosted (with the board's permission) the first integrated audience in New Orleans when, in 1949, United Nations delegate Ralph Bunche spoke at Temple Sinai.

I remember with particular vividness the way Christmas 1946, when I was eleven, changed my life. That morning, as usual, the first thing I saw when I opened my bedroom door was the Christmas tree. The short hall in our one-story house cut my view into the living room. On Christmas morning, Gail and I weren't allowed to leave our rooms until Mom and Dad were with us; that was the rule. At six o'clock I was so excited I tried to bend my eyesight around the hall corner by squeezing up against the doorjamb.

By seven thirty, when I heard Mom and Dad stir, I was exhausted from the excitement and waiting.

"Okay, kids, you can come out of your rooms now." Finally...
the call. But only after they had put on their robes, gone to the
bathroom, slipped into the living room, plugged in the tree lights,
turned on some lamps, started up the phonograph, made coffee,
and poured glasses of orange juice for Gail and me could we enter
the room.

The presents were piled high. As we approached the tree, reflections from the lowest string of colored lights glistened off the
biggest box. It was wrapped in the metallic-looking silver paper of
Maison Blanche, a large and prominent New Orleans department
store. The ribbon was a big blue band. I had an idea that the gift
was for me. Up close, the card confirmed in Mom's handwriting:
"For Petie—your big present, hope you like it, happy Christmas.
Mom and Dad."

I always saved my most important present for last, just as I did
the maraschino cherry in a sundae. I was never one to rip off the
paper in an excited frenzy; I liked to carefully undo the ribbon and
wrapping paper, then refold the paper along its seams to save it if
possible.

After opening our stocking gifts and presents from relatives and
a few smaller ones from Mom and Dad, it was time for our main
present. I had mine tucked behind the lounge chair. I said, "I'd like
to go last."

Gail was always more spontaneous, so I was surprised when she
said, "Not fair!"

"Why not?" I retorted.

She said, "Because."

I didn't budge, and Gail commenced to unwrap her last gift.

As soon as Gail finished, Mom said a bit impatiently, "Now take
your turn, so we can clean up. We have to get this place shipshape
before the relatives arrive."

The Maison Blanche's outer wrapping was thick and stiff. Packing tape covered the seams because the box was heavy, more like a

shipping carton. The ribbon slipped off in one piece. When I opened the lid, two layers of crisp white tissue paper were folded around the contents and bound with a round, silver Maison Blanche sticker. My expectations were mounting.

At first, I couldn't guess what was in the box. It felt soft, like clothes, but bulky. When I pulled back the tissue, I saw a blue blanket with beige wires sticking out of it, hooked up to a separate dial that said LOW, MEDIUM, HIGH. I was perplexed, then crestfallen. My parents were staring at me. Gail was playing with one of her new dolls. My big Christmas present was an electric blanket! I couldn't lift my eyes from the box, and didn't speak for what seemed like an age. Then I tried to smile in Mom and Dad's direction. I was still sitting on the floor next to the box. I was afraid they'd see the tears welling, so I lowered my gaze. Carefully refolding the tissue paper back across the expanse of blue, I pressed the Maison Blanche sticker back in place. The tissue papers flipped up again. I pressed them down harder, wanting to seal them forever. Then I put the lid back on the box.

On cold nights, I had been in the odd habit of taking the seat and back cushions off the living room couch and piling them like an extra layer on top of my bed. Then I'd arrange the top blanket over them and tuck it under the mattress before I'd slide my body between the sheets, under the heavy stacked-up cushions. I was very skinny, and in the winter my body got cold easily. Those cushions were weirdly comforting, like having someone hold me. "Use an extra blanket if you're cold," my parents would say when they came in to say good night. "How can you stand those heavy cushions on top of you?"

"They feel good," I'd answer. "I like the weight."

"Well, put them back on the couch when you get up" was always the last line of that discussion. I'd try to remember to plump them back into shape.

I suddenly realized that the electric blanket was a solution to *their* problem. I'd no longer mess up the living room couch.

Somehow I found the courage to say, "Thanks, Mom. Thanks Dad. . . . Uh . . . I'd never thought about wanting a new blanket." Then I hesitated. I couldn't help going on, "Would you mind if I traded it in for something else, if it doesn't cost any more?" I wasn't sure how I managed to get the words out.

At the time, I didn't realize what a novelty the gift was. Electric blankets with thermostats went on sale for the first time that Christmas. It was a cutting-edge gift, akin to giving a young boy these days a watch that registers true solar time.

They looked at each other, surprised.

"What is it you want?" Dad asked in a hesitant voice, tinged, I thought, with irritation.

"I don't know . . ." I felt as if I was going to sob, but I took a deep breath and wished I could curl up in a corner all alone.

Everyone was quiet for what seemed like an hour. Then it came right out of me as a sudden impulse: "I want a dog."

They looked at each other again. I could read no signal between them.

"Would that be okay?"

Dad replied quickly, "A dog! We're not going to take care of a dog."

"I will," I said.

"I mean feeding and washing and cleaning up the poop," he said. "House training . . . everything."

"I know. I'll do it. I'd like that," I said cautiously, not letting my hopes get too high.

They looked at each other again. I thought I saw Mom make a very small, weary affirmative nod toward Dad.

He said, "If you can find one, we'll think about it, but let's talk about that later. Right now, we've got to get this place shipshape."

I was excited. It was possible! Not certain, but possible; only now I'd better learn something about what kind of dog was best and how to care for one. I decided to look up dog breeds in the school library and talk to my friends.

As Dad began to stuff the used wrapping papers and ribbons into a box, I watched Mom plump up the couch pillows.

* * *

After New Year's, Mom drove me downtown, and I lugged the big box to the returns office at Maison Blanche. The clerk posted a forty-dollar credit to my parents' charge account, taking the blanket back with no questions asked. It had been an expensive present.

Before we left the store, Mom gave me four ten-dollar bills. "Okay," she said, "the rest is up to you." I wondered how an eleven-year-old-boy would ever be able to convert this cash into a puppy.

It proved surprisingly easy. As soon as I asked, Mom drove me to see litters I'd found looking through the *Times-Picayune* classifieds. After visiting one kennel with cocker spaniels, we looked at Dalmatians in the garage of a woman named Mrs. Thurgoux. By the time we got there, three of the four puppies were spoken for. The one remaining, which she identified as "the runt of the litter," was smaller than the rest and had more dark spots than the others, so many that he appeared splotched rather than discretely spotted— too many, any Dalmatian breeder would have said, I later learned. The puppy shimmied over, looked at me with watery eyes, stuck out his tongue, and emitted a tiny, excited whine. I could feel my heart open up. I patted his short, soft coat and felt his warm body under my hand.

Mrs. Thurgoux said we should leave him with his mother for two more weeks, and that she would arrange for his initial shots. "Come back in three weeks," she told us, "to be safe."

"That's fine," I said, and gave her three ten-dollar bills, the price she and Mom had agreed on.

That same morning, we went to the pet store. With the money left over, I bought two tin bowls, a collar and leash, and a cozy dog bed. The Saturday we brought him home, the first thing he did was wander all over the house. So I called him Ranger. That proved to be a good name. As he grew, he roamed the neighborhood far and wide, as did all the other dogs around Brockenbraugh Court.

Dalmatians were famous in magazine pictures I'd seen as the dogs that would lope beside horse-drawn fire trucks to the scene of a fire. The English called them coach dogs or carriage dogs. By instinct, a young Dalmatian will trot alongside the shoulder of a horse. My bicycle was Ranger's coach. When I headed off on my bike, Ranger always ran beside the front wheel. Before long, Ranger assumed, quite correctly, that if I was going someplace on my bicycle, he was going, too.

Ranger was quiet at night. Even as a puppy he never barked, and he always slept well. Maybe it was all the exercise. He slept in my bed, even at full size, which was about sixty pounds. And I mean *in* my bed—not on the floor or at the foot of the bed as many dogs do. In fact, he slept between the sheets next to me. He preferred to sleep with his head down under the covers, near my feet, which meant that his rear end rested on the pillow next to my head. This drove my parents to distraction, but I saw nothing odd about it. I never minded the occasional odor. I didn't even notice it.

A couple of months before I got Ranger, my friend Merrick's parents had given him a Doberman Pinscher puppy that he named Rusty. Merrick's puppy may have been what made me think about having a dog of my own. Before Ranger was six months old, Merrick brought Rusty over. We were talking on the patio under the fig tree in my backyard when we heard snarling, then howling. I heard Ranger cry out and whimper.

Merrick and I ran to our dogs. Ranger was on the ground, one leg bleeding and both ears nearly torn off. Rusty was standing nearby, looking defiant. Merrick grabbed Rusty and shouted, "What the hell have you done!"

I realized how foolish I'd been to leave them alone. Ranger was much smaller, a gentle animal from a gentle breed. Rusty was the progeny of warriors, a breed used as guard dogs and watchdogs and police dogs, even attack dogs by the marines in World War II. Neither of us had thought about what could happen. Merrick leashed Rusty and got on his bike to go home. "Petie, I'm sorry," he said. "Ranger will be okay. I'm sure."

Ranger's leg healed, but after this skirmish he was deaf.

His disability worked to make the two of us even closer. From then on, we communicated in our own private sign language. I could beckon Ranger with a hand gesture toward my chest. I would ask him to sit or lie down next to me by pressing my outstretched hand through the air in front of me toward the floor.

We also communicated by gaze. He would look into my eyes as if he could read my thoughts, and by something in his eyes he'd let me know what he wanted. If he saw me come into the front yard, he'd look at me from the far sidewalk, and, if I stared back at him, it was like a call. He'd come running from wherever he was, often bolting across the street—ears back flat, head lunging forward. When he got to me, he'd jump up, standing on his hind legs, and rest his head on my shoulder and lick my neck. Sometimes, Ranger's momentum would knock me a few steps backward. We were nearly the same size when he stood up.

I kept my promise to Mom and Dad about taking care of Ranger. When he was a puppy, I forced the worming pills down his throat. Every weekend I bathed and brushed him in the backyard, and dried him off with a frayed towel Mom had thrown away. I fed him breakfast and dinner. Every morning I put out fresh water in both of his bowls, one in the kitchen and one on the back steps.

Though my parents never knew it, Ranger and I sometimes even ate supper together. His usual dinner was the smelly contents of a can of Alpo dog food. But sometimes he had a special treat. I'd take a package of horse meat from the freezer compartment of the refrigerator, which Mom sometimes bought just for Ranger, and defrost it in a pot of boiling water, stirred together with leftover rice. Then, before Mom got home, I'd sit at the kitchen table and eat a portion out of the same pot while Ranger had his supper at my feet. The warm meat was tangy and stringy like stew, but so bland I usually added salt. He loved it and so did I. My mother would have been horrified.

One Saturday morning, Ranger was roaming the neighborhood as usual. It was a beautiful fall day. The leaves on the line of trees in our front yard were just starting to turn brown. My bike was in the garage. Before going to get it, I stepped out of the front door to determine whether I'd need a sweater. Ranger happened to see me from across the street, where he was playing in the DeBardelabens' yard with their dog, Mike. He perked up his head as soon as I opened the screen door. Our eyes locked. He abandoned Mike and rushed headlong toward me. At the same moment, I saw a dilapidated red pickup truck traveling fast in his direction.

I watched, transfixed. I screamed, but of course Ranger couldn't hear me or the vehicle. It happened so fast. I saw it all and heard the dreadful thump as Ranger's body was thrown, mangled and broken, to the side of the street.

The truck driver screeched to a stop and jumped out of his cab. Visibly shaken, he said, "I didn't see your dog until the last minute. I couldn't stop in time with this old truck. I'm so sorry, son!"

I kneeled where Ranger had landed and touched his shoulder. His head was twisted backward, blood streaming from his mouth. His eyes were open, but there was no breath. I couldn't bear to look for more than a minute.

"He was deaf," I said between deep breaths. "He couldn't hear your truck, and he couldn't hear me scream. He was looking at me all the while, and at nothing else."

Then I broke down and ran inside. Dad was reading the newspaper in the living room. He didn't say anything as I rushed past him. I slammed my door shut and lay on my bed and wept. I felt as if I were going to suffocate. I wished someone would come in and hold me, talk to me, ask what was wrong, help me.

No one came into my room.

A little while later, when I could, I went back outside. I wanted to see Ranger one more time. But he wasn't there. Dark bloodstains marked the concrete. I saw Dad pushing the wheelbarrow with the shovel sticking out and Ranger's legs off to one side. His crushed head drooped over the edge.

"I'm sorry, son," Dad said. "He was a nice animal, but the way he wandered, and being deaf, something like this was bound to happen. What do you want to do with him? I can call the vet and they'll take care of his body."

"No," I said. "I want him to stay here."

As Dad stood by, I dug Ranger's grave in the empty lot between our house and Malcolm's, the lot that had always been a happy place for me until then—the safe and private carefree place where my friends and I had built our fort and played mumblety-peg when we were younger.

Back inside, I felt horrible and went immediately to my room. I looked at my bed, where Ranger used to be. I looked at the door panel where he had long ago, as a puppy, scratched his nails into the soft wood when he wanted to go out. After a while Mom came home. I don't know where she had been. She came into my room and looked at me just sitting there on the bed. "Dad told me what happened to Ranger," she said. "We're both so, so sorry. Maybe you should think about getting another dog."

At that moment I couldn't imagine such a thing. I know she was trying to console me, but her suggestion made me sadder. How could any other dog ever replace Ranger?

* * *

When I started Sunday school in September 1948, all I knew about Judaism was what I had picked up at two family Passover seders hosted by Aunt Ida, whom I had not seen for a couple of years. My parents and their friends made no effort to conceal their Jewish identity. But neither did they speak about being Jewish. They never told Jewish jokes. They never referred to Jewish issues in the city or in America. Only in the weeks leading up to Mardi Gras did I ever hear mention of our family being in any way special because of being Jewish. At that time of year, excluded from the social festivities, many Jews in the city planned to be away.

The first time I had to show up for Sunday school was the first and last time either of my parents accompanied me to temple. To do so, Dad had to get up at eight thirty, dress, eat breakfast, and drive thirty minutes from Metairie into the city. The class started at nine thirty sharp.

This was not a welcome addition to my parents' routine. What my mother and father did look forward to all week long was Saturday nights on the town, gambling at the Beverly Supper Club out along River Road, usually with Melanie and Sidney Marks (Sidney was the manager for Prudential Insurance for Louisiana) and Byrde and Joe Haspel (Joe was a prominent member of the family that produced Haspel Brothers' ubiquitous seersucker suits in New Orleans and sold them across the country). After dinner, roulette, and craps, they'd drive downtown to Bourbon Street to hear jazz at the Famous Door. Later they'd leave the French Quarter and drive across Canal Street to the Roosevelt Hotel, where the evening would end with a nightcap in the dark piano bar. During the fall and winter, when the Fair Grounds was open, they would linger over Saturday lunch through late afternoon at their clubhouse table, eagerly studying the racing form, socializing with friends, and betting their hunches. I went with them sometime, and Dad taught me how to read the racing form. On nice Sundays they liked to play golf at Lakewood, our country club.

As my father and I drove up to Temple Sinai, I saw a tan brick façade so bland that it disguised any aura of sacredness. "Go home with Charles after class," Dad reminded me as he stopped at the corner to let me out of his yellow Olds convertible, no doubt nursing a stiff hangover. "We'll pick you up sometime in the afternoon on our way home from the club."

I got out of the car, and faced a dark doorway a few yards away, beyond the protective curb and sidewalk. Dad had let me out at the corner rather than turn into the circular driveway leading up to the entrance, as if he didn't want to be seen near the place. He also may not have felt either steady enough or patient enough to maneuver into the line of other cars turning into the drive, discharging kids. I felt all alone before this strange structure. If Mother and Dad didn't bother to come here, I wondered, why should I? I was also wishing, instead, that Dad and I would be going off on a fun Sunday adventure, maybe just the two of us. Dad did love to fish, and he did take me with him sometimes. Once or twice he joked, "I can't wait for you to get big enough to carry the outboard motor." On those very special days with Dad we had a great time, and usually caught speckled trout and redfish.

The first day of Sunday school was the second time I had been inside the temple. The first occasion had been my cousin Peter Mayerson's confirmation the year before. I had to start my own relationship with the temple by registering in the office downstairs, at a beige Formica counter. A lady smiled at me as I completed the various forms. Her hair was a shiny copper color and stiff with hairspray. She scanned my sheaf of papers in her file. After she nodded okay, I handed over Dad's tuition check. As she put it into a drawer underneath the counter, she said to me, "I'm Mrs. Schaeffer. As you've not been in the school before, I'll take you upstairs to your classroom."

Mrs. Schaeffer led me through a gray metal door. Behind it, linoleum-covered stairs were edged with a double tubular metal railing. Our steps echoed in the empty stairwell. The paperwork had taken so long that I was going to be late for class.

When we got there, the classroom door was already closed. Mrs. Schaeffer pointed to the door, turned around, and went back down the hall. As I walked into the room, the teacher, who was seated at a broad wooden desk, stopped speaking. Everyone looked at me. There were two rows of kids, about fifteen students in all. Except for Charles Marks and Teddy Alcus, who happened to be the children of couples my parents socialized with, I'd never seen any of them before. As it turned out, they all lived in town and were all in the same class at Newman, the rigorous private school ten blocks from Sinai, with the largest Jewish student enrollment of any school in New Orleans.

Each kid was seated at an old-fashioned, wooden combination chair and desk, and each had an open workbook and a Bible on his desktop. On the slatted racks beneath each seat I saw identical, hardcover paired volumes with gold writing on the spines: *The Union Prayerbook*. No one had told me to bring a particular text, so all I had with me was a pocket-size spiral notebook and a pen. Before long, I learned that these volumes were called *Gates of Prayer* and *Gates of Repentance*. The subtitle of the second volume, *The Union Prayerbook for the Days of Awe*, appealed to me.

Everyone stared at me with what I imagined to be both curiosity and disdain. Who was this guy who got to begin Sunday school in the last year, the big payoff year of congratulations, of bountiful gifts and liberation? I felt simultaneously embarrassed, out of place, and abandoned. I wondered, What will it be like to be closed up in this dreary classroom every Sunday morning with Jewish kids I don't know instead of out fishing with Grandpa or exploring my neighborhood on my bike? I wanted to go home.

After Mr. Hirsch introduced me as "our new class member, Peter, who lives out in Metairie," I took the last seat in the back row. For the rest of the morning, I listened to stories about Old

Testament characters and events I knew virtually nothing about. I struggled to follow the meaning of the questions and answers.

When class was over, Mr. Hirsch called me to his desk.

"Peter," he said, "you've got a lot of catching up to do. Everyone in this class has been getting ready for confirmation for at least two years."

I didn't know what to say. At that awkward moment, I recalled how I happened to end up standing there that day in front of Mr. Hirsch's desk.

At supper a few weeks before, my mother had looked over at me and said, "All of our in-town friends send their kids to Sinai. Just last night Melanie and Sidney told us Charles likes being there, and they think it's good for him. They asked why you weren't in that class." Then Dad had chimed in: "Because of Country Day and living in Metairie, you don't know any of the Jewish kids from our crowd who live in town. You'll get to meet some new kids, some you might enjoy."

In talking to their friends about the social advantages of my going to Sunday school at Temple Sinai, my parents hadn't bothered to find out what I might need to bring to class, or any reading I should do to try to catch up. Maybe getting me admitted to the class was quite enough to foreclose what my parents may have sensed as criticism from their friends. They were also likely aware, in a way that I was not, of the impending need to expand my social contacts with young people in the Jewish community. I had no sense of who first got the idea of my going to Sunday school. It certainly wasn't me. And being the kind of kid I was, I didn't think to find out, or to object. For my parents, sending me to Sunday school was likely the equivalent of offering an extracurricular social opportunity to meet their uptown friends' children who went to Newman, rather than a way to begin to consolidate my religious heritage and identity, concepts not very important to them. Because we lived in Metairie and because I did not go to Newman, my parents may have possessed a slight sense of regret that I was absorbing absolutely nothing at home or in school of Jewish customs, rituals, and history.

"Here's your workbook," Mr. Hirsch continued, handing me a sturdy paperback volume with a shiny green cover and a gold menorah stamped on it. "You'll find a weekly assignment sheet inside. The other thing you need to bring every week is the Bible. We'll be reading out loud every class from the Old Testament. I'll have prayer books here for you next Sunday."

"Okay," I answered, without much enthusiasm.

Mr. Hirsch persisted. He evidently had an agenda. "Now come with me and I'll show you the sanctuary."

"Charles is waiting," I answered. "I have to go home with him."

"It'll just take a couple of minutes," he said. "I'll ask Charles to wait." He guided me down a much larger staircase than the one I had climbed with Mrs. Schaeffer. "You probably won't see it again until next spring when you'll be confirmed before the ark by Rabbi Feibelman."

The cavernous, vaulted, Byzantine-looking sanctuary seemed big enough to hold half the city on the high holy days. It looked as if it might have been based on an etching of some ancient holy place like the Blue Mosque in Istanbul, which I'd seen in *National Geographic*.

A pinkish-beige stone clad all the walls and massive columns in the sanctuary. It looked nearly as empty and cold as it had on the morning of my cousin's confirmation. On that morning, wearing a necktie and tight leather shoes that pinched my feet, I was forced to watch Peter and his classmates sitting stiffly onstage. They faced the audience from the elevated platform in front of the ark, where the temple's Torahs were enshrined. Peter and his classmates looked uncomfortable and unnatural, hardly even allowing themselves to blink. The boys wore black robes over dark suits and the girls wore white robes over dresses. All of their heads were bare, including the rabbi's; there was not a yarmulke to be seen on the stage. Rabbi Feibelman's thick white hair and wide silver-rimmed glasses gleamed. The class remained quietly seated as Rabbi Feibelman reported their remarkable progress and praised their accomplished learning. Then the group of twelve students stood as he proudly read their names. No recitation was expected, and certainly nothing was said in Hebrew. Satisfied parents, relatives, and friends beamed restless approval at the stage. Temple Sinai families did not throw a party either before or after the confirmation ceremony. They did what everyone else did after church let out: go home or to Galatoire's for Sunday dinner.

The evening after my first class I found a copy of the Bible at our house, shelved with some Time-Life picture reference books about Africa and World War II, and a whole row of *National Geographics*. I got really lucky: the preface explained how the Old Testament in English had been based on Hebrew and Aramaic versions first fixed in the Christian era and revised by Jewish scholars (the "Masoretes") of the sixth to ninth centuries. Those scholars had, in turn, referred to more ancient versions that had been translated into Greek, Aramaic, Syriac, and Latin. Now that was interesting, even though *Masoretes* sounded to me like a high school drill team with cute drum majorettes. Just as striking was the engraved topographic map of Palestine in the back of our Bible, its graphic scale showing that the territory's entire length was about 275 miles. I measured with my ruler just to make sure. I was astonished that the whole country, where all of the world-shaking events we were studying were supposed to have taken place, was not so much longer than a round-trip on the highway to Baton Rouge.

Two other small maps appeared on the double-page layout of the map of Palestine. One showed "Ancient Jerusalem" in topographic format with its walls and nearby mountains and valleys. The second inset in the top left-hand corner listed the names of the Jewish tribes and the locations of their territories. That got me to wondering what original tribe my forebears had wandered about with. The name of that map was "Palestine as Divided Among the Tribes of Israel."

After that inaugural trip to Temple Sinai, my parents let me know they had planned different regimens for subsequent Sundays. "Melanie and Sidney have a big house on Robert Street near the temple," Dad said, "and they've offered to have you stay over on Saturday nights with Charles. You can then go to confirmation class together Sunday mornings."

"Melanie reminded me," Mother added, "that the big playroom downstairs has Ping-Pong and pool tables, so you and Charles will have a great time."

If my grandparents happened to be staying in town for the weekend, another option was for my parents to leave me at their house on State Street Saturday evening. From there I could take the streetcar or walk on Sunday morning to the temple. As Gram and Grandpa usually left for Pass Christian on Friday afternoon, though, this rarely happened.

Usually, my parents dropped me in town at Charles Marks's house on Saturday evening before they went out. Since my parents spent many Saturday nights with Charles's parents anyway, this was a convenient alternative for them. However, this plan was based on the assumption that I wanted to spend Saturday night at the Markses with Charles, which was not always the case. He was simply a conveniently located son of friends of my parents. Indeed, at the time I scarcely knew him. The Marks plan had a further catch: it depended upon us two boys getting up on time, making our own breakfast, and taking the streetcar down St. Charles Avenue to Calhoun Street by nine thirty.

Despite my personal misgivings about spending so much time in an unfamiliar house with a kid I hardly knew—which I didn't consider discussing with my parents (if they said I should go, I should go)—for the next four Sundays I went to Sunday school with Charles after having spent the previous evening with him. As time went by and we grew closer, I learned to have fun playing games with him. We played Ping-Pong and pool on Saturday nights, and stayed up later than we were supposed to.

In class we'd begin by taking turns reading passages that Mr. Hirsch preselected from *The Union Prayerbook*. By then I knew that it was the Reform Jewish prayer book. Mr. Hirsch would explain each passage afterward. After that part of class, Mr. Hirsch would go around the room a second time, in the order of our seats, and ask each of us to read a few paragraphs from some part of the Old Testament relating to the prayer-book section we'd just reviewed. I accepted whatever odd and mysterious protocol was given me at Sunday school without questioning, assuming it had been established well before the Louisiana Purchase, or maybe even before construction of the Second Temple in Jerusalem.

I kept hoping Mr. Hirsch would talk to us about "the Days of Awe," mentioned so frequently in *Gates of Repentance*, our liturgy for Rosh Hashanah and Yom Kippur. Or about Awe itself and the spirit behind the prayer book. About the idea of the "Ineffable" that was also mentioned from time to time. About the times in which the early Jews lived. About an ancient people spread out across the desert being called to prayer in a shady tent by the haunting sound of the shofar, the ram's horn, which made a low-pitched tone that traveled far across sandy terrain. If we'd each been given a turn at trying to push our breath through a curly ram's horn to re-create that sound, I think we would have felt more of a personal connection. I know I would have.

I also kept hoping Mr. Hirsch would talk to us about contemporary things I'd been pondering since the end of the war, such as the horrible experiences that Jewish people all over Europe had endured less than ten years before. I hoped he might say something to us like "You kids being in this class means survival of the Jewish people," or "You kids are the lucky ones, you just don't know it yet," or "You kids, for the rest of your lives, watch out. The world has wanted to kill Jews forever."

He did not raise these topics. He talked about nothing but the assigned lessons in our workbook and the passages that we read out loud.

After one month, my attendance record began to waver. It wasn't just that I resumed frequent trips across the lake with Gram and Grandpa, with no objections from any quarter of my family.

It was also that the sleepover plan devised by my parents was based on a flawed premise: that Charles and I would exit the streetcar at Calhoun Street. We didn't always do so. Charles certainly knew enough, after four years in Sunday school, to get confirmed with his eyes closed. He was a star pupil, always prepared. So when I slept over he didn't seem to mind my occasional suggestion that we allow the St. Charles Avenue streetcar to rumble past Calhoun, with neither of us reaching up to pull the cord. It was two stops farther to the Katz & Besthoff drugstore at the intersection of Broadway and St. Charles. Katz & Besthoff, with its beckoning purple awning, harbored a soda fountain, comic books, and a good collection of pencils and notebooks. K&B, as everyone called it, had long been the dominant drugstore chain in town (it was founded in 1905 and sold to Rite Aid in 1997). It was owned by good friends of our family, a situation that made me a little nervous; I didn't especially want to be seen in that store, just then.

* * *

As I've said, my relation to Judaism had always been casual at best. I was eleven when I went to my first seder, held in 1946 at the big brick-and-plaster house at the corner of Palmer and Loyola avenues that belonged to Aunt Ida, as we called her, my grandmother's aunt and the oldest member of our family. Her real name was Ida Weis Friend. I don't recall ever having met her earlier. I'd never seen anything like her Victorian drawing room with its green velvet-upholstered furniture, a dark beamed ceiling, and leather banquette seats around the huge fireplace. Before the meal began, she took me aside. She had a straggly collection of wispy gray hairs growing out of her chin. I remember her raspy voice, her thin, bony hand in mine, her skinny, bent body, her jaw, which looked as if it had grown more protruding in recent years, and her droopy ears stretching downward even without the weight of earrings. Behind the thin silver frames encircling her eyes, Aunt Ida had dim gray irises that nonetheless flickered with warmth and wisdom and light as she sized me up. She was the oldest and thinnest lady I'd ever met.

"Petie, I'm your old aunt Ida," she started out. "Finally, we get to meet."

"I know," I answered a bit shyly, as I felt her cold, bony hand.

"Tonight you're going to hear the story of the Jewish people escaping into a new land and a new life. They were saved from slavery by a miracle. Your grandmother tells me this is your first Passover. Do you know the story?"

"No, I don't," I said.

"Do you know all the people here?"

"No, not all of them."

"These are all relatives of yours who live in New Orleans. They're part of the Godchaux-Weis family, just like you. You must have met some of them before tonight." She continued, "Haven't your parents told you that your great-great-grandfathers Weis and Godchaux, once they got established over here, were among the founders of Temple Sinai?"

"I didn't know that. And the only people I recognize here are Gram and Grandpa, Gram's brothers and sisters, and Uncle Jimmy, Aunt Catherine, and Aunt Caroline and Uncle Hy and their kids, my first cousins. I don't know anyone else except my parents and my sister." I was only eleven. We'd lived out in Metairie nearly my entire life, while most of our extended family in that room lived in town.

"Well, during the evening, I'll introduce you to some of the young people. There are eighty-six family members here tonight, all related to you through your grandmother. None of your grandfather's kin ever moved down from Bayou Sara to New Orleans."

Then she stopped and looked at me carefully, searching my face. She was silent for what seemed forever; then she continued in her squeaky voice, gazing intently at me as if to drill her points into my brain: "You need to learn about your own Jewish people and their journey from Europe to the New World and New Orleans," she said. "Think of it as your own personal Passover." I remembered vaguely some of the early family history Gram had one time talked to me about, but only vaguely.

That night, in sentences so short and cryptic it took me many days (and lots of new questions for Gram) to understand it all, Aunt Ida told me about her father—my great-great-grandfather Julius Weis—who as a boy in the 1840s had traveled by stage from Germany to Paris and then voyaged from Le Havre to Natchez. My great-great-grandfather Leon Godchaux arrived a few years earlier in New Orleans from France. Originally, his name was spelled "Godchot." Both boys started out as peddlers to the plantations up and down the Mississippi River. I did recall that part. Both prospered, and Weis moved to New Orleans. After the Civil War, when they were each grown up and had families, they founded Temple Sinai in 1870 with some of their friends who had also come to Louisiana from France and Germany. Sinai was the first Reform congregation in New Orleans. Julius Weis, Aunt Ida's father, was the temple's first vice president and its second president from 1874 to 1876, and served again as president from 1890 to 1898.

I didn't know what Aunt Ida meant by "Reform," but I thought it would sound stupid to ask, so I didn't.

Aunt Ida seemed pleased to pass along glimpses of our family history to me. I wanted to remember what Gram had told me and to grasp what Aunt Ida was adding, but with all the people around and the many strange names to take in, I felt quite bewildered. Her guests swirled around us. "Petie, don't you see?" she said in a voice that sounded suddenly and miraculously as clear as a bell, "I'm the founder Julius Weis's daughter, and your grandmother is Leon Godchaux's granddaughter. Besides that, your grandmother's mother was my sister. Now, do you see?"

I was struggling to keep up. This was a very New Orleans conversation. Everyone in the city talked all the time about family lineage and history. Although I didn't realize it at the time, never again would I have access to such a direct account of my family's founding "first arrivals."

My mother and father were probably both uneasy being surrounded by so many family members and indeed had never bothered to tell me about most of them. They didn't like to spend time with the big, extended Godchaux-Weis clan, but rather preferred their social time with friends at the country club, out partying, gambling, bowling, and playing cards—primarily within their select segment of the older families within the Reform Jewish community. That's another reason why I only knew my most immediate relatives. My parents chose friends around personal interests and activities. They were not clannish, unlike my grandparents and most of their older friends, who tended to spend a lot of their time with family members. Still, because he had lived in New Orleans all of his life, Dad had a passing acquaintance with most of the people at the seder. To my mother, many of these relatives were in fact virtual strangers. I imagine at this and other extended family gatherings she felt a bit awkward, like an unknown, recently arrived (in New Orleans terms) outsider who wasn't particularly eager to be much more.

My mother's family had a rather parallel history, and her generation possessed, as I learned later, a similar indifference to its Jewish roots. Earlier generations of her family, much like mine in New Orleans, had been much more involved in Jewish culture and religion in their hometown. My mother's own mother was born Minnie

Eisenstein. She grew up in the South, in Savannah, Georgia. Her parents were part of a prominent, well-established Jewish family there who had been long and closely associated with the local temple, Congregation Mickve Israel. Minnie's mother was named Carrie, just as was my own grandmother in New Orleans. My mother's family, just like mine in New Orleans, never made any effort to disguise their Jewish identity. They too primarily identified their lives with their own towns and with America, having been resident and prominent in the United States for many generations.

During the seder at Aunt Ida's, I heard the story of the persecution and miracles. I was nervous when I realized that I'd be called upon to read out loud. When my turn came, I was hesitant and stumbled over a few words but soon relaxed. I loved it that everyone in all three rooms was part of one family and eating the same ritual meal, one filled with symbolism. We seemed to me like a scattered tribe called together to give thanks and encounter one another on this special occasion. I began to imagine that I had journeyed from the desert of Metairie to meet my far-flung, scarcely known kinsmen beneath Aunt Ida's big tent.

The next year, during Aunt Ida's seder, my grandmother, Carrie Godchaux Wolf, joined our table. To my delight, she sat down next to me. I could never get enough of her.

"Aunt Ida told me she had such a good conversation with you last year," said Gram, all smiles. I wondered, though, if she was teasing me.

When I looked at her, it seemed impossible that she could be related to Aunt Ida. Gram was what people in those days called stout. Instead of her clothes hanging loosely from her frame as did Aunt Ida's, Gram's clothing fit closely around her voluptuous bosom and ample hips. While Aunt Ida's eyes were often tired-looking and a faded gray color, Gram's were bright blue and lit up like fireworks. Aunt Ida's hair was so thin that I could see her scalp through it. Gram had piles of luxuriant brown and gray hair piled and plaited all over her head and held in place by long, dark tortoiseshell pins. Aunt Ida spoke with a squeaky sadness, the kind of sound a dull Victrola needle makes on an overused record. Gram's clear voice was full of spunkish laughter.

"She told me a lot, Gram. About the beginning of Temple Sinai, when it was downtown, and how you two are related."

"But she didn't tell you the most important part of the story, about herself. I knew she wouldn't. But that's the part I want you to know about tonight while you're in her house and while she's still here."

It turns out that Aunt Ida was among the small group of Temple Sinai members who selected its current uptown site twenty years earlier and helped get the new temple built.

"It opened its doors in 1927 at the corner of St. Charles Avenue and Calhoun Street," Gram said, "two years before the Depression. It might not have been built later. It surely wouldn't have been so grand."

I said, "I've seen the temple on the outside sometimes going to your house, but I never knew what it was."

"The main thing you need to know about Aunt Ida is how much she's done for New Orleans and for Reform Judaism."

I discovered that Aunt Ida, born in 1868, was a big-time New Orleans celebrity in so many areas. One of them was in her commitment to our Jewish heritage. She was president of the National Council of Jewish Women and of the New Orleans women's chapter of B'nai B'rith. In 1917 she founded and then served as the first president of the New Orleans Hadassah.

"All through the war," Gram continued, "Aunt Ida worked to help Jewish refugees. She collected money and clothes and books. Last year, after peace was declared, Aunt Ida told me she'd felt sick for four years. In honor of her service, the year after the war, she received a national award from the American Red Cross."

"Sick with what?" I asked. "Is she sick? She does seem frail."

Gram looked straight at me and said, "She has suffered because of the killing and because of the Holocaust. We all should have."

Now I looked blankly at my own grandmother. All during the war, while we talked about European battles and speculated about where my father might be fighting in the Pacific, I had never once heard the word *Holocaust*. I had never been aware of the Nazis' hatred of Jewish people. I'd heard nothing about the possible formation of the State of Israel.

Aunt Ida, it turned out, was even more of an honored celebrity than Gram let me know, for her service in support of Jewish causes, the national war effort, and the well-being of so many in New Orleans. In 1946 alone, at age seventy-seven, a year after the war was over, and two years before the founding of the State of Israel, she was declared by the Quota Club the New Orleans "Woman of the Year." The *Times-Picayune* publicized her honor with a front-page picture of her receiving the paper's annual silver Loving Cup award.

After Aunt Ida's seder, my interest in World War II grew and switched focus. Instead of thinking about Fiji, where I knew my father had spent much of the war, I began to imagine the horrors the Jews had experienced in Europe. I began to wonder more about why my own ancestors had left the Continent. I started to feel closer to my big immigrant family and curious about who they were.

I did discover eventually what seemed to me at the time to be an odd contradiction: my relatives, for all of their well-earned prominence in the Jewish community, didn't much care to observe their religion in their own Temple Sinai. Aunt Ida loved to gather the family for seder at her house to talk about the family's role in founding the temple, but she herself did not go to temple, except on the high holy days. Her sister, Henrietta Weis Godchaux, my great-grandmother, taught Old Testament Bible classes in her home but didn't care to participate in any of the temple rituals. They were both dynamic activist women, proud to be Jewish and interested in

Jewish history and culture. But they, like the other Jews in my family, and those in my mother's family as well, were not particularly devoted to their religion's spiritual rituals or beliefs. Gram had told me, "We're Jewish, but not in an obvious way."

I eventually came to understand that my ancestors, who had fled the chaos of Alsace-Lorraine in mid-nineteenth century as it passed from French to German hands, were seeking a cultural homeland where they could speak the local language. They did not come in quest of a religious haven. From the beginning they sought to fit in, to become successful on American terms. They wanted to look indistinguishable from other residents of their adopted homeland. So they embraced Reform Judaism, inaugurated temples where the service was conducted in English, and broke old tradition by having men and women sit together. They wanted to remain Jewish on their new and own terms. Organ music filled their new hallowed spaces with rarely a yarmulke or tallis visible.

Many years later I found out that in 1880, around the time that Julius Weis and Leon Godchaux were most active, two-thirds of Louisiana's 7,500 Jewish residents were concentrated in New Orleans, then the largest Jewish population in the South. This small community of ambitious commercial and professional people made a large, distinctive imprint as they prospered and became part of the dynamic growth of the South's most powerful nineteenth- and early-twentieth-century city. Though Jews had comprised only one percent of the New Orleans population, their imprint in medicine, law, the arts, and commerce was very much larger.

When my great-great-grandfather Leon Godchaux died in 1899, at the age of seventy-five, newspapers reported that that he'd established the largest sugarland holdings, with one hundred thousand acres of cropland, and the most modern refinery in the South. At his death he had been the largest taxpayer in Louisiana. He'd also built a private railroad system, which came to be known as the Mississippi River Sugar Belt Railroad, to gather the cane on his vast property holdings and bring it efficiently to the refinery. The *American Jewish Historical Quarterly*, in its special bicentennial issue, published in September 1976 and focusing on American Jewish business enterprise, concluded its piece on Godchaux: "His impact on Louisiana cannot be measured. Judging him on his career, it is possible to say that he was the most important person in the economy of that state in the nineteenth century."

* * *

Besides my founding relatives, there were other extraordinarily gifted, generous, and ambitious Jewish leaders in New Orleans during the prime years of our family. The most nationally prominent in the early days were Judah Touro (real estate and patron of Touro Infirmary in New Orleans; his father, Isaac Touro, led the famous Touro Synagogue in Newport, Rhode Island, dedicated in 1763), and Judah P. Benjamin, the first avowed Jew elected to the United States Senate, and subsequently a member of the Confederate cabinet. In the religious realm there was scholar linguist Hermann Kohlmeyer, among a small number of rabbis who joined rabbi Isaac Meyer Wise to begin the Reform movement in Cincinnatti before settling in New Orleans, where he taught college and served as a rabbi to various small congregations. Within the professions, early distinguished Jewish practitioners included lawyers Felix J. Dreyfous, Montefiore Mordecai Lemann, Charles Rosen and Alfred David Danziger; in architecture Emil Weil, Moise Goldstein, Leon C. Weiss, F. Julius Dreyfous, and Solis Seiferth; and Abraham Louis Levin in medicine.

There were many other commercially oriented, successful Jewish émigré settlers who made a permanent contribution to the city of New Orleans. Many if not most of them or their descendants were friends, colleagues, or fellow trustees and board members with my ancestors, other family members, or of mine, or whose contribu-

tions mingled with our family. Among them were Isidore Newman (cotton broker, financed the institution that became Newman
School); Moise Waldhorn (Waldhorn's, the first antique shop in New
Orleans); Theodore Dennery (confectioner, founder of nationally
prominent Charles Dennery Inc.); Isaac and Samuel Delgado (sugar
agents; Isaac was founder of the Isaac Delgado Museum of Art, later
renamed the New Orleans Museum of Art, and benefactor of Delgado Community College, the oldest and largest community college
in Louisiana); Gustave Katz and Sydney Besthoff (ran the largest
drugstore chain in the city, later managed and sold by third-gener-
ation family member Sydney Johnson Besthoff III, who in recent
years contributed the former K&B warehouse as the Contemporary
Art Center, and in City Park with his wife, the Sydney and Walda
Besthoff Sculpture Garden); I. and M. B. Sontheimer, and Henry and
Alfred S. Tharp (Tharp-Sontheimer-Tharp Funeral Home, the larg-
est mortuary in the South); Samuel and Emanuel Pulitzer (Wembley
Inc., which became the largest men's tie manufacturer in the world);
Henry Stern (Henry Stern's Antique Shop); Joseph Haspel (Haspel
Brothers, which dominated the seersucker garment industry); Jacob
Aron and Leon Israel (J. Aron & Co., nationally prominent coffee
merchants); Samuel Zemurray (founder of Cuyamel Fruit Company,
and ultimately president of the vast United Fruit Company); Stephen
Goldring and Malcolm Woldenberg (Magnolia Marketing Company
leading alcohol distributors and both in later years dedicated phi-
lanthropists through the Goldring Foundation and the Dorothy and
Malcolm Woldenberg Foundation); Abraham and George Shushan
(Shushan Brothers Toys and Huey Long insider); Seymour Weiss
(principal owner and managing director of the Roosevelt Hotel and
Huey Long confidant); Edgar Stern (a cotton merchant) and Edith
Rosenwald Stern (daughter of Julius Rosenwald, who was head of
Chicago-based Sears, Roebuck & Co., Edith founded Newcomb
Nursery School and Metairie Park Country Day School; she and
Edgar created and donated Longue Vue House & Gardens, and es-

tablished the Stern Fund, which contributed generously to charitable causes in and away from New Orleans); and Coleman Adler (Adler's, the finest jewelry store in the city and one of the few historic Jewish-owned businesses that remain there).

A variety of these landmarks, civic contributions, and commercial forays twined directly into my life:

Touro Infirmary is where I was born. My grandfather, father, and sister served as trustees. That's where my grandmother had her mastectomy; my father had cancer surgery, which, unfortunately, was too late; and I had my tonsils out.

Newman School: practically all the Jewish kids I knew in New Orleans went there.

At Waldhorn's and Henry Stern's antique shops you could find the most trustworthy antique furnishings (Stern's) and best antique jewelry (Waldhorn's). These men and many family members who followed were personal friends.

Dennery's had my favorite chocolate sauce, the one everyone wanted. Dennery's thick, rich chocolate sauce was the best topping on anything. Family members were close friends for multiple generations. Charles Marks is a descendant.

New Orleans Museum of Art, originally the Isaac Delgado Museum of Art: Where our family has donated works of art, where I have been friendly with the curators, where my mother worked as a volunteer for many years.

Sydney and Walda Besthoff are lifelong friends of mine, and both sets of parents were friends of my parents. Katz & Besthoff is where Charles Marks and I played hooky from Sunday school. It is where everyone in town bought their drug supplies. The Contemporary Art Center and the Sydney & Walda Besthoff Sculpture Garden are two of the top cultural attractions in New Orleans.

Tharp-Sontheimer-Tharp Funeral Home is where all of our family funerals have been held. Stephen Sontheimer is my friend and was the last Sontheimer proprietor. His parents were close with mine. The business has been sold to a chain of funeral homes.

The Pulitzers and the Wembley tie company: We all wore Wembley ties. So did much of the nation. Sidney Pulitzer is a longtime friend going back to our days in Tau Beta Phi, a high school Jewish fraternity in New Orleans. We sometimes talk about gold, his passion. I was close to his deceased sister Melanie, who married one of my closest friends in New Orleans, Judge Martin L. C. Feldman.

Haspel Brothers: Peter and Barbara, the children of my generation, went to Country Day with us, and Peter bought my sister and brother-in-law's country cabin in Mississippi. Byrde and Joe Haspel and Muriel and Leo Haspel were good friends with my parents. At one time practically everyone wore Haspel seersucker.

Jacob Aron and Leon Israel: Coffee from J. Aron & Co. was everywhere in New Orleans. Descendants of Leon were among my parents' closest friends. Their son, Larry, and I played tournament tennis together in our youth.

Temple Sinai was designed by Emil Weil, Leon C. Weiss, Solis Seiferth, F. Julius Dreyfous and Moise Goldstein. Goldstein was the architect my grandparents selected to design their Victorian house on State Street. Weiss, Dreyfous and Seiferth were the architects for the expansion of Touro Infirmary where I was born and family members long served as trustees. That firm also built from scratch, under the patronage of governor Huey Long, Charity Hospital in New Orleans which served generations of the needy, where I recovered from shock after being attacked by a rabid dog, and the imposing Louisiana State Capitol in Baton Rouge.

Coleman Adler: His family jewelry shop, now merged with Waldhorn's Antique emporium, is where we got Ronson lighters repaired when I couldn't manage. Multiple generations overlap as family friends.

Edgar and Edith Stern were friends of the family. I attended both Newcomb Nursery School and Metairie Park Country Day School, both founded through their foresight, dedication, and munificence.

Herman Kohlmeyer Jr., one of the last cotton futures brokers working in New Orleans, is a longtime friend as well as a scholar of New Orleans history.

* * *

Like every other Jew in New Orleans, no matter how successful or civic-minded, my grandfather Albert Wolf—a senior partner of the nationally prominent brokerage Merrill Lynch, Pierce, Fenner & Beane, a firm that became a cornerstone of the New Orleans business and social communities—was not invited to join any of the elite white, male, Christian-only social organizations that sponsored not only the public Mardi Gras parades but also the lavish costume balls that followed, and that functioned as the de facto power centers that controlled the city. Zulu, the one prominent black social club and the group with the most colorful parade of all, did not invite him, either; they had their own restrictions.

During the Mardi Gras parades, we'd stand along the curb with everyone else. The floats of the most socially elite "krewes" (as the social clubs' carnival float riders were called) were filled with Grandpa's half-drunken business associates, costumed as knights and squires. They threw trinkets down into the crowd. Later, while his investment banking partners were attending their fancy-dress balls in the Municipal Auditorium, Grandpa and I and the rest of the family would be in the living room with Gram, looking over the beads we'd snatched from the air as the floats passed by. A lot of Jewish people left town during Mardi Gras.

Once I said to Gram, "I don't like that Mr. Hirsch reads to us all the time in confirmation class about the Jews being the chosen people."

"The traditional Jews believe that," Gram told me. "It's a big thing with them, and the Passover story is used as proof."

"Does anyone believe that stuff? That it really happened?"

"Yes, many do. Lots don't, too. We certainly don't."

"Gram, don't you think my friends at Country Day would be pretty irritated if I went around school saying we Jews always have been God's chosen people?"

"I imagine they would, so I wouldn't if I were you."

"I couldn't possibly," I said, satisfied that Gram was my ally in this.

*　*　*

When spring came around, the redfish began running at first reef. I had not found my way back to either Charles Marks's house or to Temple Sinai for weeks in a row. I resumed fishing, working the jigsaw puzzle, chatting with Gram and Grandpa on the screened-in porch, and riding back to New Orleans while listening to the opera rebroadcast on the car radio.

One Monday evening toward the end of April, I was at home in Metairie doing homework after supper when Charles called.

"The kids have been talking for a few weeks at Newman," he told me. "It came to a head yesterday at Sunday school."

"What came to a head?" I asked, detached and uninterested in Newman School gossip.

"Mr. Hirsch brought up the question," he said with a little quiver in his voice, "of what we thought about your obvious lack of interest."

"Mr. Hirsch asked about me?"

"Yes." Then he waited, as if to summon up courage. "The class decided that you aren't interested enough in learning about Judaism to be confirmed. Most of the class didn't think it would be fair if you were."

"How was this decided?" I inquired, with increasing curiosity.

"Mr. Hirsch asked, 'Does anyone think Peter Wolf deserves to be confirmed? If so, speak up now.'"

No one spoke up. But Charles couldn't say that. Instead, in an apologetic voice, he told me: "I think everyone was shy. No one said anything." When I didn't respond, he continued: "Mr. Hirsch then announced, 'I'll report your decision to the rabbi.'"

Charles had one more thing to tell me, but he waited before doing so, maybe to let me reply or curse or whatever he thought I might do. "Oh," he then added, "as we were gathering up our things to leave, Mr. Hirsch walked over to me and said, 'Charles, you're Peter's friend. Give him a call to tell him about the decision. Will you do that?' So that's how I got stuck with the job of telling you."

"Thanks for letting me know." I'd never been dismissed from any place before. This news that I'd been excluded from a Reform Jewish Sunday school left me unfazed. I felt the class was right, even if they had been manipulated. And I felt relieved that I would no longer need to travel into town on Sunday mornings. I had never felt that I deserved to be confirmed, given my meager effort. My parents had nothing one way or another to say about Charles's news. I suspect they had been ambivalent all along about my acquiring a semblance of a Jewish religious education. Surely, arranging for me to begin at the end, in the last year, indicated a lack of fervor.

My family sent Charles, who'd been set up as the hapless messenger, a beautiful confirmation present. My mother picked out a light blue cashmere sweater from Godchaux's department store that she said matched the color of his eyes.

Part II

AWAY: UP EAST

5

Exeter

For my twelfth birthday, our parents took us to a restaurant downtown where I'd never been—a really good one, Galatoire's. The room we walked into was a bright space that glistened: white tile floor, walls hung with huge mirrors, and electrified gaslight chandeliers. I would not have another meal there until the night before I left for Phillips Exeter Academy, the boarding school in New Hampshire I would attend up north three years later.

When the last of the crème brûlée lay in a soft, sticky puddle, Gail, growing restless, implored, "Let's go. It's time to leave. Dessert is over."

Dad wasn't ready. He pulled out his Dunhill lighter from his trouser pocket and leaned down to light a Camel he'd lipped out of the pack he carried in his suit jacket. Only it didn't fire. "Now my lighter's on the fritz," he murmured, as if accusing the belligerent god of simple mechanisms. "So are most of the ones at home."

Feeling grateful and now grown-up, I offered, "Let me try to fix your lighter when we get home, Dad."

"That's a nice offer, son, but no," he said. "The Dunhills are delicate. When we get home, I'll show you how the Ronsons work. They need help, too. Maybe you'd take that on?"

"Okay," I answered, wondering what he had in mind. I was already raking the leaves in the fall and taking out the garbage on Sunday nights when Georgie was off. But those were unskilled jobs.

"Half the cigarette lighters at the house aren't working," he continued, as he scraped his thumb across the sparkless wheel that would not engage with the flint. "I'll show you what to do when we get home."

"Okay," I said. As a souvenir of the meal, I took the candle I'd blown out (Galatoire's offered one to everybody, no matter what age) and put it in my pocket.

At home Dad showed me the workings of a Ronson table lighter. He took one apart. He pointed out how the serrated steel wheel spun against a flint to create a spark that ignited the wick. Then he depressed a lighter's trigger to show me the action. He turned it upside down. He peeled back the oval green felt pad on the bottom so I'd see the big flat-headed screw that conceals the cavity stuffed with cotton wadding. He unwound another, much smaller screw at the base and extracted the delicate spring that pushes the flint up against the wheel. "This screw," he told me, "is the one you tighten to compress the spring as the flint is used up."

My responsibilities, Dad made clear, did not include their precious Dunhills—his solid gold and Mom's sterling silver. Mom moved her Dunhill from pocketbook to pocketbook, and Dad kept his with his keys and change. "Adler's," he told me, "will continue to service them. The whole mechanism is very delicate." My job was to keep all fifteen Ronson table lighters, scattered about the house, in good working order.

The next Saturday morning right after breakfast, which I always ate alone on weekends while everyone else slept late, I picked out as my workbench one of the mahogany and brass Chinese rice-chest side tables next to the living room couch. It was quiet there, with good light from the big window facing east. I'd extracted the classified section from the morning *Times-Picayune* and folded it to cover and protect the table.

After my parents left for the country club, I gathered every table lighter and placed all of them on the side table. As I did this, for the first time in my life I realized that our house reeked from stale smoke and tobacco flecks left in ashtrays. Every side table downstairs held the same contents: a lighter, a hinged-top box (usually from a foreign country) filled with cigarettes, a ceramic or glass ashtray, and a small sterling silver sleeve that enclosed a box of short, thin wooden matches, in case the lighters weren't working.

I collected all maintenance paraphernalia that my parents had scattered around the house and arranged it in one place, scoring four flint packs from Mother's dressing table alone. Flints came in cellophane-wrapped cardboard strips of six, with a tiny horizontal depression for each flint. In all, I found seven flint stashes—some packs partially used, some new—in various other places, including Mom's top desk drawer and the medicine cabinet in the downstairs powder room. Dad kept a can of lighter fluid handy in the top drawer of his dresser and another next to his toolbox in the garage. Both cans had been opened and were grimy from dripping fluid. I cleaned them up.

I consolidated my supplies in an unused back corner of the cabinet next to the fireplace. My parents used the front of this cabinet, the part they could reach easily, to store poker chips, mah-jongg tiles, the cribbage board, canasta double-card-deck holders, and stacks of new and used playing cards. Another shelf in the cabinet was well stocked with Dad's favorite cognac, Rémy Martin.

I arranged the lighters in a horizontal row at the back of the table and the supplies I wanted to use in a line perpendicular to them. This configuration left most of the tabletop clear to serve as my work surface.

On first examination, I found several problems. Two lighters needed new springs. They were already tightened to the max, and I didn't have a spare. Those two would have to go to Adler's repair department downtown. Three others had clogged wheels, the spaces between their serrations congested with flint fragments. I fixed these by rubbing them with a piece of fine steel wool and blowing on them to dislodge the flint dust. Later, I used an old tooth-brush to improve upon this part of my routine.

Next, the wicks. Half had burned down to the metal plate sur-rounding the wick aperture. I got eyebrow tweezers from Mom's medicine cabinet and pulled up all that had burned down too low. There was plenty of extra line in the body of each lighter, coiled into the cotton stuffing.

I searched in Dad's toolbox to find a screwdriver with which to open up the fluid well. Ronson table lighters have a large screw with a narrow slit at the base. The bit on Dad's only screwdriver was too large, but a silver dime worked fine.

Then I filled all the lighters with fluid. The reservoirs were all pretty dry, some completely. It seemed that no one had bothered filling them for ages. Though I tried to trickle each drop squarely into the center of the exposed cotton patch, occasionally one would escape along the side of the can. I was glad I'd been careful to have a double layer of newspaper under the lighters to protect the pol-ished surface of my worktable from fluid and flint dust.

Those oval-shaped Ronsons were heavy, solid sterling silver, each with the same scalloped design along its outer edge. They felt substantial—cool to the touch and well made—as I held them up-side down to refill them. Georgie kept them polished.

When I finished these tasks, I lined them all up and tested them. I brought paper towels from the kitchen and wiped off my fingerprints until each lighter was spotless, shiny, and dry. Then I checked all the screws to be sure they were tight and flipped the release latches one more time to be sure they ignited on the first try.

I put each lighter back where I'd found it, one on each side table in the living room, one on each table and one on the bar in the solar-ium, and one in the entrance hall. Upstairs, I returned a lighter to the combination lamp and table in my parents' dressing room next to Mom's chaise and one to each of their identical, square, pickled white bedside tables.

Over the next week, in their own indirect way my parents thanked me for getting all the lighters working. Dad smiled when he told me, "I see you got the hang of it with the lighters. Good job." Mom offered: "I'll drop off the two you couldn't fix the next time I go to Adler's and ask if they sell springs. How many do you want?"

"Six should be plenty for now," I answered, glad for the assistance.

A month later, they gave me their Dunhills. "Take care of these, too," Dad said. "You've got the knack now. We'll let you know whenever one of us has a problem. But be careful: they're expensive." I had proved myself.

* * *

Several years later, a critical day arrived for me. At the breakfast table that morning, I felt a strange tightness in my stomach. As usual, Dad was dressed in a close-fitting, dark gray double-breasted suit with a black silk tie and white shirt with gray stripes; he had purchased it at Charvet in Paris the previous year. Georgie served him a whole pink-meat grapefruit just the way he liked it, with the top off and each section cut, together with a cup of black coffee with chicory. He scanned the *Times-Picayune*. It was lodged in an upright mahogany reading stand on top of the antique cherrywood dining table that he and Mom had bought in London a few months earlier. The table was so highly waxed and polished that I could see the reflection of the newspaper in it. My father's sharp blue eyes were shielded and dimmed by his round, tortoiseshell reading glasses. His full, almost pudgy face and short thick neck were directed squarely to the morning's news; only occasionally did he glance my way. Not a word regarding the importance of the next twenty-four hours was exchanged. Between us it was quiet and tense.

I was thinking about what he'd told me many times since he'd returned from the war five years earlier. He disliked my school, Metairie Park Country Day, thought it too soft and easy, certainly compared to Fortier, the public school where Dad had gone before Exeter. He had lectured me on the advantages of finishing the last two years of high school not at Country Day but at his alma mater, Exeter. "Exeter," he was fond of telling me, "is tougher and more important than college as a place to learn how to think, a place to learn how to study. After Exeter, Yale was a cinch for me. It will be for you, too."

I loved Country Day. Each morning, as school began, it was my job to conduct the class meeting. Well built but skinny, I was the shortest boy in the class and the lightest. Yet maybe because I had fun at it, year after year I'd been reelected class president. I felt accepted by my friends, even though I was small and Jewish. I was happy in the light, airy classrooms. The teachers didn't use pressure tactics, and they talked to us about what we were doing—not like at home. Since the class was small, half boys and half girls, they knew each of us well. Most of us had been together for ten years.

But that day of the tense breakfast, when I got to school I felt oddly like a spectator. As I conducted the class meeting standing in front of the green bulletin board, I felt separate from my group, isolated and nervous. On edge, I hissed, "Ellen, stop talking out of turn! You know the rules." When she didn't stop giggling with Judy, I felt like throwing my chalk at her, and then . . . I actually did it! I watched it sail end over end, hit her shoulder, and fall to the ground, where it snapped in half at her feet. My impulsive action frightened me for a moment. I wondered if Ellen would get mad or cry. She did neither. In fact, she hardly seemed to notice, though I was ashamed to have lost my cool.

In the afternoon, at tennis practice, my attention wandered. I was usually fast and strong. Even though I weighed only 120 pounds and was just five foot five, I loved tennis and had a talent for it that became evident in school. My parents encouraged me to explore my potential. They recognized and even told me that tennis would be a good sport for me because I was athletic, but small. They also understood, I am sure, though we did not talk about this, that being able to excel in a sport would be good for my self-esteem, especially how I would feel among all the bigger boys, and later in life, men. After I did very well on the Country Day team, they sought out the most eminent pro in New Orleans, Emmet Paré, the Tulane University coach, and offered to pay for weekend lessons if he would take me on. After a successful tryout, I became one of Paré's few children pupils and began to be instructed by him on weekends at the New Orleans Lawn Tennis Club. By the time I was in tenth grade, and maybe leaving town to go to Exeter, I'd become the top-ranked player city-wide in my age group. I was the city champion after winning the *Times-Picayune* tournament in City Park, prevailing over eighty of the best players in the region.

Though I was generously and continuously encouraged to play, my parents did not take the time to come to a single tournament match, not even the city championship. Curiously, I did not especially want them there. I think I did not want them to see me fail, if I lost. Perhaps they understood.

I had a long-standing, ongoing crush on Betsy Stirratt, a classmate and the most beautiful girl in all twelve grades at Country Day. My one date with Betsy had been a double date with our classmates Herb Schneidau and Barbie Ott. Barbie was a daughter of Mel Ott, the Louisiana-born Hall of Fame slugger for the New York Giants. We had tickets for the Pulitzer Prize–winning stage play *Harvey*, by Mary Chase, the first play any of us had ever seen in a commercial theater. Our seats were in the dark balcony. During the performance I thought about holding Betsy's hand. When her parents picked us up afterward, I got to squeeze in close to her in the backseat. Her thigh, right next to mine, was soft and warm. One day that fall on a school outing we were walking together in the great allée of Pakenham Oaks, where the Battle of New Orleans was fought. There was no one else around, and so I put my arm around her waist. When we stood that close, though, it was clear that Betsy was so much taller; I felt ashamed.

After school on this critical day, Betsy drove me home. As I started to get out of her car she said, "You look sad, Peter. Is something wrong?"

My tentative answer: "Well, there's something going on at home that I'm worried about." I considered saying more but couldn't.

Only Georgie was there in the kitchen at our new house on Woodvine Avenue, which my father's brother, Uncle Jimmy, had designed. By 1950 Dad had earned enough to afford more space, a brick house, in a much nicer neighborhood, Metairie Club Gardens, nearly across the street from Country Day. Georgie was at her usual post, sitting at the red Formica counter stringing beans and listening to the radio. I was so glad to see her. She made me feel calmer just by being there. What do you think, Georgie? I wanted to ask. Should I go up north to New Hampshire, where it's cold, where maybe I can't play much tennis, and I'll have to study really hard to keep up with a bunch of very smart boys from all over the country?

I would even have liked to say to her, I'm afraid I won't be able to keep up. I hate the idea that no girls will be around, especially Betsy. Should I leave home to learn how to study, to pave the way for college?

Sitting next to Georgie after drinking half a glass of milk, I noticed how pleasant the kitchen smelled with dinner cooking and how inviting the room looked. The cork-tiled floor next to the stove was splashed with yellow slats of bright afternoon sunlight that had filtered through the dense magnolia leaves outside the window. It was comforting to come home to Georgie's late-afternoon radio installment of *Our Gal Sunday*, followed by my favorite program, *Terry and the Pirates*. "Did something bad happen at school today?" Georgie asked in her low southern lilt. "Your face is all stiff." I didn't answer, as if I was too busy listening to our serials. While our programs progressed, I watched the kitchen clock, watched time run by, and felt each minute as a loss of indescribable significance. Georgie couldn't give me the answer. I knew that.

When Gail had turned ten and I was twelve, we began to have dinner in the dining room with our parents at six thirty on those rare evenings when they stayed home. Tonight was one of those. When I said, "I had to stop practice today; I felt bad on the court," my voice sounded hollow and faint, like a distant echo from some faraway person in another house. I glanced at my father at the head of the table. He was still wearing his business trousers and dark tie. His bright blue eyes, which could sparkle like sun-tipped waves on Lake Pontchartrain, were guarded and seemingly calm.

I thought about how, within the few short years since he had returned home, Dad had not only invented a brand-new business, but had made it a success. During his tour of duty as a communications and intelligence officer, he had been trained to operate the gigantic new IBM computers. Back home, he had applied his knowledge of computer codes and information-storage potentials to keep track of all the war-surplus cotton stored in warehouses throughout the United States. Now he was the only one who knew where all of it was. He'd become the most powerful cotton broker in America. People from all over the country called regularly. Dad had made a lot of money, enough that we'd moved into our new, two-story brick house at the edge of the country club's eighteenth-hole fairway. Those days, even while admiring his business skill, I was unable to imagine the fear, the loneliness, and the danger he must have experienced and endured out there fighting the Pacific war. Had I seen William Wyler's Oscar winning 1946 World War II film, *The Best Years of Our Lives*, I might have understood some of the emotional stuff Dad was going through as he re-entered civilian life. But I hadn't, and I didn't.

* * *

During the night, toward morning, I had the dream I always had when I went to bed frightened. I saw the enormous mad dog flying through the dark night, his drooling, snarling mouth aimed at my left eye. I felt his rabid fang slash into my face.

I awoke cold, with sweat soaking into my pajamas. The sheets were damp. I looked around. I stared at my books on the built-in shelf at the foot of my bed. In the dim light I could barely see the smooth, wide, honey-colored cypress boards that covered the walls on either side of my bed and around the rest of my room. I touched the wall and felt better. Outside my door, down a short hall, my sister and parents were asleep in their own rooms.

The air-conditioning had come on. As the compressor whined, it stirred the air. A chill ran through me. It was first light outside. In a half hour, my father would be at the head of the breakfast table, grapefruit and black coffee before him, the *Times-Picayune* upright in its stand. This morning I had to tell him either "Send in the tuition deposit" or "Don't do it."

I dressed slowly. I thought about my class, about Betsy, the tennis team, this new, beautiful room, and other things I didn't want to give up—even the warm air and the hanging moss. I had lived in this wonderful new house for less than one year. I pictured Betsy— long-limbed, lovely, golden yellow hair and creamy white skin. I felt exciting warmth deep in my groin at the thought of her. The fresh cypress-wood smell in my room blended with the tawny sisal aroma of the rug, a mixture that followed me past my sister's room and down the hall to the bathroom.

Downstairs, my father was at the table, dressed immaculately for work, as always. But today he hadn't opened his morning paper. As I entered the dining room, he looked directly at me. When I got to the table and pulled out my chair, he said, "Well, son, what have you decided?" There it was, the question. To me, it sounded like thunder and lightning cracking over a sugarcane field.

"Dad, what do you think is best?" was all I could manage to answer.

"I went to Exeter," he replied evenly, calmly, confidently. "So have many members of our family for five generations." His vivid blue eyes were trained on me in a forceful, unyielding gaze.

I poured milk over the Rice Krispies topped with fresh Louisiana strawberries that Georgie had left at my place. I didn't lift the spoon. Unable to look at my father, my own gaze fixed on the coarse red berries instead, I whispered, "Okay, I'll go."

"Fine!" he responded in a full, rich voice tinged with triumph. "You've made a good decision; I know it was hard for you. I'll send in the check this morning. Let's talk later and I'll tell you more about Exeter." He unfolded the *Times-Picayune* and began to read the front-page news.

I rose from the table. He didn't seem to notice. I wanted to call Betsy. Instead, I walked into the powder room under the stairs, closed the door tightly, and threw up, as quietly as I could.

* * *

When I got off the train at the dingy, bleak station in Exeter, New Hampshire, three other boys had already stepped out onto the platform.

I felt inadequately prepared for the trials ahead; next to those guys in tweed jackets and with their ties askew over button-down oxford shirts, I felt out of place in my wrinkled khakis and striped polo shirt. I worried. I didn't know anyone in the school except for Charles Marks, who was also a new student. We'd come north separately, because I'd spent a few days in New York with my mother's sister, Aunt Margaret, and her husband, Uncle Benet Polikoff. At Country Day I'd known everyone, not just in my own class but in several classes up and down. I knew most of their parents, too.

I wondered if I'd survive in this remote place that Dad had always praised. I longed for the familiarity of home. I wanted to hear Betsy's voice. I felt like an exile, sent away by Dad to be toughened up.

As the taxi pulled up to my Exeter dorm, I noticed that a tricycle and a baby carriage cluttered the front walk. A man of average height in rumpled brown corduroys and a loose-fitting gray crewneck sweater appeared, holding open a screen door. As I dragged my bags up the short concrete walk, he extended his hand and smiled cheerfully. "You must be Peter. We've been expecting you. I'm Colin Irving, your housemaster."

Sleeper House, where I'd been assigned to live, was one of four ramshackle clapboard dwellings perched on the edge of Faculty Circle, a block-long cul-de-sac across Main Street from the Phillips Exeter campus.

"We'd better stop talking," said Mr. Irving. "Dinner is available in the dining hall only for another half hour, so take your things upstairs. Then you'd better get over there." He pointed across the street. "Wheelwright Hall." When I looked in that direction, I saw boys standing at the curb, waving good-bye as their parents drove away. So that's why no one was at the station. Their parents brought them to school.

In my first days at Exeter, I kept thinking back, longing for the nine girls and nine boys in my class at Country Day, most of whom lived within a few blocks of my house and had been my friends since I was six. Above all I longed for Betsy.

At Exeter at that time there were no girls. (It did not become coed until 1970.) I was sequestered in a class of 230 bright guys from across America, and two-thirds of them had been together since being members of the junior class—ninth grade, also called the prep class. Cliques had formed. Sports had been mastered. Extracurricular club memberships were full. I had gone from being president of my class to being a nobody.

In those first months I didn't have time to think about participating in an extracurricular activity like student government or debating or the school paper—the *Exonian*—where guys got to know one another outside of class. My time was filled with trying to keep up with homework and to understand what was going on in the fast-paced classes conducted predominantly as seminars around the large oval-shaped Harkness Tables.

The Harkness Table, I came to realize, was at the heart of the special teaching focus that dominated an Exeter education. It began when philanthropist Edward Harkness wrote the following in 1930 to Exeter's principal, Lewis Perry, regarding a substantial donation. "What I have in mind is (a classroom) where (students) could sit around a table with a teacher who would talk with them and instruct them by a sort of tutorial or conference method, where (each student) would feel encouraged to speak up. This would be a real revolution in methods."

The idea was accepted. Every class in my day was taught around a large, magnificent wooden oval table designed to seat twelve students and an instructor. By the format of this specially constructed furniture, we students were placed at the center of the learning process, under the guidance of a teacher seated among us. There were no lecture classes at Exeter.

My most challenging class was English. I was assigned to H. D'Arcy Curwen—appointed in 1924, B.A. Harvard, 1915—the same teacher my father had proudly survived twenty-five years before.

Mother had been indifferent as to whether or not I went away to prep school, whether Exeter or anywhere else. She never advocated my going, and in my hearing never objected, either. I think she was programmed to believe that this was what happened to boys in my father's family. Generations had been sent north to prep school, specifically to Exeter. I think she believed something like "It's a tradition that I have to accept." The same tradition did not prevail for girls. Dad wanted Gail to go east, too, for the last two years of high school, to Dana Hall School, in Massachusetts. But she refused, and so completed high school at Country Day.

The first winter at Exeter seemed to last for eight dark months. It was more than a season; it was a foreign way of life. Winter to me meant that the grass turned a rusty shade and that poinsettias bloomed instead of camellias. But at Exeter, month after month, shoulder-high snowbanks defined the campus walkways. Ice was everywhere underfoot. It was dark when I got up and dark when my last class was over.

At Exeter, the whole school was required to go to chapel, which was held in the Academy Building Monday through Friday morning. Little about it was ecclesiastical, except a hymn after morning announcements. Church attendance on Sunday morning in the school's chapel building was mandatory, unless an excuse was obtained. An excuse usually consisted of validation of weekly attendance at another church in town, or a synagogue.

The core spiritual principles of Exeter, which was founded in 1781 and opened its doors in 1783 with fifty-six students, had lingered on in mandatory Sunday chapel. Exeter's own private Anglican-looking stone chapel sat squarely facing Front Street at the edge of the campus. Each Sunday the school chaplain conducted a proper service, with the sermon often delivered by a visiting cleric or scholar. As a Jewish student, I had the option of going to a synagogue in town. Since I didn't do that in New Orleans and had no particular interest in the ecclesiastical tenets of my religion, I went to chapel, usually with my close friend Stephen Friedlaender, also a nonobservant Jew from the South. I felt a bit strange walking into that sacred space, but not nearly as odd as when we started to sing about Christ. In those parts of the hymn I'd go silent. Steve did, too. After chapel, I'd go downstairs to the basement of the nearby Academy Building, where there was a little snack bar called the Buttery. I'd treat myself to a vanilla milk shake. The smell and the taste of it reminded me of Claren's drugstore and of home. New Orleans: how I missed it!

Yet when I got home at the end of that first year, my household seemed even colder than Exeter. My parents were not welcoming in any special way. Gail, too, was unusually reticent. Something was wrong; I could feel it.

I fled to see my friends, and stayed out until two in the morning my first night home. We drank in the French Quarter. We were underage, of course, but that mattered little to most New Orleans bartenders. Between drinks at three different bars, as we walked around Bourbon Street, we listened to jazz blowing out into the moist night. That evening I told Herb and Larry and Ken, "From now on, I'm not Petie anymore. Call me Peter or Pete. I don't care which." What people should call me had been complicated from the beginning of my life, and maybe that's why Petie got started. My father was known by everyone except his parents as Pete, though his real name was Morris. My first cousin, two years older than I, who lived down the street and also went to Country Day, was named Peter.

The second morning home Dad came to breakfast, his face covered with red blotches; his eyes were watering; and pale, skin-toned makeup was smeared into creases down his cheek. Gail didn't raise her head from her plate of cereal.

"Kids," he said, "your mother and I had a terrible row last night. Neither of us slept. She clawed down the side of my face."

"I've heard you two screaming for weeks," Gail said. "I can't stand it."

"It's over," he whispered. "It's over, kids."

"What?" I asked.

Mother came sweeping into the dining room, hair uncombed and in her robe, looking wild-eyed. She never came downstairs for breakfast and wasn't usually awake this early.

"Your father's a disgrace!" she yelled at him but addressing me, then swiveled her head toward Gail. "I don't want him to lie to you. I found out last night what I'd suspected for months. He's been having an affair, a miserable rotten affair with his secretary."

"Christ," I said, wanting to hear, and at the same time wanting not to be there.

Dad was dressed in a well-tailored gray suit and had on a dark tie and striped dress shirt. From the neck down he appeared as he always did. But he sat impassively, head down, seeming sad and angry all at once. "Calm down, Ruth," he said. "We've had this out. I'm going to let her go today. It's over . . . It's over."

"You're goddamn right it's over!" she howled. "You're goddamn right it's over, or you're out of here forever!"

At that moment I felt that all of my hard work, the entire grueling year, had been for nothing. I felt that my family had just been obliterated. I felt so shocked, angry, and disappointed with my father that I couldn't look at him. And I felt so ashamed of him that I wanted him to leave forever.

But I said nothing. I was in shock and still tired from the long trip home and the late night out with my friends, and a little hungover. Dad finished up his coffee and folded his paper and told us good-bye by saying only, "I'm going to the office and will be back as usual for dinner."

As soon as he left, Gail and Mother started to cry. Gail's was a soft, frightened sob. Mother's was a raging outburst that doubled her over until she had to hold on to a dining room chair for stability.

I sat listening to them for what seemed like ten minutes. Finally, I went around the table to Gail and put my arm around her shoulder, and she leaned into me, her brown curls touching my chest. I stood there next to her for a few moments. Then I went over to Mom, who was still bent over but at least quiet now—bent as if she lacked the strength or will to straighten up, maybe ever again. I took her hand and pulled her a few steps, then helped her to sit at the head of the table by sliding her through the space left vacant by Dad's pulled-out chair.

I whispered, "Dad said it's over. Let's believe him. Let's hope."

* * *

For most Exeter boys, the ultimate drama of life is admission to college. "Where ya going to apply?" was the predominant, most intensely asked question. According to friends, college admissions mania had begun much earlier—often before birth for many of these guys. One told me, "My parents tried to get me on the Harvard waiting list for the class of 1957 the week I was born."

In my house, college was rarely discussed, except for Yale, where Dad had enjoyed the course in Shakespeare. Maybe it's more accurate to say it wasn't discussed so much as it was assumed. The Exeter-Yale, one-two automatic sequence was a given, an expectation that I had lived with from the earliest days.

How it was decided where each Exeter student would apply to college seemed on the surface to be quite straightforward. Each boy met alone with the venerable dean of students, Edwin Silas Wells Kerr. He was the gatekeeper. For most of us, it was the only time we would ever be ushered into his cavernous office on the main floor of the Academy Building. The few who were so smart they had enough spare time to get into trouble were already well acquainted with him.

The morning of my interview with Dean Kerr, I arrived ten minutes early. I presented myself at his assistant's outer office, dressed in the requisite uniform: blue oxford button-down shirt, Exeter maroon-and-gray regimental tie carefully looped under the collar with the knot pulled all the way up to the neck, blue blazer, and pressed gray flannels. Exeter had no formal uniform, but this was the eastern prep school attire that we all knew constituted the right thing to wear for a serious occasion on campus.

Inside the office, Dean Kerr sat behind a vast mahogany desk, in front of a wall of books.

"Well, Peter," he said looking over the thin silver frames of his glasses, "where are you interested in going to college?" I had done no research. I wasn't prepared to discuss that question. I was prepared to be told where I should apply. I hesitated. He glanced down into his lap at my file. "Your father, your uncle Jimmy, and most of your other New Orleans relatives who came to Exeter went to Yale." He was quiet for a moment; then he added in congenial afterthought, while he bent his head to reinvestigate my file, "Your family has sent many boys to Exeter over the years. All have gone to Yale. Would that suit you?"

"Do you think I can get in?" I asked, squirming in the dark wood chair with the school seal engraved in its back. To my considerable discomfort, he didn't answer me immediately. Instead he deliberately riffled though my file, taking a few minutes to read my evaluations and look over my grade charts. "Well," he finally said, looking straight at me, "contrary to expectations, you seem to be something of an overachiever, so I'd say yes."

His remark stunned me. It hurt my feelings to the core. I thought Dean Kerr was saying that I wasn't very smart, and that's why I'd had to work so hard at Exeter. I thought he might also be telling me that I'd been admitted because my family had a long record of sending sons to Exeter, a kind of unspoken sinecure. I wondered if, from Exeter's point of view, I had been admitted because they also liked to demonstrate the wide geographic reach of the institution. And there I was, a live one from way down south. It never occurred to me to think, Peter, you worked hard, you did well, and Dean Edwin Silas Wells Kerr, of all people, is paying you a compliment.

Weeks later, I realized that Dean Kerr and I had not actually decided where I'd like to go to college, even where I should submit applications for prime-choice and backup schools. I realized this when I found a manila envelope from his office in my mailbox. It contained only a Yale University application form.

Graduation morning, Sunday, June 14, 1953, was clear, cool, and beautiful in New Hampshire. In New Orleans, the temperature was ninety-five degrees. I didn't see my mother and father until I was walking down the stone aisle of Phillips Church, the school's chapel, where the annual Anniversary Service, as the morning ceremony was known, took place. I could see their faces turn toward me as they spotted me in cap and gown, marching with my classmates into the front pews.

World War II had been over for exactly eight years. Dad was not the only veteran in the audience. They were all over the place, some still in uniform, some with missing arms, and several in wheelchairs. We were in a somber, Christian, ecclesiastical building full of survivors. I felt like one of them.

6

Yale

As my cab wove through New Haven, Connecticut, toward the Yale University campus, which I'd never before visited, I could see Harkness Tower in the distance. It beckoned like a herald, calling me to a new life. I got out at Phelps Gate, the formal entrance to the Old Campus, across the street from the New Haven Green. Outside the gate on that bright, early September morning, cars were parked all over the sidewalks along College Street. Proud parents were helping their boys unload.

As I stood inside the gate, the Old Campus, where all freshmen lived, looked like a gigantic medieval cloister. Set side by side, sealed one against the other and blocking out the deteriorating city of New Haven, dormitories of austere architectural styles enclosed a minimally landscaped common space the size of two football fields. The huge green and its enclosing stone-and-brick dormitories were accessible to New Haven only through iron gates at each side of the large quadrangle. Mature oak, sycamore, and London plane trees in dark leaf shaded its stone paths. As I stood there getting my bearings, ten o'clock chimes tolled from the belfries of the three churches on the New Haven Green, just beyond the Old Campus, along with the carillon from Harkness Tower. Their mingled sounds filled the air and put me in mind of a new student being called to studies in Paris or Bologna or Oxford in the earliest days of university education.

Using the campus map that had been mailed to me, I spotted Wright Hall, my assigned dormitory. It was to the right, diagonally across the Old Campus from where I stood. I began to drag my two suitcases, Olivetti portable typewriter, and tennis racquet in that direction. Up close, Harkness Tower loomed like a stone belfry, the sort of marker in the landscape that I imagined had called the faithful to prayer at a lacy Gothic church like Tintern Abbey in England.

As I climbed the broad steps up to Wright's raised-flagstone entrance, I noticed that my new home looked like a stone fortress, softened slightly by its generous bay windows into a semblance of chateau domesticity.

I also sensed a level of social comfort I'd not felt since Country Day. I was wearing a dark blue polo shirt (Yale blue); a lightweight, charcoal-gray jacket with no shoulder pads, worn through at the elbows; and unironed but clean khakis. My soft Bass Weejun loafers were scuffed enough to be recognized as "shoe," meaning very Ivy League and in style beyond belief. I knew at least twenty guys from Exeter roaming around the freshman campus out of the incoming class of a thousand. None of them, though, were close friends. I was following the family tradition by going to Yale, not the Exeter tradition of going to Harvard.

I arrived feeling a new confidence; at the same time, I felt alone, just as I had all of my life. I felt separated from the camaraderie I saw across the Old Campus as guys met, exchanged smiles and handshakes, and clasped one another's shoulders. I watched with envy as parents who had driven to New Haven helped carry luggage through the maze of paths, or proudly waved good-bye to sons who had made it into Yale.

I carried my gear up three flights of stone steps to my room. It was very different from my single in Wheelwright Hall at Exeter, where I had moved senior year. This was a suite, if only a spare one. I entered an oak-paneled living room that held three large oak desks and three oak bookshelves. Two small bedrooms completed the suite, one with a double bunk, the smaller room with a single bed. The single was taken, so I deposited my stuff on the lower bunk. We each had an oak dresser with six drawers and a small mirror on top. Our bathroom, which we shared with three other suites, was on the entryway landing.

I left my suitcases on the bed and walked down one flight to meet my freshman counselor, John Dixon. After knocking on his open door, I entered his spacious living room, which had a bay window with a window seat overlooking the Wright Hall courtyard.

John was dressed just as I was. Only he was tall, lean, blond, Aryan. With his angular jaw, chiseled lips, thin, elegant nose, and lively blue-gray eyes, John looked like an über-WASP. In defiance of the stereotype, though, his eyes were warm and his handshake welcoming. I liked him at first sight. At Exeter, where for the first time I had met a lot of new people I knew nothing about, I'd learned that I could trust my first impressions. With John, as it turned out, I was right.

"Hi, Peter," he said, smiling and motioning me to sit in a rickety chair near his desk in the bay window alcove. "Welcome to Yale." He'd studied the photos in the freshman class book.

"Thanks," I replied in my best, clipped New England style, wanting to come across as self-assured and calm.

"Did you find your room?"

"No problem," I answered, confident on the outside but inside feeling alone in a strange new land. I needed this guy. I had an immediate urge to depend on this tall, handsome Yankee. Maybe I'd already found a sympathetic surrogate authority figure in New Haven.

"I'll be around, in and out of the dorm between labs," John explained to me in a chatty collegial way. "I graduated last spring, but I decided just before graduation that I wanted to go to medical school. Since I was a history major, I have a lot of science to make up." As he spoke, I noticed his athletic build and a well-used lacrosse stick, squash racquet, and two tennis racquets propped in the corner.

"Sounds like a tough year," I answered, recalling my own painful encounter with science at Exeter.

"I'll be busy, for sure. But I'm here to help you guys in this entry," John answered. "That's my job, in exchange for room and board. Let me know if you have any problems. You're my guys."

"Thanks," I said. "Nice to meet you." With that, our first encounter ended. "My only problem," I reported, standing close to John on my way out, "is getting my trunk out of the basement storage room where the shipping service left it and lugging it up three flights to my room."

John smiled at me. I wasn't sure why. Then, moving toward his open front door—either to usher or accompany me out; I wasn't sure which—he said, "We'll find your pal, Charlie . . . It's Charlie Maderer, isn't it?"

"Yes. Is he here already?"

"You guys—the lightest-weight Exeter wrestler and the champion heavyweight wrestler in one room—scary. I'll warn the rest of the entry not to mess with you." John had prepared. He knew that Charlie had been the champion heavyweight at Exeter and that I'd managed a decent record on the All-Club wrestling team in the lightest category, 123 pounds and lighter. I was proud that my Exeter tennis team had defeated rival Andover, but even more delighted that we'd swept them in wrestling 35–0, a triumphant end to my participation in a new sport where I'd learned how to overcome strength with agility.

"It's worse than that," I teased back. "In tenth grade back home, before he came to Exeter, Charlie was the high school heavyweight wrestling champion of upstate New York."

"Well then, I'm sure he'll be able to carry up your trunk,"

John added with a wink. "Let's go find him. He was just here."

While I was unpacking my trunk that first afternoon, I heard a faint tap on the door. I thought it must be our new roommate. But out in the hall I found a guy I didn't instantly recognize, although he did seem familiar. Slightly taller than me with a stocky build and broad chest, he was dressed in a light tan jacket with wide lapels and padded shoulders. It was cut like the sport coats worn by most young men who stayed in New Orleans for high school. "Hi, Peter," he said, extending his hand. "It's me, Bud. Bud . . . Calvin Trillin . . . from Kansas City." When I didn't immediately respond during our handshake, he continued, "Remember? We met last winter at the Sugar Bowl basketball game in New Orleans while I was visiting Jerry, our mutual friend."

I remembered. Bud stood there for a moment, then entered the room. I began to unpack as we caught up. He talked about Southwest High in Kansas City. I told him about Exeter. I began arranging my clothes on the bed before putting them away in the dresser. Looking over my Exeter wardrobe, Bud made an oblique request for help, saying, "We couldn't find the Ivy-look eastern-type clothes in Kansas City people wear here, so my folks and I decided I'd buy some new stuff when I got to Yale. Where do you suggest I go?"

I stopped unpacking. We left my room. We walked down the stairway to John's room. He told us where to go. Five minutes later we were inside J. Press, a couple of blocks away on York Street. Under the hovering, appraising eye of George Feen, one of the great haberdashery salesmen of all times, Bud replaced key parts of his wardrobe.

Bud was to serve as one of my guides into what turned out to be a new world for me. Before Thanksgiving I had acquired, by some kind of osmotic chemistry, three new friends to whom I felt especially close: Bud, Gerry Jonas, and Henry Geldzahler. Henry and Gerry had been classmates at Horace Mann School in New York and friends for years. We were busy learning about one another's lives, even busier talking through the academic excitement we each felt but would never have admitted to. Instead, we tried to appear ironic, cool, and masterly about our studies. Bud argued that Dostoyevsky was too young to write *Crime and Punishment*. Someone must have helped him, maybe an insane older brother. "Besides, the structure is shabby," I remember Bud arguing. "He needed more help." Henry, my most European friend, liked to say that the French Revolution had been an international disaster because it allowed despots to take over Europe. We didn't know what he was talking about, but we also had no idea how to challenge his knowledge of European history.

When Bud, Gerry, and I got into a heated disagreement about *Hamlet*, arguably Shakespeare's best play, Henry sat back with a quizzical smile, his head cocked to the side, before saying, "You guys sound like the Horace Mann debate team attacking a trick question. There ain't no answer, guys." Gerry liked to tackle both sides of intractable questions on subjects like the nature of God, and could carry on for paragraphs about who had said what on the topic. Bud's forte was the irreverent quip, his eyes twinkling as he related almost any subject back to life in Kansas City.

On Sunday nights the four of us got into the habit of escaping the three-meals-a-day, seven-days-a-week routine in the cavernous freshman dining hall, known as Commons. Commons, where freshmen had been expected to take their meals since the 1930s, was a cold, impersonal, neoclassical monster of a building surrounded by a long colonnaded entrance, like the side of an immense Greek temple. Inside it was an imitation Gothic-style Oxford or Cambridge dining hall. We ate at large round oak tables that seemed puny beneath its soaring, vaulted ceiling. Yale College's heraldic flags were draped from poles high up on the walls that extended from ornate brass brackets. The flags gave the hall an exalted atmosphere at odds with the frenzied, noisy feeding that took place below.

Once we started our Sunday night routine, we'd usually treat ourselves to pizza off campus. I'd never had pizza before. In New Orleans, when I wanted a cheap, hearty restaurant meal, I'd eat an oyster loaf—French bread stuffed with fried oysters and dressed with lettuce, tomato, ketchup, mayonnaise, and sliced dill pickle. After meeting at Phelps Gate at six, we'd walk along the campus edge of the New Haven Green, then on past the Taft Hotel, sauntering through downtown New Haven into the Italian section. After two years of virtual lockup at Exeter, being allowed to walk through the Old Campus gates and out into the city felt to me like going AWOL. To Bud and Gerry and Henry, who had lived at home all through high school, this routine experience didn't register as a privilege. Along Wooster Street, we'd pass benign winos lingering in Wooster Square. Fifteen minutes from the freshman campus, Italian was the street language. We were in a different world. Hungry and excited, we'd enter the Spot.

The Spot was a dilapidated shed slung low across the back of an unnamed dead-end alley, its tin roof wedged between five-story brick tenements. Inside, Formica tables lined the light brown, faux-wood-paneled walls. Above the tables, though, I was introduced to the best architecture in Sicily. Smudged, faded posters of the Cathedral of Palermo, the glorious classical remnants of the Greek temples at Segesta and Agrigento, and one huge poster of the Cathedral Cloister at Monreale created colorful swatches on the cracked walls.

Three Sicilian brothers owned and operated the Spot. Nearly indistinguishable in their tattered overalls and drab short-sleeved shirts, they looked as if they'd just walked down the hill from their mountainside village. They had squat physiques, dark skin, high Asiatic cheekbones, powerful shoulders, and thick forearms ending in fleshy hands with which they made the best pizza in town. In those days, that may have been the only culinary distinction that any New Haven eatery could claim. Set into the back wall of

the one-room restaurant was a gigantic brick oven, hot and glowing, from which the brothers withdrew their masterpieces on long,
wooden-handled platters. I'd never seen three guys work so hard
or so silently, becoming interchangeably waiter, crust shaper, gar-
nisher, and cook. The brothers saw no need to speak English while
conducting business, and it was not easy to coax a smile from any of
them, even when we lavishly praised their pies, which we generally
did while paying our modest bill.

Far away from the Yale campus, sitting around a grungy table in
the center of Little Italy at the back of a dark alley, Henry, Bud, and
Gerry used words like *schmoozer* and *macher,* as if Yiddish was our
lingua franca. They shared Passover stories and bar mitzvah recollections. Each of them could read Hebrew, a language I'd scarcely
been permitted to see and had never heard, except the routinized
four lines of the Shema prayer known as "Shemaa Yisrael" during
my brief tenure at Temple Sinai Sunday school.

Bud, Henry, and Gerry became my rabbis, of a sort. They never
formally took on the role (they never even noticed assuming it),
but they were my teachers, the unwitting coaches who introduced
me to the nuances of what it means to be culturally Jewish. They
taught me some of the fun about being simultaneously assimilated
and Jewish in the modern world, without the burden of being an
observant Jew, a transition I could not have made given my absence
of background about Jewish traditions, and my ingrained indifference to organized, doctrinaire, ritualistic religious practice. They
regaled me with stories of Jewish life among their families, of Jewish food—the good, the bad, and the ugly—and told me Jewish
jokes, something entirely new to me. I'd never heard a Yiddish joke,
a joke that deprecated Jews, or a joke that lampooned Christians.
Being Jewish was no laughing matter where I came from, because,
I suppose, it wasn't particularly spoken about at all.

Late in the fall at the Spot, they taught me about Sukkot, the
feast of booths, which celebrates the bounty of the harvest, and

the makeshift shelter, or sukkah, erected by the ancient Jews wandering in the wilderness. At Sukkot, observant Jews recite their prayers inside the sukkah, and often eat and sleep there as well. After numerous attempts by Jonas, Trillin, and Geldzahler to explain it to me, I finally got it. I amused myself by imagining I'd build my own sukkah in our backyard in New Orleans. I imagined dragging in my recalcitrant family to recite our Sukkot prayers of gratitude. I imagined our backyard shelter would be supported by sugarcane stalks from Godchaux property (in the town of Reserve, Louisiana), covered with green cotton-plant leaves, and festooned with lush white bolls. I wanted to tease my grandmother, too, to tell her all about the distinction between Sukkot and a sukkah.

I learned to say the word *tzimmes* ("stew" or "fuss"), found out that I preferred *shiksas* (most of the girls I'd knew at Country Day), was told that a *mohel* had circumcised me even if my parents didn't want to call him that, and asserted that there was likely no *shochet* (kosher butcher) in Metairie or maybe all of New Orleans.

Just as I found their Jewish identities intriguing, my pals were appalled at my ignorance. One Sunday evening during pizza, Henry asked, "How is it possible that with two Jewish parents and a large extended Jewish family and all that history down there founding Jewish institutions, you can be so dumb about your heritage?"

"My whole life," I told him, "I lived in a suburb and went to school at Metairie Park Country Day. There were no Jews around. Plus, my parents, who disdained Jews they considered low status, were full of *mishigas* about being Jewish."

"Good one, Peter," they exclaimed in unison.

Henry looked like a soft Dutch boy, though he was actually from Antwerp, Belgium. His blond hair fell in straight lines across the top of his round head. Behind his light blue eyes there seemed always to be bons mots waiting in the wings, about to burst forth from his lips, and they often did. Through Henry's pale apricot tortoiseshell glasses you could see his mind flickering in amusement and astute engagement with the topic at hand. Though he had been fat as a young boy, as a college student Henry was merely pudgy. He was also a little bent forward, pulled in that direction, it seemed, by the velocity of his mind.

"No one went to temple in my family," I answered. "I tried Sunday school for a few months but got kicked out for not showing up."

"What's this about temple?" Gerry wanted to know. "Didn't you have a synagogue or a shul? Was this the Masonic temple you guys shared or what?"

"No one gets kicked out of Sunday school," Bud chimed in. "It ain't kosher."

"Your deplorable absence of a Jewish identity is so bizarre," said Henry from Antwerp, Horace Mann, and New York's West Side. "I want to go down there to see Metairie and New Orleans for myself."

"You're on. How about next Christmas?" I gamely took up the challenge, turning up the volume on the word *Christmas* and delivering the invitation with a broad grin. "We give the biggest Christmas party in town." Though it was true, they didn't believe me. "Henry," I added, "I'll teach you how to decorate the Christmas tree." He rolled his eyes as we proceeded to order one large pepperoni pie and one large half-mushroom/half-anchovy, our usual shared combination.

I observed Passover during sophomore year at Henry's house. Most of the evening was conducted in Hebrew. When my turn came, rather than resort to English, Mr. Geldzahler, who was leading the seder from the head of the table, suggested, "Peter, try to sound out the phonetic Hebrew. You'll see it below the Hebrew script. See what it's like. We can help you." The company was so congenial, their encouragement so overwhelming, and Henry's smiling face so reassuringly fixed on me that I went for it. The room became silent, a rarity for that loquacious bunch. The whole table, including many of Henry's Antwerp relatives, his parents, and his brother, were there with me. When I stumbled, someone offered up the appropriate sound. No forks clanked while I struggled. When I finished, cheers were heard all around the table: "Yes!" from the younger kids, "Bravo!" from Henry and his brother, and "Mazel tov!" from his parents. That night at Henry's apartment, at 66 Central Park West, in the most privileged neighborhood of New York's heavily Jewish West Side, surrounded by Jews who had been through it all in Europe—some of them Holocaust survivors with bluish ID numbers tattooed above their wrists—wearing a loaned white yarmulke on my head, I went through my own rite of passage, my own oblique bar mitzvah.

In the midst of that lively, singing, celebrating, grateful family, sipping my third-blessing cup of sweet kosher Manischewitz, I could feel the shame, fear, and *mishigas* that reverberated through the cultural and religious denial that gripped not just my own family but most of the Temple Sinai congregation in New Orleans. The fun and pride of being Jewish, and the long, dramatic, creative, sometime tortured past of the Jewish people had been all but dissolved in the New Orleans culture that I was a part of. I felt deprived, but on the trail of a lost part of my past. Mr. Geldzahler concluded the seder with the traditional cry, "Next year in Jerusalem!" It was a ritual statement that would have given Rabbi Feibelman—on his perch on St. Charles Avenue, surrounded by his own congregation—the willies.

As I got to know Henry's parents, I learned firsthand about the Holocaust, whose name I recalled hearing only once in New Orleans and never at Exeter. As prominent and well-established Jews, Henry's parents had fled Antwerp before the war. But many of his relatives did not, and had been exterminated.

Mr. and Mrs. Geldzahler were the first adults I'd ever known who contained within themselves deep pain mixed with palpable gratitude. It took a while before I could understand that part of them. At first, all I saw was their stylish, urbanized exterior. As I watched Mr. Geldzahler leading us through the ritual seder meal,

I remembered my own father's double-breasted, dark gray suits. Henry's father wore a perfectly tailored, gray pinstriped light wool suit, a polished white-on-white dress shirt, and thick Italian silk Borsalino tie, all a bit shinier than I was accustomed to. Henry's father, through and through, brought Europe with him: his elegant if a bit slick dress, his discernible accent, his overseas commercial connections, and his devotion to Judaism. My father, by contrast, considered Europe a holiday playground, suits tailored at Godchaux's quite correct (though he preferred Charvet shirts and ties), and his own Jewish identity nothing to celebrate.

Mr. Geldzahler brought something out of Europe that I'd never heard of. He was a member of the De Beers international diamond syndicate, a wholesale client known as a "Sightholder." As Henry told me in awe, "My father receives a shipment of diamonds in a plain box every month."

"You mean diamonds—the real thing?" I asked. "In a box like a pound of candy?"

"Most are cut and ready to set," he continued. "The uncut ones are full of risk," he explained, a devilish expression on his round face. "In the second floor of the Diamond Club on Forty-Seventh Street, the cutter must find the way into those. He examines and reexamines the rough stones in daylight, close to the window. Deciding to cut here and not there, he takes the plunge. A false cut can reduce any fabulously valuable stone to dust." I believed Henry's account, and it might have been true.

"The 'merchandise,' as the syndicate calls it, comes in a little green box," Henry continued. "It's called a sight. My father is entitled to examine the contents for twenty-four hours. He has to decide to accept the entire shipment and pay for it at De Beers's wholesale prices, or send it back. It's all or nothing."

"Does the box come in your mail?" I asked, fascinated about this precious cargo.

"No, a special courier brings it to him at the Diamond Club.

If he keeps the box, his job is to market the diamonds however he wants, at whatever price he can negotiate, so long as he doesn't sell one carat of stone below the established De Beers retail minimum."

"In our family, where we have dealt in cotton for a long time," I told Henry, trying to leverage my limited commercial sophistication, "we'd say once he accepts the 'sight,' your father is 'long the market.'"

"Dad walks around New York with all those diamonds in his trouser pockets as if they were loose change," Henry confided, with the only awe I ever heard in his voice about anything or anyone.

Henry had seen therapists since high school. He knew all about psychoanalysis before I had ever heard of it. He knew how to size up character and personality—something I was just beginning to learn. I was too timid and too psychologically naïve and distant from myself to know how to do well what Henry seemed to do without effort.

During our Christmas vacation in New Orleans, after he had observed me for a few days in the midst of my family, Henry said to me in a conversation that I will never forget, "Peter, you're an island." It wasn't until years later that I realized he'd immediately seen how I was rather isolated from my parents, how I sometimes shriveled into myself, shrinking for need of the love and care that I felt I rarely got from them, no matter how hard I tried to be a good son.

Neither athletic nor interested in conventional competition, Henry spent his time at Yale reading, talking about, and looking at art. He developed a loyal band of followers. I never saw him alone, even walking to class. Unlike most of us, after a couple of college dates, Henry didn't bother to meet women. He may have experimented with girls in high school, but he never told me about that. Indeed, we never discussed women. I didn't recognize that Henry's apparent lack of interest in our obsessive longing for female company and sex was a signal that he was possessed of an entirely different sort of sexual longing. Henry was the first gay person I ever knew well.

* * *

The first winter at Yale, I decided to try skiing. Before Exeter, the only skiing I'd done was behind a motorboat on Lake Pontchartrain. In his room one day, when I told Henry I was going to try it but had no equipment, he instantly offered his. "I've got all the stuff. Never used it. Take it."

"Thanks, Henry," I said. "I'll borrow it for the weekend at Dartmouth."

"Peter," he replied, "I ain't no way, no how, ever going to use this stuff. Not the skis, not the boots, not the socks, not the long johns, not the cap. Use it. Keep it."

"You might want to ski sometime," I said when I came back to pick everything up. Looking over the big cardboard box full of clothing and boots and two gleaming skis propped against the wall, I asked, "Are you sure?"

"My parents thought this was a sport I could do. Something I'd like," he answered. "There's no way I'm riding in some guy's car six hours into a snowstorm [Henry had never learned to drive] to wait in a long line and get on top of a freezing, friggin' mountain just so I can fall on my ass or break both legs. This stuff is yours."

* * *

Freshman year, philosophy was a new subject for me, the only one. It blew my mind. I was being introduced to a secret language that seemed to unlock the mysteries of ancient and modern wisdom long hidden in a vault I never knew existed. I felt like Aladdin being offered the magic lamp. We read Plato and Aristotle first; they set the scene. Then came a big jump, as the semester proceeded, to Martin Heidegger, Søren Kierkegaard, Karl Jaspers, Arthur Schopenhauer, and, my favorite, Immanuel Kant. During that first term, my philosophy class friends and I would debate late into the night about things like whether or not Kant's categorical imperative did, in fact, provide a sound basis for making all future life decisions. Just before Christmas break, we read Jean-Paul Sartre. Taken also with Kierkegaard, I wrote on the flyleaf of my text these seven notes:

1. Why have faith?
2. Is there salvation?
3. Is there eternity?
4. Faith in conflict with modern morality?
5. What comes after?
6. If God is the condition, what can man do? How to reach God?
7. What kind of a God is this? Is there justice and choice?

On my flight back to New Orleans at Christmas, I couldn't wait to tell my grandparents about the categorical imperative and existentialism. It never occurred to me to discuss either topic with my parents. They would find philosophy tiresome and irrelevant. At my grandparents' house my second evening home, I said to Gram and Grandpa, "Have you ever heard of Immanuel Kant? He's got a great idea; he calls it 'the categorical imperative.'"

Gram looked at me quizzically. "We have a good encyclopedia. Let's see what it says about him. And what was it called?"

"The categorical imperative," I proudly reminded her.

"Oh, that doesn't sound like something the encyclopedia would help us with," she said, smiling. "But let's check." Gram loved to look up things in her reference books, which took up part of one whole shelf in the dark, built-in floor-to-ceiling bookcase that spanned the length of her living room.

"How about existentialism?" I laid it on. "What about looking that up, too?"

Grandpa got into it. With a merry look in his eye, he asked, "Can you spell that?"

When I had finished giving my self-satisfied summary discourse

about the essence of both the categorical imperative and existentialism, Gram let out an endearing "Oh, Pete."

* * *

In the middle of freshman year, I decided to try to join the *Yale
Daily News*. My grades were good. I was finding my classes stimulating, especially philosophy, but I did have spare time to do more.
I thought it would be a fun and interesting challenge to work on the
paper, something I'd wanted to do at Exeter but had not had time
for. Even though we never discussed it, Bud and Gerry had come
to the same decision.

One didn't wander over to the *News* building and volunteer to
become a staff member. The only way to become part of the organization that put out the official daily Yale paper was to "heel." Until
then I'd thought "heeling" was what my Dalmatian, Ranger, was
supposed to do after I'd trained him to walk obediently at my side.

The first step was to attend the heelers' orientation meeting in the
News building. The evening of the meeting, after supper at Commons, Bud and I walked over, nervous and uncertain of what to expect. I'd never been inside the light brown stone building; indeed,
at that point, I had to consult a campus map to find it. Inside there
were about fifty of us, including, to my surprise, Gerry. The meeting,
held in the downstairs heelers' room, was chaired by the managing
editor, Ted (Edward) Whittemore. He was thin with a fine, chiseled
small nose. Ted wore a tweed jacket that hung loosely over rumpled
khakis, dark brown loafers completely scuffed, and a tie hanging
loose inside the collar of his button-down blue oxford shirt. His beige
horn-rimmed glasses melded into his shaggy light brown hair. As he
stood there before us conducting the meeting, I was sure he was one
of the most elegant, understated men I'd ever seen. "This is going
to be more difficult than you can imagine," he barked. "It's going to
take thirty hours a week. Can you handle that? If you're the right

guy, your grades won't suffer. If they do, you'll have to drop out."

Then Whittemore reiterated, after a long pull on his dark Cuban cigar, "If you fall behind in your college work, you must stop heeling. And you're going to be exhausted all the time."

He then stopped and, like a drill sergeant, looked into each terrified face one by one and said, "Leave now if this isn't for you." Some did. Bud and I stayed. Gerry decided to drop out of this first round. He came back, though, to heel in the last heeling period for our class in the fall of sophomore year.

Heeling consisted of showing up at the *News* building at seven in the evening Monday through Thursday, and on Sunday afternoons. We had a daily paper to put out. We reported to Whittemore, as a cadre of free, willing workers with no rights and no status and most of us with no experience. As heelers, we stood trembling in awe before him. As we proposed story ideas, he seemed infallible in judgment, unflappable no matter what the apparent crisis; night after night he confirmed my original instinct that he was the coolest guy in New Haven.

To heelers, Whittemore was all-powerful. He was entitled to ignore any suggested story without comment. He was entitled to give us any assignment for that night or for the next day. The assignment could be anything: write a story, research a story for one of the editors, go out and find out about something that the managing editor wanted to know, clean up the building, bring back pizza, take the final pasteup to the printer. Regardless of the eventual tasks, you were required to be on duty most of the night.

The *News* building was a freestanding structure on York Street at the outlet of Fraternity Row, a narrow semicircular road giving access to six other relatively similar stone buildings. Opposite the *News* building, across fraternity row, was the Yale Theater. Unlike the fraternities, which had been failing for years and had mortgaged their properties to stay in business, the *News* owned its building free and clear.

Under Ted's authoritarian command, we got whipped into shape as the future custodians of the paper. Inside the heelers' room on the first floor, a wooden counter fifteen inches wide ran around three walls. Each heeler had a workstation on that ledge with a Royal or Underwood typewriter supplied by the student. We each considered being assigned a workplace an immense privilege, the first step into membership, into being an inhabitant of those sacrosanct portals—if we made it. Between seven and eleven each evening, as we hammered out our work, our sturdy, ancient typewriters went click, click . . . click . . . click, click, as if, independent of us, the transitory occupants of their abode, they were holding a conversation with one another. There was simultaneously camaraderie and intense competition among us heelers as we struggled to prove ourselves.

Once he entered the fray, Gerry made the biggest scoop of any heeler in our class. He noticed a report in the *New York Times* that forecast an expected bulge in the U.S. college-age population. He showed it to Whittemore and told him, "I want to find out what this might mean for Yale."

Whittemore generally dismissed heelers' proposed story ideas with a wave of his hand—he'd heard it all before—or simply with a blank stare that said it all. Gerry expected Ted to yawn, maybe to draw deeply on his stogie, then at best to say something like "Okay, check it out in the library and let's see what you come up with."

Instead, he became alert. "Go see the university secretary; see what he says. Find out what Yale is going to do about it. If you can find a way to wrangle it, take an interview with Griswold [Alfred Whitney Griswold, the president of Yale]." Gerry did manage to get that interview—a full half hour—the only heeler in our class who got in to see the president of the university. Gerry's story ended up as the front-page lead with his own byline, a major triumph.

Of the fifty-five heelers in our class, spread over four induction periods, twenty-eight finished. Of those who did finish, not everyone was invited to join the *News*. Making it to the finish line did not automatically get you in. Twenty-three of us ended up members of the *Yale Daily News* class of 1957. I'd found an energetic affinity group of bright and practical men. I'd found a way to move beyond the boundaries of Exeter acquaintances and to expand my inner circle beyond Henry, Gerry, and Bud, although Bud and Gerry were right there with me at the *News*.

The *News* became my second home. Without realizing it, I'd learned new skills—how to manage my time more efficiently than ever, how to write clearly and briefly. I'd become alert to nuances in interviews and skeptical about what I was told. Eventually I learned how to run an organization with other men, and how to manage the financial necessities of a business for which we became responsible during our final year in office.

Before our tenure was over, I came to understand that the *News* was set up in a most curious way. It had no official connection with Yale University. It owned its own building. There was no Yale faculty or administration oversight of management, news reports, or editorial content. A bunch of often half-baked, soused undergraduates ran the show at this for-profit enterprise. At the end of each term of office, the *News* board was entitled to split whatever profit had been earned, the lion's share of it by custom distributed to those who put in the longest hours and held the most responsible positions: chairman, business manager, and managing editor.

When I left New Haven in June at the end of my first year, I thought of New Orleans in a new way. It was a place to which I was returning for just a few months. It was still home, but now I'd found a place where I could be independent, and I'd come to understand more about my Jewish identity. With it, I was gaining a new idea about my own history and my family's journey over the ages. I had found a new world filled with peers. Academically, I was no longer scrabbling from the bottom of a steep hill, as I had been at Exeter, forced to climb to save my life. In the way of a newly graduated freshman, I was feeling pretty grandiose all the way around.

* * *

When I moved from the Old Campus to Jonathan Edwards College, one of Yale's ten residential colleges, at the beginning of my sophomore year, I elected to live with near-strangers for fear I'd be discovered by my closest friends to be a fraud. If Gerry and Bud and Henry truly knew me, they'd be disappointed. They couldn't possibly care enough to accept my undisclosed foibles or my well-concealed intellectual shortcomings.

Sophomores were allowed to have cars. My parents had generously offered to pay for a new car to use at college and to drive back and forth between New Haven and New Orleans on long vacations. I found a beauty at the Don Allen Chevrolet dealership in New York and believed I'd negotiated a good price after considerable days of haggling to fit into the budget I'd been given. This snappy, shiny black convertible with lots of shimmering chrome and white-wall tires was my ticket to visiting women's colleges, and to getting around New England on short holiday excursions.

Undergraduate Yale after freshman year was organized on the college system, like Oxford and Cambridge, its venerable reference points. Each college was a distinct residential unit with its own dining hall, common room, headmaster, and affiliated faculty, though all undergraduate classes were open to all qualified students. Once assigned to a college before the beginning of sophomore year, a student remained there in residence until graduation. Quite naturally, because one lived, slept, and ate in one's college (though there were ways to exchange meals to go to another college for the occasional dinner), friendships and relationships were most easily formed around the college unit. And since each college was composed of sophomores, juniors, and seniors, this setup was an excellent means of getting students to mingle across class boundaries.

At the end of freshman year it was possible to select roommates for the next year, but not to select the college in which you would live. The university had to fill rooms based on availability, and if one did not select a full complement of roommates for the assigned suite, the university filled in whatever space remained available. I "pinned my name" together with two young men I'd met in my entryway in Wright Hall who had become casual friends: Mac Mc-Gowan, who was headed for engineering, a field I knew nothing about, and John Leinenweber, an ardent Catholic who wanted to become an architect. Sam Morley, a government major and already a junior, was assigned to live with us—a piece of good fortune. Sam was an openhearted, cheerful westerner from Portland, Oregon, and had graduated from Vermont's Putney School. His family was in the lumber business.

Bud, Gerry, and Henry also split up, and, as it turned out, each got assigned to a different college. Although we lived dispersed around the campus, we managed to remain very close through classes, extracurricular connections, and, when all else failed, the telephone.

Yale College wisely required that, before electing an academic major, each student fulfill "distribution requirements" during the first two years. These were a set of academic hurdles intended to assure the college administration and the larger world outside that every Yale undergraduate would leave New Haven an academically well-rounded graduate. The imposed requirements included two years of a foreign language, two years of English literature and composition, and two semesters of science. I was delighted to continue French, and fine with English, but I knew from Exeter that I was not overwhelmingly capable within the admittedly important domains of physics, chemistry, and math.

No doubt it was champions of the liberal arts within the Yale administration who had arranged a gentle, nonquantitative, two-term sequence for the scientifically challenged, which consisted of astronomy first semester and geology second. This particular offering was known affectionately by all grateful liberal arts students as "Rocks and Stars."

I got through astronomy—just barely—my first term.

Geology was competently taught by an enthusiastic, ramrod-postured full professor whose last name happened to be Flint. Richard Foster Flint was famously known to all as "Rocky Flint." Mr. Flint divided us miserable excuses for science students into two-man teams. Each pair was expected to collaborate in lab, on field trips, and on the final paper, which served as the final exam.

Bud and I teamed up. Our project was to unravel the geologic history of a rocky outcropping we'd seen on the shoulder of Route 146 north of Branford, Connecticut, one early sunrise while returning from Wellesley College. Our plan for the final draft of our paper was simple. After each wrote his respective section, we'd meet on Sunday evening to jointly knock out the conclusion.

At nine on Sunday evening, just as we'd agreed, Bud gave his double rap on my door. We never locked the door—knocking was just a form of casual greeting or warning. The door handle turned. From my unsteady perch on our beat-to-pieces couch, I vaguely saw Bud, all fuzzy in the doorway. He looked over at me and noticed that I remained prone. "Hey, guy, you ready to wrap this thing up?" he asked quizzically.

"Bud?" I said, still not quite able to move.

"Yeah, it's me, Bud," he answered. I heard quizzical go to nervous.

He looked around at the empty Miller beer cans all over the living room. He sniffed the stale air. Guys from up and down our stairway entry had been in the room drinking and listening to the radio since Sunday afternoon. Me, too. I was sloshed.

"Can't work . . . Can't do it, pal," I giggled. "I'm consumed with the consumption."

Horror quickly washed over Bud's astonished face. I wasn't much of a drinker, but that Sunday I had been one of the guys. I lay flat on our lumpy couch, incapable of collaborating.

With Bud's indulgent help and escorted by his steady arm to the

United Greek Diner for black coffee, I gradually sobered up. Back in the room, I tried to settle into our collaborative edit. It took us until two in the morning, and Bud did most of it. That's how we finished our final paper, the one that would seal our fate for the term and liberate us from science forever, one way or another. Rocky Flint knew his audience well. Armed with low expectations going in, he gave us a B-plus, good enough to get both of us through the Yale science requirement.

* * *

During the winter of my third year, after I'd elected to become an English major, I noticed a poster pinned to the English department bulletin board. The beige flyer announced an international summer school in Oxford, England. The focus was seventeenth-century English literature. I was attracted to more than the study. The idea of living in Oxford for a summer gripped me. The poster mentioned afternoon punting on the Thames and a summer pass to the Bodleian Library, which I'd heard reverential mention of in English class. St. Hilda's, the women's college where participants would live and study, was described as a relatively new, small Oxford college set amid a spacious lawn that descended to the banks of the Thames on one side and ended in two grass tennis courts on the other. It was the grass tennis courts, I must confess, that clinched my determination. Rather than expecting me to find a summer job, my parents made my summer in Oxford feasible with generous willingness to foot the third-class ship transport and modest room, board, and tuition.

During the first week there, at the end of dinner, I noticed a thin woman who looked to be about my age sitting alone at the next table. I'd seen her seated quietly and alone in class since the first day. I was alone as well. She was reading and dawdling over the remains of her boysenberry cream custard, the gelatinous dessert that had capped each bland meal in the St. Hilda's dining hall since we arrived. She seemed oblivious of the dinner remains and clutter that had been left on her table by departed students. The young woman was so slight that her behind, tucked tightly into khaki Bermuda shorts, didn't protrude beyond the edge of the narrow wooden bench upon which she sat.

"Hi," I called over. "You wanna sit together while you finish dessert and I finish my tea?"

"Sure," she said with a smile. "Come over."

As I sat down across from her, the bespectacled girl closed her book.

"Hi, I'm Deirdre Frome. I live in New York and go to Radcliffe. What about you?"

"Peter Wolf. I'm at Yale and from New Orleans, between junior and senior years."

She considered this information, then said, "I was reading this John Donne poem, 'A Valediction: Forbidding Mourning,' for class tomorrow. Heavy stuff. Have you read it yet?"

I had. We began a first conversation.

"He's gloomy and so morose in that poem," she began. "I like that. He reminds me of Schopenhauer."

In my mind I immediately imposed the Radcliffe-type cliché: smart, verbal, intellectually intimidating. In New Haven, I'd never seen one, but we imagined all Radcliffe girls carried heavy book bags and wore thick blue stockings.

"I know he gradually turned away from dissipation, cynicism, and worldly ambition," I said, trying to rally by drawing on a recollection from English 201. "Maybe 'Valediction' illustrates him in transition."

"Did you know he got kicked out of Oxford?" she parried. "It took him a long time to become a devout Christian. He eventually became a great churchman."

Before we parted an hour later, she had read me two romantic John Donne poems, "The Message" and "Lovers' Infiniteness." She'd also told me two risqué jokes. This skinny, ribald creature, an intense, smart, and funny woman from Riverdale, in the Bronx, was much more complex and appealing than the stereotype of the Radcliffe woman we'd manufactured in New Haven. As we left the dining hall, we agreed to meet for lunch the next day.

Deirdre's straight, flyaway chestnut hair, flat chest, contourless body, and austere metal glasses frames would not have been considered particularly attractive features by most of my classmates, or by my parents, who always appraised the girls I took out as being either pretty or not. Her sharp wit and inquisitive nature more than made up, in my estimation, for her plain and, I thought, attractive appearance.

"Have you ever seen Tintern Abbey?" she asked two weeks later, as we left class. We'd been analyzing William Wordsworth's "Lines Composed a Few Miles Above Tintern Abbey."

"No, I have no idea where it is."

"Let's go," she whispered exuberantly. "Let's go next weekend. It's not a long train ride."

I'd never gone to the country for the weekend with a woman anywhere. Nevertheless, I answered, "I'm game. Let's go." I was full of expectation and fear about the personal part. Sitting beneath a big weeping willow down near the river, we'd kissed a couple of times, period. Now we were going away for the weekend.

We found that we could go by train to Bristol, ten miles from Tintern Abbey, and bike the rest of the way. We used our rental bikes daily, as did most students around Oxford. I'd never taken a weekend bicycle trip, either, but in England it was very simple; the whole country seemed to be doing it. Automobiles were not yet crowding the roads in 1956, as the English economy was slowly emerging from wartime devastation.

At the Oxford station, we bought a bicycle-supplement ticket for almost nothing and were told by the stationmaster how to stow our bikes. As the train pulled in, we spotted the bicycle transport car lodged in the middle of the other coaches. One snap of the outer latch and the sliding doors opened, revealing bike racks. We loaded ours into the retrofitted freight car, snapped the latch shut, and hurried on to a second-class passenger car.

After a four-hour train ride and a brief bicycle jaunt through the Wye Valley, we shared a late picnic lunch inside the ruins of Tintern Abbey, founded in 1131, and which in its current romantic desolation looked, apart from an absence of foliage, very much as it had when brilliantly portrayed in pencil and watercolor by the massively talented seventeen-year-old draftsman-trained J. M. W. Turner, who visited the site in 1792. No one else was there. It was a moody Saturday afternoon. Dark gray cumulus clouds raced over us. I spread my biker's poncho over the grassy carpet on the floor of the abbey's nave. Deirdre pulled cheese and bread from her knapsack. I fished a bottle of Chianti from mine.

We were in the midst of a roofless, majestic church, its decomposing Gothic nave surrounding and sheltering our quiet meal. The stained glass was long gone, leaving a sequence of lacy stone-tracery silhouettes as window frames, made vivid by the hills and dark sky beyond. Instead of the blue, red, yellow, and green filtered light that the parishioners had long ago experienced in this place, we saw the early afternoon's overcast light through the west façade and, outside the huge east window, sheep grazing and trees bending in the wind.

As we sipped wine and ate our provisions, we read to each other lines we selected on the spot from Wordsworth.

In a clear, singsong voice, Deirdre read:

For I have learned
To look on nature, not as in the hour
Of thoughtless youth; but hearing oftentimes
The still, sad music of humanity. . . .

Moved by the architectural ruins surrounding us, I responded by reading:

These beauteous forms,
Through a long absence, have not been to me
As is a landscape to a blind man's eye;
But oft, in lonely rooms, and 'mid the din
Of towns and cities, I have owned them. . . .

After a while, we stopped speaking. We kissed and then we kissed again, hard, as we held tight to each other. Then we watched the light and listened to the wind all around us. Nearly dozing, we sat leaning against a column shaft, unburdened by anything other than the slight pressure on our backs.

We stayed until it was nearly dark, eventually lying on our backs, clasping hands as we gazed at the turbulent sky, and from time to time holding each other close and kissing. Above us, the clouds turned from mildly threatening to menacing. Then it poured.

By the time we arrived just before dark at the only bed-and-breakfast for miles around, we were drenched. Just one small room was available, containing one double bed. We'd not previously discussed sleeping arrangements; neither of us knew what to say.

Soaked by the rain and secretly filled with enthusiasm for our imposed communal experience, Deirdre and I looked at each other. She nodded at me. I nodded back and said, "Okay, we'll take it." For the rest of the summer, each weekend, we traveled into the English countryside, usually to visit a cathedral or a historic village.

After summer school, Deirdre and I maintained our relationship. During the fall she visited New Haven for the first time. I met her at the train station on Saturday afternoon. When I got to her arrival platform, there were a lot of excited students milling around, waiting to meet their dates. It was a football weekend. Neither of us had any interest in going to the game. Indeed, during my Yale career I never saw the Yale Bowl, or the tennis courts, which were far from the campus. I'd made a basic decision to do new things, and to concentrate my limited time not on sports but on whatever new things I wanted to learn, in and out of class.

When Deirdre stepped down from the train, her metal-framed glasses shining in the light, she looked more like an old-fashioned, book-bag-carrying, bluestocking "Cliffie" than she'd ever seemed to me in Oxford, England, or in Cambridge, Massachusetts (where I had by now spent time with her).

"Well, I made it," she said and smiled at me cheerfully. "Class got out late. I nearly missed the train—what a panic! So, this is where you Yalies hang out," she said, looking around at the grim rail yards and dilapidated railroad station. It looked as if it hadn't been repaired since it was built.

"Welcome to our shabby city," I said. "I hope Yale won't be too boring for a Harvard-Radcliffe woman."

"Peter, I'm so happy to be with you," she answered, dissolving my defensive tension with a tight hug and kiss right there on the station platform.

Over the weekend she met Bud, Gerry, and Henry and my colleagues at the *News*. She met my roommates at a small postgame cocktail party that we organized on Saturday afternoon, although Deirdre and I did not attend the game. Dressed like a Quaker in drab cotton clothes of a neutral brownish gray and wearing neither makeup nor ornaments of any kind, she looked nothing like the other female visitors. She was more intense than anyone else's date. She never uttered a platitude. Indeed, Deirdre said very little when there were other people around, as if she were continually gauging the universe she'd been led into. When she did speak up, though, she was interesting and her remarks substantive. She displayed her knowledge lightly, often with intriguing phrases laced with teasing wit.

* * *

When it came TIME to think about Yale senior secret societies, I had a lot of background from New Orleans to consult before moving ahead. As soon as I was old enough to drive, which in those days in New Orleans was fifteen years old, I began to get the picture. Suddenly my social life was not confined to Metairie and to my friends from Country Day. Just as suddenly, I realized that my closest male Country Day friends were being invited to join certain high school fraternities while I was not. Instead, I received an overture from Tau Beta Phi, the Jewish fraternity whose members lived primarily in town. The invitation to pledge came from Leon Rittenberg, the only Jewish boy in the class ahead of me at Country Day. From then on, almost all social occasions to which I was invited were populated primarily by Jewish kids. When in New Orleans, through high school and college, I was not invited (nor were any other Jewish boys or girls whom I knew) to participate in the feeder fraternities, sororities, and social organizations that prepared girls for their debuts and boys to become krewe members, who assumed the roles of courtiers, queens, and kings at Mardi Gras. Nor, in later years, was I or any other Jewish boy or girl of my generation invited to join the roster of prominent and powerful social clubs in New Orleans that sponsored the spectacles that the general public associates with Mardi Gras. It dawned on me back then that those finely costumed Mardi Gras kings and dukes riding spirited horses in the streets, and those courtiers up on the parade floats throwing trinkets down to us in the crowd, many of them business colleagues and casual friends of my parents and grandparents, were all members of the parade-sponsoring social clubs that excluded Jews. At about the same time, it occurred to me that my family and all of my Jewish friends belonged to one country club, Lakewood, while all of my Christian friends belonged to either the New Orleans Country Club or the Metairie Country Club. Only then did the paradox dawn on me that my family lived along the eighteenth hole of a beautiful golf course belonging to a lovely country club down the street that we were not permitted to join. My parents never once talked about this to me. There was no expression of resentment that

I heard. But I wonder how they felt, way inside. For my part, just like my parents' apparent indifference, I accepted discrimination without consciously thinking of it as such. To me, that was the way it was. My Country Day friends went to Metairie Country Club, or New Orleans Country Club; I went to Lakewood.

Sometimes at Tau Beta Phi meetings someone would mention a Christian fraternity or sorority or something about a society party held at the Metairie or New Orleans country club covered in the social section of the *Times-Picayune*. But not once in those years did I ever discuss with any of my lifelong Christian friends this cleavage in our social life that came with being able to drive. Nor did any of them ever broach the topic with me. That's simply how it was.

Years later, at Country Day reunions, we did talk about it. My Christian friends told me they too accepted the situation as it was. Ruth Hardie told me that implicit but firm social discrimination starting in ninth grade separated her from her best friend, Judy Schwarz, and that she felt helpless to do anything about it, even to discuss the situation with her socially prominent parents. On both sides of the divide, it seems, my group at that time went along to get along, rather than get overtly upset. It was not an era or a culture in which kids acted up. We chose to accept discrimination and adjust to it. We knew and considered no alternative.

So, at the beginning of junior year, when I began to think about the secret societies at Yale and to wonder how my being Jewish might affect my prospect of being asked to join one, I knew more about the impact of the anti-Semitic social clubs and their associated Mardi Gras parade krewes in New Orleans than I did about the attitudes of the secret societies at Yale.

The seven major Yale secret societies each owned a headquarters near campus known as its "tomb." Skull and Bones, Scroll and Key, Berzelius, and Book and Snake, all founded between 1832 and 1863, inhabited nineteenth-century neoclassical temples. Skull and Bones and Scroll and Key, the most famous and the oldest among them, were rumored to possess substantial endowments and to wield mysterious influence in government, politics, and finance far beyond the confines of New Haven. As far as I could gather from my casual inquiries at the time (and confirmed by research in later years), none of the Yale secret societies in those days were overtly "restricted," though Skull and Bones, the most famous of them all, was rumored to be the least likely to seek out Jewish members.

Each year, after solemn and determined deliberation, the seniors in each society selected and admitted fifteen new replacements from the junior class. Admission was governed by the arcane, mysterious rules and rituals of Tap Day. It was in the early evening of Tap Day that outgoing seniors revealed their selected replacements from the class below.

The central action of Tap Day had occurred for generations on a particular late spring evening each year. Until 1952, Tap Day had been held in Branford College courtyard. By the time I got to Yale, the visible part of this sacred event took place (if it took place at all for you) in the relative privacy of your college dorm room around eight in the evening, under cover of darkness. Tap Day was a once-in-a-lifetime occasion; it was a day of reckoning and recognition that could enhance one's senior year immeasurably. For anyone who wanted to be tapped but was passed over, however, it was a disappointing day that could mar your Yale experience.

In the middle of junior year I began to consider how I felt about the seven senior societies and what my chances for acceptance to one of them might be. I walked past the tombs and tried to imagine what it would be like to be a member. I eliminated the thought of tying my preference to their architecture, though clearly Skull and Bones and Scroll and Key occupied the most eerie, truly tomblike, windowless buildings. Anyway, I was sure that I wasn't a prominent enough member of our class to be selected by either; nor was I especially interested in what I accurately or inaccurately had come to understand about their distinct cultures. I'd looked through a couple of class books to see if I could figure out what each of the societies was like: what kind of people they admitted, who had been invited to join in the past, what their attitude toward Jews might be, and what their culture entailed.

Secret societies were so integral to Yale life that each major society was allocated a lavish two-page spread near the front of the class book, the concluding official record of each class. On the left side of that layout was a full-page picture of the tomb's façade. On the facing page, in an elegant typeface, were the full names of each member. For some reason lost in the history of time and the traditions of Yale, each society admitted exactly fifteen members each year.

The society called Manuscript was looking for a different sort of guy from the others. It honored writing, music, drama, and cultural and creative endeavors. I was intrigued; it sounded like a place where I'd fit in. After doing my research, I decided I'd like to join a secret society, but only if the right one came calling. For me, the right one would be Manuscript.

Manuscript had been founded in 1952, the first major secret society since the founding of Elihu in 1903. Its appeal was to young men committed to the primacy of academic work but who wanted to mix their sociable instincts with participation in creative aspects of campus life. Manuscript's unannounced (and still to me vague) ideology fit the pattern I'd forged for myself, not by design but simply by instinct, as I made my own path through Yale.

Just before Tap Day, every junior pretends to be indifferent. When the evening arrives, however, a surprising number of them happen to be in their rooms. Study carrels and the reserved-book reading room in Sterling Library are uncharacteristically empty on that night.

By long-standing gentlemen's agreement among all of the societies, no one is tapped before eight in the evening. Nor, according to the code of the realm, is there supposed to be any commitment requested or obtained from any junior prior to the tap.

During the weeks before Tap Day, in spite of our close friendship, Sam Morley, my roommate and a member of Manuscript, maintained the honor code of silence. I assumed I was cooked—that is, likely to be passed over. I didn't know if Manuscript had an attitude toward Jews or even a Jewish quota, as Yale did in my day. (I later learned there was a quota of approximately 10 percent to 15 percent per incoming class per year, a number that ran consistently through the admission statistics going back to the 1920s.) As Tap Day approached, I couldn't get the painful idea of those ethnically exclusive New Orleans clubs out of my head. I was prepared to attribute my failure to the faith of my fathers.

The arithmetic wasn't encouraging. At a limit of fifteen boys each, the seven majors tapped a total of 105 guys, roughly 10 percent of the class. Men who wanted to join a senior society but had the distinct feeling that it wasn't in the cards and didn't want to be humiliated, elected to spend that particular evening at the movies, no matter what was showing. On the fateful night, I sat alone in our living room trying to read. Eight bells chimed from Harkness Tower. Moments later it seemed as if it was eight ten. My odds were diminishing each second. Then I heard a firm knock on the door. I stood so fast that I dropped my book on the floor. I tried to walk slowly to the door. I opened it and saw a guy I knew slightly, dressed in a three-piece dark gray flannel suit, wearing a tie whose emblem I didn't recognize. Was this it?

He ritualistically called out, "Are you Peter Michael Wolf?"

I responded, "Yes, I am Peter Michael Wolf." I felt a chill of eagerness. But where was this guy from?

He slammed his hand on my shoulder (the tap) and announced, "Manuscript." He waited a moment. "Do you accept?"

I felt a surge of relief course through my tense back.

For some guys, this is where the most intense gamble of their entire Yale career takes place. If he's hopeful that a different society will come by any second later, one he prefers, he might say, "No, I do not accept." But who could be sure? No one else might appear.

You've got to decide right then, at that moment. The senior standing before you has alternates on his list.

I had no doubt. I answered firmly, "Yes."

"Come to the tomb in an hour," my envoy directed. Then he
was gone, rotating on the heel of his slightly scuffed black loafer.
I watched him slam through the entry door at a full run to report
back. I felt relief and pride surge through my body.

That night, as part of the introduction, I was given a key to the
front door of Manuscript's tomb, a vernacular, modest New England white clapboard house at 344 Elm Street. I discovered to my
immense pleasure and great surprise that both Gerry and Henry had
also been tapped by Manuscript and had accepted. Over drinks, we
were welcomed by the outgoing members, including Sam Morley,
who I only then learned had served as secretary, and Henry Cooper—a casual friend and a direct descendant of the writer James
Fenimore Cooper—who had been chief strategist as chairman of
the tap committee for the class of 1956. We were given a tour of
the house and the garden out back, and advised about house rules.
We were also informed that one-time "battels" of two hundred dollars for the year had to be paid to help defray the cost of meals and
the salary of our Swedish housekeeper-cook, whom I knew only as
Mrs. Josephson. I had never heard that rather pretentious archaic
English word *battels* before, even though I learned years later that
it emanated from Oxford and was meant to denote an "account for
expenses or dues."

That evening we shared with the outgoing members a luxurious
home-cooked meal, a Swedish buffet with headcheese and meats
and vegetables, topped off by a massive Swedish apple cake for dessert. This was way beyond anything I could have imagined after life
in Commons and the college dining hall.

The next day, in whispered conversation, Bud let me know he'd
accepted Scroll and Key, and Gerry told me that he had turned
down Skull and Bones. "At one minute after eight, when I said,

'No, I don't accept,'" Gerry told me, "the guy spun on his heels and took off."

Manuscript became a continuation of the best parts of my life at Yale, a mixture of satisfying social interaction and seminar-like engagement. We met formally at the tomb each Thursday evening, as did each of the other major societies. The Thursday night meeting was compulsory. A predesignated member would present a paper or theory or idea that the group would discuss, debate, and criticize. After the presentation, we would share a full-scale dinner around the big communal table in the dining room. Mrs. Josephson was on hand to cook each of our Thursday evening meals. During dinner, intense conversation continued—until the wine took hold, that is. All over Yale on Thursday nights, 10 percent of the senior class was mysteriously absent from the library, from extracurricular meetings, and from social gatherings, but nevertheless learning something of immeasurable importance.

Entering the house and smelling the aroma of freshly prepared food often put me in mind of Georgie dutifully taking care of the family from her post in the kitchen. Each week one of us, taking turns, would accompany Mrs. Josephson to the market, helping to carry groceries, select food, and, for most of us, to engage in learning the beginning of domestic skills.

On Sunday evenings we also met at the house, but attendance was not compulsory. Mrs. Josephson prepared a cold buffet or more casual fare for anyone who wanted to drop by for supper. The informal buffet dinner would be followed by casual conversation.

For me, being in our tomb was like being in my own private house. Manuscript provided a welcome escape from Yale institutional life and a ready-made community of peers. We had our own refrigerator (refrigerators were not allowed in the dorm rooms). We had a living room and a dining room. We had a little garden out back.

In quiet moments at the house, especially when no one was around, I'd sometimes feel a deeply familiar pang of loneliness. It was a feeling I'd lived with for so long—the feeling of returning to or being alone in an empty house, as I had been during much of my childhood. Looking around at my privileged and appealing surroundings, I could practically hear the animated voices of my fellow members. I would tell myself that I was among the chosen, among a group of interesting companions who were also becoming friends. In such moments, when the darker parts of me took hold, what I told myself could not make the emptiness disappear, but my feelings of acceptance and achievement at Yale did make it subside considerably.

* * *

Like publications all over America, the *Yale Daily News* made a distinction between "upstairs" editorial functions and "downstairs" business functions. In our building, the business office was literally on the ground floor across the hall from the heelers' room. The editorial offices were upstairs. That arrangement may have been symbolic as well as practical.

When it came to selecting successors, the cultures were different as well.

New downstairs officers were selected by the small, now-experienced group of graduating seniors. New upstairs officers were selected by the class of juniors about to take over the paper.

Our *News* class elected Bud our chairman. It was a big honor and an enormous task, as he assumed the daunting responsibility of becoming the spokesman for the paper and writing a daily editorial. As chairman of the *News,* Bud became the most visible member of the class of 1957 for the students, the faculty, and especially the university administration.

Gerry was appointed features editor. He shared a coveted, centrally located office with our managing editor, Charlie Abuza, down the hall from Bud's immense, dark-paneled office. Gerry assigned longer stories and wrote extended pieces about whatever interested him. He also took over writing the traditional feature editor's weekly humor column, called "Sound and Fury." Gerry used his column to lampoon campus stodginess, ineptness, and pretension—a breath of fresh air during the complacent 1950s.

As I'd grown increasingly interested in downstairs operations, I was appointed publicity manager. I became one of the five guys responsible for the business survival of the *News*. My downstairs colleagues were Charlie Trippe (who as the son of Pan American World Airways founder Juan Trippe was considered to have a legitimate business background), Henry Von Maur, Howard Gillis, John Neumark, and Morris Raker.

I opted to participate in the business affairs of the *Yale Daily News* even though I was deeply engaged in my academic life as an English major and thus writing papers all the time. Something in me sought a balance between upstairs and downstairs. I felt an innate familiarity with the attitudes and activities of the *News* business office, as if it were in my blood. Indeed it was, coming as I did from a mercantile family. Not following a consciously conceived plan, I fashioned a mixed intellectual and extracurricular life at Yale that reflected the contrary impulses and capacities within me. In making the choice to go downstairs, I revealed my heritage—that long line of sugar, cotton, retail, and securities careers stacked up behind me—while forging a new and unfamiliar role as an English major in the world of literature and scholarship. It was an exciting and satisfying time. Without recognizing what I was doing, I had managed to find a sense of balance by getting my component parts aligned.

* * *

The most concentrated time I spent with the intellectuals in our class and with members of the Yale faculty was inside the Lizzy, as the Elizabethan Club was affectionately known. Since its beginning, the Lizzy, a refuge of civility and English customs, had been domiciled in the midst of the campus in a small two-story white clapboard house facing College Street. From the outside it resembled Sleeper House, my first dorm at Exeter, and its plain white New England façade also looked a lot like Manuscript's tomb.

The mission of the Elizabethan Club, as envisioned by Alexander Smith Cochran when he gave Yale the house, his library, and the initial endowment in 1911, was "promoting among its members and in the community a larger appreciation of literature and of social intercourse founded upon such appreciation." Cochran in his heyday was known as America's richest bachelor. A Yale graduate, after college he assembled an astonishingly fine collection of original editions of plays and poems published during the reign of Queen Elizabeth I.

Every afternoon, under Queen Elizabeth's watchful and frightening gaze, high tea was served. Dainty cucumber and tuna sandwiches on crustless white bread squares, along with tea and cookies, were arrayed on the dining room sideboard. The resident steward, dressed in a short white serving jacket, kept both the sandwiches and the tea samovar replenished. His wife assisted in the kitchen. Both lived at the club and functioned as combination stewards and guardians of the building and grounds.

Studied modesty began at the Lizzy's portal. A narrow three-inch brass plate read THE ELIZABETHAN CLUB in thin, ornate letters so faint and small that you could read them only standing close. The letters were chilling enough in their effect to discourage tourists and unaffiliated students from knocking on the locked door. We members, students, and selected faculty of this decidedly noninclusive, semiprivate club all proudly carried our own door keys.

Inside, understatement reigned. A short, narrow entrance hall dulled down by a shabby Oriental runner led straight back to the dining room. There, over the long, wide tea table, one encountered the imperious gaze of the club's namesake, Queen Elizabeth I. This stunningly detailed portrait, painted about 1585, was part of Cochran's original gift.

The parlor was to the right of the front door. A vivid orange, blue, and camel Oriental carpet covered its dark-stained oak floor, and clusters of brown leather couches and overstuffed, faded chintz chairs hugged its edges. Sprinkled among them were tall, round tea tables. I quickly learned that the low-standing coffee table, the kind my parents and everyone else in New Orleans had in front of their couches, was a debased and decidedly pedestrian modern American contrivance.

The crown jewel of the club was a world-class collection of rare editions of English-language manuscripts. These were protected at the back of the house inside a walk-in fireproof vault, the kind I'd seen only in banks. The vault door was open at four, teatime, each Friday afternoon and closed at the end of tea at six. I could walk into the vault and touch or even open and read some of the foundational documents of English literature. Among the club's most valuable prizes were four folios of Shakespeare, including the finest known copy of *Venus and Adonis* and the unique first edition of *Troilus and Cressida*.

A skinny flight of stairs climbed from the narrow entrance hall. Upstairs, once-modest corner bedrooms had been converted into quiet reading rooms. Shelved books covered every wall. A variety of dark Oriental carpets filled the center of each room. Comfortable chairs were arranged around standing lamps, their shaded goosenecks bending toward the reader.

One upstairs bedroom was different from the others; it was reserved for membership meetings and the conduct of club business. Membership decisions were made at a long wooden table in the center of that room. A polished wooden box about the size of a container for two decks of cards, the kind with a sliding top that I'd seen used by my mother's canasta group, sat innocuously atop the table. In the center of its rectangular lid was a round hole. The first time I saw it, curious to learn what the mahogany vessel might contain, I slid off the top. Inside I saw twelve white marbles and twelve black marbles, each slightly smaller than the hole. This was the first time I'd ever understood the term *blackball*.

Standing there, I imagined the scene. After reading files and discussing each candidate, twelve austere men in tweed jackets sit in judgment. As each candidate's name is called out and discussion wrapped up, the box is passed. Each admissions committee member drops in a white or black marble concealed inside his closed fist. When the chairman opens the lid, if enough black marbles are found, the candidate is not admitted—no discussion, no appeal. Blackballed. I realized that this voting procedure, historic though it was, was congenial to arbitrary abuse: no committee member ever had to reveal or to justify his decision or his bias.

I don't know who proposed me, who seconded me, when my name was posted for club-wide comment, or why the admissions committee found me acceptable. I had no idea what a special privilege it was to be asked to join the Lizzy, and I didn't think to inquire, once admitted, what the admissions procedure had been. It stuns me today to recognize that I wasn't more inquisitive. At the Lizzy, back then, I was more terrified by the brainpower around me than proud to be considered worthy of being a member.

In this serene and unabashedly exclusive place, faculty members from all departments of the university gathered. Most of them quite willingly, even enthusiastically, talked to student members, especially to the big brains—guys in our class like Richard Arnold, whom we expected to become the youngest-ever chief justice of the Supreme Court, and André Schiffrin, sure to be the most brilliant philosopher, liberal editor, or left-wing political activist in America. I expected a couple of the other big brains to divide up the Pulitzer and Nobel prizes for several generations as well.

Most of my fellow undergraduate members seemed to know how to make amusing remarks at just the right time. I usually sat in a deep brown leather chair, way too big for my small body, pretend-ing to read the *Times Literary Supplement* while I tried to figure out how to participate. By furtively watching my powerhouse intellec-tual peers perform, I learned how to talk to brilliant scholars and famous academics. In the Lizzy I got to engage with some of Yale's best undergraduate minds and with accomplished faculty. As I did so, it was precisely there that, to my surprise, I found I had un-consciously partially absorbed my father's disdain of the academic world, an attitude with which I struggled, not always successfully.

* * *

Before I left New Orleans in the fall of 1956 for my senior year, my parents and I did not discuss life after college. They didn't raise the issue of what I would do after graduation, and I didn't bring up that subject with them. Indeed, my parents seemed grateful that this would be my last year at Yale, maybe because, as Dad told me a few days before I left for New Haven, "I'm going to get the biggest raise of my life at the end of this school year when I no longer have your college tuition to pay."

As I headed back to Yale and to my privileged senior single room, I, like my parents, wasn't ready to confront the issue of what I wanted to do when college was over. That I could and should decide what I wanted to do, my own deep wish, did not occur to me. I was in denial about my own personal responsibility. Nor did I realize how fortunate I was that jobs were available at that time to college graduates in all sorts of endeavors.

As I began my last year in college, Dad's business as a cotton broker had become a terrible struggle. The previous spring, the federal government had indicted his company, along with his larg-est customers, for restraint of trade. In addition, as he'd told me over the summer, the government had run out of war-surplus cot-ton, so that the opportunity to market an abundance of baled cotton long stored in warehouses across the Cotton Belt was lost entirely. He was trying to figure out what to do to reinvigorate his business and to clear his name. Dad was deeply preoccupied fighting the antitrust indictment with a group of other firms, with the assistance of their collection of more than fifty lawyers.

When I saw the Yale campus again, I felt as if I'd come home. As an aware upperclassman, I knew the shortcuts through buildings in and out of side exits, between the colleges on narrow stone paths, and across various courtyards accessed via unguarded iron gates.

I settled into the academic year I'd been long awaiting—finally, mostly electives. I signed up for advanced English literature and composition, which together constituted half of my course work. The rest was scattered between subjects I'd been curious about and waiting patiently to be able to include in my schedule, among them the history of religion survey and, most of all, Vincent J. Scully Jr.'s thrilling undergraduate survey of the history of art and architecture, with an especially large dose of architecture, Scully's specialty. Scully was already known by everyone on campus as a spellbinding maverick. He would link Greek myths and primitive cultural practices to expose the meaning he found, and presented to us, in architecture and art. He had spent a year in Greece just before I took his course. That year he was awarded tenure.

As the fall evolved, I found myself both more self-assured and engaged in my studies with greater pleasure than at any other time I could remember. In English class, as I pursued my major, I kept thinking, I'm never again going to be able to work on a piece of writing and obtain such careful criticism of it and discuss it in this depth.

But most of all, with refreshed vigor, I threw myself into engagement with my friends, with my responsibilities at the *News*, and with colleagues at Manuscript. Though I was still mildly intimidated inside the Elizabethan Club and often hesitated to join in repartee with the most imposing undergraduate intellectuals and the suavest faculty members, I found myself more comfortable there as well. During tea I'd look around and realize that I had not been selected by a chance lottery, and that I knew enough people and was accomplished enough. I no longer felt compelled to hide in a chair behind the *Times Literary Supplement*, forever the invisible observer.

After the Christmas holiday, I was coasting along happily, engrossed in my busy daily life as if my existence at Yale would continue just as it was, forever. I was scoring credible grades in all of my courses that involved words and ideas.

I loved my art and architectural history class, too, but never considered this a serious enough subject to study rigorously. Out of all the art history courses offered, I'd signed up only for Scully's popular lecture class, as if it were permitted entertainment earned by being a senior. I was certain that my parents would think spending money to send me to Yale to study the history of art and architecture was a betrayal of what I was expected to do, which in their lights, I believed, was to study something that could be applied later in business or law. I, too, held the conviction that art and architecture were too pleasurable to waste time and effort studying diligently; they were a reward. I knew from years inside the family that art and architecture were the subjects my father's brother, my architect uncle Jimmy, had studied and enjoyed, the kind of thing my father and grandfather did not respect.

Then, before I knew what had hit me, the spring of senior year came up like a squall in the Gulf of Mexico. Brilliant green ivy suddenly covered the ochre and beige stone walls of Jonathan Edwards College, which just moments before had been drab brown and dormant. My years on the *News* were ending. The 1958 board had been elected; I couldn't ignore that reality. Every evening we were training our replacements. The schedule of farewell teas was posted at the Elizabethan Club. Like each preceding cadre of Senior Society members, at Manuscript we had dutifully evaluated, discussed, winnowed out, and tapped our fifteen successors.

* * *

During that last spring vacation, I spent ten days in New York as a guest at Henry Geldzahler's home. His parents welcomed me as always. Away from my busy college life, though, I grew uneasy. I began to comprehend why the cluster of warm tan stone edifices in the middle of gritty New Haven were referred to as "Mother Yale." It dawned on me: I was going to have to leave home, again. At night I was tense, irritable, and had trouble sleeping, even after long evenings spent drinking at McSorley's with Henry and Gerry and their friends from Horace Mann.

Seeking relief from my status as a man without a country, I found myself trying to convert the relatively unknown city into a familiar place. I had an anchor there: Henry's comfortable apartment on Central Park West and his warm, supportive family. His mother and father seemed to be home all the time, to me a totally unfamiliar quality in parents. I liked that, even if Henry didn't. His parents always wanted to know where we were going and the next day what we'd done. Mrs. Geldzahler, who had grown up as a very protected bourgeois young woman in a prewar, conservative Jewish Antwerp household, lit up with a gracious smile when we described McSorley's dark, unmarked entrance door and long, seedy bar with sawdust on the floor and assorted Greenwich Village characters ten feet deep at its rail.

With Henry and Gerry as guides, I began to feel less overwhelmed by New York. I took buses across town to the Metropolitan Museum of Art. I rode the subway to Greenwich Village to meet Bud for supper downtown, where he was staying with friends. I ventured beyond Mott Street down to the Bowery, where I discovered Freeman Alley, a dead-end, half-block-long street of two-story brick factory buildings that even Henry and Gerry had never known existed. One day I rode the subway to Wall Street to see what my father and grandfather had been talking about all these years. I wanted to see where Grandpa's stock orders were executed and the Cotton Exchange, where Dad's clients hedged their inventories and speculated on price trends. The financial district downtown, with its immense gray granite buildings and drab airless, skyless streets devoid of shops and obvious public restaurants, impressed me as the coldest and most intimidating part of any city I'd ever experienced.

I had several dates during the holiday with Barnard College girls, sisters of Henry's and Gerry's New York friends. This was new to me, easy and pleasant—real dates with beginnings, middles, and ends all in one evening. No complex hotel reservations for girls to stay in town, or train arrangements; no worry about how to keep my dates entertained over what always seemed endless weekends. No long, dangerous late-night drives back to New Haven, half soused, full of food and usually horny. No, I did not have to face the inevitable prospect of 2, 3, or 4 a.m. returns that left all of us exhausted and wiped out the next day. The normal nature of the encounters in the city reminded me of social life in New Orleans, only with a formal edge that was nothing like the easy familiarity I'd known with girls before I left for Exeter.

I became interested in the big, distinctive uptown towers and began to notice the astonishing diversity of New York City architecture, rather than experiencing the street as hemmed in by towering, undifferentiated monoliths. On my previous visits, most midtown buildings had seemed to be sheer masses blocking the sky above and leaving me feeling minuscule in their shadow. I visited the Chrysler Building, walking up and down Forty-Third and Forty-Fourth Streets to glimpse different views of its shiny, eccentric art deco spire.

I walked along Riverside Drive, where I noticed an enticing mix of low-rise and high-rise stone buildings, their façades facing Riverside Park, and beyond, the sunsets over New Jersey and the Hudson River. At the start of the new season, the park was a radiant green. I watched the tide flow out to sea from the Hudson. The river looked almost as wide as the Mississippi where it bends around the wharves below Canal Street in New Orleans —the long, lazy arc in the center of town from which New Orleans got its nickname, Crescent City. I began to fantasize about this quiet neighborhood and thought to myself, This peaceful place, with its lovely riverfront promenade, wide boulevards, and charming architecture would be a great place to live . . . maybe someday.

I could feel New York's social diversity, manic pace, and energy, so unlike the laconic rhythm of New Orleans. Here was a place where I felt simultaneously challenged and intimidated, a place where I had no special connection, no social advantage, no deep family history. All of this intrigued me. Whatever I might do here would have to be achieved on my own. I sensed risk, and adventure.

Before the end of that vacation, I mused, Maybe I won't go right back to New Orleans. But I also feared that I was unprepared to do anything else. Then there was also the issue of the draft, waiting for anyone who exited the shelter of a college deferment.

I couldn't imagine my next step, much less how to initiate a completely new direction. My family history and cultural traditions were so deeply rooted in Louisiana and New Orleans. Most of the men in my family—uncles, grandfather, and father—had left the South to be schooled in New England, but they always intended to return and they did so.

* * *

When I got back to my room from that New York spring break, John Leinenweber, whose hometown was Joliet, Illinois, greeted me at the door. On scholarship throughout his years at Yale, John hadn't been able to afford to leave campus during spring recess.

John had entered Yale with a plan for life. He wanted to become an architect and work in Joliet, where his parents were schoolteachers. But by the end of freshman year he was dismayed to discover that, while he had been able to master high school math in Joliet, he couldn't fathom calculus at Yale, an architectural prerequisite. John, a deeply committed Roman Catholic, also found that he could not reconcile his fundamentalist Catholic beliefs with many of the assumptions and assertions embedded in his physics, astronomy, biology, and philosophy course work.

So John abandoned pre-architecture and expended great effort throughout the next four years threading a delicate, eccentric path through the abundant and enticing undergraduate course catalogue offerings. By the spring of senior year John had managed to complete a liberal arts education that left his religious beliefs unshaken.

As he came through the door, this mild-mannered, lanky, blond midwesterner with thick round glasses all but commanded, "Sit down, Peter. I've got to talk to you."

"Okay," I answered. "Can I at least put my suitcase down?" I heard urgency in his voice and uncharacteristic energy in his manner.

As soon as I got settled, John said, enigmatically, "I'm not worried about next year anymore, or my career." He told me this with a quiet confidence that I'd never before heard in his voice.

His statement drove me down onto the decrepit couch, which now rested flat on the floor, its wooden legs broken off long ago. I always imagined they'd been extracted for firewood one cold New Haven night, maybe by someone in my father's class, before the living room fireplace had been permanently sealed. I asked, "What are you talking about?" I couldn't fathom what he might say, but I could hear the certainty in his voice. It was so strong that envy seeped into my curiosity before he could continue.

"I had a vision near West Rock." He hesitated, looking at me with steady eyes, trying to gauge my stunned reaction. We'd debated miracles for four years, with me consistently taking the rationalist, agnostic position. "I received a calling," he continued. "It came to me distinctly, the voice of an angel."

"Are you kidding?" I gasped, now more incredulous than envious and instantly aware that this was no time to talk about Descartes or Galileo, certainly not Darwin.

"No," he said, his cornflower blue eyes so calm I couldn't doubt his report, even though I couldn't understand his experience. "I'm going to become a monk."

"My God," I said, though I should have put it some other way. Holy shit was what I was actually thinking, but that would have been worse.

"I've already talked it over with my priest," John answered quietly, now sitting next to me, his knobby knees spiking up awkwardly within his rumpled khakis from our low seat near the floor. "He's going to contact the abbot at Portsmouth Priory. I'm going to enter the Benedictine novitiate there."

"John," I whispered, "this is fantastic," meaning that word as both wonderful and unreal. John was too excited to be awake to the ambiguity of what I was saying.

"There's one more thing," he went on in a tone as hushed as my own now. "We must relinquish our given names as we go through the novitiate. I've been thinking of calling myself Peter, eventually Brother Peter." I knew from art history all about St. Peter as the apostolic embodiment of the Catholic Church.

That's how my longtime roommate John unraveled the end of his Yale career. He had a plan. A plan for life, again. On a long, solitary afternoon walk, John had received the bounty of his steadfast faith. I, on the other hand, with Jewish ancestry on both sides of my family going back as far as could be traced, wasn't getting any help from my own heritage. At that moment, I envied whatever his faith had delivered and regretted the agnostic, rationalist views I'd been educated to follow and embraced.

True, it was at Yale that I'd become aware of my Jewish heritage, but that was of no specific use to me in this crisis. I knew that my blend of Judaism was a homegrown, southern variety, a determinedly assimilated brand not especially familiar to Jonas,

Trillin, and Geldzahler. They were guys from the East and the Midwest whose grandparents spoke English with a European accent, and who knew and embraced matter-of-factly their religious lineage and culture. But my newly and scarcely grasped sense of self as a member of the Jewish Diaspora seemed incapable of helping, as John's miracle helped him, in this troubling time. I was not in possession of any doctrinal faith. Indeed, metaphorical stories, Christian and Jewish alike, that were expected to spark a sense of faithful wonder seemed to me irrelevant and insubstantial. At that moment, though I'd often disdained John's blindly held beliefs, I envied the mysterious channels through which he was resolving the biggest problem facing both of us: how to shape the rest of our lives. Though I was another Peter, the pipeline was blocked for me.

* * *

Four days after John's (shall I call it) revelation, as Bud and I shared breakfast at the United Greek Diner, Bud told me: "I've lined up a summer job at Time Inc., so I can stick around New York for a while. Then I'd like to go to Europe until I'm drafted." "Great plan!" I said, knocking his shoulder with my fist. *Time* magazine, I knew, had been founded in 1923 by two *Yale Daily News* veterans, Briton Hadden, who had served as chairman of the *News* in 1920, and Henry Luce, a close friend of Hadden's and one of the editors the same year. Everyone at the *News* was aware that *Time* had been pleased to hire *News* chairmen ever since, and Bud was qualified beyond doubt. He was already a gifted reporter and a fine writer. His hopes were fulfilled. In the fall he was posted by Time-Life International to their London bureau and four months later to Paris, all before his army service began at Governors Island, in New York Harbor.

A week later, while we were walking home from the post office, known as Yale Station, Gerry let out a whoop as he read his mail. He snapped his finger against the letter in his hand and with a broad grin said to me, "I've won a Henry Fellowship! I'll be going to study English literature at Pembroke College in Cambridge, England, next fall!"

"Kudos!" I answered, applauding right there in the street and shaking his hand, which was trembling with excitement.

"What about Joan?" I asked. All year Joan Edwards had been his focus in an intense romance. She was an attractive and talented artist and dancer a year behind us at Mount Holyoke College.

"I'm not sure," he said, suddenly quiet and contemplative. "She'll finish college in a year. We're talking about getting married after that."

This was the first I'd heard of a possible marriage, the first ever discussed with me by any of my friends. "Oh," I exhaled. "I had no idea you guys were talking about that."

"I don't know how she'll react to my being out of the country for most of a year," Gerry answered, now thoughtful, his exuberance muted. "Leaving her is the downside for me, but I can't reject this offer. I think she'll be supportive; she's great."

The idea that one of my friends could imagine himself sufficiently settled in life and in his own mind, and who knew his heart well enough to contemplate marriage, stunned me. That was a state of development way beyond anything I could fathom.

The Harvard graduate art history program captured Henry by telegram less than a week after he filed his application. In September he'd be starting his Ph.D. work.

As my friends in the class of 1957 reported their post-undergraduate successes and plans, I realized: I've had my own great run, but Yale is really over now. I felt like the graduating high school football hero who failed to get into college or find a job.

In the midst of feeling left behind, I tried to assess what I cared for most about my years at Yale and what my experience might be telling me about myself, and where that might lead. As I thought about it, I realized that the most important and valuable aspects had been unintended—the extracurricular activities that emerged from and ran parallel to my course work. Manuscript, the *News,* and the Elizabethan Club had all enriched my academic life. I realized that they, along with my friends, represented the sources of my deepest pleasure at Yale.

As my activities and classes rapidly closed down, I felt more and more like a helpless, lost, lonely guy about to be thrown out of the house, someone who couldn't take care of himself. I wasn't friendly with this guy. I didn't want to know him. I was deeply bewildered about my own next step, immobilized not just with uncertainty but also with an element of denial that my life would soon be changing whether or not I wanted it to be.

In the late spring, in desperation, I took a battery of career tests at the Yale guidance office, spending a morning answering personality-related queries either true or false, followed by an afternoon of "Select your preference" from a battery of statements with four options each. The results (surprise of all surprises) suggested a career related to words and ideas.

* * *

As I entered that (for most students) sublime final spring period when seniors are permitted to coast to the finish line, I spent more time with Deirdre and her parents in Riverdale, their leafy northwestern Bronx suburb.

Our romance had ripened into a calm, consistent intimacy that allowed me to be part of Deirdre's life at Radcliffe and with her family on special weekends. I'd come to understand why she didn't wear the simplest jewelry, not even earrings, or colorful clothing of any kind. Just like her mother, she let her thin brown hair hang straight down from her scalp to her shoulders. Her clothes were usually light brown as well, or various shades of gray. Skirts, dresses, shorts, blouses—all were the same limited tones and everything matched, or nearly. Neither her mother nor her two sisters wore makeup, but all had bright, alert blue eyes. The entire family was highly educated, broadly read, quick-witted, and shared the same lack of pretense and finely keyed humor. They were an impressively evolved community, one that expressed genuine warmth and affection, in which they generously allowed me to share.

Each member of the family played a musical instrument, and well. Deirdre could make a harp sing and her listener weep. Together, the five family members would play chamber music after dinner, taking their places behind their music stands, permanently installed in the living room bay window overlooking the Hudson.

The weathered, gray-shingled Frome residence seemed anchored in the ancient shale cliffs above the river, enveloped and shaded by massive hickory, black walnut, and oak trees—a true refuge within New York City limits. It was a large-scale, rambling house whose interior levels changed to accommodate the falling contours of the cliffs on which it was built. Its generous-sized rooms and irregular Victorian floor plan reminded me of my grandparents' home on State Street in New Orleans. From her spacious screened porch, Deirdre and I could watch lurid, spectacular sunsets across the Hudson as seagulls careened over the Palisades of New Jersey. In her parents' garden, the forsythia was in bloom.

Deirdre and I had arrived at a stage in our romance in which we assumed we'd spend free weekends together. We had met each other's close college friends. We'd been able to share stories about our childhoods and prior romantic relationships, though neither of us had much of a dossier to offer in that department. I told her about my schoolboy infatuation with Betsy. She told me about being fondled behind her house one bright fall afternoon by a boy she liked, then his never touching her again. She told me how frightened that had made her; how she had worried that she was undesirable. She told me that her parents were happy that she had a boyfriend.

Deirdre's father was a distinguished doctor, chairman of the surgery department at Columbia University's College of Physicians and Surgeons (known throughout the medical world as P&S). A patient, kindly, thoughtful, good-natured man with a trim mustache, muscular shoulders, and quiet manner, he was not much taller than I, but more solid, even stout. What I saw was a success: the scion of an intellectually engaged and deeply cultured household; a physician with an accomplished and secure practice and teaching affiliation at a distinguished medical school; the father of talented and loving children; the head of a beautiful house (not an apartment) within a stone's throw of Manhattan, a place to which I'd become attached. As my final year of college was fast ending, he was a man of the world whom I admired and respected.

Sitting on Deirdre's sunny porch late one afternoon, I allowed myself a wildly magical thought. Why not become a physician like Dr. Frome? Why not go to P&S? Then everything would be settled, except how to pay for it. Okay . . . what kind of doctor? I'd be a psychiatrist, I decided. They dealt in words and ideas, and I would end up with a special sort of training that would pave the way for a successful career.

Daydreaming on into twilight, I began to feel an immense relief. I didn't bother to ask myself how I could possibly qualify to enter medical school, much less succeed at it. I simply decided, Yes, I will go to medical school. I will become a doctor—not a hard-science guy, but a psychiatrist.

Two nights after my apocalyptic decision, Deirdre and I went out for pizza and a movie. At the Pizza Palace of Riverdale, between bites I said, "You know, I think I'm about to solve my life."

"Oh, that's a good opening line," she said, smiling as she took a sip of her Rheingold.

"No, I mean it. I've decided to become a doctor, to live in New York. What do you think?"

"A doctor?" she asked, incredulous, thinking no doubt about my love of English literature, art, architecture, and our wonderful summer in England studying seventeenth-century poetry.

"A psychiatrist. From what I know, they aren't tied to hard science and use their imaginations. I'll admit, I've never met one. My parents' physician friends are either pediatricians or surgeons."

"Maybe you should discuss this with Dad," she counseled, "and some other people before you go much further."

The next day I was having lunch with the Fromes around the family table in the bay off the kitchen. Deirdre's father asked in a most congenial but nevertheless direct way, "So, what are your plans after graduation, Peter?" I wondered if Deirdre had confided in him.

Now, manufacturing my own epiphany, I answered, without knowing precisely how I'd arrived at this announcement, "I'm going to go to medical school, to become a psychiatrist." I didn't add that I hoped to go to P&S—it was after all in New York and, perhaps most important, not far from the Fromes—and then, having secured a way to make a living, to reside in New York forever.

Deirdre, who still had one more year at Radcliffe, looked at me in what I imagined as surprise that I was sticking to yesterday's brash decision. She smiled, I thought, but in a qualified gesture of support as if to say, So now go on and tell him your thoughts. Her father's eyes did not flicker, nor did his smile fade, but with what must have been considerable skepticism and astonishment, laced with practiced restraint—knowing as he did that I was an English major and philosophy minor with special interests in art and architecture, that is, 100 percent liberal arts—he answered, "Oh, I see."

I wonder if Dr. Frome had any more insight at that instant than I did about the significant role he and his family had played in my unpredictable decision. Perhaps he didn't bother to give the matter any thought, although I imagine he did wonder what my decision might mean, if anything, for his daughter's future.

"Well, that's quite a departure from all of your college work, isn't it?"

"Yes. I decided, sort of out of the blue," I answered, trying to look him right in the eye but having trouble holding my gaze steady. I didn't want to betray the terror I was feeling, while talking to this accomplished surgeon whom I so admired, about entering his world.

In a professionally constrained tone, which I imagined was so appreciated at postoperative bedsides, he asked me, "How do you expect to become qualified to apply to medical school?"

"I'm going to apply to take a postgraduate year at Yale, two if necessary," I told him. That part sounded solid and sensible to me, though I was churning inside, unsure whether I could be admitted to the required courses, much less pass them with grades that would qualify me for medical school consideration. Even if I did, could I obtain enthusiastic-enough recommendations to succeed at the cutthroat contest for admission to medical school?

I had classmates at Yale who'd been grinding away for four years to qualify for acceptance to a top medical school. Most of them had relinquished all but the most modest engagement in Yale's rich extracurricular life. They'd focused from the start on an intensive science curriculum, and all had been accepted into good medical schools that graded downward from the three top choices, Harvard, P&S, and Yale. I'd be competing against those same kinds of guys with the same obsessive determination, only now they'd be from one or two classes below me.

That's the last I ever talked about my startling decision with Dr. Frome. Yale gamely went along with my gamble. I was accepted as a freshman counselor, the role John Dixon had played with such meaning in my life. In exchange for my advisory services to about thirty freshmen, Yale would waive my room-and-board charges and house me on the freshman campus.

The university's pre-med advisor sculpted a special one-year crash program for me, taking into account my prior course work at Exeter in chemistry and physics, as well as my Yale brush with astronomy and geology. "If you manage to do well enough in biochemistry, statistics, chemistry, and biology," he told me, looking grave, "you'll qualify for a medical school application. That's the most I can promise at this point."

I'd decided before I told my parents about my decision that I would pay for my course fees out of my savings account.

After I had wrapped up all the arrangements with Yale, I called my parents. "I've made a big decision about next year," I began. "It's going to be a surprise to you."

"We were wondering," Mom said. "You'll be out of college in a few weeks. I've had your room thoroughly cleaned and your desk straightened up and dusted."

"After graduation I'll be home for a while in the summer, but then I'm coming back to Yale."

Dad jumped in, "What in the dickens will you do at Yale? Has there been some snafu with you graduating?"

Then he paused, and I wasn't sure how to proceed.

"We've got our plane tickets," he continued. "What's wrong?"

"Nothing's wrong. I've decided to take an extra year here after graduation to try to get into medical school. I think I want to become a doctor, maybe a psychiatrist."

A long, stunned silence followed. They were responding appropriately. I knew that they couldn't see each other, because Mom was in her bedroom and Dad was downstairs in the solarium. Both were literally speechless.

I was terrified and wordless, too. What was I doing? I could unwind all those plans right now, I thought. Yale would understand; they had more applications for freshman counselor slots than places available, and surely I was a long shot for medical school. I could make all this go away. I held the phone and I held my breath. I said nothing.

Then Dad spoke, slowly, "Son, you'll never be a doctor."

"Dad," I answered weakly, "I'm going to try, and I've arranged to pay for next year. I know you said long ago that four years of college was the end of your financial responsibility to me. And I agree with you."

"Son," he replied, "think about this some more. I have a desk for you at the office. This isn't anything like you. You can't even stand the sight of blood."

"That's true. It's a problem. One of a number I'll have to get over."

"It's terrible, hard work, years and years of training and a huge expense—before you ever earn a dime." Dad's voice was coming through louder as he regained his wits and tried to counsel me.

"I know, Dad, I know. I have to try."

"Let's speak again tomorrow," Mother chimed in. "Think about this overnight."

* * *

As I began my year of cramming to qualify for admission to medical school, I optimistically and naïvely decided my first choice would be Columbia's College of Physicians and Surgeons. I thought it was the best in New York and I wanted to be in New York. Albert Einstein College of Medicine, in the northeastern Bronx, didn't appeal to me. It was too far from Manhattan. Nor did New York University, downtown. It seemed seedy when I visited.

As my postgraduate year got under way, I struggled to master the basics of biology, chemistry, physics, calculus, and statistics. As I did so, my previous struggles with science came flooding back. Centrifuges, Bunsen burners, delicate scales, arcane computations, and chemical formulas swarmed through my days and snuck into my dreams at night. Over and over I'd say to myself, I enjoy reading about science in the *New York Times*. Shouldn't that be quite enough? No, I had to put the weakest side of my brain to the ultimate test and take it into the woodshed to teach it the ultimate lesson. Whereas my undergraduate work at Yale had been a pleasure, I studied and struggled now with a determination I'd not had to exert before, except during those first months at Exeter. I was way behind again.

I studied through the weekends. I befriended advanced students who could offer helpful advice in the evenings. Unlike in my liberal arts training, where I had learned to debate, question, and speculate, I now learned to shut up and listen, take notes, and memorize. It wasn't fun, but it was interesting. I was learning the science that governs the natural world and my own body. Science stories in the *Times* did, in fact, come alive in my course work. So did the natural world and the physical environment, for the first time in my life.

During the medical school application process, I couldn't bring myself to ask Dr. Frome for help or advice or even a letter of recommendation. I was afraid that I would not measure up, and I didn't want to embarrass him. My first cousin Peter Mayerson was already in medical school at Tulane. I asked his father, my uncle Hy, who was a fine scientist and chairman of the Tulane physiology department, to write one. When I called to discuss whether he'd be willing to risk his reputation with colleagues in New York at P&S, he gave me a piece of advice I've cherished ever since. "Peter," he said, "if you really want something, use every resource you have to obtain it."

Deirdre was back in Cambridge for her last year at Radcliffe. We spoke only occasionally on the phone about her final year and my new struggles. The previous spring, while she was visiting New Haven for my graduation, we'd had an important conversation.

"I'm going to be away from the East all of this summer, and next fall I have to be glued to labs and slide rules," I said.

"I know, I've been thinking about that. Don't suppose we'll be seeing each other much."

"Maybe it's best," I said, after anticipating this conversation for weeks, "that we assume our romance is graduating tomorrow, too."

She was quiet for a moment and looked into my eyes, questioningly. Her blue eyes were full of emotion but I thought softened a little with a sense of relief.

"You've been a great companion, Peter, but I think you're right. I've been feeling we should talk, too. I want to try to work very hard next year, and I don't think it's a good idea to try to maintain our intimacy with you gone all summer, then with the Northeast Corridor between us, especially as I'd have to do most of the traveling."

"I'll always love you, Deirdre. You know that?"

"Me, too. You're the first love of my life."

It was a situation that had served both of us well. Even before this conversation, our feelings had resolved themselves into a pleasurable friendship that neither of us wanted to relinquish. Nor did either of us want to adventure beyond this point romantically. I could never quite figure out if Deirdre also thought I'd lost my way with this medical school idea.

Perhaps it was my heroic study effort that did it, or maybe I was lucky enough to come before a risk-taking P&S admissions committee that year. Whatever the reason, I was admitted to P&S in the first round of acceptances.

When I picked up the letter at Yale Station, it was early spring. I promptly took the day off from class, the first time ever. I wandered the streets. I stopped in for tea at the Lizzy, where I'd not been all year. I bought a ticket for the seven o'clock showing of *The African Queen*. Late in the evening I used my key to enter Manuscript. Some guys from the class of 1958, the ones we'd selected, were there, feeling mellow, contemplating leaving Yale and starting new lives themselves. I drank far too much Jack Daniel's while talking with them, before wandering back to my room. When I got into bed I felt dazed, triumphant, and frightened. Now I'd done it. I wanted to call Deirdre to tell her I'd made it, but I didn't. For all I knew, she was someone else's girlfriend by now. A pang of jealousy wafted over me.

7

Round the World and Medical School

During the summer of 1958, before I was to begin medical school that fall, my parents celebrated their twenty-fifth wedding anniversary with a six-week trip, mostly in Asia. Dad sold cotton all over Asia.

The catalyst had been a Pan American Airways round-the-world ticket special, a huge discount if you went all the way. Over lunch during the prior Christmas break, while Mom and Dad were talking about their plans, I'd asked, "Why don't you take along a couple of healthy, inquisitive kids to carry your bags?"

Gail chimed in, "I can spare six weeks this summer. Take us!"

They looked at each other, stunned. Obviously, the thought had not occurred to them. I could understand that they might have preferred to have this amazing experience free of children, though by then Gail was nineteen and I was twenty-two, so we were beyond needing a lot of special attention.

"Do! Take us," Gail added with an eagerness that I know got to Dad. "We won't be any trouble."

Gail had a way with Dad. So we were given a life-enhancing opportunity to take a round-the-world 1958 mega-trip, a tour of exotic places from Tokyo to Istanbul, with a luxury rest stop in Paris on the way home. This was before jets; before massive global tourism; when it was much less common for Westerners to visit many of the places we were going to. Dad had arranged with the mayor's office for him to present a key to the city of New Orleans to Madame Chiang Kai-shek in a ceremony at the new Imperial Palace when we were in Formosa. After that, our plan was to see highlights in India, Nepal, Cambodia, Thailand, and Turkey before the final stop in Paris. In those days Nepal was utterly remote with no international communications, tourist accommodations, or roads.

Almost immediately, as detailed planning got under way, I began to have ideas about going to see special places beyond the highlights that my parents' New York–based travel agent had proposed. Once we were part of the trip, in fact, I started to make suggestions focused on my own interests in art and architecturally distinguished places, including proposed side excursions to more remote locations.

"Let's check out the Buddhist caves outside of Bombay. There are incredible sculptures in them."

"We're not going to Bombay," Dad snapped. "It's too far south, way off the path that the Pan Am ticket permits without extra cost."

"You'd go all the way to India and miss those glorious carved and frescoed ancient Buddhist caves at Ellora and Ajanta?" I said, incredulous.

"Not only would I," he said. "We will."

"Come on, Dad," I begged. But Gail didn't support me in this one, so it was "no dice," as Dad liked to say. I was being troublesome, a generously invited interloper disturbing their carefully considered—and for that era before jet planes were used commercially—extraordinarily adventurous plans.

Nevertheless, before we left, I'd plowed into deep visual research, scanning my basic art history world survey texts, as well as specialized Asian art and architecture volumes like the recently published magisterial two-volume edition of *The Art of Indian Asia*, by Heinrich Zimmer, to identify the most important monuments and sites along the way and just beyond our itinerary.

* * *

I hit upon THE IDEA of contacting architecture schools all over the country, and procured a list of names and addresses from the Yale Architecture School secretary. I wrote to every school, offering to provide Kodachrome slides for them to supplement their teaching-slide libraries. We were going to places in Asia that back then, in 1958, were poorly represented in many of their visual archives. I made detailed three-by-five-inch index cards for each major build-ing. I prepared area maps for the places I wanted to see and photo-graph. I plotted the distance of any potential out-of-the-way target site from our group destinations. My business plan was to set up a mail-order operation. I made a catalogue of places we were going to, or places I hoped to go to as a special side trip, and listed all the important monuments in each location. I made up a simple order form. I would keep the master original slide and sell duplicates on an approval basis. Payment would be expected only if the images were satisfactory.

My camera was a 35 mm Contax single-lens reflex with a 50 mm lens. I had an interchangeable 35 mm wide angle and 135 mm telephoto lens, too. I bought a couple of filters to enhance clouds. I found a beautifully made stainless-steel tripod whose legs tele-scoped inside themselves so effectively that when closed down it measured just eighteen inches; fully extended it was a solid forty-two. The tripod came with its own finely sewn leather case and was just the right size to fit under my arm when strapped to the top of my Sears camera bag, which held the rest of my equipment. I didn't have a flash system to light up interior spaces. I hoped I could do the job with natural light, using my tripod, very slow film, and long exposures. If I could pull it off, I imagined that those pictures of remote locations and isolated monuments would be very much in demand.

Toward the end of the trip, we had scheduled four days in Istan-bul, where I would meet my greatest photographic challenge: the dark, immense, complex interior of the Hagia Sophia. I was going to see it, to be inside the last Roman and the first Byzantine building—Justinian's immense, domed Palatine chapel. The Hagia Sophia represented a staggering, luminescent volume of layered space and would be the ultimate challenge for the architectural photographer I hoped to develop into. I knew, however, that my experience, my camera equipment, and the meager, filtered light inside the church-turned-mosque were inadequate to my ambition.

I proudly phoned Dad from New Haven to tell him the full scope of my income-producing, cost-defraying photography scheme.

"We're not going to have you dictate what we do and what we see," he said.

"I don't expect that. But I will need a long time in some places to set up and get the pictures I want."

"We agreed to bring you and Gail along so that we'd all be together," Mother interjected. "With both of you in college, you never see each other, and we don't see much of you, either."

"I'll be with you at meals and in the hotel, on trains and planes, in taxis and on camels and donkeys," I answered. "*Most* of the time."

"Don't make this difficult for us," Dad snapped, ending the call.

Obviously, a lot was going on inside me that I didn't fully recognize, including the temporary suspension of thinking about medical school, and inadequate appreciation for all that our parents were doing for us. I needed to have a rationale and a plan to explore my emerging fascination with architecture. Even though I was being taken along as a guest, it felt irresponsible to be going around the world without a purpose. The idea of doing so as an appendage to my parents' whims made me feel both infantilized and like a spoiled brat. I wanted to find a financial justification, a possible monetary payoff, a way to use my interest in art and architecture, as if that would render my passion acceptable to my father. He'd understand and admire a successful new business venture.

My slide business was also, of course, a genuine expression of my deep interests. I longed to pursue my idea, in part as a way of allowing me to accept my parents' generosity and custodial guardianship in these strange lands. Grandiosely, I imagined that I'd eventually pay my own way. Even if my idea turned only a modest profit, I decided I'd offer to reimburse Dad for some of what I cost him on the trip.

As soon as I assembled and sent out my catalogue, I received quite a few orders. "Send us slides of . . . ," the department chairmen would write, and they would also check the box that read, "We agree to remit $1.25 per slide for each one we keep." Encouraged, I estimated even greater success once I'd created an inventory. After all, we were going to places, some quite remote, that few architectural photographers had visited in years for all sorts of reasons, not the least of which had been global depression, followed by the chaos of World War II, which had ended only thirteen years before.

We were among few tourists in Thailand, Nepal, and Cambodia. I had the most perfect clear blue sky and white clouds to set off my photographs of Angkor Wat, a sacred temple of the Khmers. It was a Kodachrome day, with the soft afternoon light making the temple stones glow. No other tourists visited the site all day. I took a long time with the huge building in the jungle, which consisted of concentric stone-walled squares within squares—each wall intensely decorated with carved images of voluptuous, animated female figures—leading ultimately into the small central court that contained the four-foot-high, abstract, upright *linga* ("phallus" in Sanskrit). The single silent stone was a symbol of the creative energy of Shiva ("auspicious one" in Sanskrit) and represented a material emblem of the presence of the divinity across the ages. When my family finished walking through the sprawling, empty monumental site, they were tired and understandably impatient as I scurried around setting more shots. They and our driver were ready to return to the hotel, which was thirty miles away. I scored some fantastic photographs that day, though, and must have sold at least fifteen sets upon my return, bringing in more than one hundred dollars, enough to pay for all of our rooms that night.

In the three weeks after we got back to New Orleans and before I had to leave for New York City to begin medical school, I had all of my slides developed by Kodak. I spent days labeling each original. Then I bought ten rectangular gray metal containers, also produced by Kodak. In each box there were eight plastic subcompartments, four to a side, each large enough to hold all the slides from a single roll of film. Each subcompartment flipped outward independently so that it was easy to extract the slides. Pasted to the inside of each box top was a paper register ruled into squares, one square directly above each compartment. I identified each film by country or subject, or both.

I also selected the fifty best family images—pictures of my sister, my father, my mother, and me linked with people from all over the world whom we'd met along the way. I had enlarged prints made from these. Then I made a book for my parents, with each photograph labeled and put into a glassine sleeve. The book, which I titled *The Family of a Man in the Family of Man* (I'd been to the touching, impressive Museum of Modern Art photo exhibit *The Family of Man*, which led to the celebrated book of that name), was a thank-you gift. Mother kept it on her coffee table for the rest of her life.

* * *

In early September, I reported to Columbia's College of Physicians and Surgeons. I was issued a short white coat, a long list of texts to buy, and a shiny new dissecting kit. I was also given a key to a small, single dorm room in a high-rise next to the hospital.

That September—while Bud was writing for *Time* in New York, Gerry was blazing a distinguished trail at Cambridge University in England, and Henry was captivating the graduate Harvard art history faculty—I spent all day in labs and amphitheater lectures. I studied deep into the night in my room at Broadway and

168th Street. Within weeks, as I got into the work, I began biting my nails and picking at my cuticles. My fingers became so raw I had to wear surgical gloves (to which I now had access) while I studied, to try to break this habit. At the end of the evening, the inside of the gloves would be crusted with blood from my chewed and mutilated fingers.

The first day I walked into the anatomy lab, I was dazed and upset by the scene. In a cool, antiseptic room, male and female cadavers laid out on metal tables were waiting for us, wrapped in thick cloudy plastic sheets. The instructor assigned me to a team of four at one of the tables.

"What'll we call him?" Newell called out. He was a friend from Yale and the other man in our dissecting team.

Marjorie said, "How about 'Cutup'?"

Mae Woo disagreed. "No, we must be respectful."

We settled on "Thomas," a ghost Newell remembered from one of his favorite children's books.

I could hardly look at him lying there, greenish brown, gnarled, stiff, reeking of formaldehyde, and enveloped in the greasy, thick plastic sheet in which we'd rewrap his remains every day after we'd taken more of him apart.

I thought of the antiseptic mummies I had seen in the Cairo Museum and summoned a remote setting to my mind. I saw the glowing tan stones and encroaching green jungle of Angkor Wat. Another instant I envisioned myself inside the dim majesty of the skillfully layered architecture of Hagia Sophia. All places I'd so much rather be, I realized.

Soon the all-too-real sights and pervasive odor of formaldehyde, which made me slightly nauseated, pulled me back. I felt as I had as a child riding in my mother's smoke-drenched Buick. I was part of a grim scene of death, putrid odors, and deterioration that could not be denied.

Even though I studied constantly and never missed a day in

the dissecting lab, I had great difficulty remembering the names of Thomas's nerves, arteries, veins, and even muscles. When we were required to walk around an unfamiliar test cadaver that had been tagged with numbers and question marks on various parts of its grainy, decomposing insides, I could not call up the correct names in order to identify the body parts on my test sheet. In spite of studying hard, I was testing badly.

As a special privilege after six weeks of class and lab work, we were taken in groups of five to the hospital maternity ward. Most of my classmates were thrilled. They were going to witness birth from very close up. Our small group scrubbed with the doctor. He told us that his patient had given permission for us to observe, but we were to say nothing during the delivery. "I'll explain what I'm doing," he told us. "I'll point out whatever we can see of her anatomy. I'll go slowly, so you can watch the emergence of the baby and the whole procedure. But don't ask questions," he admonished us, "until after we're out of the operating room." We fell silent in our baggy blue gowns and white plastic shoe covers. "Also," he added, "don't touch anything in the room . . . nothing." Then we marched through a pair of metal swinging doors into the brightly lit OR. I hung behind everyone else, but finally went in and stood at the back of our group.

Inside, there she was, lying on her back, legs wide open, feet strapped into stainless-steel stirrups. The doctor motioned us into a semicircle just beyond the edge of her cracked heels and pulpy footpads. As she pushed and screamed, he probed and blood flowed out. I began to feel dizzy. Hoping I'd be able to distract myself, I tried to remember the details in Thomas Eakins's masterly arrangement of figures and light in his painting *The Gross Clinic*. In it I remembered Dr. Gross's cool engaged demeanor as one of the figures turns away, unable to watch the surgery. Moments later, I fainted onto the hospital floor.

What I took pleasure in at this time was my architecture-slide business. In one corner of my medical school dorm room, I'd set up a portable desk on a wheeled typing table that I bought at a nearby used-furniture store on Broadway. On top of the table I had placed a set of files: New Orders, Correspondence, Invoices to Send, and Checks to Deposit. In front of the manila files held up by a pair of metal bookends I had made space for my old portable Royal typewriter, the one I'd used to type college papers. That was the world headquarters of Wolf Worldwide Architecture Slides Associates.

I sent a revised catalogue and order form to every architecture school in America, and one to every college art department I could find. Inquiries and orders began to come in volume as word got around about my service. I loved holding up each duplicated slide to the dorm window during the day on Saturdays. That glimpse served as my quality-control check before I packaged and sent out each order. I looked forward to receiving mail orders, and corresponding with school slide librarians and archivists all around the country. I liked to open the check envelopes and felt proud and pleased when I made a deposit. I sold sixteen sets of my Hagia Sophia slides—ten slides to the set—and gave one set, plus a few additional slides, to the chairman who'd helped me obtain permission to photograph that grand building.

* * *

Before the academic year was over, I knew I couldn't go on. I felt as if I was having a nervous breakdown, but I didn't talk to anyone at P&S, or anywhere else, about it. My work was obviously not up to standards, but no one on the faculty or in the administration discussed with me my ongoing subpar performance. I assumed that by the end of the year I'd be summoned to the dean's office. Toward the end, my memory refused to work. I think I was gripped by an emotional and intellectual panic. The long names of chemical compounds made no sense to me. Their expected biochemical reactions in the body retained their mystery. Tagged nerves on Thomas, whose function, source, and destination I tried to memorize, were, in my eyes, merely colored wire fragments sticking out of a putrid grainy gray wall. I couldn't watch instructive surgical procedures on living patients for fear I'd tumble to the floor again.

In the late spring, I called Dad at his office from the pay phone in the dorm.

"You were right," I said. "Medical school isn't for me. I can't remember anything. I can't concentrate. I faint at the hospital."

"I knew you wouldn't like it," he replied, sitting, I presumed, in his high-back tilting office chair on the fifth floor of the New Orleans Cotton Exchange Building. I couldn't tell if he was mad at me or feeling vindicated or feeling a flash of pity for me. I'd worked so hard to get there. He said so little, and asked nothing. I imagined just then that his feelings were a mixture of compassion for me that I had failed, and relief that I was getting out sooner rather than much later from demanding, expensive training for a career he was sure all along would not appeal to me.

"I don't have any other plan, Dad," I said, as bravely as I could. "I think I'd better come home."

"Okay," he said. "Come home. Start to learn the cotton business. As you know, I have a desk for you in the office. I've kept it here all year."

At that moment I felt like an immigrant, an orphan, a high school dropout with no prospects. I felt as if someone had found me sitting dejectedly against a peeling wall on a decrepit street corner in the neighborhood around Broadway and 168th Street and suggested that I enlist in infantry basic training so that I'd have shelter, three meals a day, and a bed. But I was also grateful that I had a family, a place that I could call home, and a job that might work out. I knew Dad had been through horrible business difficulties, and I wasn't sure how viable his business might be. Still, I felt I had no other choice, and that maybe I could be helpful to him. Perhaps I'd like this new career following in a long family tradition, and start to build a new life in my beloved hometown.

Part III

HOME AGAIN

8

_____

The Cotton Business

I stared at the front door of room 507 before I entered, as if I'd never seen it before. Like all the others on the dimly lit marble corridors of the New Orleans Cotton Exchange Building, the upper half had a frosted-glass center panel surrounded by a dark wood frame. I was about to encounter what remained of the cotton trade—the business that had created the commercial energy and prominence of New Orleans, the career path that many of my forebears had taken. I read, with a mixture of pride and apprehension, WOLF & CO., COTTON BROKERS.

When I entered, there was one empty desk with paper clips, pencils, and a yellow pad on top. Dad had been saving my place all this time. My cousin John Godchaux, ten years older than I, had been with Dad for six years and was sitting at his desk. Also there was Dad's secretary, the only other employee, Susie de Haas, who had been with him since after the sad affair with his first secretary, in the early 1950s. I could hear Dad on the phone in the next room. Though I'd arrived at eight thirty precisely—the time I was told we opened—the others were already at their places, and working.

Dad stopped talking, his call apparently finished, and walked out into the front room to greet me, his engaging smile in full force. "Welcome to the office. Here we are. I installed your two telephones last fall," he said. "I'm glad you're back, son."

I looked over and saw two black instruments with push buttons—two separate lines and a hold button—the primary tools of my new trade. They were perched on top of a bleached-wood side table next to my desk that matched the other furniture in the room.

"Welcome," John said, extending his hand. "Welcome to the cotton business." We were standing near the front door. I was fortunate indeed to have a ready-made chance at a new career in my hometown.

"Thanks." I was glad to see that we stood eye to eye.

John's hand was small and bony like mine; it felt familiar. I looked at him carefully. He had a Godchaux physique: a slight build (he stood about five foot seven), well proportioned, with dark, almost wavy hair, pale skin, an angular face, and the bright blue eyes characteristic of my grandmother's side of the family. Except for the blue eyes, I fit the same physical pattern. I was home.

Susie, whom I'd met casually over the years, looked different today, maybe because I looked closely at her for the first time. She wore too much makeup; I could see patches of beige powder shades darker than her fair skin. Her hair was dyed a color that had a faint orange tinge. I soon found that she abhorred small talk, typed on the IBM Selectric like a dynamo, and smoked incessantly. She was all business—Dad's business first and foremost.

* * *

After college and before the war, Dad had worked for his father as a cotton broker and later in the Godchaux family retail business—in both the factory and the store—presumably training for a major executive position someday, perhaps even president of Godchaux Clothing Company. But he never liked working in his family's enterprise. I'd worked at "the store," too, as a clerk when I was sixteen. Back-office work at Godchaux's had been my first paying summer job.

Dad opened Wolf & Co. in January 1946. It was first called

Newburger, Wolf & Co. Dad had launched the cotton brokerage together with Kirby Newburger in room 507 of the Cotton Exchange Building. Wolf & Co. was still situated there.

Kirby, a few years older than Dad and an experienced cotton broker, had remained in New Orleans throughout the war. Subject to depression all of his adult life, Kirby had committed suicide only a couple of years into his partnership with Dad, on July 30, 1948, by jumping off the Huey P. Long Bridge, his delicate disposition overwhelmed by business pressures.

Dad and Kirby became important brokers in the reviving postwar cotton trade, and Dad carried on as the sole proprietor after Kirby's death. In the late 1940s and early 1950s, bimonthly auction sales were being held by the U.S. Department of Agriculture (USDA) in order to dispose of the postwar glut of surplus cotton. No longer needed were hundreds of thousands of bales that the government had purchased and stockpiled for uniforms, tenting, bandages, and other wartime uses.

Within months of opening the new business, Dad had grasped an immense opportunity. He leased a surplus IBM mainframe, the kind he'd learned to operate while facilitating Allies' messages and deciphering enemy communications. At the time, most people had not heard of IBM or computers. Impressed with the company and its innovative equipment, Dad also had the foresight to buy a few hundred shares of IBM stock soon after the war, his best stock pick ever. The IBM mechanical behemoth lived in and nearly filled an entire windowless, airless, eight-by-twelve-foot storage room Dad leased down the hall from the Wolf & Co. office.

I knew this machine. Home from Exeter, I had accompanied Dad on several Sunday evenings as he and John fed it punch cards and recalibrated its printing dials, urging it on to produce their weekly sales catalogue before Monday morning.

Using his innate brilliance for business and an entrepreneurial nerve as powerful as any I've ever met, Dad converted his wartime experiences to his own practical, peacetime application. As I mentioned earlier, he used the big IBM computer to track every scrap of government surplus cotton in the country. He remained in the intelligence business—now, the kind he could sell.

By 1947, buyers from all over the United States were dependent upon the firm for guidance as each government auction of surplus cotton approached. They needed to know how much and what kind of cotton was available at any given location, especially those convenient to their mills. The firm became the authority on price movements because it brokered so many of the bids at these auctions. This information was invaluable in advising clients as to recent market price trends for every grade and type of raw cotton sold by the United States government.

Customers from all over the Cotton Belt were content to pay Wolf & Co. for this information—at fifty cents per successfully purchased bale. If they were outbid, no commission was charged.

By 1950, at the time I was getting ready to go to Exeter, Dad had become the prime broker between the largest private merchants in America and the government agency that owned more warehoused cotton than any other entity, public or private, had ever owned. In an amazingly short time, he had created a powerful presence in American industry, and he'd also invented a money machine.

But in 1956, as I wrote earlier, Dad's world began to fall apart. I happened to be home from Yale on spring break that March. Dad and I were having one of our customary quiet breakfasts during which we shared the *Times-Picayune*. One indelible morning, jumping off page one, I saw this fat, dark, blazing headline: CONSPIRACY CHARGED IN DEALS FOR COTTON. A photograph of Morris Wolf, my father, wearing a stern and pained expression, appeared just below it. I was immediately overcome with dread and horror. Dad had given me no warning—he'd never mentioned his problems, much less discussed them previously with me. Until that morning at breakfast, I'd had no idea that Dad had been accused of anything by anyone, except by my mother years before for having had the affair with his secretary, whom he fired long ago. Now my father and his biggest customers were being indicted for restraint of trade by the Department of Justice under the Sherman Antitrust Act.

I felt deceived and disregarded. I was also simultaneously ashamed of him and sorry for him. I immediately assumed that Dad had done something really awful, or else why would the government be after him? It did not occur to me to be primarily compassionate, upset for his travails, doubting of the government indictment, and outraged that he would be publicly humiliated.

"Dad," I said, "what is this about?"

"Son," he answered, looking distant and cold and not quite right at me, "there's a bureaucrat in Washington who's jealous of my success. He's being criticized for the way he's run the CCC's surplus cotton program. He wants to ruin me to protect himself. I'm going to fight this to the end." I'd heard about the Commodity Credit Corporation for years, and I'd heard Dad complain about a guy in Washington named Frank Biggs. But until that moment I didn't put the two together.

"What happened?"

"Nothing happened," he answered. "But if you want to know more, let's talk this evening." He said this last thing as if it were an afterthought, one I interpreted as: I don't want to talk about this, certainly not now. He was profoundly upset.

Ten minutes later, he got up from the table and headed out to his Olds 88 to drive downtown to his office.

I sat riveted to my seat, mortified. I feared he was a criminal. He'd earned so much so fast. We lived in a new brick house in an upscale neighborhood. All around us were big houses and nice lawns with carefully maintained professional landscaping. Then there was the brand-new 24-foot Chris-Craft boat and our full-time cook/housekeeper, Willie-Mae. My parents, in their new wealth, spent more time in Florida and Paris than at home.

After Dad left, I read the front-page *Times-Picayune* report, dateline New Orleans, Thursday, March 29, 1956:

It is charged that the defendants engaged in an unlawful combination and conspiracy to restrain competition under Section 1 of the Sherman Act by engaging and maintaining Wolf and Company as common purchasing agent through whom the defendant cotton merchants purchase cotton.

The indictment further charges that the defendants violated the act by permitting Wolf and Company to allocate bids among the defendant cotton merchants on cotton offered for sale by the CCC and by permitting Wolf and Company to fix bid prices. . . .

The defendants are also accused of using their efforts to eliminate or discourage others from entering into or engaging in business in competition with Wolf and Company. . . .

It is also alleged that during the period 1954–1955, more than 262,000 bales of cotton, having a value in excess of $40,474,000, were sold by the Commodity Credit Corporation, and the defendants, employing the services of Wolf and Company purchased approximately 60 percent of that cotton.

As it turned out, the lawsuit would last nearly two years. It would fully occupy Dad's time and cost hundreds of thousands of dollars. So many firms were involved as co-conspirators that fifty lawyers from Washington, D.C., New York, and all over the Cotton Belt were involved in the defense.

When the suit ended, I was home for Christmas holiday during my extra year at Yale. On December 26, 1957, the *Times-Picayune* announced in an even larger banner headline (about the size I'd expect if war had been declared): U.S. DISMISSES CASE AGAINST COTTON FIRMS.

The front-page story began: "The federal government today voluntarily dismissed criminal and civil charges against eleven cotton firms." It went on to report: "In addition, there was filed a consent decree in which the defendant firms agree to not disclose to any person or organization, other than the Commodity Credit Corporation, the price they bid on cotton."

Although my father had been exonerated, this one change in the USDA's auction procedures eviscerated his once-thriving business. This one innocuous-sounding provision in the decree destroyed Dad's central position in the American cotton industry. That single clause, aimed at Dad and accepted by all of the merchants and reluctantly by Dad, made it impossible for any broker to serve as the representative of any bidder.

"Dad, my God, this is great," I said with naïve relief the next morning at breakfast. "Congratulations!" I was so happy for him, and for our family, that I had not absorbed the one most important, nuanced detail.

"We settled with the bastards two nights ago on a huge conference call."

"Aren't you pleased?" I asked.

"I'm relieved the damn thing is over," he said. "In the end I didn't have a choice. All my customers were ready to settle."

I didn't understand the profound change the consent-decree clause would bring about in the conduct of auctions. So Dad explained it all to me. From that time forward, instead of brokering wholesale auctions of World War II surplus cotton between the federal government and cotton merchants across the country, Dad's role in the wholesale cotton industry was restricted to arranging transactions between private parties and for the purchase of privately held American cotton by foreign mills, mostly in Asia. He'd negotiate for growers to sell to merchants, or for merchants to sell to domestic or overseas mills. Even though he knew everyone in the trade and remained an esteemed member of the American cotton industry (and was elected president of the New Orleans Cotton Exchange in both 1959 and 1960), what was available to him was a much-lower-volume business, and his income suffered.

* * *

By 1959, when I started working for my father, Wolf & Co. wasn't the only family-owned company beginning to falter. Times were changing in the South and in New Orleans. After years of being nationally recognized preeminent local brands, Godchaux's Sugars, Godchaux's Clothing Company, and Eustis & Godchaux Insurers, all enterprises owned and operated by my grandmother's brothers and close relatives, were now challenged by serious competition. No other department store in New Orleans was as upscale as Godchaux's. Its dignified store on Canal Street, the city's prime, wide retail boulevard, had become the regional emporium of style and sophistication. Nevertheless, new entrepreneurial endeavors with national purchasing, distribution, and advertising capabilities were entering the locally dominated New Orleans territory.

Prudential, Home Life, and other national brands, headquartered in places like Newark, New Jersey, and Hartford, Connecticut, were undercutting Uncle Paul's insurance business. As part of the great suburban exodus throughout America, shopping malls were beginning to sprout along the city's periphery, and their retail chain outlets owned by national brand companies were drawing customers away from Uncle Leon's flagship store. Privately owned family-run department stores across the nation that were located in downtowns, such as Rich's in Atlanta, Jacobson's in Michigan, and the Battelstein's and Sakowitz's stores in Houston, encountered the same problem; they were either bought out by national chains or headed toward bankruptcy.

In New Orleans the story was no different. On Canal Street alone, most Jewish owned or managed stores would be out of business within two or three decades, including those founded in the early days by Gus Mayer (Gus Mayer department store), Mayer Israel (Mayer Israel department store), Marks Isaacs (president of Marks Isaacs department store), Herbert Schwarts and later Isidore Newman II (presidents of Maison Blanche department store),

Theodore Danziger (Danziger's dry goods), and Sam, Leopold, and Max Krauss (Krauss Company). The Hurwitz-Mintz Furniture Company, founded by Morris Mintz and Joseph Hurwitz, not on Canal Street, would become one of the few Jewish retail legacy enterprises to survive.

In the town of Reserve, thirty miles upriver from New Orleans, Godchaux Sugars was having trouble, too, struggling for its life against the encroachment of much larger public companies like Colonial Sugars, American Sugar Refining Company, and National Sugar Company. My great-great-grandfather Leon, the same patriarch who began his career as a peddler, and later founded the department store, had acquired his first sugar plantation in 1861, just as the Civil War began consuming the southern economy. By the time he'd finished building the company in 1880, he owned fourteen plantations, with holdings of sixty thousand acres of timberland and one hundred thousand acres of sugarcane fields. At its height, Godchaux Sugar was the largest sugar producer from cane in the United States. Besides the Louisiana sugar, it refined raw product from Cuba, Mexico, Puerto Rico, and the Philippines, which was brought to its docks at Reserve along the Mississippi River by steamship and then transported by the private Godchaux freight railroad to the refinery. From the earliest days, Leon Godchaux refused to utilize slave labor, which he believed to be inefficient as well as distasteful. After emancipation, most of his crew, both black and white workers, remained on the job, rather than flee as many did at so many other working plantations.

When I was a young boy, Reserve was still a vibrant company town—the center of Leon's innovative refinery business. Because of this plant, which could process more cane than the family-owned fields could support in a season, Godchaux Sugar Inc., eventually listed on the American Stock Exchange, became a major player in the twentieth-century manufacture and distribution of sugar throughout the South and the Caribbean. The refinery was capable of producing approximately two million pounds of refined sugar every twenty-four hours; this was then packaged and shipped in cartons of one, two, or five pounds and bags of two, five, ten, and twenty-five-pounds, each distinctively labeled GODCHAUX PURE CANE SUGAR. The ingenious, complex refinery turned out sugar products for all needs, including extra-fine granulated, brown, and confectioners. Nearly everyone who lived in Reserve worked for my uncle Charlie Godchaux, who then ran the company. The high school in Reserve was named the Leon Godchaux High School. The town's parks, churches, and other civic buildings stood on land donated by "the sugar company," as it was referred to. Most of the public buildings in town had been built by Godchaux for use by his employees, as had the workers' houses. From the top of the levee, a Godchaux's loading dock still jutted out into the Mississippi River.

To me, the endless fields of mature cane, where Dad took Gail and me a couple of times in the fall when we were kids, were a magical site—waving in the breeze, stout and firm in row after row. Dad liked to tell us how, as a boy, he got to ride horses through the property. I could walk through the fields and touch the rough stalks that towered over me; whenever I wanted, I could take out my pocketknife and cut one down to bring home. I loved to climb into the cab and maneuver the controls of Baldwin Engine Number 3, a coal-burning locomotive that used to run on the Godchaux's private railroad, now silent; it had been restored and left on display on a short section of track near the factory. Dad showed us how to cut each segment of a stalk just above and below the knotty ring and then strip it to expose the sweet pulp inside. Gail didn't care about this part and didn't carry a knife. But I always had mine in my pocket when we went to Reserve. Then Gail and I would suck and chew, spitting out the stringy pulp onto the ground after we'd extracted the sweet sugary substance.

We always took home some stalks to gnaw during the next

week, and enough to give to friends and to take to school to show in class. We'd lodge the base of the long stalks on the floor in the back of the car and stick the upper part out of the rear windows on both sides. It being harvest time, there were huge open-backed trucks all over the River Road and U.S. 10 filled with cut cane, headed for the refinery. Most of the kids at school had never seen sugarcane growing. None of them had ever stripped open the mottled stalks, ranging in color from brownish green to eggplant-purple black, to get to the sweet, chewy pulp. So I showed them what Dad had taught me.

By the time I was working for Dad, then, change was coming fast. Like the various Godchaux enterprises, many types of non-Jewish and Jewish-owned retail stores including clothing, antique, dry goods, bakeries, pawnshops, furniture and drug stores, along with food and restaurant suppliers, as well as cotton merchants, photographers, morticians, and clothing manufacturers that had prospered since the nineteenth century, were no longer doing so. Most of the locally prominent endeavors, founded by Jewish émigrés whose descendants carried on as respected, civic-minded, often philanthropic businessmen, doctors, architects and lawyers, were facing a new national economy. Some companies would be sold to larger national organizations; other businesses and professional practices, lacking generational continuity, would fade away. Many long-established leaders found it difficult to adapt to changing conditions in the region and in the nation.

* * *

My first weeks as an apprentice at Wolf & Co. was spent reviewing files and absorbing salient facts, routines, and details of customers' business concerns and personalities. I was reassured that Wolf & Co. could still support our family, as well as John's and Susie's, and pay me a good starting salary. As brokers, we continued to function as intermediaries between private members of the cotton trade—

growers, merchants, mills, and exporters. Our contribution was negotiating skills and trade knowledge.

After a few months in the office, Dad concluded that I needed to learn how to "class" cotton. He decided to send me to Houston for training, under a friend of his. Dad told me that a classing shed is a utility building filled with samples pulled from raw cotton purchased by a merchant and stored in the firm's warehouse. "Classers," he explained, "sort and describe the identifying characteristics of freshly picked cotton. The value and use of cotton depends upon how it's defined by the classer."

When I got to Houston, I saw that the interior of the shed was furnished with large, flat wooden tables, with edges that rose two inches above the surface, so that the cotton samples wouldn't fall to the floor. I could see in the bright light that raw cotton in its natural state is not a uniform shade of white, like the swabs in a box of Q-tips, as I'd always imagined. The cotton samples ranged from beige to gray to bright white.

After three weeks, I could line up the cotton fibers between my thumbs well enough for my sample to join the others on the table, though it took me twice as long as it did the most junior professional. After eight weeks, without consulting a color chart or a ruler, I could describe a sample within one color variation and one staple length.

The "staple" is a genetic trait of the cottonseed and partly determines the cotton's potential uses and its market value; the longer the staple length, the more valuable the raw cotton and the more uses for which it is suitable once processed. The finest shirts are made of staple cotton generally more than an inch in length.

After the eight weeks of training around the classing tables, I was ready to return to New Orleans. Soon after getting back to town, I found my own apartment in the French Quarter, on Burgundy Street, home to rowdy bars and soul food restaurants, and most of whose residents were black. For the first time in my life, I had my own address.

Once I knew what cotton looked like and how it felt, my training continued at Wolf & Co. To get the hang of negotiating I was told to listen in on conversations Dad and John held with their customers. I found out that making brokerage deals took much more finesse than just being knowledgeable about who owned cotton in Vicksburg and at what price it could be purchased. The telephone was indeed the basic implement of my new trade, and conversation was the catalyst. What our customers in the countryside expected as much as the technical information was camaraderie. They wanted to chat about home and children and vacations and weather as much as, if not more than, cotton. I noticed that John and Dad had become friends with each of their customers.

I was especially eager to renew ties with Country Day classmates. Alas, I soon discovered that every one of the nine girls in my class had married or moved away, as had most of the guys. Only a couple of my male classmates had remained to work in New Orleans. Also, I quickly found that my few remaining Country Day pals were surprisingly preoccupied. The debutante season was under way and, though I knew some of the debutantes and their families, as a Jew I was excluded.

The cotton business, the securities business, and most of the law firms downtown were thoroughly mixed, with Christians and Jews working side by side, sharing partnerships, business decisions, and board positions in the city's nonprofit institutions. But even during the business day downtown, social commingling was interrupted at lunchtime, when the Christian men would silently disappear into the exclusive sanctity of their restricted clubs. The most notable of these were the Louisiana Club, the Boston Club, and the Pickwick Club. They sponsored the most important Mardi Gras parades— Momus, Comus, and Proteus—and held the top-of-the-social-season lavish tableau balls that followed the parades.

I discovered that Jewish men who worked downtown or anywhere else in the city had to establish their own meeting places, so they gathered for lunch in public restaurants. Generations back, Galatoire's had become my own family's preferred luncheon club. As a young workingman from one of the leading Jewish families, I also got invited to join a Friday luncheon group, composed mostly of men a few years older than I was. The group called itself with intended irony the Boston Club East. The "East" part meant that we gathered in a rented room on the third floor of the International House, a trade association building a few blocks east of the Boston Club headquarters on Canal Street. Everyone paid a weekly charge that covered the room fee and the cost of a preordered lunch.

During those early working days, when I wasn't having lunch with my father and grandfather at Galatoire's, or getting to know the members of the Boston Club East on Fridays, I'd have lunch alone, usually at the Acme Oyster House. I loved the place. To get there I'd walk down Carondelet one block to Canal Street, the wide shopping thoroughfare that ran in front of Godchaux's department store. Once a wide drainage artery running from the Mississippi River to Lake Pontchartrain, Canal Street separated the French Quarter from the later Anglo commercial district. My destination was just one block inside the Quarter, on Iberville. The Acme, a seedy bar and seafood joint, was located kitty-corner to Galatoire's.

No two eateries could be more dissimilar. Galatoire's was formal and sparkling, the Acme raffish, boozy, and rank with the smell of beer and fried oysters and shrimp. During the "r" months (cooler months, each name contains the letter "r"), when Louisiana oysters were at their prime, the Acme served, day in and day out, the best raw oysters in the world. They were grown (local legend asserted) in the Acme's own oyster beds, situated in secret coves deep in the Louisiana marsh.

I'd get there early, around eleven thirty, before the lunch crowd, and take my standing position at the stained and pitted white marble counter just to the right inside the entrance.

"Jesse," I'd say to the dark-skinned oyster shucker on the other side of the bar, "I'd like the coldest and the largest ones you can find."

"Yes, man, I knows," he'd answer. "How many you want?"

"Let's see how they are," I'd say. "They salty?"

Jesse would let me know if they weren't either salty or cold by replying, "What 'bout startin' with a ha'f dozen to see?"

He'd swiftly slit one open with the short steel blade of his wood-handled knife, unerringly locating the release point between the hinged shells. Jesse split clenched oyster shells as if they were made of soft butter. He'd flip off the top shell, scrape under the eye, and place the gelatinous meat—juicy and trembling in the glistening, open half shell—on the bar before me as if it were a precious gift from the gods. After giving it a spritz of lemon and nothing more, I'd taste Jesse's trial offering.

All I had to say then was "Half," "One," or "Two." Usually they were so good, especially during the "r" months, that my response was a smile followed by "Two," meaning, of course, two dozen.

After one or two dozen eaten raw, I'd still have room for a "po'boy" oyster loaf, "fully dressed," meaning with shredded lettuce, thin-sliced dill pickle, spicy mayonnaise, and ketchup. While my oysters were being fried and the fresh loaf of French bread sliced, I was enveloped in and intoxicated by the special fragrance of frying oysters and shrimp, mixed with the sweet, heavy smell of beer—mostly Dixie on tap. I'd survey the vast assortment of blinking neon beer signs on each and every wall and wonder if I could convince one of the distributors to sell me one. You'd never see a more extensive or more colorful collection than in the murky recesses of the Acme, dark even when the New Orleans sun was ablaze outside.

As part of my training during the first months of 1960, Dad and John took me on the road. It was their practice to meet personally with each of our customers at least once a year. This was a key factor in how business relationships and friendships were maintained. Over a four-month period, I traveled by car and by plane with one or both of them to California, Texas, Tennessee, Oklahoma, Arkansas, Alabama, Mississippi, Georgia, South Carolina, Florida, and upstate Louisiana.

I saw cotton growing as far as the eye could see in places like Belzoni, Mississippi, a dusty crossroads settlement whose motto was "The Heart of the Delta." As we drove into town, metal scaffolding arched over the highway. At its peak was an immense, triangular Greek delta with a cast-metal heart painted bright red at its center.

"Customers need to look you in the eye," Dad told me on the first trip.

"I want to meet the people attached to the voices," I said, "but I'm worried I won't have much to say to them."

"They're going to decide if they can trust you and if they like you."

That seemed a heavy agenda. I said, "In one meeting?"

"Yes, probably in ten minutes."

"Should I say anything special?"

"They'll want to both trust and like you," Dad said to reassure me. "They've all taken to John and will to you, too. Just be yourself; don't try to make an impression."

When I went on a customer visit with John, he'd invariably say as we walked in, "Meet Peter, Pete's son. He's ready to work with you. So now feel free to speak to any one of the three of us."

Dad would say the same thing, but add "I'm always there to help if you need me, but give my son a try."

At first I felt like an impostor with these cotton men. For the most part they were seasoned, rugged characters with big bank accounts, living in small country towns. I was sure the customers would see through me in a glance. That I'd graduated from Yale was a potential source of embarrassment, but it never seemed to come up. I wondered if they knew that Dad had gone there, too.

"You got a girl back home?" is what they mostly asked me.

"Workin' on it," I learned to answer, with a smile to let them know I was in the swim. Otherwise, they seemed content to have me just listen.

In September 1960, as my second year at the firm began, I felt more secure with the jargon as well as with the people in the trade. I spent my days on the phone with customers, making deals. I was beginning, as Grandpa liked to say, "to pull my own oar."

And sometimes on slow afternoons, Dad would call me into his office and begin to teach me something new. Sitting at his desk, with me at his side, he would use his own stock portfolio as our classroom to teach me about finance and investing. He showed me how to keep an eagle eye on the trend of price-to-earnings ratio in any given company, rather than focus exclusively on earnings, as did many analysts in those days. He cautioned me to investigate the policies and quality of top management, and to make my own judgment about its judgment. Turning to the fixed-income portion of his holdings, he explained the way to determine the underlying appeal of any bond by computing its "yield to maturity," as I learned it was called. I didn't know it then, but long before I'd heard of such noted pioneering investment analysts as Benjamin Graham or David L. Dodd, these solid lessons and on-the-job training sessions provided the foundation for skills I would develop more fully and use extensively in the future.

At the same time, I didn't feel deep down as if I was becoming part of the culture of the cotton industry, or that it was becoming an important part of my life. It was a job, and I was learning a lot, and I was earning a good salary. That was appealing—the learning part especially, and the financial independence I was gaining. Perhaps I was impatient, a characteristic I'd never been able to avoid, but I didn't feel especially congenial with most of the cotton executives I encountered. Most of the men were considerably older and their sons weren't entering the business. I felt separate and alone, still the impostor, albeit an increasingly effective and knowledgeable one.

A special workday break would occur when I was invited to lunch with Grandpa and Dad at Galatoire's. Sometimes Uncle Jimmy, Dad's brother, was invited to join us. Though the restaurant didn't officially accept reservations, Mr. Galatoire guarded Grandpa's table until twelve fifteen each weekday. It was directly in front of Mr. Galatoire's customary post in the back of the dining room.

I loved walking into this grand establishment, purveyor and custodian of upscale New Orleans style and cuisine. From the sidewalk along Bourbon Street, its marble façade appeared curiously closed, its brass and wood door decisively shut, and the two street windows obscured by a thick white lace curtain.

To push through those heavy doors, though, was to enter the secret kingdom—a lively, warm, old-fashioned ambience that was reminiscent of the most elegant Parisian bistro. The walls were hung with great numbers of beveled, gold-framed mirrors, which laughed and sparkled with the reflections of the patrons. The room was lit by brass chandeliers; originally lamp-oil fixtures, their short curved arms each held a cluster of suspended, naked, low-wattage bulbs that glowed yellowish. The original floor tiles, small white hexagonals arranged in a rosette pattern, shimmered in the incandescent light and resounded as patrons and waiters walked briskly over them. Around the room, shiny decorative brass hooks were screwed into a high wooden molding to accommodate coats and umbrellas. Centered above each mirror and leaning down graciously toward the glass, a wall-mounted gooseneck lamp with a single exposed lightbulb enlivened the surface of the wall and cast the perimeter of the room into a soft glow. Below the mirrors, a hunter green baseboard encircled the room, filling the three feet of space between white tile floor and shimmering glass. Above the mirror frames, emerald green wallpaper festooned with a gold fleur-de-lis pattern rose to the ceiling some twenty feet above us.

Yvonne Winn, Mr. Justin Galatoire's daughter, always sat behind a small, round bar at the far end of the room, facing the entrance, just behind her father. There she reviewed bills and watched over the proceedings in the empire founded by her grandfather.

At the sight of Grandpa entering, Justin Galatoire (one of three brothers who owned and ran the restaurant) would rise from his perch next to Yvonne. "You are welcome, *Monsieur*," he'd say, as Grandpa smiled and extended his hand. Then the two proceeded together to Grandpa's regular table.

"*Ça va?*" Grandpa would inquire.

"*Oui, ça va.*" He never allowed a specific response or complaint as he answered and simultaneously pulled out Grandpa's preferred chair at the table. Then, usually following a fond pat on Grandpa's shoulder and a "Welcome" to each of us, he'd return to his post. These two elderly men greeted each other like seasoned friends, but, in fact, it was just a ritual.

Laborde, our usual waiter, would come to the table. Ceremoniously he'd ask, "Would you like to see the menu?"

I learned how to brush my hand along the plane of the thick white tablecloth to indicate that a menu wasn't necessary. No regular at Galatoire's ever consulted the menu. Laborde would report what was fresh and, among the freshest options, what "looked" best to him. Every waiter spoke to his regular customers as if he'd personally examined the seafood as it had been delivered hours before.

My favorite dish at Galatoire's was called stuffed eggplant. It did not appear on the menu; its indefinite, vague, and not especially appealing name was misleading. This supreme concoction consisted of the eggplant's hollowed-out purple skin filled with an outrageously delicious mixture of strands of sautéed eggplant mixed with bountiful portions of jumbo back-fin crabmeat and perfectly boiled, peeled, and diced Gulf shrimp. It was all bound together with a béchamel sauce infused with red wine vinegar, chopped green onions, salt, a pinch of white pepper, a dash of cayenne pepper, and finely chopped parsley. A thin, top layer of fresh breadcrumbs mixed with the highest quality Parmesan cheese was applied at the end of the baking process, resulting in a savory and sensual union of soft and crisp textures.

Uncle Jimmy usually ordered a regular menu item, a Godchaux salad—iceberg lettuce, diced tomato, sliced hard-boiled egg, anchovies, boiled and pealed shrimp, and lumps of back-fin crabmeat, tossed with creole mustard vinaigrette—named for my great-grandfather Paul, who'd invented it. Dad would usually place his order, hardly looking up. "Laborde," he'd say, "you know how I like my speckled trout, only today add some spinach on the side, please."

Grandpa would add, "I'll have that too, just the same as Morris."

It was at that table—with my father the cotton broker, my uncle Jimmy the architect, and my grandfather the stockbroker—that I was inducted into the central committee of the Wolf clan. We discussed the city, the world, business, and any issue facing the family. It was there at lunch that I learned about the slow deterioration of the Godchaux enterprises. I could see, feel, and hear in their barely guarded remarks their disappointment in the current generation—various Godchaux uncles—who had taken over in these difficult times of change and were failing. Other than as board members, the Wolf men at the table had no management responsibilities in any of the Godchaux family enterprises. They had each struck out for careers independent of the family, so it was easier for them to be critical.

At those lunches I also began to recognize that Uncle Jimmy's interests were quite unlike my father's and Grandpa's. They particularly liked to discuss the cotton and securities markets, and the world affairs that were driving them. Jimmy was captivated by the delight of a recent exhibit at the museum, or a play he'd seen at the Little Theatre, or the last concert at Municipal Auditorium. He sometimes talked about his latest architectural commission or a watercolor he'd started during a vacation with his wife, Catherine, or a struggle he was engaged in as a member of the Vieux Carré Commission, preserving the architectural integrity of the French Quarter. I noticed Dad and Grandpa were impatient when Jimmy got started on one of these subjects; I found them stimulating.

At these lunches I came to realize that I shared the interests of all three men—the financial viewpoints of my father and grandfather mixed integrally with the artistic and cultural proclivities of my uncle.

After a year of my lunching once or twice a week at Galatoire's, the doorman would subtly recognize me by a slight tilt of his head when I entered. Now, even when I wasn't accompanied by my father or grandfather, he'd show me to a good table and say, "Glad to see you, Mr. Wolf. I'll let your waiter know you're here."

9

The French Quarter and Tulane

My apartment at the edge of the French Quarter was the place of my dreams—a freestanding cottage concealed behind two lush, bright green banana trees at the back of a deep courtyard.

The entrance to the courtyard was through a small, unnumbered iron gate facing Burgundy Street. Once inside the gate, you walked down a narrow brick path, damp and slick with lichen, past the side of the main house, then through an overgrown enclosed garden courtyard, and finally into my hidden space at the rear of the court.

The apartment was composed of four tilting rooms stacked on two floors inside a yellow wooden building. Van Gogh would have liked to paint it. Upstairs, the bedroom overlooked the Quarter's red-tiled rooftops. I could see all the way to Esplanade Avenue, the wide thoroughfare that bounded the north side of the Vieux Carré and intersected the wharves at the Mississippi River.

The weekend after I had returned from Houston, I'd patrolled up and down the grid of the Quarter looking at FOR RENT signs. At the second place, I rang the front doorbell and a sixtyish white woman answered the door. She'd pushed back her startlingly bright silver-blond hair and rubbed at her forehead continuously as we spoke—a hangover, I assumed. After we talked about the weather and the Quarter and the mayor, as southerners do, she showed me through to the little cottage hidden at the back of her courtyard, a place I couldn't believe existed, and loved at first sight.

To my surprise she announced, "If you want the place, you can stay for as long as you want." Hilda owned the property and lived in the front building. "We don't need to write up any papers."

As a newcomer to the Quarter, I didn't realize that black tenants inhabited most Burgundy Street properties. Not one was occupied by both blacks and whites. Hilda was happy to see a white prospect with a reliable job.

"What about the rent?" I asked, thinking back to the horrors of the annual increases I'd heard were rampant in New York.

"What about the rent?" she asked right back, as if having to endure the most absurd question. "The rent is the rent, and it stays like I said for as long as you're here—as long as I get your check by the first of every month."

"Okay," I said, confused and relieved. I could imagine growing old at 612 Burgundy Street.

"But," she said, and here comes the kicker, I thought, "you know that ten dollars every month has to be cash to pay off Mike, the cop on this block, so you can park in front between the NO PARKING signs anytime?"

"Yes, I know that has to be cash with the check. You told me that."

"No, no . . . What I mean is, that amount might change. It depends on Mike."

I'd confined my apartment search to the Vieux Carré. I'd always fantasized living in the Quarter among the small Caribbean-looking cottages with shared walls surrounding hidden courtyards, their properties lined up next to one another, but each totally private because of the imposing brick wall dividers. Throughout the Quarter these cottages mingled with the statelier two-story European-style houses still attached on both sides to the adjoining property, but decorated with wrought-iron balconies that overlooked the street. I wanted to be part of this reservoir of historically curious architecture, like none other in the nation. I wanted to find out how the Quarter had gotten its look and developed its narrow street grid. I wanted to know more about the oldest part of this city in which I'd lived nearly all my life and I was eager to become exposed to its fabled French Quarter culture.

I'd found my first home in the old center a few blocks from what had been Tennessee Williams's house at 1014 Dumaine Street, Sherwood Anderson's apartment in the Pontalba building adjacent to Jackson Square, and William Faulkner's modest yellow town house nestled within Pirate's Alley, all within a five-minute walk through the Quarter.

In New Orleans, especially after moving to the French Quarter, I often felt I was living in a tropical dream world suspended on soft, marshy soil. The French Quarter, I knew, was on relatively high ground, having been elevated over eons by silt deposits from the annual flooding of the Mississippi River before the levees were built. Much of the city, though, had been a swamp less than a hundred years before. In lower-lying areas, ordinary rains (which came in profusion, especially in summertime) and floodwater from storms and hurricanes had to be pumped up-grade and out of the streets into drainage canals. The main (but not sole) conduits through various parts of the city to either Lake Pontchartrain or the Mississippi were the Seventeenth Street Canal, the Industrial Canal, and the London Avenue Canal.

* * *

I'd felt a loss ever since I let my architectural-slide business go, a loss at not being in touch with the great masterworks of the world. So in the fall of 1960, after about a year of working for Dad and trying to help stimulate his languishing business at Wolf & Co., I did what many a young adult in search of something more does. I went back to school after work hours.

I registered as an auditor at Tulane University and signed up for a late-afternoon art history course. I had long regretted not taking more than Vince Scully's one architectural history class at Yale. Our round-the-world trip, exposure to international architecture, and the experience photographing some of the greatest buildings in the world had left an indelible longing and deep impact. Living in New Orleans, a city full of diverse and historic structures, became a stimulant and constant reminder of my latent passion.

As I assessed the options, I discovered, to my surprise, that the art history faculty offered no course focusing on New Orleans architecture. They were ignoring the intact remains of a flourishing architectural tradition, right in the university's own backyard. The department's scholarly focus, like that of most academic programs around the country in those days, was with the great European periods and works. I registered for Early Renaissance Art and Architecture; Brunelleschi had always been one of my favorites. I'd never gotten over Professor Scully's explanation of the symmetry and logic embedded in the plans, simple decoration, and structures of the Basilica di San Lorenzo and the Pazzi Chapel in Florence.

On a Friday evening three months into my experiment with supplementary education, I was studying in the Tulane library. It was the night of my twenty-fifth birthday. My parents and sister hadn't planned anything special, and I wasn't dating anyone. I was feeling forlorn.

I tried to study but kept thinking: Here I am alone in a library on a Friday night on my birthday. This doesn't feel like the Big Easy to me, where everyone supposedly parties all the time, where "the saints go marchin' in." I was working myself over but good, battered by a super-sized helping of self-pity.

As I looked up from my study carrel, a Delacroix apparition

suddenly lit up the dim reading room. Long, straight, shiny black hair, luminous white skin, and curvy legs poured into rust-colored jeans were illuminated by the soft light. Her torso was clad in a tight-fitting, thin lavender sweater, outlining full breasts. She was as close to me as the next desk.

I recognized her from class, so she was a student at Newcomb, in those days a private, independent undergraduate woman's college associated on a shared campus with Tulane. It was easy to initiate a conversation.

"Hi," I whispered, observing proper library etiquette. "We're in Early Renaissance together."

She looked at me. "Yes, I know," she whispered back with a polite smile.

"Would you like to take a coffee break?"

"Sure," she said.

When we got out of the library, she laughed. "You looked so miserable in there; I thought I'd better step out with you. I'm Camilla."

"Well, it's my birthday," I said. "I'm Peter."

"Honey-chile, you can't be spending your birthday all alone in a musty library," she said in a playful mock-Cajun accent.

That evening at Bruno's, a hamburger joint two blocks from campus that reminded me of George and Harry's, one of my favorite New Haven hangouts, Camilla unveiled her spicy sense of humor. Though only a sophomore, she'd already decided to major in art history; she wanted to write a senior paper, she said, on "female anatomy as depicted through the ages." She confided, slyly, "I'm especially interested in how they decorated it in the eighteenth and nineteenth centuries."

"Decorated it?"

"You know," she said, "peek-a-boo veils, flower petals . . . whatever."

"Is that really going to be your topic?"

"Sure, darlin'," she said. "I've even cleared it with the chairman, way in advance. She wasn't thrilled at first—still isn't, would be my guess—but they're going to let me do it."

"Well, it's art," I said. "The figure is the painter's most beguiling topic of all time."

"Right," she said. "I'm focusing on one of the most beguiling, and in some periods contentious, subjects in the history of painting."

"I can hear you in her office."

"I might come up with some of my own theories." She grinned and shot me a coy look.

"I'm new at Tulane," I confided, after a second beer. "I moved back to New Orleans last year to work for my dad in the cotton business. I tried medical school, but it wasn't for me."

"So now you're trying something else?"

"Yes, art history—mainly architecture. The cotton business alone doesn't seem to be completely satisfying, so I'm sticking with it and trying to do this, too."

"Can you do a day job and academic work at the same time? It's hard enough for me just keeping up with my studies."

"I have late afternoons and evenings free," I told her, aware that I was giving this attractive young woman personal information but hoping she would respond by providing some of her own. "I'm starting out as an auditor," I continued. "I want to see if I can at least manage that."

"This is New Orleans," she said. "You're supposed to relax and have fun!"

"It's heads down right now," I said. "I leave the office after we settle our trades with the clearinghouse, around four."

We sipped our beers and ordered two hamburgers.

"It's going to be rough," she continued. "You're going to need a ton of energy and discipline."

"I think I've got both . . . We'll find out. Dad's convinced I'm a dilettante."

"Are you?" She caught me off guard. This is a very direct woman, I thought, not your typical oh-so-sweet southern magnolia.

"I don't know," I said.

I wanted to know the things she wasn't telling me. Was she involved with anyone? I thought I'd ease into the personal stuff. "Do you live on campus?"

"No, I live at home, near here. My dad teaches at Tulane. He's chair of the Spanish department."

"You like living at home?"

"I do," she said. "I'm an only child. And I love talking with my parents, especially Dad. He's wicked funny and smart. Plus, it's practical. Even though I go to school tuition-free, professional courtesy doesn't cover room and board."

Within a few weeks, I found that this young woman—partially Cajun on her father's side, New York Jewish on her mother's— loved New Orleans as much as I did. We shared a mutual affection for the old, seedy side of New Orleans, the city's odd customs, garlic-laced food, and curious mix of Caribbean, Spanish, and French architecture.

Living in the racially mixed part of the French Quarter, I began to experience a New Orleans I'd never known. A bar called Emile's, one block up from me, was typically filled with rowdy, hard-drinking black patrons, mostly men. During my first and only visit, I felt so uncomfortable that I didn't dare go back.

Buster's was a different story. A restaurant across Burgundy Street from my place, owned by Buster, a skinny, slightly bent-over black man, and a Creole woman, became my weekend lunchtime haunt. They served meals at midday to black and Creole workmen, as well as to employees of all persuasions from local shops. These customers walked over to Burgundy for Buster's cooking, many from the white-owned antique stores and bars on upscale Royal and Bourbon streets, several blocks away. Buster's four-burner, white enamel cooking stove was located behind the bar, like a short-order house. There was no kitchen. Out of his blackened iron skillets, though, Buster managed to produce the best jambalaya and mustard greens in New Orleans. On Fridays he turned out what may have been the best red beans and rice in the United States.

Before long, Buster expected me at lunchtime on Saturdays. "You been travelin'?" he asked after my first long out-of-town business trip.

"Yes, over in Texas and out to California."

"What you doin' over in those places?" he wanted to know as he cooked my jambalaya.

"Talkin' to cotton men," I answered, falling into his rhythm.

"My people picked cotton, but never got to talk to the boss. For way too long."

"Yeah, I know."

I'm pretty sure that Buster understood I wasn't typical Deep South. He knew I'd been away from New Orleans long enough to have my own ideas about race, and that I'd elected to live in a mixed neighborhood. He liked that I lived right across the street and was a regular.

Camilla enjoyed the earthy atmosphere at Buster's, too, especially when he walked over and said to her in a low, confidential tone, "Honey-chile, why you spend so much time uptown?"

Her eyes twinkled as she leaned toward him and said, "Man, you got that right."

Then he'd squeeze my shoulder and move on to another table.

Camilla and I spent most of our time on weekends together. Some nights she stayed over, after a call to advise her parents where she'd be. She loved my cottage. At night, through my open bedroom window, we listened to the warning whistles and wails from tugboats on the Mississippi River six blocks away, many owned by my childhood friend Merrick's family. Late on Saturday nights, we'd sit at the outdoor terrace of the French Market's Café du

Monde, talking, listening to the foghorns, and feeling the terrace shake with the impact of docking ferries. A block away, above the levee, I could sometimes just barely make out the looming hull of a docked freighter, its running lights etching its bulk into the night.

We often stopped at the Café du Monde after listening to a late set of jazz and visiting with Allan and Sandy Jaffe, the founders of recently opened Preservation Hall, whom I'd gotten to know. The Hall, as we called it, embodied the Jaffes' lifelong ardor for the musical heritage and genius of New Orleans. The Hall was one small, dark room about twenty-four feet wide and forty feet deep at 726 St. Peter Street. It perched right up against the sidewalk but was separated from it by a wall penetrated by shuttered windows. The entrance was the first door on the left as one walked through a covered carriageway; farther along, the carriageway also opened into a small courtyard and apartment. The Hall was always dark, even at midday in the summer. The only light filtered in from the two side doors, which were sheltered by the roof that covered the carriageway. Inside, four rows of pews faced the chairs where the musicians played. Behind the pews it was standing room only. In front of the benches, people sat on the bare, unpolished wooden floor, knees jammed up, practically in the path of the trombone slide. The crumbling plaster ancient walls of this soon-to-be-famous front room were obscured by Larry Borenstein's collection of large oil paintings of local black musicians holding or playing their instruments and gazing toward the rapt crowd.

In that room, the Jaffes revived traditional New Orleans jazz and spread its sound and soul across America. I never felt more alive or more at home or more privileged than in that first year, 1961, when the Hall began to buzz, and only jazz fans and some French Quarter residents wandered in. The Jaffes, too, were so alive and committed and happy to have found a mission at the center of their hearts. Night after night, for the first time in decades, long-ignored black musicians drawn out of retirement (plus white Allan on the tuba) wailed it out through those walls onto St. Peter Street and into the New Orleans night, to an entranced white audience.

As our relationship intensified, Camilla moved in with me on weekends. Her parents approved so long as she got her schoolwork done. Since we were both studying, this was never a problem.

On Sunday mornings, when we stayed in town, Camilla slept late and I began playing tennis again. I joined a group of Jewish men who met at the public courts in Audubon Park every Sunday morning at nine thirty. That was my best option, since almost no Jews were admitted to the New Orleans Lawn Tennis Club, located a few blocks away from the park, and where I had taken lessons as a boy. (Several years later, I was admitted, perhaps because of that past, the quality of my tennis, the standing of our family in the city, and with the help of several influential Jewish friends who were already members and went to bat for me.)

Camilla loved it when I came home sweaty, exhausted, and happy after tennis. She'd smile at me and touch a certain spot on the back of my neck. Mutual attraction became one of the basic ingredients of our life together. It seeped into everything we did. Glances across the room, innuendo, the amount of garlic and Tabasco we used in our cooking. Because of how she moved in such a slinky manner, I eventually nicknamed her "Cat."

On those torrid Sunday mornings, feeling so accepted and embraced, I often recalled my mother's reaction the day I came home from winning the city-wide boys' fifteen-and-under tennis championship. Before I could say a word, she said to the new boy-tennis-champion of the city of New Orleans, "You smell like the dickens! Don't sit down, you'll stain the upholstery. Tell me about it after you get off those wet clothes and shower."

10

Settling In

At Wolf & Co., our business remained flat, and we began to search for new, profitable business options. We investigated buying empty cotton warehouses and converting them to new uses. The massive solid redbrick buildings scattered along Tchoupitoulas Street at the edge of the Mississippi River were magnificent vestiges of a bygone era, when New Orleans was a major port for the storage and shipping of cotton overseas. We also thought of a leasing enterprise. I proposed to Merrick on the phone that we buy barges and equipment for his firm and that they then lease them from us. Merrick liked the idea.

"Hell, yes," he said. "We'd lease a barge or a whole fleet of them from you."

"Let me get back to you with a proposal," I answered, thrilled. We were going to fill a niche: we'd free inert capital that operating companies could use to better advantage than having it tied up in machinery, vessels, and vehicles. Using a large line of credit to secure the purchase, we would earn a steady return as lease income while amortizing the capital value of the equipment. Plus, we'd have the equipment to resell in the used-equipment market at the end of the lease period.

However, in spite of having good local credit and pristine relationships with local bank executives, we found that we couldn't borrow enough capital to finance a successful leasing business. Our assets were not at the scale necessary to provide the level of security required for the loans in those days. It wasn't possible to compete with General Motors, General Electric, and the local savings and loans.

Dad and John sent me to New York to determine if we could become a branch of a major investment bank or brokerage house. Since we knew the Loeb family, I went to see Henry Loeb, a senior partner at Loeb, Rhoades & Co., a prominent investment house in those days. He was cool to my approach. "There isn't enough money in the New Orleans area, we believe, to be attractive to us," Mr. Loeb told me. "We also know that the city and state governments are incompetent and crooked. We would need state licenses and local audits. We work in a regulated industry; I'm sure you realize that," he said. "And there's another problem," he continued, now with a resolve I knew there was no way around. "We'd want to get a piece of the municipal and the state financing business if we took the risk of opening an office down in New Orleans. But I'm not willing to pay the bribes and do the favors I know are customary down in your neck of the woods."

"Henry," I said, "we wouldn't work that way, either. There's got to be some part of that business we could obtain with our family contacts and the special expertise that Loeb, Rhoades would bring to the area."

"Maybe," he said. "But from where I sit it isn't worth the gamble or the exposure. We have a sterling reputation. We intend to keep it."

After two weeks in New York, I came home and reported back to Dad and John. "No one on our list wants to be in New Orleans," I told them. "The city is too poor for another firm, they feel, and too corrupt for any of them to consider opening up a branch office." What I didn't mention is how good it felt to be back in New York.

* * *

Eventually, Wolf & Co. decided to try something closer to our proven expertise. We had always been a member of the New Orleans Cotton Exchange, but we did not solicit business as futures brokers. The exchange itself, which had its headquarters directly below our office, was suffering as it never had before in its long history. Overwhelming competition from the New York Cotton Exchange, mixed with diminished supplies of U.S. cotton sold through the futures market, was doing it in.

Dad had been elected president of the New Orleans Cotton Exchange in December 1959, a few months after I began to work for him. He'd made headlines during his first appearance on behalf of the exchange in Washington, D.C. The *Times-Picayune* declared on December 11, 1959, in a bold headline on the first page: COTTON EXCHANGE'S PLIGHT GRIM—WOLF. In his testimony before the Joint Congressional Cotton Subcommittee of the House Agricultural Committee, Dad had stated the day before, "The Cotton Exchange cannot survive under existing farm policy." What he was calling attention to publicly, as he had previously on numerous occasions in New Orleans, was a change in the government's surplus-cotton policy that enabled it to sell its warehoused cotton in direct competition with private merchants. "We want," he said, "the government-owned and controlled carry-over stock of raw cotton removed from the market as direct competition with the American farmer and held intact, unless sold at not less than 115 percent of the current applicable support price."

After Dad testified, Hale Boggs, the influential U.S. representative from Louisiana, told the committee that "present farm policy, as it applies to the marketing of cotton, puts an unnecessary and heavy burden on the cotton trade, the cotton farmer and on the taxpayer. It is socialism with a vengeance."

Congressman Boggs went on to describe the dire effect of current policies on the New Orleans Cotton Exchange: "Because of government competition, the New Orleans Exchange, that [*sic*] in

September, October and November of 1958 handled transactions covering 11,000,000 bales, in the same months this year handled only 1,500,000 bales."

We decided the best and most logical way to stimulate our business would be to try to revive the New Orleans Cotton Exchange and to become active futures brokers on it. Given all of the other limitations, it was our best shot, we thought, with our extensive contacts in the industry and with Dad now president of the exchange.

Futures would be our growth business, while we continued our traditional spot business in "actuals"—that is, baled cotton in warehouses ready for immediate sale. The idea made sense. The same customers would use both services from us. Counting on their loyalty, we set up a new corporation and prepared to win back business from the New York Cotton Exchange. No new capital was needed. In February 1961, we announced the formation of Wolf & Godchaux Inc., Cotton Futures Brokers. Our card, which we distributed to the entire industry, stated: "This new corporation is an additional facility and in no way alters the regular services of Wolf & Co." At the bottom, three names were printed: "Morris Wolf, John Godchaux, Peter M. Wolf." I was very proud to be listed with Dad and John, and to be a shareholder in this new venture.

We asked all of our loyal customers and active members of the cotton industry to place their futures orders through us in New Orleans rather than continue to trade in the New York market. As a result, we did modestly build up our own futures "book" (customer orders), but many of our merchants and mills continued to hedge their crops and protect forward purchases and sales in the much larger and more liquid New York marketplace. The largest speculators in the country worked through New York, too.

By watching the trading in New Orleans and hearing about which brokers were executing large volumes of contracts in New York, I came to understand that the role of speculators was crucial to the smooth working of any futures market. Without them, certainly in the cotton markets of both New York and New Orleans, there would have been inadequate liquidity for the market to function effectively.

To be a useful part of Wolf & Godchaux Inc.'s futures trade, I had more learning to do. I didn't understand fully what a cotton future was or, for that matter, a corn, soybean, silver, copper, or hog future. The idea of buying and selling something you didn't have and didn't even want to possess (and even more perplexing, something that could not yet be delivered) was at the outset a mysterious notion. I was a very long way from John Milton, Søren Kierkegaard, the Hagia Sophia, and basic anatomy.

The simple explanation John gave me in his succinct manner helped. "What we're selling," he told me in a raspy voice that made him sound as if he'd grown up in the Ninth Ward or in Brooklyn, "is a contract. The contract is an obligation between buyer and seller to do something in the future. We're intermediaries who bring the buyer and seller together to agree to undertake a transaction at a set price in the future, only we do it around a trading ring instead of over the telephone."

With that, John pulled open a file drawer. He took a document out of a manila envelope and handed it to me. "This is the contract for the New Orleans Cotton Exchange. One of our jobs," he continued, "is to be certain we represent only people who will perform."

I didn't know what he meant by that last part, but, since he was busy, I set about reading the four-page agreement.

I learned the following: Only cotton of specific color and staple could be delivered on a futures contract. At least I knew what that meant. I learned that delivery of the cotton and payment for it was expected (depending upon the detail of the transaction) on the first day of April, July, September, or November, and that cotton was not traded more than twelve months ahead. The seller must deliver the specified amount of cotton to the buyer at the warehouse location detailed in the contract. I learned that the buyer must pay for the cotton by bank draft to the seller's bank on the day of delivery. Each "contract" negotiated would be for one hundred bales of cotton, each weighing five hundred pounds. These were the basic terms of a futures contract entered into on the New Orleans exchange and so governed each transaction. New York had a very similar contract.

The exchange occupied the entire second story of the New Orleans Cotton Exchange Building. It was a majestic double-height space, 150 feet long and fifty feet wide. Access was either from the elevators or from an ornate white marble staircase that rose from the lobby.

Various ancestors had been active on the Cotton Exchange during its heyday, from the 1870s to around 1940, as had my grandfather. In those days, New Orleans businessmen of all sorts would visit the trading floor by using the lobby staircase. Many of them, part-time speculators, would have given orders to their local brokers; others liked to stand around watching contracts being bought and sold, money in effect changing hands, and listening to the shouting and frenetic trading. Visiting the exchange for downtown businessmen in those prosperous cotton-trading days was a form of lunch-hour recreation. Back then, cotton was king in the South, and as the preeminent warehouse and banking center in the South with a thriving international port and futures trading market, New Orleans served all the industry's needs. The introduction of Eli Whitney's cotton gin in 1793 had enabled the rapid rise of the cotton industry and the mercantile culture that surrounded it. During the peak years of the last half of the nineteenth century, about a third of all of the nation's cotton production passed through the port of New Orleans.

Some evenings on my walk home to Burgundy Street, I'd think about Dad's blazing success after the war and his subsequent pyrrhic victory in being exonerated by the federal government. His experience frightened me. I came to the vague, partially unconscious, and surely irrational conclusion that, whatever I did, I should try to remain relatively inconspicuous. I had an uneasy sense that Dad had been too bold, that he'd overreached and lost his sense of proportion, and so had been cut down. I thought of King Lear. I felt that Dad was a large figure, the King Lear of my own life, the ruler of the kingdom. Possessed by my shaken uncertainty about our future, I imagined he had handled his pride and power unwisely.

* * *

Every workday after the Cotton Exchange had closed and I had filed our futures trading report with the clearinghouse, I'd drive uptown through rush-hour traffic along St. Charles Avenue to Tulane. To most New Orleans residents, St. Charles Avenue was a congested street made all the more hazardous by streetcars and pedestrians cluttering intersections. What I saw was splendid Victorian mansions lining both sides of the broad boulevard. Bisecting the avenue was a wide swath of "neutral ground" (as it was universally called in New Orleans) in which streetcars ambled; the open spaces were filled with extravagant azalea bushes, which flourished beneath palm, magnolia, crepe myrtle, and oak trees. Moss-covered limbs arched over the street, creating a bower. Each day I journeyed through a virtually intact museum of nineteenth-century architecture and horticulture.

En route, I'd check by radio the closing prices on the New York Stock Exchange. By then, the beneficiary of Dad's helpful tutoring, I'd begun to accumulate and manage my own modest portfolio. Next, I'd turn to the classical music station to ease the transition between cotton and art. I'd often feel a sudden sense of exhaustion, a mental grating and grinding, as my two worlds collided and I had to switch gears.

Once at Tulane, I'd head for the graduate student lounge in the Newcomb art building, where I had a desk, now a fully enrolled student. Sometimes I needed a short nap to settle and refocus my mind before I could go to class or begin research. The lounge was a run-down corner space on the first floor. Along one wall stood an old couch where I'd stretch out in my business attire, after draping my jacket and tie over the back of a chair.

A full-time graduate student, who was a resident of Baton Rouge and ardent about eighteenth-century Italian painting, occupied the desk next to mine.

"You're missing everything," he said to me one day. "You show up here, take a nap, then start studying."

"What am I missing?"

"Everything," he said.

"Everything?"

"You know," he said, "most of the lectures in the department, all of the campus activities, getting to know the Newcomb babes."

"You've met Camilla," I said. "You've talked to her right in this room a hundred times. I have a girlfriend. One is enough."

"Yeah, okay, but you're not taking some of the best courses in the department because they meet in the morning. You're not getting to know the faculty, either."

"Can't do it all, man."

But even as I said it, I knew he was right. I knew I was experiencing Tulane even less thoroughly than the way day students had experienced Exeter and Yale. They had not been part of the social life of our class in any deep sense. Few of the boarding students knew them, and they had missed out on essential campus culture—the after-class and late-night bull sessions, extracurricular intermingling, unscheduled time to chew the fat and gripe.

I did miss all of that, but it didn't particularly bother me. I had an active life in New Orleans as the youngest board member of two busy nonprofit organizations that interested me: the new educational television station in New Orleans, WYES-TV, and the New Orleans Public Library. I had a steady girlfriend. I had Sunday

morning tennis. I was holding down a job. I felt little or no resentment about my circumstances.

My graduate work continued to progress well, regardless of dis-
tractions off campus. I loved the atmosphere around the art building,
a place that mixed within a single structure tidy art history scholarship and appealingly messy painting, drawing, ceramics, and glass-
blowing studios. I realized I had set up my new university life as if I
were going to a second job. I needed to straddle the fence. I couldn't
imagine making a full-time commitment to my studies in art and architectural history, or, I now realize, to the cotton business.

As our relationship matured, when we had weekends free, Camilla and I eagerly took to the road to explore the bayous and ancient communities throughout the Cajun country, the swampy lands
west and south of New Orleans and north of the constantly and dangerously receding marsh edging the Gulf of Mexico. These frag-
ile marshes, diminished by heavy storms and hurricanes, serve as a
crucial storm surge protective barrier buffer to the uplands beyond.
We'd spend entire afternoons looking at poorly maintained ancient
vernacular houses, traditional country stores, fields planted in cotton, and shady cemeteries in places like French Settlement, Presque
Isle, and Montegut—small towns huddled on low banks above turgid bayous. On Saturday nights, we'd eat "dirty rice" with boiled
shrimp in bare-bones restaurants, and two-step with fishermen and
trappers and their women to zydeco in rickety roadhouses.

On Sunday mornings, we'd find a back pew in a rural church
and listen raptly to spirited gospel singing and impassioned preach-
ing. Upon arrival, we were often the only whites. The congregants
would stare at us at first, since we were obviously strangers. Then,
almost always, one of the ushers would approach us. Ushers were
always women identifiable by their shiny, white, formal dresses,
white stockings, and highly individual hats. "Are you looking for
anybody in particular?" they'd ask, understandably suspicious.

"No . . . we'd just like to attend your service. Would that be all right?"

A long, hard look typically followed. We could see the usher thinking: Are these people telling the truth or do I need to alert someone? Troublemakers?

If the silence became too painful, I'd interject, "We're students from New Orleans on a weekend outing, that's all."

"Be welcomed" was the routine answer. "We're pleased to have you." Fortunately, we didn't encounter, or inadvertently provoke, any obvious resentment or the rage that flared so violently and so easily in those days between blacks and whites. Most of the rural bayou communities we visited were mixed populations: families of blacks, Creoles, Cajuns, and a handful of whites, all working the land or the swamps or the waterways as hunters, trappers, fishermen, and farmers—sometimes all four, depending on the season and what was profitable.

After services, Camilla and I would walk through the adjacent cemetery to examine the elevated tombs, while congregants left flowers at family grave sites. In both urban and rural Louisiana and through much of the Gulf region, people buried their loved ones in the finest and most ostentatious aboveground tomb structures they could afford, because any hole in the ground, whether dug for a body or a building, filled with water overnight. People, like houses, were set on slabs above grade and topped off with whatever else money could buy. These cities of the dead were scattered throughout the lowlands.

On special occasions, like Camilla's birthday or mine, we'd splurge on a luxurious overnight stay at one of the restored plantations. Mintmere was our favorite, an original unspoiled 1857 Greek Revival cottage in New Iberia, with grounds cascading down to Bayou Teche. It contained just three airy guest rooms. The one we liked best was furnished with a huge four-poster bed, its sides and top furled in white gauze. With Camilla in my life, each of our birthdays was a major event. When mine came around, I always recalled how bereft and alone I'd felt the night we'd met. I hoped to avoid that experience again, forever.

When we didn't have the whole weekend to spare, we still made excursions to the river's edge. It pulled both of us. We'd stand by the Mississippi not far from my apartment and watch the ships inch hypnotically up and down river, or we'd drive to the bend where St. Charles and Carrollton avenues meet. There we would climb to the top of the grassy levee and stroll for hours with the river on one side and the city below us on the other.

Lake Pontchartrain beckoned us, too. With my cousin Peter Mayerson, I purchased a fourteen-foot day sailer. We took turns using it. When Camilla and I took our turn, she liked to pack a picnic. We'd eat at the slip, either before or after sailing. I wasn't a competent enough sailor to enjoy eating on board. I worried intensely about not noticing changes in the wind or forgetting to scan the horizon for telltale signs of a squall, the kind that frequently blew up nearby in the Gulf and toppled small craft.

Much like my grandfather years before, Camilla sometimes said, "Out here I feel free—free of art history, my parents . . . everything. Don't you?"

"Yes and no" was always my answer. We were out there together, but I was aware that we were very much on our own, and I always felt some danger being in charge of a small boat at sea. At the same time I felt a spacious liberation, rocking in that tiny craft, my pleasure at being in the light alone with Camilla, for a brief time unconcerned about the future of our cotton business, or of my own life.

To introduce Camilla to my parents, I invited them to join us for dinner one evening at Galatoire's. She struggled to engage them with questions. "Peter tells me you go to Europe often, especially Paris. Which museums do you like?"

My parents didn't routinely visit museums; it was not why they went to Paris. Rather, they loved to shop on the rue St.-Honoré for Mom, and Charvet, tucked into the corner of Place Vendôme, for Dad. They strolled stylishly from the Rond-Point down the Champs-Élysées to the Place de la Concorde, and then on through the Tuileries Gardens. That the Louvre was just a step away at the end of their walk wasn't of primary interest. That they could turn left, amble through the Palais Royal gardens and shopping arcades, and arrive at their reserved table at the elegant, historic Grand Vé-four, Dad's favorite restaurant, was thrilling. Years later the Grand Véfour became my favorite, too, of the big-name restaurants.

When I spoke to Mother from the office the next day, she said, "Camilla's a lively girl. But your dad and I couldn't imagine her at your grandmother's on New Year's Eve. Have you thought about whether she'd fit in?"

Mother, who'd had her own hard time fitting in at Gram's for New Year's Eve and every other family holiday for years, said this so casually and so bluntly that I was momentarily startled. On sec-ond thought, though, I realized that she was right. Camilla would enjoy the scene with Herbert passing champagne and caviar on a sil-ver tray. But something about the style of her dress (maybe it would be tight around the bust) or her direct gaze or her habit of asking a lot of questions might irritate my grandmother. Grandpa wouldn't say a thing, but he'd be thinking, Can't Peter find a more suitable woman in this town . . . a quieter one, someone who isn't as flashy?

A little later, Dad said "Tell me about Camilla. What's her back-ground, other than Newcomb?"

I had thought he would like her sexy appearance and ready smile. "Did you like her, Dad?" I asked him.

"She's a dish, for sure," he said. "But tell me more about her."

"Well, she's from New Orleans, unlike most of the Newcomb girls, so she's not part of the regular undergraduate scene. And she's not going to be leaving town anytime soon, like most of the college girls. She lives at home."

I believed these facts would be a big plus for her, but he didn't reply.

"Her father's a professor at Tulane, head of the Spanish department, and claims to be part Cajun," I continued. "Her mother is from New York, the child of a well-off Jewish family. Camilla's an only child and a good student. Anything else?" I also thought he'd be pleased to hear that her mother's family had been affluent, at least at some point, and from the Northeast.

"Son," he said, "there are lots of attractive young women in town. I think you could do better. What about one of those Country Day girls?"

"Dad," I said, "Camilla is great. She's earthy. She understands me. We're both interested in art and New Orleans. Plus, she's real—no pretense, no attending coming-out parties, no debut, no anti-Semitism, no racism, half Jewish but totally agnostic. She bridges New York and New Orleans, Christian and Jewish, downtown and uptown, art and . . . I could go on and on."

"However you describe her," he said, "she's a faculty kid and I've never heard of her father."

To me, Camilla's father was a man of value, and I admired him and enjoyed his raffish, irreverent humor. But I, like my father, could not place him in the same idealized category as the well-off, highly regarded lawyers, judges, doctors, and businessmen my family had known for generations. I had to be honest with myself. I placed Camilla's father in a large field of achievement, but inside a small universe, one subsisting in a soft fog and separated from what I thought of at the time as "the real world"—the one that counted. I was becoming a chip off the old block.

My folks never warmed to Camilla. The sexy way she dressed in tight jeans and tighter sweaters was too provocative, her hair dyed too black, her language too earthy and off-color. So I stopped inviting Camilla to family events. We began instead a downtown lifestyle in the Quarter with local artists, young entrepreneurs, people from the music world like Allan and Sandy Jaffe, and a few others who, like me, were withdrawn from their more conventional families. Our circle eventually consisted of locals and friends from almost every state, plus a few from abroad.

We also drifted away from my old Country Day crowd, who were mostly inaccessible anyway due to the discriminatory social strictures that prevailed—the tacit social segregation of Jews from Christians ruled, especially at night. By this time, I could become angry when I thought about this, so I tried not to, just like so many other Jews living comfortably in New Orleans. Camilla couldn't be of much help in this regard. Her status wasn't high enough on her father's side to be accepted in the elite Christian sphere, nor would she have been comfortable there. But because her mother was from New York, neither was she local, old-family Jewish enough to be accepted into the inner sanctum of New Orleans–based, so-called German Jews, to which I had well-established credentials. From the outside it might not have been apparent, but I felt very much on the margin. I was once again different from my peers—in being a student at this late age, in having a girlfriend who didn't fit any particular traditional mold of eligible young woman, and in residing in the Quarter rather than the Garden District or uptown or the desirable parts of Metairie.

Had I been more self-aware, I'd likely have realized that it was precisely because Camilla did not fit into one of the accepted categories that she particularly appealed to me. She, too, was an independent, finding her way in a stratified social setting that depended upon labels to confine each individual to just the right box. Camilla belonged there with me—she, too, was odd and marginal. We were each finding our own way.

* * *

Toward the middle of my second year at Tulane, I discovered my master's thesis topic. Inadvertently, Camilla led me to it.

"You know the Napoleon House?" she asked one Saturday night. "It's near your apartment."

"Yes," I answered. "I've played chess there with Leo." Leo Roos was a local lawyer, a Jewish man a couple of years older than myself, who lived in the Quarter. I'd known him casually for years, and he was one of the guys I played tennis with on Sunday mornings. "Why?"

"Did you see the old courtyard in back?" she asked.

"Sure. I've sat in it, had a drink in it, read in it," I said. "I love it."

"But have you ever looked at it? Have you ever been in it at night with a full moon lighting up the walls and turning that one big banana tree silver-green? It's wonderful."

Encouraged by Camilla's affection for the place, when we stayed in town we adopted the Napoleon House as our regular hangout on Saturday evenings. Back then it was a quiet, off-the-tourist-path bar and bistro. We met friends there, especially those living in the French Quarter. We'd eat fried oyster po'boy sandwiches and drink beer, wine, or Jack Daniel's as we played chess. I imagined us being as free, intense, and raffish as Jean Cocteau, Pablo Picasso, Simone de Beauvoir, and Marcel Duchamp had been in Paris.

I loved the look of the bar's musty old rooms—its ochre-stained and peeling plaster walls, its dimly lit courtyard and finely proportioned exterior. I was drawn to the way the wooden staircase at the corner of the courtyard unfurled elegantly upward to the second-floor gallery.

Camilla was right about the courtyard in moonlight. The sturdy palm trees became inky silhouettes against flaking, multicolored plaster, like an ancient planting in a Moroccan *ksar* at the edge of a river below the Atlas Mountains. Across its life span the plastered and painted brick wall had obviously had many incarnations, each of which was visible within the building's irregularly peeling layers—sepia, umber, bisque, light orange, ochre, yellow. The undulating staircase, protected under its overhanging balcony, cast its own jagged shadow when struck by the yellowish New Orleans moonlight. I wondered who the architect had been.

I called Uncle Jimmy to ask what he knew about the place.

"It's a splendid building," he said. "I've always wondered who designed it, but I never bothered to look it up. I'm not sure who would know." He then gave me ideas about research sources both in New Orleans and beyond.

I launched an investigation and eventually learned that a Frenchman named Jean-Baptiste-Hyacinthe Laclotte was the architect. After a lot of digging, I discovered that he had designed three of the best buildings in the Vieux Carré, each in the historic center of New Orleans. One of them was the Girod residence of 1814, built for Nicholas Girod, mayor of New Orleans from 1812 to 1815. In 1821, a rumor floated through New Orleans that an expedition was being subscribed in the city to rescue Napoleon Bonaparte from his forced exile on the South Atlantic island of St. Helena. Girod publicly offered his home at the corner of Chartres (in New Orleans pronounced "Charters") and St. Louis streets as a refuge for the former emperor. Legend asserts that three days before the rescue ship (the allegedly super-speedy, two-hundred-ton schooner *Seraphine*, financed by Girod) was to sail, word got to New Orleans that the emperor was dead. The expedition was thus abandoned. From that point forward, Laclotte's building was known as the Napoleon House. When it was converted into a bar many years later, it quite naturally assumed the name by which it had been known for a hundred years. History, lore, and fine architecture were wrapped into a great hangout.

My research revealed that Laclotte, born in Bordeaux in 1766, trained in architecture there and then may have attended the École des Beaux-Arts in Paris. He immigrated to New Orleans in 1804 and practiced in the city until about 1816, when he left for Paris for a spell to supervise the engraving of a renowned picture of the Battle of New Orleans that he'd painted the previous year. He turned up briefly in Philadelphia in 1818 before returning to his hometown in 1821. He died there in 1829, at the age of sixty-two.

Until I introduced him, no one at the Tulane School of Architecture or in the art history department knew anything about Laclotte. There was not a single book in the city or university library about him. Indeed, only one pamphlet mentioned him. I realized, with gleeful amazement, that I'd found a prime thesis combination: a gracious, overlooked New Orleans building of undeniable architectural quality and an elusive international architect of merit whose work in New Orleans had not been previously studied. More than that, I'd found a topic I was eager to explore for reasons far beyond the purely academic. I would be smack in the middle of an inquiry that was bound to teach me a great deal about the city I'd come to treasure and identify with, and in which I'd made my home. Furthermore, as a special bonus, some of my fieldwork would require spending time at the Napoleon House. Close observation of details and building analysis would, of course, be essential.

When I suggested the topic, my department chairman said, "Are you sure an architect who worked in the French Quarter is worthy of your time and our review?" Her department's focus was on better-known, usually well-documented figures in the history of art, especially those working in Europe and sometimes in Latin America.

"I've checked out his buildings," I said. "They're better than anything else of the period in the Quarter."

Although the art history department was skeptical about my homegrown topic, it gamely approved my proposal. Because my subject and local focus were unusual, the department chairman then asked me to put together a special committee that would include architectural experts to oversee, evaluate, and guide my work, subject to her approval. The final group comprised Samuel Wilson, Jr., a long-established, practicing New Orleans preservationist architect; Bernard Lemann, a New Orleans native and architectural historian at the Tulane School of Architecture; and two art history department members: Prudence Myer , a specialist in French art, and Cecilia Davis, a scholar trained in Europe and at New York University's Institute of Fine Arts.

My research progressed, though slowly. I had to fit in time after work for classes and research. Camilla and I tried to coordinate our studies to make time for the occasional late-night hamburger together after the library closed.

A greater problem, though, was logging the research hours I needed in the New Orleans Notarial Archives, housed in the Civil District Court building. That office was open during the same hours as Wolf & Co. I began to spend my lunch hour, sometimes consecutive lunch hours, three blocks away from our office, deep inside the Civil District Court building. The staff there got to know me well and set aside a small desk for me. Mrs. Courtal, the chief clerk, who had once worked at Godchaux's, let me leave documents on my table there during the week.

As I dug deeper into primary sources, I began to uncover Laclotte's unaccountably ignored trail in the early city records, many of which were more than 150 years old and stuffed into the Notarial Archives (in early days New Orleans legal instruments were known as Notarial Acts, as they were in France) in the Civil District Court   Building. These were the original commercial transaction records, undertaken in the presence of a notary. I found, for instance, a building contract of December 16, 1815, that mentioned the "New Home of M. Girod." Instead of simply recording the transaction and the deed, the act contained a description of Monsieur Girod's property, indicating that the corner site was empty at the time of the sale. Bingo! I knew then that Laclotte had designed the Napoleon House from scratch.

Laclotte had not always been an independent practitioner. Between 1810 and 1813 he had a partner, Arsène Lacarrière Latour. By 1813, though, the partnership had run into financial difficulty. I was able to trace their plight through City Council records at the New Orleans Public Library. I knew about these particular records because of my work as a trustee on the library board. In checking the proceedings of the New Orleans City Council, housed at the main branch of the library, I came across a petition for bankruptcy relief that Laclotte and Latour had filed at the end of their partnership. It amounted to a plea, a list of assets, and a schedule of liabilities that exceeded their assets by twelve thousand dollars. Their plea was rejected and the partnership forced into bankruptcy. Their inventory of assets revealed a cameo of the culture about which I was writing and with which I was fascinated. Their worldly goods were listed as:

A lot on Burgundy Street, 90' front by 63'8" in depth [I wondered, but had no way of checking, if this could have been where I was currently living];

A Negro named "Bosom," age 20, a fair mason [I also wondered if "fair" described this man's skin tone or his masonry skills];

A sand pile;

A lime pile;

Some bricks;

A quantity of planks and lumber;

Two dump carts;

A box containing some old iron pieces;

About 60 lbs. of nails of various sizes;

Five old pick axes;

Four pulleys;

About eighteen feet of tin piping;

Four masons' hoods;

Seventy squares of marble, some good and some bad.

But it was in Washington, D.C., thanks to the interlibrary loan system, that my research hit pay dirt. I found that late in the Depression, the Historic American Buildings Survey had produced measured drawings of each of Laclotte's principal New Orleans buildings. I analyzed earlier architecture in France and Italy to discover sources and to find stylistic influences on Laclotte.

My work downtown at the office was intense at this time. We had recently opened our futures trading business, hoping to expand our profitability. I had become increasingly comfortable with my mastery of the intricacies of our spot cotton business. Yet that challenge held no thrill. It was in my studies that I came alive. My excitement, energy, sense of fulfillment, and delight were sparked by reading, looking at architecture and art, and investigating Laclotte and his milieu. Their impact on the character of the city was fascinating to me.

I felt both conflicted and ashamed to tell my parents how much I enjoyed my work at Tulane. I wanted them to think of it as an extracurricular activity, as I, too, had originally; something akin to learning the Tibetan language—an interesting, harmless pursuit that would never prove practical. I often thought to myself, Maybe I never will use what I am learning; maybe I'm just having a good time. Is my father right? Am I, in fact, a dilettante at the core of my being?

From time to time I talked with Camilla about the possibility of my continuing in architectural history. In spite of persistent self-doubt, it was on my mind, and I imagined it was on hers, too. I was deeply entangled in my studies. Most weekday evenings I worked in the library until it closed at eleven. When she and I were together, I couldn't stop talking in relentless detail about my research discoveries. Camilla didn't complain. She, too, was very busy with her art history studies.

Camilla believed in what I was doing, and she understood the strain I was under in trying to hold a responsible day job and simultaneously pursue graduate studies. I was grateful that she was generously giving our relationship a great deal of time especially tailored to those periods when I was available.

Still, in spite of goodwill on both sides, and great affection, eventually our relationship suffered. I was unable to imagine that she was thinking about our future as a couple. I was so engrossed in my own dependencies on her—partially assuaged by keeping manically busy at a mixture of school and work—that I found ways to avoid feeling the pressure of time and the appropriateness of our talking seriously about a possible next stage. It was beyond my confined imagination to step into her way of thinking.

I was comfortable with her in limited spheres: sharing our probing academic life at Tulane and the bohemian world of the French Quarter. Our romance had allowed each of us to step into unknown worlds. I contributed an out-of-town education, enthusiasm, and a glimpse into the New Orleans Jewish establishment. She brought a rakish, sensual verve, together with gaiety and freedom from social convention. Camilla was right for me then and there, and perhaps I for her. I was self-absorbed enough to believe that she was equally satisfied. I was also infected by some of the same doubts that my parents had aired about Camilla and that I surmised my grandparents shared. I had no idea what kind of woman I'd want as a permanent companion, as a wife. I wasn't disposed to think in those long-range terms. I was too absorbed in my own quandaries to think deeply—much less ask—what it was that she would like. At the very least, it would have been utterly appropriate to acknowledge her need to talk about our romance by asking something like "Would you like a deeper or more formal commitment between us?" or "I'd like us to think about a future together. Would that interest you?" Instead, I felt I was in the midst of a passage between what had been and what would be. In the deepest recesses of my imagination, I felt temporary and unsettled, very preoccupied with my own needs—like an island.

11

Mosca's

In late November 1962, I proposed a mini reunion weekend with Henry, Bud, and Gerry in New Orleans to celebrate Bud's and my birthdays. We were each born in early December, one day apart. Henry was too busy to get away, having recently joined the staff of the Metropolitan Museum of Art after graduate work at Harvard; Bud and Gerry were game.

Gerry had married Joan Edwards, then becoming a sculptor, when he returned from his Henry Fellowship in England, and gone to work as a reporter for the *Boston Herald*. By the time of our reunion, he and Joan had returned to New York, and he had secured an entry post on the editorial staff of the *New Yorker* magazine, from which he soon advanced to become a "Talk of the Town" reporter there.

When I suggested the idea to Bud, who was then back in New York as a member of *Time* magazine's staff, he said, "Yes, yes; are there any good places to eat that aren't the usual tourist traps, or the big-deal restaurants I know about?"

Bud had always loved to eat authentic local food. I'd known that for years and from our travels together.

"I'm gonna take you to a restaurant so genuine and so good you'll never forget it," I assured him.

In those days, even though it had been serving remarkable food since just after World War II, Mosca's was unknown outside the city and all but unknown to most white-shoe New Orleans sophisticates who fancied themselves arbiters of taste.

"Yeah," he said, sounding dubious.

"Bud, trust me on this one."

My friends arrived on a Friday in early December. We walked the Quarter, visited plantations up the River Road, hung out at the Napoleon House, and consumed two grand meals—at Galatoire's on Friday evening and at Antoine's for Saturday lunch.

I saved Mosca's for Saturday night, their last in town. I steered my Volkswagen Beetle through town and past the low wooden houses of Jefferson Parish, continuing onto U.S. Route 90 over the Huey P. Long Bridge, then headed southwest. The little car was crowded, with Camilla in front and Bud and Gerry squeezed into the backseat. After passing through the Bridge City traffic circle at the base of the bridge, I swung right on the west bank of the Mississippi in the direction of the towns of Paradise, Des Allemands, and Boutte. I drove past the Avondale Shipyard. We cruised the darkening highway until our headlights and those of passing cars provided the only illumination.

"Where the hell are you taking us, Pierre?" Bud asked.

"We're nearly there," I said. "Hang in."

The swamp was evident on both sides of the dark road, which grew dimmer as we passed fewer and fewer cars.

Camilla asked, "Can you guys see the cypress knees out there?"

"The what?" Gerry asked.

"The darkest shapes out there—part of the root system of old cypress trees sticking up in the water," she said. "I love them!"

Ten miles after the bridge, I turned left off the road, negotiated a drop of about a foot, and descended into a shadowy parking lot made of crushed and layered oyster shells. The man-made ground cover rose just a few inches above the level of the swamp. We stopped in front of our destination, a low-slung, one-story roadhouse with cracked and peeling white paint and wavy clapboard walls: Mosca's. In the streaked, intermittent light of passing cars, you could just make out the murky swamp behind the roadhouse and weedy, mushy land on either side of it.

"Is this it?" Gerry asked, looking at Bud as if to say, "The guy's been down here too long—he's lost his compass."

Bud was more hopeful. As I parked amid the few other cars in front of the building, he eagerly asked, "Do they serve alligator, muskrat, and rattlesnake? What about nutria? Never had possum." He was on a roll.

Gerry was uncharacteristically quiet. He was a less adventurous eater and by now noticeably nervous.

"You'll know soon enough," I said to Bud as we stepped out of the car onto the iridescent oyster shells. Their sun-bleached insides reflected whatever light was available, making them appear dimly illuminated by some interior source.

Mosca's was set thirty yards back from the road and marked only by a single light fixture next to the front door, with one paltry bulb. A rusty tin sign swinging from a metal pole read, DRINK BUDWEISER.

"I like this," Bud whispered, as if to keep the news from Gerry. "But what is it?"

"A Mafia hangout."

"A what?" Gerry said, looking more nervous than before.

"A Mafia hangout," I said again, this time whispering, as we were close to the screened front door. "Don't make any comments inside about the way anyone looks. Believe me."

"Okay, okay," they both said, a muted chorus.

"Johnny Mosca has impeccable credentials," I explained. "They say his father was Carlos Marcello's chef. Marcello, the Mafia chief in New Orleans, is here all the time. He set Johnny's father up in the swamp when the heat got too intense in the city."

"Jesus, Peter. You sure we'll be safe?" Gerry asked.

"It's not just his credentials. He's got a bona fide heritage to live up to," I told them. "Provino and Lisa Mosca, Johnny's mother and father, established deep connections in the restaurant business with the Chicago Mafia going back to the 1930s before coming down and opening this restaurant in 1946. Some say Provino was Al Capone's chef, but that's a local rumor, I think."

We opened the front door and shuffled single-file through the vestibule. Johnny Mosca was working behind the bar, looking, as usual, as sad as a bloodhound. He worked up a smile as he saw us enter the bar area and came around to greet us.

As we shook hands I said, "Johnny, you know Camilla, and these are friends from New York, down for a visit." I wanted him to know they weren't locals, snooping.

"Okay," he said, as if they'd gained his permission to be there. He picked up four stained menus from a side table and motioned for us to follow him. We crossed a clean, bare wooden floor—it always looked recently mopped—and entered the dining room. On the way in, I could see Johnny's sister, Mary Mosca Marconi, the chef, standing at the kitchen door. I waved to her. She brushed her hand against the apron around her waist, as if to clean it before waving back.

"Peter," Johnny said, motioning, "go to that corner four-top so Sally-Jo can take care of your group."

The wainscoted walls were painted dark green. Small windows high up in the wall were covered by dark burlap curtains, as if to conceal the goings-on within. Three naked bulbs in each round chrome ceiling fixture threw an even light across the room. Atmosphere was not a concept that had crept into the Mosca family's marketing plan.

Twelve tables of various sizes filled the room, most seating four to six people. In the back left corner was one large table. I'd never seen anyone who looked as if they were from uptown New Orleans sitting there. The night we came, like every other time I'd been to Mosca's, it was inhabited by corpulent men in dark pants, their white shirts open at the collar and sleeves rolled up, their dark jackets slung over the backs of their chairs. Each man bulged over the edge of his seat. They didn't speak much, concentrating instead on the food heaped on their table.

When Sally-Jo came over to us, she said, "Hi, what'll it be?" She was short and intense, with dark hair that looked naturally curly. Her impatient dark eyes said, "I'm a busy lady in a busy place." She carried a carafe of water for another table.

I said to my pals, "You want to have a go at the menu or shall I order for us?"

"Whatever. What's good, Peter?" Bud asked.

Sally-Jo stood there waiting.

Camilla said to Bud and Gerry: "He'll order. You'll be glad."

"Think Chinese," I said. "This is communal eating. No one orders individually."

"Should I come back?" Sally-Jo asked, her tone tinged with impatience. People came to Mosca's knowing what they wanted: no silly questions were tolerated about how something was cooked; no one asked, "What's your recommendation?"

With a touch of resignation, Bud folded his menu. So did Gerry. I hadn't opened mine. Neither had Camilla.

"Sally-Jo, how you doin'?" I asked.

"Good," she said. She stood there, her patience at its limit.

I said, "Two Oysters Mosca, one Italian Shrimp, one Chicken Grande, two Crabmeat Salads, and one Bordelaise." (To Sally-Jo, that meant Spaghetti Bordelaise.)

She wrote down nothing. "Red or white?"

"Red," I said.

"Okay," Sally-Jo said. As she left, she picked up our menus with her one available hand.

I motioned discreetly with my head toward the big round table in the corner. "Those are some of the types I was talking about. You see what I mean?"

"Yeah," Camilla said, "they're the real thing. . . . Maybe why the food is so good."

Bud and Gerry tried to slant their eyes in the right direction. They knew enough not to move their heads.

"What you drink with supper at Mosca's is wine. Just wine," I said. "Sally-Jo will bring us a bottle of whatever they happen to have. It's usually very good and very inexpensive. I have no idea what their source might be. Maybe it goes through special channels."

Gerry said, "You think it's stolen?"

I said, "Let's talk about the weather."

At Mosca's there was only one style of glass for wine—a thick, kitchen-supply-house tumbler, the sort most places used as a water glass. At the bar, these same glasses were used for highballs or martinis. At the table, they appeared as both water and wine glasses. Johnny didn't believe in a lot of diverse tableware.

After our first bottle of red wine was delivered to the table, Camilla poured full tumblers all around. Holding hers up, she said, "To the birthday boys," flashing a smile at Bud and then at me. "Bud and Gerry, I'd never have met you if I hadn't rescued the local birthday boy from the Tulane library exactly two years ago tonight."

After Camilla told them the story of our first library encounter, she charmed them with a Cajun story about her father, a self-pronounced master linguist, getting lost on a driving excursion through bayou fishing villages and not being able to understand the directions he was being given in the local Creole patois. Then we settled in for the meal.

Sally-Jo brought the first course. I didn't have to specify. The cold crab salad is always the first course—shredded back-fin crabmeat tossed with lettuce, chopped green peppers, celery, light oil, and vinegar. No choice of dressing is ever offered.

The secret to Mosca's signature cooking is oil and garlic roasted into absolutely fresh seafood and fowl, laced with wine at just the right time. Johnny Mosca, who never goes into the kitchen, always says, "Wine is the secret. Wine is the secret in all of our cooking." Oysters Mosca is a tight assembly of large, freshly shucked Louisiana oysters roasted with oil, garlic cloves, and shallots, topped with a light breadcrumb coating cooked in and served on the same large round or oval dented nickel platters that have been used since the restaurant began. Italian shrimp is made with the same basics, only with more oil and no shallots. It consists of large Gulf shrimp roasted in their shells, with no topping and only the head removed. If you know what to do, you eat the shrimp, shell and all, chewing slowly to coax out the flavor and thoroughly shred the tangy husk. Chicken a la Grande is pan-fried bird cut into eighths laced with olive oil, garlic, oregano, and rosemary, and basted with a smoky-sweet, garlic-infused marinade. Big cloves of fresh roasted garlic are sprinkled all over the ancient metal platter between the oddly cut chunks of glistening chicken, still on the bone.

The purpose of the Bordelaise is to mop up the garlic and oil, as well as the remnants of the oysters, shrimp, and chicken left on your plate. The dish is simple: thin spaghetti lightly tossed with more oil and garlic.

At the end of our meal, there wasn't a scrap of food left on any of the tin platters cluttering the table—not even one oily garlic clove. The bill, with pencil notations for each item, came to thirty-eight dollars. Those who try to replicate Mosca's dishes at home end up in despair, proclaiming that it's the seasoned cookware that makes all the difference.

Bud said, "You guys weren't kidding. This is way beyond barbecue!"

Gerry was holding his stomach. "I haven't eaten so goddamn much food since my brother's bar mitzvah." Then he offered a fanciful quasi-scientific experiment of the type he was always coming up with. "Maybe I could take home some of that roasted garlic flavor by exhaling into a paper bag for a couple of days."

"You think it'll spice up your chopped liver at the Madison Avenue Deli?" I asked. We all laughed, though Camilla looked at me quizzically as she joined in. I later filled her in on New York's late-night deli fare and the Jewish connotation of chopped liver.

When we left, we could see that Johnny had been afflicted by drinks he'd had with customers who were waiting to be seated. His sad eyes were even droopier and more watery. He now wobbled a bit. But he was still there at his post behind the bar near the door, both to greet people and to scrutinize who was coming in. For some people—certain judges, for instance—there didn't ever seem to be a vacant table. My good friend, whom I'll call Judge Cross to assure his continued security, despaired of ever going to Mosca's, he said, because he had "put away Marcello's brother." Johnny held his hand out to me. "Thanks for comin' by," he said graciously as the old screen door swung open to the oyster-shell plateau.

It wasn't necessary to worry about how Johnny would get home safely that night or any other. He lived, along with his sister, wife, and mother-in-law, in a house adjacent to the restaurant that his father had built.

Outside I was relieved to see that there was no fog. I'd been to Mosca's before when fog, rising from the marsh all around the little white building, seemed to drive wet air right into the dining room. When it was foggy, the narrow, steep ramps that rise up the Huey P. Long Bridge alongside the railroad tracks don't seem wide enough even for a Volkswagen.

In the car, Bud said, "How far is Mosca's from the airport?"

"The airport's halfway to Mosca's from the city," I said. "Why?"

"Because this is so good I might come down just for supper," he said. "This is the best goddamn meal I've had . . . maybe ever. No bullshit, no jive."

12

Challenged

By late fall of 1962, the beginning of my third year at Wolf & Co., I'd completed my thesis research. After a year and a quarter of visiting archives and seeking to unearth Laclotte's story and achievements, I began to write. I wanted to prove that Laclotte was a skilled architect who deserved great appreciation. This was the stylistic part of my study. I had looked hard at other buildings in New Orleans contemporary with his time and was convinced that he had superior design skill. I'd become familiar with his École des Beaux-Arts sources and with the studio system of French architectural training in which he'd been educated. I was sure that his formal training set him apart from most of his provincial colleagues in New Orleans. To prove my beliefs, I traced Laclotte's sources, the buildings and architectural theory that influenced him most in early-nineteenth-century France, and then traced those stylistic sources back to their inspiring late Italian Renaissance roots. In Andrea Palladio I found persuasively similar building profiles to Laclotte's Girod residence in particular. I knew that French architectural students had studied Palladio's *Quattro Libri dell'Architettura* (The Four Books of Architecture), published in Venice in 1570, the most famous treatise on architecture for generations of early nineteenth-century French students and practitioners, and surmised that Laclotte had as well. I believed I'd nailed his sources, a must for any budding architectural historian.

As Laclotte's New Orleans buildings had not been found distinguished by other investigators in the past, I struggled to illustrate
the unique quality and individuality of his work. I analyzed his use
of balanced proportions based on European influences that looked
back to Roman column-and-arch sequences. I wanted to demonstrate just how his design was superior to the casual Mediterranean
styles that pervaded the Vieux Carré, products of less schooled
vernacular builders and their speculative clients. I also wanted to
establish that I had a discerning eye—a tricky matter in art, but the
only basis for my own aesthetic pronouncements about Laclotte's
quality and achievement.

In rummaging around in the New Orleans Notarial Archives, I
made an exciting discovery. I found that Laclotte should be cred-
ited with having a major role in the design of a once very prominent
French Quarter building that had not been previously ascribed to
him, the majestic Théâtre d'Orléans (1806–13). This new attribu-
tion, which would become a permanent part of the history of the
French Quarter, lent heft to my paper and gave it the solid underpin-
ning of original documentary research that it needed. This successful
sleuthing gave me a first taste of a kind of intellectual thrill at the end
of a hunt, a payoff for all the time spent rummaging in dusty rooms
with frayed archives under inadequate light and poor ventilation. I
found also his plan and graceful rendering of a tower proposed by
the city to be constructed in the prison yard of the Cabildo. But this
project was not commissioned. The Cabildo, built under Spanish rule
(1795–99), had been the seat of colonial government in New Orleans,
and served as city hall, a courthouse, and then as a prison in Laclotte's
day. Since 1908, it has been the Louisiana State Museum. Its neighboring counterpart, the Presbytère erected in 1813, flanks the other
side of St. Louis Cathedral. Today this suite of nationally prominent historic buildings forms the monumental civic edge of Jackson
Square, the iconic heart of the French Quarter in New Orleans.

To my surprise, I learned that Laclotte achieved his greatest recognition during his lifetime not as an architect but as a painter. This didn't please me. I was much more interested in architectural history, but I had to pursue this line to present a credible account. Laclotte, as it turned out, had been present on the field at the Battle of New Orleans in 1815, and had sketched on-site that decisive day when the well-trained, pristinely uniformed English forces were defeated by a ragtag collection of American volunteers. I'd been out to the battlefield years before, during a Country Day field trip to Chalmette, Louisiana (where the battlefield is located). Betsy, the girl I'd had a crush on, and I had walked hand in hand down the center of the grand allée of oaks. That corridor of majestic trees had been known forever, it seemed, as the Pakenham Oaks. Now I learned that the planting of the allée had been a generous gesture honoring the defeated general of the English troops, Sir Edward Pakenham.

That fateful day, January 8, 1815, became a famous moment in American history. Within weeks it came to be known throughout the country as the day marking American victory at the Battle of New Orleans—the final bloodshed, final battle, and final day of the War of 1812. The stunning American triumph against overwhelming odds marked the beginning of General Andrew Jackson's march to the presidency. At the time, no one knew that the bloody battle, humiliating to the English and uplifting to the Americans, was irrelevant. Peace had been declared weeks earlier in Europe.

Based on his field sketches from a nearby vantage point that day, Laclotte painted a magnificent panoramic view that he called, appropriately, *The Eighth of January 1815*—a title that would have meaning in both Europe and America. I learned that he then took the picture to Paris, where he commissioned a fine engraving of his painting and hurriedly had prints struck from the plate. Taking advantage of American exuberance following the victory, Laclotte sold hundreds of prints in the United States and Europe at a very handsome profit. I couldn't be certain, but I suspected that this profit liberated Laclotte from further struggle to obtain architectural commissions.

From Paris I traced Laclotte to Philadelphia, where he lived and worked briefly. After that he seemed to disappear for a while. I was very interested in his intercontinental journey and immigrant's story. I was thinking of my family and its own immigration, also from France just a few years after Laclotte found himself in New Orleans. I wanted to know the rest. Finally, I found in two Bordeaux newspapers, *L'Indicateur* and the *Memorial Bordelais* of September 6, 1821, this notice: "Avis divers. J. H. Laclotte, ingénieur-architect, vient de rentrer dans sa ville natale. . . . Il a été au Mexique et aux Etats-Unis." (Varied Announcements. J. H. Laclotte, engineer-architect, has just returned to his native city.... He has been in Mexico and in the United States.)

Eager to complete the biographical part of my story, I contacted the Municipal Records Office in Bordeaux. Weeks later, I received a brown envelope embellished with a row of engraved stamps depicting the Louvre. Xavier Védère, evidently one of those competent and dutiful French civil servants, had obliged me beyond my wildest expectations: he had enclosed a copy of Laclotte's death certificate, which I incorporated into the text just as I was finishing the final draft of my thesis. As a result, I was able to include this last footnote: "111, *Op. Cit.* Védère, Letter to the author, May 9, 1963, p. 2. Original certificate in Bordeaux, Archives Municipales, registre 3-E-95, acte 1505."

Laclotte had died at the age of sixty-two, eight years after returning home.

I wrote my thesis on my Royal portable, using carbon paper to create the three required copies. After much typing, retyping, and Wite-Out touch-ups, I pasted the photographs and visual documentation onto heavy paper and presented the work—text, footnotes, bibliography, and photographic documentation and credits—in a black binder.

I concluded my paper with these words: "The architectural tradition of eighteenth- and early-nineteenth-century New Orleans is sophisticated and complex. It is also, in its specific architectural historical references, largely unclarified and neglected. As the last and most refined representative of this important American regional architecture, Jean Hyacinthe Laclotte deserves careful attention."

All three readers signed off on my paper on August 7, 1963. They were pleased, and so was I. I'd spent two years, while working for my father in the cotton business, reliving Jean Hyacinthe Laclotte's sojourn into the land of my ancestors. It had been a thrilling experience. I discovered authentic satisfaction in the study of art history, in the research and conceiving of an independent paper, and in the writing of the story itself. I could focus in a way I'd never been able to do at medical school. I felt an ongoing surge of energy in my body as I produced with success at both Wolf & Co. and Tulane University. At the same time, the level of intellectual stimulation I found in my studies brought me a heightened sense of enjoyment and contentment. I'd walked into this territory all by myself. It didn't belong to my father or my family. I'd staked a claim.

On May 1, 1963, May Day, Cecilia Davis, a very scholarly member of the Newcomb art history faculty and one of my thesis advisors, called me into her office. She'd been reviewing a near-final draft of the second half of my thesis. School was winding down for the year. My completed paper was due in less than five weeks. I was working nights and weekends to finish. Even at that late hour, I was hedging my bets in my own mind, thinking: This has been interesting, writing a thesis and focusing on French Quarter architecture. It's been fun, but I don't know what to do next, if anything. Camilla and I are getting along well, too. She's about to graduate. Will that make a difference in what she wants, or even in what I want?

When I went to see her, Professor Davis asked, "Peter, what are your plans for continuing art history after you get your M.A. this spring?"

"I don't have any."

"You're doing a good job. We're impressed with your paper.

Have you thought about going on? We have no doctoral program here," she said, as if the only question was what I'd do next in the field of art history. "You'll have to leave New Orleans to continue."

"What do you suggest?" I asked, all of a sudden aware that this conversation was entering dangerous territory, the potentially destabilizing realm I'd heretofore avoided.

"Go to the Institute in New York," she said, without a moment's hesitation, "the Institute of Fine Arts, New York University's graduate school in art history. It's the best in the country, probably the world. Go there. Apply now—it's late. The deadline was February, but go ahead and apply. I'll call them and tell them about you and your work. Some of the faculty are friends of mine; I'm a graduate."

"Let me think about it," I said. I was feeling rushed and grateful and appreciated and frightened, all at the same time.

What flashed through my mind was the thought I'd had many times over the past few years. After a dinner at Gram's or a lively weekend with my grandparents at Pass Christian, I'd think, When Gram and Grandpa die, there will be nothing left for me in New Orleans. Camilla's lovely smiling face also came flooding to mind, and I shook my head as if to try to ward off the extra level of confusion that she provoked within me.

At other times I'd think, As much as I love my life in the French Quarter with Camilla, being a cotton broker is not enough. At those moments I'd realize I wasn't looking for another job in New Orleans, one that would enable me to stay with Camilla and have a vibrant career in my hometown. Maybe New Orleans wasn't enough, either. Maybe those years in and around New York had gotten deep under my skin—the vibrancy of the place, the competition, the range of art and culture. It was where so many of my friends from Exeter and Yale lived and worked. There I imagined I wouldn't be hemmed in and sometimes humiliated and infuriated by the anti-Semitism that dominated social life in New Orleans.

Nevertheless, at that crucial meeting with Cecilia Davis, I still thought of myself as a person pursuing art history as a side event and one who thought of New York as the big time—out of his league. I was not able to accept, much less imagine, my hard work at Tulane as a first step toward commitment to a new future. More than anything, I feared a major change in a life in which I'd grown comfortable and successful. I couldn't precisely define either my fear or my ambitions. As I tried to contemplate a next step, I recognized that I also felt myself to be a part of the South more than I had ever realized, even though I had well-founded disdain for parts of its culture: the racism (black and white), the redneck disregard for learning, and the preoccupation with the Confederate past, especially old family histories and the constantly reinvoked injustice of the outcome of the Civil War and its immediate aftermath. I couldn't imagine what it would be like to lose this identification and become a part of the national immigrant pool, to undertake all the striving that I imagined necessary to obtain anything close to the access provided by my automatic pass in New Orleans.

"It's late, Peter," Cecilia said, interrupting my thoughts. "If you're interested for next fall, I'll ask them to airmail an application. Shall I do so?"

There it was. I had to answer. I sat for a long, silent moment in the hard wooden seat next to her metal desk stacked with papers, in a small room lined to the ceiling with bookshelves. Kodachrome slides spilled from every shelf in her personal working library. There were real art history books in French and German and Italian, fat, scholarly books in the languages of the world. I was in the presence of a true scholar, and I was present at a professional juncture I'd created.

"Yes, thank you," I said.

13

Restoration Dreams

On a warm Saturday morning in October 1961, a year after I'd begun taking classes at Tulane, I left my apartment for a stroll. I'd wanted to stretch my legs and check out the neighborhood after a long and intense business trip to New York. As I walked the run-down blocks of Burgundy Street toward Esplanade Avenue, the downriver boundary of the Vieux Carré, sunshine glistened off puddled rainwater.

In the middle of the 1100 block of Burgundy Street I saw an awkwardly hand-lettered FOR SALE sign on a West Indies–style house. The dwelling, despite its poor condition, held my gaze. The proportions, distinctive deep gray color, and moody profile of the broad, low building appealed to me. I couldn't believe that I'd never noticed it before. The sign, hung by a rope over the handle of the latched cypress door shutters, seemed to be aimed at me, like Uncle Sam's pointed finger calling for World War II enlistees.

I turned around and trotted home in the morning sun, briskly sidestepping puddles and people. I immediately dialed the number on the sign. The line was busy. I was sure negotiations were under way; maybe the deal had already been sealed. A minute later I dialed, then dialed again. I never took my hand off the telephone.

"Laurent Arceneaux," he answered finally. His voice sounded

weak and distant and held a drawl that sounded like New Orleans for the last two hundred years.

"I'm calling about the building at 1118 Burgundy Street," I said. "Are you the person I should be speaking to?"

"I am."

"Is it still available?" I asked, sure that the answer would be "no" or "probably not" or "I should have taken down that sign."

"I've had calls," he said. "But it's still available. Are you from New Orleans?"

"I live down the street and I'm from New Orleans," I said, wondering if that was good or bad from Mr. Arceneaux's point of view.

In the way of New Orleanians, we then commenced a conversation about Burgundy Street, the Quarter, and the likelihood that the neighborhood was improving. As custom demanded, we touched upon both of our stories—his family history and mine.

After a while he said, "I know your grandfather. I was once his accountant way back in the cotton business days."

"I see him all the time," I said. "He still lives in the same house uptown on State Street and thinks I'm nuts to be living down here on Burgundy Street."

"I've gotten stiff and sick," he said. "I'm retired and the building is too much for me now, so I'm selling."

We met the next day. In ten days, after I had consulted with Allain Steinslevsky, a lawyer acquaintance, I made a good-faith deposit to purchase the house. We had a deal.

A rational observer looking at my impetuous acquisition would have seen a run-down, single-room-occupancy cluster of tenement buildings consisting of a primary house built to the sidewalk line, like nearly all the other structures in the Quarter, and two smaller structures in back facing a disintegrating courtyard. The backs of the narrow rear buildings were flush with a tall wall that circumscribed the property. They and the desolate, trash-littered courtyard were reached from Burgundy Street through a rusty iron gate and a broken brick path running alongside the front house.

The main house, made of plastered-over brick, retained its original West Indies character, dating from the 1840s, the time my ancestors had arrived in the area. It had probably been built and owned, as was the entire neighborhood, by freemen of color, as Creole craftsmen and merchants were known before the Civil War. Its irregular, wavy slate roof was a beautiful relic of that period.

The two identical redbrick buildings in back, in addition to being just one room deep, were four small rooms long and two stories high. Unpainted wood second-floor balconies ran the full length of each building. On each, a wooden stairway rose from beneath the balcony through it to the second floor—the only means of accessing the upstairs rooms. The balconies created shady corridors below, much-needed and welcome places for people to sit shielded from the sun.

Not a single line was in plumb. The back buildings leaned every which way, as if swept by a gale, and the main house had settled unevenly into the soft ground beneath it.

Throughout the French Quarter, every building behind a principal street-front residence was called "slave quarters." Whether or not they had ever sheltered slaves was uncertain. Some Creoles from this neighborhood may have owned slaves. Certainly many whites who originally occupied much of the Quarter did.

The property's privacy barrier was a rough-textured, two-brick-deep, twelve-foot-high redbrick wall, thickened for extra support every ten lateral feet into a distinct four-brick-deep square pilaster. Though still effectively surrounding and protecting the cluster of buildings, this wall was old and neglected. Many of its bricks were soft and crumbling and there were many chinks and gaps in what remained of the binding mortar. At its foot, abandoned flower beds consisted of little more than parched earth holding a few struggling azalea bushes and coleuses amid plentiful weeds and wild grasses.

Climbing up from the meager soil were occasional determined ivy and jasmine vines, which clung to dark crevices in the wall.

In my mind, the compound was transformed into an assembly of three elegantly proportioned historic buildings whose interiors could be faithfully renovated. The majestic wall would enclose a brick-based courtyard whose flower beds would bloom year-round with native flowers and whose open space would be shaded by banana, lemon, and orange trees.

I would fit the newly installed, dark-stained cypress front doors of each re-created apartment with brass hinges and knockers. Tall, thin French doors would open onto the brick patio, and on the second floors to balconies edged with simple but elegant wrought-iron railings. The French doors would alternate with double-hung, twelve-light mullioned windows spaced above one another on the two floors. All openings would be protected by adjacent Louisiana cypress shutters in perfect working order, able to shield the doors and windows from threatening storms or blazing sun. The shutters would be secured by finely tooled black, nineteenth-century cast-iron ties. All of the bricks throughout the property would be crisply pointed, sealed, and protected.

The worn wall would become as beautiful as any I'd seen previously in France or Italy. I'd cap each pilaster with a big terra-cotta urn filled with English ivy and fragrant jasmine that would cascade down the old brick. At night the jasmine would emit a sweet, seductive aroma that would spread throughout the courtyard, mingling with the murmurs from the fountain I would install. The fountain would replicate traditional mid-nineteenth-century French Quarter courtyard design. The waters would fall gently into a surrounding lily pond, creating a melodious, velvety mood.

One afternoon, once the clearinghouse sheets were delivered and we'd closed Wolf & Co. for the day, I said to Dad, "Would you take a short drive over to look at a building with me?"

"Okay," he said. "Where is it?"

When I gave him the address up the street from my apartment, he responded with a bewildered expression but said nothing.

"I'll meet you there in fifteen minutes," I said.

I was waiting out front when he pulled up. I proudly escorted Dad into the property. The gate from Burgundy Street was always unlocked, but of course we couldn't do more than walk through the courtyard. Tenants stared from their windows and less obviously from the shady spaces where they were lounging below the balconies.

For fifteen minutes or so, Dad and I inspected the exterior of the premises to the extent that we could. I pointed out what I saw as the property's assets and market potential. He offered no comment. Finally I asked him, "So, what do you think?"

"Son," he said, as we headed back to his car parked in front of the rusty gate, out of hearing range of the various tenants, "have you lost your marbles? If you go through with this, you'll be taking on mortgage debt and a dilapidated group of buildings filled with black tenants—most of them probably transients or jobless. How do you expect to collect rent?"

"I'll do it myself," I answered, "week by week. That shouldn't be so difficult."

"You'll have to," he said. "No decent management company would take on this job."

I continued to plead my case. "I don't mind. I have Saturdays free. It's just up the street."

"You don't know how hard it will be to work with these people," he answered. "You don't know how much it will cost to maintain this dump. What about liability of every kind?"

"Dad," I argued, "this place can be magnificent. It can be a moneymaker, too."

"Never" was his clench-jawed reply. I wasn't sure which part of my statement "never" applied to. Maybe, in his view, to both.

"After I finish renovating, I plan to live here," I said, figuring

I had nothing to lose. "All the new tenants will be upscale—enlightened young people who want to live in the Quarter and work across Canal Street, as I do now." (I'd not yet considered the social consequences of gentrification; didn't even know that word.)

"You're dreaming. I don't know what's wrong with you," Dad said, his strained voice revealing his concerned frustration. "We brought you up in a safe, beautiful suburb. Now you want to restore a dump and live in one of the worst neighborhoods in New Orleans. The place your sister has moved to uptown near the river is nearly as bad, but not this bad." To me, Gail's modest traditional one-story clapboard "shotgun cottage" on Camp Street, where she'd recently moved with her new husband, Harvey Lewis, a young lawyer from Houston, was a perfect starter house. It was well located but affordable, being situated in one of the many mixed-race neighborhoods in uptown New Orleans.

"I'm about to sign the contract, and I've already made a good-faith deposit to hold the property off the market," I finally confessed, having been reluctant to do so before.

"You've what?!" Dad exclaimed. Then he was silent for a moment, digesting this bad news. He continued, "My best advice is get out of this. Forfeit your deposit if it comes to that."

"Dad!" I said, voice rising, but the lid still on. "I know what's going on—I see it every day. There's fresh paint on three buildings in the next block, and two are being renovated by white families who are moving in. Another is being turned into modern apartments inside a beautiful old shell. That's what I want to do."

"For this neighborhood to change," he answered, "you'd need an act of Congress."

"I'm studying the French Quarter for my master's thesis," I said. My voice now tight and edgy.

"That's another matter," he said. "That's studying; this is spending money—taking on liability and risk."

"Can't you remember?" I asked, trying to remain calm. "The

Quarter's been through hell, but it's coming back. We're smack in the middle of the Vieux Carré, the second-oldest historic district in America. It's going to come around. Someday this will be incredibly sought-after, valuable real estate."

It was futile. I knew that Dad, having lived through the Depression, did not trust real estate. As he eased into his yellow Oldsmobile, relieved to escape the neighborhood with his tires and canvas convertible top intact, he said over his shoulder, "The war's over. It's been over for fifteen years and this is still a slum."

Regardless of what my father thought, for me the Vieux Carré, with its cultural diversity, historic buildings, and French-Caribbean flair (making it *tout ensemble* a unique community), plus its historic-district designation, which most people in New Orleans didn't seem to care about or even have much awareness of, made for an irresistible opportunity and challenge. The financial success I envisioned would admittedly take some time. I wanted to prove my independent entrepreneurial flair. Way beyond that at-the-time-unconscious goal, I was becoming intrigued by the potential for historic preservation and deeply attracted to this idiosyncratic and, I thought, lovely part of New Orleans. Most of all, I'd fallen head over heels in love with this collection of needy, long-neglected, splendid vernacular residential buildings arrayed around a protected courtyard.

I had something else on my mind as well. By now I knew from family talk that Godchaux Sugars was locked in a struggle to survive. It was up for sale and facing the threat of extinction. Godchaux Clothing Company, no longer managed by my diligent, dutiful, merchandising-wizard great-uncle Leon Godchaux, was also losing market share. Retail malls sprouted in vacant flood zones in the Lakeview district and across the river. Canal Street, still the grand principal downtown shopping thoroughfare, was in decline.

The family cluster of power and prominence that had allowed me to feel safe and recognized in New Orleans—part of what appealed to me and drew me back to the city—was crumbling like an old, airy plantation that was unable to adapt to new uses. I seized upon the traditional architecture of New Orleans as a figment of stability. I felt that I could secure my own identity if I preserved, honored, and owned a piece of the city. But not just any piece: a very particular building and neighborhood in the ancient urban core, the location of first settlement, the source.

* * *

After the contract was signed, I called Camilla and asked her out to dinner. "I have a big surprise," I added.

"Tell me!" she commanded.

"Nope. Not until tomorrow night. Can you meet me at Galatoire's for dinner?"

"Galatoire's? Oh . . . oh! Yes, but what is this?"

"How about at seven, so we don't have any trouble getting seated?" I proposed. "By then the lunch crowd will have passed out or gone home, and the dinner gang won't yet have arrived."

Lunch at Galatoire's on Friday was more special than on any other day of the workweek. Local businessmen arrived at noon and didn't go back to the office. Some of the most distinguished lawyers, brokers, port executives, and society ladies in New Orleans could be found visiting from table to table all afternoon, sipping their Sazerac and bourbon.

To ensure a seat for lunch on Friday, executives sent their secretaries to stand in line. After eleven thirty you couldn't reach most of them. No one was answering the phone, at least not until a few minutes after noon, when the secretaries were back at the office covering for the boss. I learned during my first months at work that this was a fact of conducting business and social life in New Orleans.

"Okay, deal," Camilla said; then, *click.*

My strategic plan worked. We walked right in. The last stragglers from the lunch crowd were abandoning their tables. The tourists were still in their hotels dressing or in Bourbon Street dives enjoying a predinner drink and live jazz. The locals came later.

By then I'd been back in New Orleans long enough to be recognized by Julian Galatoire's brother Gabriel, who held the prestigious position of controlling the door in a world-famous restaurant that took no reservations. No exceptions. We were conducted to the most desirable part of the room (to the back and on the left side as you walked in) without my saying anything other than "Good evening, Gabriel."

Gabriel nodded and replied, "Good evening." He guided us to the corner I liked, two tables away from Grandpa's usual spot.

Richard, by then our family waiter, arrived promptly. He was tipsy, as many of the waiters habitually were on Friday evenings after the long luncheon sessions with their regular customers. Galatoire's maintained a permissive policy about help drinking on the job. Richard managed to ask us if we'd like a cocktail.

"Champagne for the lady." I knew it was her favorite on big occasions.

Camilla echoed, "If he says so, Richard."

"Yes, miss," he said. "And for you, Mr. Peter? Jack Daniel's old-fashioned on the rocks?"

I smiled at him, nodded.

Though Camilla was looking at me expectantly, or maybe apprehensively would be more accurate, I waited to share my news. We ordered identical dinners: Oysters Rockefeller followed by stuffed eggplant, followed by a shared Godchaux salad.

At the end of the meal, Mr. Julian Galatoire approached. I had a second old-fashioned in front of me. Camilla had switched to white wine.

"I see we drink the same drink," he said. "The same as your grandfather."

I stood to speak to him, honored by his visit to our table. While standing I introduced him to Camilla. "Good evening, *chère*," he said as she smiled and bowed very slightly.

"I love an old-fashioned with the stuffed eggplant," I answered. "It seems to go."

"Now . . . ," he said, then hesitated. He looked more serious than I'd ever seen him look before.

I stood there, uncertain about what he might be thinking and wanting to tell us.

"You've become, these past few years, a part of our family here at my restaurant. You're the next generation in the long tradition between your family and the Galatoires that goes way back. I want to allow you to sign for your check."

I'd seen Grandpa sign our lunch checks. Dad, too, but I'd never given it much thought. Suddenly I felt my face flush, and I felt flustered. Camilla was looking up at us.

"Do you mean my own personal house charge account?"

He didn't answer. He smiled and pushed on my shoulder to tell me to be seated. "Sign your check this evening. At the end of the month you'll find your bill at your office, addressed to you." Then he walked away with a bounce in his step, I thought.

As I sat down, Camilla smiled her most restrained and deeply personal smile. She touched my hand and said in a hushed voice, "You've been knighted a prince of New Orleans."

I felt she was right. I'd been accorded the highest status I could imagine in the city's social firmament. It wasn't quite the same as being invited to be the first Jew in modern times to join the Pickwick Club, the Louisiana Club, or the Boston Club (a few had been admitted in the nineteenth century), but then that wasn't ever going to happen. But this had. I felt as if I'd been admitted to a special club as a full-fledged member, and to this day I love going to Galatoire's and signing my bill.

On the way out, Camilla said casually, "Come on. You've made me wait too long. The surprise—what is it?"

"Let's take a walk," I replied, as casually I could manage. "I need to show you."

We walked through the warm evening down Royal Street, window-shopping at Granet's French Antique Shop, where the jumble of furniture, elaborate crystal chandeliers, and marble-topped sideboards filled the display window. We continued on past Keil's, Waldhorn's, and Rothschild's, all antique emporia with enticingly illuminated windows, some of them containing beautiful antique jewelry. I guided Camilla past those windows and then turned left onto Burgundy Street, as if we were headed back to my apartment. It didn't occur to me even at that point that she might be thinking or hoping that the "something" would be an engagement ring from one of those places.

As we walked hip to hip toward my gate, I held her arm. When we went past it, I felt her pace slacken and her body pull away from mine very slightly. I was oblivious to the disparity between what she might have been wishing for and my engagement with a gem of an entirely different sort.

"We passed your entrance, you know," she said.

"I know. What I want to show you is farther along."

Camilla was quiet and seemed distant during the rest of the short walk. When we got to the 1100 block, I took her arm more firmly. I walked across the street from my new building, then stopped and turned Camilla ninety degrees so that she faced 1118 Burgundy.

"See that?" I asked.

"What?"

"That building we're facing, the dark gray one. What do you think?"

"I think it's beautiful . . . at least the façade is," she said. "That's all I can see in the dark. Why?"

"Because I'm in contract to buy it."

"What are you saying?" she squealed, excited.

"That's right. I'm going to close in a few days. I'm going to fix it up, all three buildings and the courtyard. It's a long-term plan."

"It's beautiful, Peter. I love it. Are you really going to buy it and fix it up?"

"Madame," I said, "that's my plan."

"Will you live there?" she asked. I sensed this question as dangerous.

"I don't know about that," I said. "We'll just have to see how things go. At the least, I think it will be a great investment when I'm finished fixing it up."

After standing there gazing for a long time, we turned around, then followed the cracked sidewalk back down Burgundy Street. We were quiet on the way home, holding hands. Since it was a Friday night, Camilla was staying over. We were quieter than usual, and in bed there was a curious familiarity, as if the fact of the house—a domestic residence, possibly to share—had altered and even diminished the uninhibited sexuality that generally heated up between us.

All she said that night, as we drifted amiably off to sleep, was "Did you even think of showing me the house before you got into contract? I love it, but I have no idea what's it's like inside the gate." I did not recognize this sleepy question as a window into Camilla's serious hope for our future. I was wrapped in oblivion, having traveled far down the narrow road of my own determined isolation.

14

Unsettled

Toward the end of my studies, Camilla and I were avoiding the subject of my possible departure from New Orleans and our future. I was stuck. I decided my head needed to be stretched or shrunk—whatever the phrase was.

More troubled than I was when I left medical school, but a little wiser for that experience, I decided that I needed help and got a name from a friend "for a friend" and went to see Dr. Eugene Cohen.

Dr. Cohen's office was on the first floor of a raised uptown "cottage" near Touro Infirmary; it was an expansive wooden house with a wide, shaded porch, sensibly elevated off the ground. The front door, at the top of a broad flight of eight steps, was painted a dark green and opened onto a central hall. Dr. Cohen's office was the first door on the right, in what was once probably the parlor. The magazines in the communal waiting area, sculpted out of the broad hallway, were out-of-date, dog-eared copies of *Field and Stream*, *Life*, and *Time*. Not promising, but I trusted my source. I was too nervous and agitated to run out of the building, although that option did cross my mind.

When Dr. Cohen had concluded his prior appointment, he appeared in the waiting area, turned in my direction, and said, "Do come in."

His nearly bald head was shiny with a semicircular fringe of dark hair. By five in the afternoon, my appointed time, his pale face was spiked with bristles from his heavy beard. He wore a gray cardigan over his button-down blue oxford shirt and dark tie. When he closed the door, I noticed a tweed jacket hanging neatly on a brass hook on the back of the door. Papers were piled up on one side of his desk and a stack of copies of the *American Journal of Psychiatry* towered on top of the pullout writing leaf. It's more scholarly and thoughtful in here, I thought. Maybe the magazines in the waiting area belonged to another practitioner.

Dr. Cohen motioned me toward two chairs. I chose one and he sat in the other. His eyes behind metal-rimmed frames were gray and partially concealed by hooded upper eyelids, and so I had to peer closely to see what they were expressing and even where, exactly, he was looking. This made me uneasy, as if he could see right through me. I couldn't guess what he was thinking.

After a few introductory pleasantries, he asked for some biographical details. When I had finished, he asked, "So, why are you here?"

I gave him the gist of it and ended by saying, "The trouble is, everything in my life is fine, except I don't know what to do. I don't know why. And I'm not happy. I've got an impending crisis, and I need to make some major decisions about both my career and my girlfriend."

"Is that all?" he replied, after a well-timed pause. From that moment I liked the guy. I had appointments to interview two other doctors, but decided to cancel them.

I told no one except Camilla that I was seeing a psychiatrist. I felt ashamed, defeated, and bewildered that I needed one. She must have suspected that a possible future for our relationship was part of what I was confused about.

"Break it down," he said at the beginning. "Your childhood, your mother, your father . . . ?" We started there. Before very long, we were in the midst of trying to unravel the reasons, connected to my parents' relationship and my upbringing, that I was so nervous about talking more openly with Camilla. I began to learn that my own deepest feelings were indeed a mystery to me. I couldn't conjure them into conversation. I spent a lot of time in the beginning answering, "I don't know." Or "I can't feel anything about that; I just have ideas about it." And I didn't and I couldn't.

After I had seen Dr. Cohen twice a week for four months, I began to recognize how repressed and how remote from my inner self I'd been since childhood. He'd listen patiently as I'd characterize my parental conflicts, my bottomless craving to feel loved, my uncertainty about the depth and nature and even reliability of my feelings for Camilla, my instinct that I wasn't being challenged by either New Orleans or the cotton business, and the looming possibility of my moving out of the city. We also talked about how amazed and incensed I'd become, as I began to understand how I'd been suddenly excluded in my teens from the vibrant social life available to my Christian schoolmate friends.

I struggled to face more about myself. I began to know when I was feeling angry or hostile, even when appearing composed and sociable. I began to understand that, at those times, I'd reexperience the frustration and disappointment that consumed me perceiving myself, accurately or not, as the neglected child who slaved for desperately wanted affection, rarely bestowed by my parents. I gained enough understanding of my romantic dilemma to admit to myself, after considerable work on the part of Dr. Cohen, that the best I seemed able to manage in my relationship with Camilla was more like a child's longing for a dependable caregiver, the mother I felt I'd never had, who would be admiring and consoling. Yet—even before I understood what I was doing—the grown man in me, hating that dependent feeling, wanted to flee, to be on his own and to prove himself. I learned, too, that I was only dimly aware of Camilla's needs, fears, and romantic expectations, encapsulated as

I was in my own urge to be encouraged, appreciated, taken care of, and loved. As Dr. Cohen put it at the end of one session, "The lights of empathy are not yet on in your house."

I got accepted into the Institute of Fine Arts doctoral program practically by return airmail, on May 28. I was thrilled. I was also miserable. Now I had only a two-week window to decide and send in my 50 percent tuition deposit, since this was a very late admission, determined outside the normal process. If I said yes, I would then have two and a half months over the summer to wind up my affairs.

The storm had hit. My protected world had cracked wide open. I ratcheted up my schedule with Dr. Cohen to three days a week.

"No one in my family has ever left New Orleans," I said. I was going over old ground, forgetting what I'd learned. Indirectly, over and over, I'd been asking Daddy Dr. Cohen to tell me what to do as the deadline approached. "And what about Camilla?"

"Think about this as going away to school again, not necessarily a lifelong decision," he suggested. "And remember, you don't have to do anything. If you decide to stay, we can take time with the rest." He was feeling the deadline, too.

"I can't think of it that way," I said. "If I leave, it will probably be forever." I had a deeper and uneasy sense that graduate school and Camilla were only a part of the issue. My once-unambiguous love of New Orleans had grown more complex and less accepting. The prospect of being a successful part of my community's business life and an enthusiastic participant in its vibrant cultural activities, yet excluded by a vast silent historic understanding from much of its social ambience because I was Jewish, had become less and less acceptable as a lifelong proposition. I imagined, as well, limited options for exciting work, for continuing educational challenges, for exposure to highest-quality creative endeavors—considerations I've come to understand were not necessarily accurate, but rather an expression of my lack of energy and imagination at the time, symptoms of my depressive state.

"Whatever you decide," he said, "it won't be life-threatening."

"New York frightens me, but it pulls me," I said. "I think it was largely because it was in New York that I went to P&S."

"Well . . ."

"And look what a disaster that was."

"Was that the same as this?"

"No. I wasn't interested in science or medicine," I admitted. "I was ill-matched and out of place."

"That's notable," he said. "Big difference."

"I think it's again about New York first, maybe, and the IFA second. My best friends, Bud Trillin, Gerry Jonas, and Henry Geldzahler, are in New York."

"But the IFA is in New York," he said, "and it's a fine program, from what you tell me."

"If I'm mixing up my motives, I could call one of the cotton firms that trades futures on the New York exchange and ask for a job interview instead. We know everyone up there in the cotton business, and I'm sure I could find a position." Even as I spoke, though, I understood that I was creating a smoke screen and being petulant, attempting to deflect my crisis. I had no intention of moving to New York to work on Wall Street in the cotton business, but I wanted him to push me, to say it for me.

But he wouldn't do it. "So you want to continue in the cotton business in New York?" Dr. Cohen asked me.

"Okay," I admitted. "I don't know why I said that. I keep thinking that maybe Dad is right. Maybe I am a spoiled dilettante and architectural history is just my latest obsession."

"You've worked too hard and too successfully for it to be just a fetish. Could it be that you're afraid to compete at a higher level and perhaps even more afraid that you've found something that you love, at which you could excel, could be a powerful figure, like your father, or greater?"

I was quiet then; I was tired of thinking. Dr. Cohen shifted in his chair and directed his partially occluded gaze seemingly straight through my pupils and into my brain. I tried to hold his stare, but a few moments later I had to lower my head. "It could be," I said very quietly.

In the session before my reply to the IFA was due, I said to him, "I did all right at Yale and that's the big leagues." I knew he'd gone to Vanderbilt, and even though my friend Sam Morley was teaching there, it wasn't the Ivy League. I was so miserable that I was pathetically resorting to academic snobbery to try to demean him. I knew what I was up to as soon as I said the words, but it was too late. I felt ashamed and wondered if I'd insulted him. In some needy way, I understood that I was competing with Dr. Cohen, probably wanting to overpower my professional authority figure and surrogate father. The problem was, he was trying to help me. I couldn't ever quite accept that reality, just as I hadn't most of the time with Dad.

"It is," he agreed, without a trace of rancor and without any unkind or critical edge to his voice. "If you could enjoy yourself at Yale, not feel overwhelmed, and do as well as you did there, don't you imagine the IFA will be manageable?"

I sat there, surprised, but now feeling capable. Thoughts of my gratifying years at Yale and the deep pleasure I imagined receiving from new cultural contacts and studies burst through my reverie. I imagined in a flash listening to the great Dr. Richard Krautheimer lecture about the architecture of ancient churches in Rome. I saw myself standing in the Metropolitan Museum of Art, closely scrutinizing a real Velázquez and then the Manet influenced by it, as we'd studied in class. I also saw at that moment having lunch with Bud, Gerry, and Henry on Sunday in Chinatown, as we had on college weekends, laughing and talking.

"I'm going to go," I said. "I'm going to take the risk."

I saw the flicker of a smile cross Dr. Cohen's impassive face. His gray eyes gleamed a little as he lifted his heavy lids to look me squarely in the face.

The next morning, I mailed my check to the IFA.

That afternoon after the market closed I was in the office as usual. I decided it was time to tell my father. "Dad, I need to talk to you," I said at the entrance to his private office. He motioned me to the couch. I closed the door and sat down. My father, seated in his tall, leather executive chair, leaned back, closed his eyes, and was quiet for a few moments.

"Dad, I hope you won't be disappointed or too upset, but I'm going to go to graduate school in New York, in art history, starting in the fall. I've been thinking about this for a long time."

He didn't ask any details about the program or the school or the arrangements I'd need to make, and he didn't say anything about money. Then, looking right at me, he said in a quiet voice, "Son, go, if you think it is the right thing for you. Our business is uncertain. But you will be giving up all of this—our family firm and your place in New Orleans, a lifetime base for you—and you'll never be able to get them back."

"I know" was all I could manage.

* * *

I was unable to tell Camilla for another week, bringing the total duration of my cowardly delayed disclosure to two weeks. It had been torture keeping my secret from her, but I was also afraid of her reaction.

Camilla knew I'd applied to the IFA, and had even encouraged me to do so. Those isolated times that we'd broached the subject of my possible departure, she'd always said she wanted to stay in New Orleans, at least until she finished college. Yet I was nervous at the thought of telling her I'd decided to leave town to go to graduate school. Somewhere inside I knew I'd not been forthright or caring enough to fully discuss this decision with her. But nervous is as far as it went. Though I'd worked diligently with Dr. Cohen, I was still incapable of empathetically considering her side of the equation. Even if she had no intention of moving from New Orleans, nor a strong enough wish for a future with me, I'd not had the courage or the self-awareness to be open to a frank conversation with Camilla. Encapsulated in my own needs and uncertainties, I had concluded that I had to do this alone.

I felt on the verge of a deeply frightening journey away from home, probably for the last time. This wasn't like going to camp for the summer, or to Exeter or college one semester at a time. It had the feel of a permanent break with all that I knew, with all of the credentials I brought to any gathering, a stripping away of any advantage, of no longer being a privileged person in the known world. Engulfed in that way of feeling and thinking, it was beyond any boundary I possessed to imagine becoming a permanent couple, of bringing my girlfriend with me, even if she would have agreed to go.

"I got accepted and I'm going to go," I said to her, when we met. My words came out rapidly, and, to my amazement, were tinged with defiance. I was behaving as if I were talking to an adversary, as I did at times with my father.

I reached over and took her hand. She allowed it, but her hand went limp and wanted to draw back; it began to, then stopped. She was silent for whole minutes. I could look at her, but not full in the eye. I was feeling guilty and sad and disappointed with myself.

"Sounds like you're getting straightened out, *cher*," she said, her tone cold as ice.

I dimly understood that she had packed at least two levels of scornful critique into that remark. And only then did it finally dawn on me that she had expected much more for these past many months, masked by a brave façade of cheerful intimacy.

"Camilla," I said, "I hate leaving you. I hate leaving New Orleans. I'm operating on instinct here."

"From the way you've been acting lately," she said, "I thought you'd made your decision. You've been so distant. Why didn't you talk to me and discuss all of this with me? You're presenting me with a fait accompli."

"The acceptance letter came two weeks ago," I said, avoiding her real question, "but I didn't decide right away. It's been a struggle. I just told Dad a few days ago, and I've dreaded telling you."

"I imagined that this was what you wanted to tell me. Face it," she said, "part of what you've decided is to leave me."

She was right and I knew it. So I presented what I could of a larger picture, one I'd been trying to frame for myself.

"I think I've got risk-taking in my background, maybe even in my genes," I said. "Perhaps it's connected to my ancestors leaving Europe to start over in Louisiana. My ancestors, my father, my uncle, and my grandfather each pioneered in his own way; now I feel I've got to seek my own path. It's something I have to do."

"I know," she said, pouting, tears welling up in her eyes. "It doesn't help to tell me all that old crap about your ancestors, though."

"Whatever the reason," I said, "I've got to go, even though I love this town and I love you."

"Only you don't love me enough. Is that it?"

At age twenty-eight, I was determined to continue graduate school, possibly train for a new career; at the very least I was about to embark upon the intensive work required to earn a doctorate in one of the most demanding programs in my field. At the same time I was upending a settled existence in my hometown, moving to New York City to confront the challenges doing so would bring. I felt this was not the time—nor did I have the capacity—to make any other life-transforming decisions.

Then she said, with a touch of irony, "I know it's a great achievement to have been admitted to the Institute of Fine Arts doctoral program. I know how great the faculty is. Still, is being a professor like my dad what you want to do for the rest of your life?"

"Darlin', I don't know. I wish I did."

Then I realized it was late. "I'm sorry," I said, after glancing at my watch. "I can't continue right now. I have to go out to Metairie to have dinner with my parents, and I'm already late. I'll call you after dinner. Maybe we'll talk more later."

"Maybe," she said. She got up from our bench in Audubon Park and began walking away, but turned with a sad wave before continuing down the darkening path, sheltered by low branches draped in silver-gray moss, the kind she and I both loved so dearly.

* * *

As Camilla faded from view, I confronted another painful subject: what to do about 1118 Burgundy Street. I wanted to hold on to my house. I thought of it as my last remaining hometown anchor. When I'd bought the buildings eighteen months before, I'd believed I'd probably be living in New Orleans forever.

So that I'd have help as soon as I left, I had worked out a shaky temporary plan with Alphonse Gautier, my loyal tenant. When we'd discussed my departure and the increased responsibility of interim management that I'd like him to assume, he'd wisely said, "Yes, Mr. Peter, I could do that fo' you, but what does I do with the rent money? I ain't got no bank account. I ain't got no telephone. What I do if they be a problem?"

"Would you be willing to do it for just a few weeks until I arrange something else?" I'd asked. "Let's say you live rent-free during that time."

"I'm willin'," he'd said, "but what if'n I needs to call at the 'lectrician? You know the 'lectric's not so good, specially afta they be a storm."

"Miss Lincoln downstairs from you has a phone," I'd said. "Would you mind asking her to call? I'll tell the plumber and the electrician and my general contractor that you might have to reach them. And I'll give you their telephone numbers. I'll also ask them to send bills to me care of the office until I have a permanent address."

"That'd be all right," he'd said.

At dinner that evening, I decided to ask Dad for help. "What do you think I should do about my investment on Burgundy Street?" I started out. He sensed what I had in mind—he generally did. His response was fast and blunt. His blue eyes locked on to my brown ones as he said, "You've decided to leave town, to leave Wolf & Company, and to leave us. I think you should take your profit on that slum property, if there's one to be had, and get out. Get out, even if you have to take a loss. In the brokerage business, as you know by now, we call that 'talk, trade, and travel.'"

I wasn't thinking clearly enough to do what any experienced owner would have considered a reasonable stopgap: call one of the management companies that handled French Quarter real estate and beg them to handle my buildings until I could renovate and upgrade, maybe a few years. Pay them whatever they asked. I did know that it wasn't the kind of assignment the respected companies in town would want to take on.

* * *

At a farewell party I threw for friends and colleagues shortly before leaving for New York, I spotted Allain Steinslevsky, the lawyer who'd helped me close the property purchase. His silk suit and white-on-white dress shirt, partly concealed by a broad Countess Mara tie, reflected the ambient light and created a glow down the front of his body. Everyone else was dressed in casual clothes. Hand outstretched, he grasped my hand as his free arm swung over my shoulder. He steered me away from the crowd.

When I told him about my imminent departure he said, "You've got a problem, pal."

"I know," I said. "The whole thing is a mess." I looked around, feeling tense and angry, especially angry with Allain. He hadn't returned my call from weeks before; he hadn't tried to help me.

"Those buildings will need lots of work over the next few years," he continued. "No one's given a shit about them for so long."

"I know," I said. "In the past six months I've had to do expensive repairs on one roof and overhaul part of the electrical system."

"Those buildings you've got, they're hungry and they'll be needing to be fed," he said in a tone so heavy it sounded like millions of dollars of liability and capital-expense exposure to someone who had just lost his sole source of income.

"Well," I said sharply and moved in front of him, "you're the real estate expert. What should I do? Tell me. It's getting late."

"That's up to you," he said. "If you don't have a better idea, I'll take the place off your hands and handle the whole thing. No extra charge for the transaction."

It occurred to me at that moment that this was precisely what Allain had been scheming since the telephone call he had not returned weeks ago.

"Allain," I sighed, energy depleted and sadness and anger coursing through me, "so you wanna represent both sides of the deal?" Disarmed and desperate, my innate self-destructiveness reared its head.

"I don't mind," he said cheerfully. "No *problema!*"

An image flashed through my mind: a prized hatchet I'd been awarded as Best Camper at Camp Kennebec in Maine, slashing into the soft earth, severing my roots to New Orleans.

"How about I start managing the property tomorrow, take on the mortgage, pay you what you put down in cash, and take it off your hands?" Allain suggested, in what was probably his first-stage offer.

I didn't have the presence of mind to remind him that I'd made costly electrical and roof improvements. Nor did I have the energy to negotiate or argue. It was too late in a very difficult month, week, and day. I was leaving New Orleans very soon.

"You have all the numbers in my file," I answered, trying to hide any trace of my wrenched emotions and crushed heart. "Let's do it," I said. "Okay? I'll use the money for graduate school."

Allain, like Dad, knew how to talk, trade, and travel. He didn't suggest a friendly drink to celebrate, nor did he propose adjusting the offer to cover my expenses. In fact, he said nothing further, fearing, no doubt, that I might regain my sanity. His arm slipped off my shoulder as he edged toward the door. At the threshold he whispered, "Have a good time up there in Yankee-land. I'll take care of everything down here." Then he walked quickly out to St. Louis Street, and into the dark night. I could hear a street band somewhere nearby playing "When the Saints Go Marchin' In."

Part IV

GONE AWAY

15

Paris

I'd dug into my studies at the Institute of Fine Arts, and the work had gone well. I'd been selected for a graduate teaching assistantship at Pratt Institute, which helped pay my way. I made up the gap by trading cotton on the New York exchange and was slowly drawing down capital from my reluctant sale of the Burgundy Street property in New Orleans.

At the Institute, I'd followed my interest in architecture and was one of six advanced students moving toward a specialized doctorate in architectural history. As I progressed, I'd found that unlike my fellow candidates, I was less interested in individual buildings like cathedrals and palaces, the hallmark focus at the Institute's architecture program, than in a broader range of issues loosely gathered under the discipline called "urbanism," or city planning. And making this burgeoning fascination even odder from the viewpoint of the traditional, classically trained faculty, I found myself most concerned with a relatively recent period: the late nineteenth century and first decades of the twentieth century, when major cities around the world were forced to confront the private motorcar, that monster of industrialized productivity and eventual annihilator of urban centers.

As my course-work requirements were being fulfilled, I began to nose around for a dissertation topic. At first I was stumped. I didn't want to spend the two or three or four years required working on a topic that didn't interest me deeply.

One day I found a six-page essay in Françoise Choay's brand-new survey called *L'urbanisme, utopies et réalités: Une anthologie* (1965), about Eugène Hénard, an architect and urbanist who'd been prominent in Paris between 1900 and 1915. Choay was known to be one of the few reliable published authorities who presented a survey of Western urbanism. There were plenty of art history, architecture, and artist surveys, but a relatively sparse literature about the history of both practical and utopian planning. What I read grabbed my attention. This man Hénard was something of a visionary, and influential enough at the beginning of the twentieth century to have addressed the first international town-planning conferences in Berlin and London. What excited me most was that his vision was anchored in the certainty that the newfangled motorcar would invade his beloved Paris. What disturbed me most, and appealed to me as a challenge, was that he welcomed the new contraptions.

I could find nothing more than a few other references to Hénard in libraries at the Institute, at Columbia, and at the New York Public Library. This was encouraging to an embryonic doctoral candidate in search of a topic elusive enough to merit serious research, obtuse enough by conventional standards to have not been previously exploited by other scholars, and seemingly interesting enough to warrant the time and commitment required. I liked that the scale was urbanism; that the problem could be focused on one man and the car; that through these I could write both an analysis of the era and a critique of early planning; and that the study would require my living in Paris for a least a year. This last consideration, like my wish during college to study English literature as a way to spend a summer in Oxford, was far from inconsequential.

Next I compiled an argument to try to convince my advisors that Hénard was worthy of study and that I had to go to Paris to do the work adequately. In New York there was no original Hénard material. The argument I mounted asserted that this was a bigger subject than the study of a once-prominent activist architect-planner now forgotten. Hénard had presided as the most prominent urbanist in one of the most vibrant and progressive cities in the world during the introduction and early impact of one of mankind's most momentous inventions. No other device in the history of civilization, with the exception of the wheel, I proclaimed, had affected human settlement and land development patterns as drastically as the automobile.

Like many a doctoral topic, Hénard was also a convenient excuse; I desperately wanted to taste life in Paris. I had long dreamed of being part of the fabled milieu of the Sorbonne and the École des Beaux-Arts. I wanted to study in the beautifully reflected light under the immense cast-iron and terra-cotta domes of Henri Labrouste's Bibliothèque Nationale. Since living in the French Quarter of New Orleans, I'd imagined roaming narrow Left Bank streets, wearing somber clothing and sitting in smoky bistros arguing philosophy and art. I fantasized admission to the world of Jean-Paul Sartre, Ernest Hemingway, and Jean-Paul Belmondo, and romancing current versions of women like Simone de Beauvoir, Jeanne Moreau, and Simone Signoret.

I fantasized as well about my historic family ties with Paris and wanted to be part of the city my grandmother loved more than any other in the world. I wanted to know firsthand the shadowy, twisted streets of the Marais, the city's ancient Jewish quarter, where I was sure some of my ancestors had lived and worked. Some of their descendants were probably still there. Maybe I'd find members of a long-forgotten branch of the Godchaux family.

I was recommended by the Institute and won a Fulbright Scholarship to Paris. I sailed into the adventure—with my typewriter, my French-English dictionary, and my overcoat—along with other Fulbrights going to Europe, third class on the SS *France*.

Once there, we Fulbrights had to register at the university and had to obtain student identity cards; we had to settle in university residential accommodations, or find our own. On the wide boulevards lined with still leafy London plane trees, dotted with outdoor cafés at the corners leading into the medieval twists of the fifth and sixth arrondissements, there was mystery and excitement to be investigated in these student-dominated *faubourgs*, which in those days had not yet been gentrified.

The third week I was in Paris, I was seated with some Fulbright friends at Au Coin, a seedy café located near the overrun convergence of boulevards St.-Germain and St.-Michel. While chatting with new friends, I watched the confrontation between the too many people who now worked and played in the city and the far too many cars, which took over the open urban space where strollers and carriages had once ambled. Notes connected to my thesis were already forming in my head. I even jotted down a few on one of the index cards I carried everywhere at all times, just in case.

Henry Pillsbury, director of the American Center in Paris and a friend from Yale, spotted me before I noticed him. "Pierre, old guy," he called out. "Come over here!"

"Henry," I said, taking the few steps to his table, "thanks again for your help in getting me an apartment. I owe you forever."

"Here's another favor." He smiled. "Meet Victoria Barr."

From an Institute friend's promising characterization of her before I left New York, I wasn't prepared for either Victoria's baggy, understated clothes or the arresting intensity of her green eyes. She was sitting quietly at Henry's table in the midst of an extremely chatty, boozy group of people.

Firmly ensconced in a woven-cane bistro chair, Victoria twisted her upper body toward me and extended her hand. "I know who you are," she said, smiling. "I just didn't know when we'd meet." That was it . . . no ensuing introductions. I knew more about who she was, too, but this wasn't the time to say much of anything.

Henry had resumed carrying on about the successful and fascinating art opening that had taken place the night before at the American Center.

Victoria relaxed her rather intense expression. I joined the conversation, but lamely. She did not respond to my vacuous platitudes. I had nothing else to offer just then, off-kilter as I was.

Then, as I got up to leave, as casually as I could manage and aware that I knew nothing about her relationships with any of the others sitting with her, I asked, "Shall I give you a call for a drink?" I imagined myself as Humphrey Bogart delivering the same line to Lauren Bacall with graceful indifference during the opening scenes of *The Big Sleep*.

"Do," she said after a pause, grinning, as she wrote out a phone number on a napkin. "I'll show you around."

I called the next afternoon. Bogart would have disapproved of my doing it so soon—a distinct lack of cool. Victoria quickly established that she would be busy for the next several weeks. That intrigued me, too. Was there a man in her life? This young artist, the daughter of Alfred H. Barr Jr. —famed as the first director of the Museum of Modern Art in New York, from 1929 until 1943, and thereafter for several decades serving the museum in a variety of other esteemed positions—and a second-year Fulbright who'd become completely established in Paris, instantly seemed the center of the art universe to me.

"Okay," she said at the end of our phone conversation, which ranged from the latest Left Bank gallery opening to the juiciest New York art gossip. "How about Au Coin two Fridays from tomorrow? Is that good for you?"

At that point, any evening in the next fifty years would have been good for me.

As I waited for our date, I continued to scurry around Paris, lining up to obtain permits to prestigious libraries to which I needed access and to archives and institutes that I learned I would have to consult. In Paris, you don't arrive and set up shop, nor is everything conveniently situated in any one central repository like the Library of Congress or the New York Public Library. I ran smack into centuries of red tape—forms to be filled out, documents to be certified, cards of admission to be notarized by the French Ministry of Culture, applications for workspace at two libraries, two archives, and four institutes.

Finally (it seemed like months) Victoria and I had our rendezvous in mid-September at Au Coin. The café's terrace was crowded with circular white marble-topped tables, each supported by a wrought-iron base from which you could peel layers of green paint while nursing a *ballon de rouge*. We sipped wine. Then she explained her remark of two weeks ago. "I knew about you from friends in New York, the Chases. Jane is an art dealer on Madison Avenue and Charles is an adjunct at the Institute. They were here last month."

"I took his course last year. They're friends of yours?"

"Sort of," she said. "They're more my parents' friends. Charles says your thesis idea is so original that no one at the Institute knew what to make of it—too modern. But they took a chance because your Michelangelo discovery and Frick talk were so fine." She'd done a little investigation.

The year before, in looking through Leonardo da Vinci's sketchbooks, I'd discovered a fragment of a drawing of unusual paired inset columns. They looked to me like the ones Michelangelo designed some years later for the staircase of the Laurentian Library in Rome. The discovery of Michelangelo's likely borrowing from Leonardo prompted the Institute faculty to nominate me to represent the Institute at the Frick Collection's annual graduate student art history symposium. Each major graduate art history department in the country sent one representative each year to present a paper. Being selected was an honor that had likely helped support my Fulbright application.

Victoria looked down at the marble tabletop and scraped at a wine stain with her thumbnail, letting me absorb her remark and its implications. As several people passed by, they greeted her from the sidewalk. She responded with either "hello" or "ciao," but engaged no one in conversation, focusing instead on us.

"I know. They took a chance on me," I said. "Now I'm the one taking the risk. I hope I can pull it off and find enough information."

"So you're a cautious type."

I wasn't sure how she came to that conclusion.

A light breeze pushed her wavy chestnut hair across her left shoulder. When it fell in front of her eye, she teased it back, a delicate gesture.

"Not all that cautious," I said. "But I am nervous. Maybe that's what you're feeling. I'm worried about finding enough material, about organizing it, writing it. About screwing up. It's scary coming here with almost nothing to go on and no faculty structure to review what I'm doing."

"How's your French?"

"Fair," I said. "I can read okay, but my accent sucks."

"Prepare to be mistreated," she advised, without a trace of sympathy.

"I'm finding out," I said. "So . . . tell me about your painting."

"Abstract, with heavy color fields" was her automatic answer. One she'd given a hundred times before, I was sure.

"Top floor, one bedroom, no kitchen, a tiny decrepit bathroom, but a studio with northern exposure" is how she described her living quarters.

This is not one of your most talkative women, I was thinking. Maybe she's shy. Maybe she's boring. More likely she's indifferent, just having a dutiful drink.

"Mine's a three-room garret, up six flights at the back of the courtyard of 12 rue Dauphine. I think the last improvements to the building date from 1645 or thereabouts. It's great!"

My fellow Fulbrights had been less fortunate. They'd found

rooms with French families, often far from the center of town, or in a student dormitory. By remarkably good luck with Henry as the catalyst, I was established at what for me was the center of the center of academic and intellectual Paris.

Victoria and I began seeing each other as like-minded students with friends, either hers or mine. We weren't dating. Sexual attraction did not develop during those early encounters. We were carefully and cautiously getting to know each other when time allowed.

One evening three weeks later, hanging out at Au Coin with the regular crowd, I felt more warmed and expansive than usual, likely due to successive refills from the communal carafe. Victoria mentioned that she'd never been inside the nearby Church of St. Sulpice. I arched one eyebrow, looked straight into her greenish eyes, and said, "Come on. Nothing simpler than to show it to you right now. Let's go, before it gets dark."

She nodded and shifted her eyes toward the street.

As we rose from the table simultaneously and quietly, without a traditional ceremonial good-bye to the others, by some mysterious alchemy related to red wine, the fastidious new boy in town imagined himself to be on the brink of turning into a dangerous, urbane flaneur—the one he'd always wondered if he could be, always wanted to be.

We walked the few blocks in silence, hands held lightly, gliding along the narrow sidewalk.

Inside the majestic church, I steadied her hand as she lit a votive candle, a charmingly agnostic but worldly gesture by this WASP only-child from a family atop the dizzying heights of intellectual and artistic New York. This, after all, was a woman whose parents were dotingly admired by everyone from Peggy Guggenheim to George Balanchine. I was thinking, I like her quiet manner. And there's a playful personality underneath all that reserve.

Lingering in the Place St.-Sulpice after exiting the church into the lowering twilight, I pointed out the tiny Hotel Récamier next door.

"That's where Bud Trillin and I stayed for a week one summer during college," I said. "It was totally dingy back then."

"What were you guys doing in Paris?"

"Bud was playing the pinball machine over there in the Café Androis."

"And you? What were you doing while your friend was loitering?"

"I couldn't stand relaxing," I admitted. "I scurried around Paris with my index cards, one card per church arranged in arrondissement order and color-coded by historic period. I went looking for the most important capitals, the most revealing arches, the most authentic, unreconstructed façades."

I'm not sure she believed me. But that's what I did.

Six weeks after we met, we shared a pastry and tea in my tiny shambles of a living room late one afternoon. A bottle of red wine followed the chaste tea, as did one very agreeable kiss—like that of old friends who'd found each other after years of separation.

As we shared the falling light and more kisses in my little garret, try as I might to feel some electricity, some faint instinct of arousal, it did not happen. Something was holding me back, and it seemed the same was true for her.

In the weeks that followed, I began to understand more about my absence of sexual ardor for Victoria, and hers for me. We weren't the only ones onstage. Her celebrated father—vastly esteemed as a scholar, tastemaker, connoisseur, and museum curator, and a legendary champion of modern European art—hovered in my imagination. One day this issue slithered from my mind to my mouth. Before I knew it, I was forming a question: "Do you think your father would approve of me?"

"Probably not," she said without hesitation. "He hasn't approved of any man I've ever gone to a movie with or sat next to in class."

"I'm serious." I was willing to get into it.

"So am I."

As we got to know more about each other, I could see that her apparent confidence was a bit wobbly, too. After a couple of *ballons*, she sometimes referred to herself as the "Daughter of the Great Museum." Her struggle, I eventually figured out, was between her desire to separate from the power of her father's esteemed position in the international art world and her inability to relinquish its seduction.

"My mother and father," she told me one night, "think I should be a painter. I've thought it was because they were disappointed in my performance at Wellesley. I wasn't ever all that interested in the academic side of college life."

"What do *you* think?"

"I don't know," she said. "They're both brilliant and famous."

"Do you like painting? You do it every day."

"I'll never be either brilliant or famous."

"Who knows?"

"I know one thing," she said, surprising me with her firm tone, "I've been more trouble to them than anything else. Still, I can't imagine giving up my painting and my life to take care of kids— whatever I'm able to do, brilliant or famous or not, I wouldn't be a good mother."

Right then I knew she was dedicated, but not to any reproductive biological destiny. And right then I knew that I hoped to have her as a friend forever, but nothing more. My traditional family life, bleak though it was at times, had left me committed to enjoying my own children someday, to being a father.

* * *

One winter afternoon, walking down rue Dauphine I happened to meet Larry Bensky, another college pal and now a young editor at the *Paris Review*. After the usual what've-you-been-doing kind of chat, he said, "Come to the anti–Vietnam War demonstration tomorrow. There's a girl from Texas you should meet." It was February 23, 1966.

"What time and where?" I answered, immediately tempted. Political rallies were not my bag, but the way he said "a girl from Texas you should meet" had a promising ring. Bensky didn't mess around. Because of my friendship with Victoria, I felt a twinge of guilt at my unhesitating response. I was marginally ambivalent but susceptible and restless. The latter impulses won out easily.

Forever the dutiful boy, despite my curiosity about this woman, I was apprehensive about giving up a precious workday. I wished the rally were being staged on Sunday, when the libraries and archives were closed. Even worse, Bensky's invitation coincided with a eureka moment in my research. Two days before, while rummaging through the stacks of the Musée Social, I'd found—misshelved and mislabeled—a complete set of Hénard's illustrated *Études sur les transformations de Paris*, all eight pamphlets published between 1903 and 1909, the ones I'd been searching for since I got to Paris. Signed by Hénard himself with the salutation "À monsieur André Hallays, homage amicable." I'd hit pay dirt!

Suddenly I was paralyzed with fear. What if on the day I was goofing off at a political demonstration a competing scholar found the *Études*? What if the librarian reported my discovery of the long-lost documents to the French government under something like a Precious National Documents Act, and the minister of culture decided that no foreigner could have access, especially a troublemaking, dilettante, political rabble-rouser?

Despite my anxiety, I went to the demonstration, horny and hopeful. I arrived at the Gare du Nord, dressed in what I thought a perfectly reasonable *costume de manifestation*. I was quick to recognize, however, that my crisp Brooks Brothers khakis and light green, long-sleeved Lacoste shirt were not black, rumpled, stained, or torn. I was conspicuous.

Before I could retreat, Bensky grabbed me by the shoulder. He steered me toward a noisy group. "Hey, Sandra," he called out to a young woman at the center of the crowd who was holding a clipboard and handing out assignments to lieutenants, "here's the one I rustled up for you. Peter, meet Sandra." Then he moved away, on to other pressing responsibilities as the American organizer of the international march, or *manif.*

Finding myself marooned among this throng of intense strangers, I moved closer to the protective cover of Sandra's circle. "Hello there," she said, extending her hand over the shoulders of two people standing between us. I saw a petite blue-eyed blonde with fair and faintly freckled skin whose luminous smile dominated her round, open face. I was living the parlor joke of 1966: I'd come to a political demonstration to pick up a woman.

"Stay with us," she said. "We're marching as a group, unless you have other plans."

"No," I answered, "I came alone. It was Larry's idea."

"I know."

She knew.

Right away I felt accepted, welcomed, and taken care of. Sandra's self-assured safety net encircled me from the start.

"Then come on," she said, waving. "This is important. We have to stop the Vietnam War. Today we're looking for publicity, not trouble." This was a powerful young woman. I could feel it. One who wanted to include me, even if I had little to offer.

It was an overcast morning in Paris. Clouds were moving fast, dark ones soon replaced by darker. I found myself enveloped in the mayhem of a rowdy, uncompromising bunch of students from all over the world who were also taking the day off from their studies.

I marched next to Sandra through the bleak, predominantly communist northern suburbs. The jovial, enthusiastic liberated students of the 1960s around us shouted out slogans to the thin cadre of sympathetic residents lining the streets. Sandra and her group, along with all the others, shouted in unison. I shuffled along quietly at her side.

I'd never met a WASP from one of the old Texas families. Most of the cotton men I knew had been relatively new to the West, buying up cropland in the early twentieth century. I was curious about this lively lady. As I would soon find out, she was a radical contrarian who no doubt was giving her family fits—not just living in Paris but struggling against the U.S. government.

Sandra and I started to meet frequently after her day of work as an author's assistant and mine in research.

I'd never been inside one of the limestone buildings in Sandra's fashionable neighborhood around the Arc de Triomphe, although I knew what it looked like before the wide boulevards were cut through the dense medieval city under Baron Haussmann's direction.

Her apartment, to me, epitomized the essence of upscale nineteenth-century Paris. Even in the fading light it was luminous. A file of paired French doors opened in one continuous sweep from the living room and bedroom onto a balcony that extended eight feet over the sidewalk. The generous width of the balcony made me think of the screened porch at Shackling, my grandparents' weekend house on the Gulf of Mexico. Her ornate black cast-iron railing surrounded the balcony. It reminded me of the French Quarter. I was at the source.

Once, as we walked around the bookstalls along the Seine, she said to me with a tease in her voice and a sidelong glance to watch my reaction, "I'm just imagining what fun it'll be someday to show our kids this very spot, this incredible view across the river to Notre Dame. I don't want Paris to ever change for them."

"Our kids?" I asked, light and easy.

"You never know, buster. Anything can happen in this world."

* * *

One morning as we left Sandra's building on our respective ways to work, she stopped on the sidewalk and turned to me. "You don't mind, I suppose," she said, with a glint in her eye, "if you have an active file with French intelligence?"

As it turned out, she was asking me and telling me at the same time.

"What do you mean?" I said, with unconcealable panic.

"My little old concierge . . . she's a spy," she said, her voice light and happy. "They all are. She reports everything. They know when you sleep here. My phone is tapped. They know all about you, just from that. At every demonstration, plainclothes guys take pictures, especially of those of us marching in front. It all gets funneled into a Secret Service dossier and probably shared around the world." She continued walking with a gay nonchalance.

"Do you mean a spy?" I repeated with a long, slow drag on the last word.

"I mean a spy. Exactly. Me, our pacifist group, all of us. We're under constant surveillance. Now you're included." Still smiling, she looked over at me with not a trace of concern. Rather, she loved the intrigue and absurdity of it.

"You like this!" I said, after watching her manner.

"I don't mind."

"No, you like this," I said. "It's part of your Texas rebellion. I think you're waiting for the principal to call your father to tell him that you've skipped out of school again."

"Never thought of it that way."

"Do they have a political agitator's file on you? Tell me."

"I've seen Xeroxed photographs of me marching at the front of the American group last year," she answered. "And a few of the reports. One of our antiwar people works for them. We have spies, too."

"How will your dad take the call from the president of the republic when they deport you?"

"My smarmy concierge probably has a good full-face picture of you by now and a file a mile long," she retorted. "Maybe the police have copies already."

"I didn't know this was a police state," I said, lowering my voice and quickly scanning our surroundings.

"They're on to you now, bub" was her rueful rejoinder. "So enjoy it."

As our relationship matured, Sandra introduced me to her gritty, fearless antiwar community, which was about to become world-famous. She also introduced me to talented left-wing student artists inside the École des Beaux-Arts whom Victoria did not know. I, on the other hand, was on deadline, racing the clock to uncover the second-greatest story ever told—the first one, I was willing to concede to Genesis.

One day in mid-March, after we'd known each other almost a month, Sandra said, "My parents are going to think I've had a lobotomy if they meet you." I'd just invited her to join me at a reception for Fulbright students at the Académie Française, the hallowed center of French scholarship and culture.

"Would I be that unpresentable at your Waspy River Crest Country Club in Fort Worth?" I asked, knowing how much she disdained the place.

She said, "They're accustomed to my boyfriends being high school dropouts, cowboys, or starry-eyed political and religious fanatics. Usually some combination."

"By the time we meet, perhaps I'll qualify. Are they coming over?"

"No, I'm only imagining how surprised they'd be, and pleased. You realize that's a strike against you in my book?"

"What about the Jewish part? Maybe that'd help disappoint them."

"Score one for you," she said, as she swatted my shoulder. "Okay, I'll go with you to the A F."

My work was going a lot better than management of my social and romantic life. I had obtained the research bones for a credible doctoral dissertation. But I had not been successful in discovering any family diaspora in Paris. There were no relevant entries in the Paris telephone book. My inquiries at archives led back to many eighteenth- and nineteenth-century people with the surname Godchaux and first names such as Guetschle, Joseph, Lazard, Hanna, Mayer, Isaac, Adolphe, Raphael, and Henrietta. Most of them had lived and died in and around the French border region of Alsace-Lorraine, the precise terrain from which my adventurous young Godchaux ancestor had emigrated. It seemed pointless to investigate my ancestry more deeply in Paris.

Toward the end of March, I said casually to both Sandra and Victoria that I'd been spending time, albeit of different sorts, with another woman.

Victoria said, "I wondered why you'd not been going to more events with me."

Sandra said, "Who is this woman? Tell me about her. And tell me the truth."

I felt relief that my secret was out. After the disclosure, I tried to be cool and matter-of-fact with each of them. Yet I was, nevertheless, nervous all the time and darted frantically between Victoria, whose cachet I didn't want to relinquish, and Sandra, who was so warm, self-assured, and sexy. I couldn't shake my desire to possess what each of them offered, and I feared losing either one. I also experienced heart-stopping terror at the idea of losing both and being alone again. These fears preyed upon me when I wasn't studying, so I never stopped. My self-imposed predicament was definitely advancing my research.

For a short while, nothing happened. But one evening, two weeks to the day after my disclosure, Sandra yelled at me: "Cut out this running around with Victoria. I don't care how special the event or how infrequently you see her. I can't believe there isn't more to it."

Forever eager to avoid a conflict and unable to withstand Sandra's wrath, I meekly replied: "There ain't any sex. We just have a good time together at cultural stuff, so why do you care? You're turning into a control freak."

"You can't have it both ways, Peter," she answered in a shrill rage of jealousy. "So don't try, at least not with me."

Two days later, at the French Ministry of Culture's annual reception, Victoria took me aside, worked me into one of its gilded corners, and whispered in a congenial but firm tone: "I don't want to be taking you around Paris any longer as my escort when you're sleeping with someone." My grandiose and naïve experiment was over.

I returned to New York on schedule and alone, but with enough research to complete my dissertation.

* * *

It was November, twelve weeks to the day after I'd landed in New York, back from Paris. As I walked home from the Institute at Fifth Avenue and Seventy-Eighth Street across town, I reached West End Avenue, turned west at my Seventy-First Street corner, and looked down the dead-end block toward the once-handsome, now-tawdry row of town houses.

An REA Express delivery truck had stopped in front of my brownstone apartment building. It was blocking traffic on the narrow street. Approaching, I looked on and heard the unbridled impatient honking of horns. A uniformed driver was standing at the curb near Mrs. Freimer, my frail eighty-year-old landlady, who was seated on our stoop in front of him. He was gesticulating wildly as if to overcome her faulty hearing.

Mrs. Freimer had been taking the late afternoon air, as she did daily in the company of her yappy Maltese, Monroe. She raised her head, looked up the street, and pointed toward me. As I approached, I heard her say, "There he is."

"Good evening, Mrs. Freimer," I said to her. "Were you pointing at me?"

She looked toward the deliveryman.

I turned to him, "What's the problem?"

"Are you Mr. Wolf?"

"Yes," I said. "What's this about?"

"Just sign here," he barked, thrusting his clipboard toward me, obviously agitated at having had to wait.

I took the clipboard and found the line with my name.

"What's this about?"

"It's a delivery for you, so sign there." He pointed at the correct line on the page.

As I began to sign he turned away from me and walked hastily toward his van. Moments later he was struggling up the curb, his handcart loaded with two coffin-sized trunks. He deposited them on my stoop.

"What's this?" I asked, astonished.

"Your delivery," he replied as he extracted his dolly from beneath the trunks and took back his clipboard. Before I could ask more, he was seated back inside his truck and gunning the engine to get into gear.

Mrs. Freimer saw my bewilderment but said nothing.

I kneeled down to examine the pile deposited at my feet. Each trunk had pasted on one side a commercial shipping label with my name and address. Then I noticed that each was also tagged with an engraved visiting card. In florid, oversized silver-gray script I read, SANDRA CANTEY, and below that in dark red Magic Marker, IN CARE OF PETER WOLF—HOLD FOR ARRIVAL.

16

Wedding Day

Your father couldn't keep down his Ensure last night," Mother announced, as I sat by her bed while we shared café au lait with chicory. Dad was sound asleep next to her. Our wedding day, June 29, 1967, had begun.

The gray-blue walls of my parents' bedroom shimmered in the sunlight. My mother's right hand held her first Camel of the day. She was wearing the silk off-white bed jacket I'd given her for Christmas, its lace already tinged yellow-brown from nicotine.

"Your father kept me up all night groaning," she complained. "His pained sounds make me feel so helpless. Did he bother you?"

"Yes, but not much."

Here was the reason we happened to be getting married on this particular June day and why the ceremony was to be held at my parents' house, at 1000 Falcon Road (now an empty lot, thanks to Katrina) in Metairie, rather than in Fort Worth, Sandra's hometown. It was all about Dad's cancer.

My parents scarcely knew Sandra, but they liked her quick wit, trim appearance, and prominent family background. They liked being able to tell friends that when she was in college she'd sold Jack, her big black prize jumper, to the American equestrian team; that she'd earned an undergraduate degree at Vassar; that she'd completed a master's degree in social work at New York University; and that she was honorably employed as a guidance counselor at Brooklyn College. Sandra loved Paris—that appealed to them, too, maybe the most. But they knew nothing about her commitment to radical politics: that she'd quickly earned admission to the inner circle of the New York radical left as Bella Abzug's first lieutenant. They would have been horrified to learn that on many a night, shaggy pacifist Vietnam War draft resisters en route to Canada could be found sleeping on the living room floor in our West Seventy-First Street apartment.

In that apartment a few months earlier, over tea, chocolate croissants, bacon, and the *New York Times*—all part of our Sunday morning ritual—sitting unceremoniously in our robes at the small round oak table in front of our Pullman kitchen, I'd nervously and quietly asked Sandra to marry me. Not coincidentally, Dad's weight had been dropping precipitously. He was no longer able to leave the house. I wanted Dad to see me married before he died.

"I'm good to go," she'd answered, looking up from the Week in Review section with a smile whose offhand spontaneity perfectly matched my casual proposal.

Then, an unpremeditated thought popped into my mind. "Darlin'," I asked, "I wonder how you'd feel about us having a Jewish family? I'm suddenly finding that important to me."

Without a moment's hesitation, she'd answered, "I can talk to God in any language."

"And so you have," I said, smiling at her, mindful that she'd already taken turns at being Episcopalian, Baptist, and Catholic.

"I'll study and learn all about Judaism, go all the way and formally convert. And we'll go together to counseling at the Jewish Theological Seminary," she continued teasingly, "so you'll know something, too." She knew all about my sterling record as a Jew. "At the end, I'll be cleansed in a *mikvah* and you'll be right outside the door to receive me, a newly consecrated Jewess, purified and sanctified and ready to bear authentic Jewish children."

Had she been preparing?

Now here in Metairie I stood up and walked to Dad's side of my parents' bed. Standing above him, I saw the outline of his shriveled body beneath the top sheet—once a portly 175 pounds now shrunk to 90. I didn't feel comfortable that close to him. I felt uninvited, as I'd often felt in his presence. I also felt helpless and guilty. Would he be more at peace if I sat by him and said, "Dad, you're dying, you know that. Can't we talk? There is so little time. I love you; we all do." Instead, I whispered, "Hi, Dad, can I do anything for you?"

In his drowsy, morphine-muted pain, he didn't respond. I couldn't be certain if he even noticed me. I said nothing more. As I saw his cheek pressed into his pillow, I wanted to ask, more than anything else, "How do you feel about me now? Are you glad that I'm your son, that I'm going to be married today, here, so you can be part of it? I'm going to carry on the Wolf name. Dad, now at the end, do you love me?"

Although only fifty-seven, he looked so very old; he was so shriveled and helpless. Dad, I thought, how long has it been since we touched? I have no recollection of a hug or the feel of your hand in mine. You did the best you could between us. How sad for us both. I forgive you. I don't even know what for. I just forgive you for all of it and I hope you can forgive me. I was never the son you wanted, I know that. But thank you for tennis lessons, for giving me a fine Exeter and college education, for teaching me the cotton business and how to strip a stalk of sugarcane, for taking us around the world . . . and, yes, how to make a strong drink at the bar and how to send out a warm, open smile. I leaned down and under my breath whispered, "Thank you for taking the time to explain security investing, and showing me how to operate among men in the world."

I decided right there that I would hold our children until they can't stand it. I would hug and kiss them their whole lives. And now, many years later, I have, and I do, and they expect it. I hold them tight when we meet, and I kiss them, and I sometimes think what might have happened if only Mom and Dad had experienced this joy.

Without trying to speak to Dad, I returned to the gloomy room assigned to me, a cave of a place known as the guest room. I opened my suitcase. I knew exactly where I'd packed the Purple Heart that Gram had crocheted for me. I lifted it out of its leather box and held it in my palm. The wool loops were still a glossy purple. The safety pin was still attached neatly to its back, just as Gram had sewn it. How small it seemed, and how delicate. I brought it close to my face. For a moment, I was again being abandoned by my friends on a dark suburban sidewalk. Then I saw my father's concerned face the day he returned from the Pacific, when he was met by a battered, bandaged son. I remembered feeling that I had ruined his triumphant homecoming as the family's World War II hero.

Half an hour later, with Mother now somewhere else in the house, I walked back to Dad's bedside. I leaned over his body, not sure if he was awake or aware that I was in the room. I held his shriveled hand. Then I lifted the flap of his pajama pocket and pinned my Purple Heart over his emaciated chest. As I backed away, I patted his bony foot under the sheet. I felt my throat tighten. Tears that I couldn't release welled up inside me.

After leaving Dad, I checked my watch. I still had five hours. "Willie-Mae," I said, passing through the kitchen, "don't worry about lunch for me. I'm going for a walk."

"Where you goin' like that?" she asked, questioning how I was dressed so close to the big event: faded polo shirt, bleached-out khakis, tennis shoes.

"I'll be back in plenty of time."

I left the house and drove over to Brockenbraugh Court. I needed to see, one more time, the gigantic oak tree where my friends and I used to meet and play. Once there, I lingered at the spot beneath it where I'd mastered my fear of swinging. I couldn't get Dad's wasted body out of my mind. In the shade of the tree's big, overhanging limb I felt bound to my past. Here I'd flown free of the earth for a few minutes, in control and happy. I thought, Maybe I'll feel like that again tonight after our wedding.

Then, for the first time in my life, I saw myself as a lonely boy grown into a lonely man. I felt a sudden compassion for "Petie." I sensed him begin to breathe and claim a new life of his own as my companion. I mourned my childhood, so full of what I recognized as—rather than disdain for me—my father's and my mother's own unhappiness. Standing there all alone, I realized that Dad's unexamined misery had at times been communicated and transferred to me as disapproval, and that Mom's own problems had come through to me as indifference. I felt both saddened and calmed by these realizations.

I walked once around the great trunk, then again, before returning to the sidewalk. Back in the car, at Metairie Road I took a left and headed toward the Jefferson-Orleans Parish line. Crossing the Metairie Road bridge above the Seventeenth Street Canal, I could see between the slanted concrete walls down into the brown, murky water being drawn toward the pumping station where it would be lifted up more than six feet and out to Lake Pontchartrain. The city was not yet liberated from the heavy rains of earlier in the week.

Minutes later I arrived—to my surprise, as I had no special destination in mind—at Metairie Cemetery, a miniature city of elaborate mausoleums. I parked and walked. A muddy canal, twenty or thirty feet wide, of nearly stagnant water with weed-choked banks, separated the cemetery from the road. On that bright morning, I was riveted by the reflections of spires, gargoyles, and winged angels cast by the front rank of proud, tall tombs. The watery images were distorted and fragmented by the warm breeze pulling across the surface of the canal. The gleaming, white marble houses of the dead were lined neatly along narrow lanes of crushed oyster shells. I knew Aunt Ida was buried here. So were my grandmother's brothers, my uncle Leon Godchaux and his brother, Paul. But I wondered why my Jewish relatives were interred way out here near Metairie in a predominantly Christian cemetery.

Years later I found out. In Julius Weis's self-published *Autobiography*, printed in 1908, I came upon this revealing passage:

In 1884, Mr. M. Frank, Isador (*sic*) Newman and myself, formed a
plan to purchase a plot of ground in Metairie Cemetery, to be used
as a burying ground, and together with thirty-seven other members
of Temple Sinai, we bought forty lots in Metairie Ridge, which we
dedicated to this purpose. The move created considerable opposition
among some of the members of the Congregation, as they thought
it was not proper for our religion to be buried in a Christian burying
ground. The matter was finally left to the decision of our Minister,
Rev. Jas. K. Gutheim, who decided that it was perfectly proper, as it
was in a separate lot from the balance of the Cemetery.

This cleared things up. The term *minister*, used instead of *rabbi*,
jumped off the page for me.

As I gazed at this curious burial ground, I knew in my gut that
my father could not live much longer. In my heart I felt the impending loss of both of my elderly grandparents. I could see myself years
from now as a withered survivor, the Wolf family name disappear-
ing with me, unless today changed all of that.

When I got back to my parents' house, it was nearly three
o'clock. Through the dining room's picture window I saw the flo-
rist's staff positioning large terra-cotta urns. They were filled with
yellow and white chrysanthemums. I noticed three chairs and one
wide, empty space in front of the portable podium where Rabbi
Feibelman and Sandra's minister would preside. The chairs were
reserved for my mother and Sandra's divorced parents. The space
was for my father's wheelchair.

The afternoon sun burned into the large, western-facing glass
sliders. The living room's orange-umber walls glowed like a church
façade in Tuscany. The cedar roof emitted a light haze of evaporat-
ing moisture.

Back inside, I adjusted the air conditioner to full blast. Was I the
only one feeling the heat?

I began to dress: dark gray suit, new white shirt (made, I knew,
from long-staple Egyptian cotton), black-and-silver-striped silk
tie. My heavy, solid gold cufflinks were the shape of cotton bales, a

trophy of Dad's stunning business success after the war. They had been a gift from Mom to Dad in 1950, when he signed the contract for a vacant lot on Woodvine Avenue, enabling us to move from Brockenbraugh Court and build a two-story brick house across the tracks in the Metairie Club Gardens subdivision. Ten years later they bought the house around the corner that I was in right now.

"You might as well have these now," Mom had said earlier that morning, passing me the Adler's box with one freshly manicured hand.

"But they're Dad's."

"He can't wear a French-cuff shirt any longer. Take them."

"Mom, I brought my own from New York."

"Peter, you're responsible for this family. You have been ever since your father got so sick. Wear these; they're yours. Take them."

Once I pushed the back clasp of the heavy gold cotton bales through my shirt cuff, I took a deep breath. I checked my gold pocket watch, a family heirloom given to me by my father when I was fifteen and which I had never used. It was a wind-up Patek Philippe, engraved on its round back in scrolled lettering with MW, my great-grandfather's initials. Morris Wolf was the name shared by my father and his own grandfather. I was dressed and ready. I still had twenty minutes.

I opened the bedroom door and walked out into the hall. I was steps from where the ceremony would take place. In the sudden bright light, everything and everyone was in silhouette.

Before I could fully grasp what was happening, someone attached a large white boutonniere to my lapel. Then someone else took my elbow and guided me gently toward the makeshift altar. The house blurred, and all the guests seemed to merge.

Sandra was suddenly standing next to me in a short, pink-sequined wedding dress. I hadn't seen her arrive at the podium. She quickly curled her arm firmly into mine, like the lead partner of a ballroom dance team. Someone was speaking to us. I started to tremble; an unstoppable shaking crept upward through my legs. She must feel it, I thought nervously. But there was no sign that she did. No tightening of her hand, no worried glance.

Someone else was speaking. The rabbi? The minister? Me? Suddenly, on cue, there was my best man, my father, below eye level in his wheelchair, at my side. What appeared to be a huge shirt collar was wrapped around his skinny neck, all bunched up by the loosely hanging black necktie. His suit jacket sagged across his shrunken shoulders. In his lap there were mounds of fabric, no longer needed to envelop his formerly heavy frame. His glasses looked far too wide for his face.

Using his skeletal index finger and thumb, Dad extended the flat gold band toward me. He couldn't raise his arm. Is Dad's hand shaking or is the ring blurring like a top spun off its string? I reached down to grasp the unruly band.

At that moment I felt Sandra tighten her grip and at the same time lean away from me, as in a dance. She succeeded in rotating my body a quarter turn toward her. At first I resisted. Then I realized: I've been staring at Dad too long.

On quivering legs I eased into her lead and faced the podium.

17

Dominique Calls

Is that Peter Wolf?" a female asked in a warm, engaging French accent.

"Yes," I answered from my cluttered back-room study on West Seventy-First Street, where I was writing the last stages of my doctoral thesis. "Who's calling, please?"

"Dominique de Menil here, in Houston," she answered. I did not know who she was. "I'm chair of the *histoire* of art department at St. Thomas University. I just read your article in *Art in America*. It's on *précisément* the material we've been looking for someone to speak about."

"Speak about?" I asked, surprised.

"Yes," she answered. "We'd like to invite you to teach a five-week course open to the public, one lecture per week."

I listened, bewildered.

"We know you're going to be showing some of the material at the Museum of Modern Art next fall. It fits right in."

How could this lady in Houston know that Arthur Drexler, the director of the architecture department at the Museum of Modern Art in New York, had just decided this?

"I'm not sure I have time," I answered, stunned at this sudden invitation from someone I knew nothing about, to do something I had never done. "I'm trying to finish my dissertation, I'm studying

for my orals, and I have a part-time job teaching at Pratt Institute."
I didn't think it relevant to add that Sandra and I had only recently
been married and that my father had died not long before of cancer,
so I was traveling back and forth to New Orleans to liquidate Wolf
& Co. and to help settle his estate. I had my hands full.

"It won't take any time at all," this forceful lady said. "You
won't lose time traveling, either. We'll collect you and bring you
back to New York in our plane."

I remained silent for a moment. Then: "What?"

"There is an endowed honorarium for the course," she continued. "You'll stay with us overnight after each lecture, and we'll
have you back in New York before noon the day after."

"That is so very generous," I gasped, "and tempting."

"We'd like you to talk about the people you're writing about,
especially Eugène Hénard and his circle. This man Hénard you've
discovered, this man that MoMA is going to reveal . . . I'd never
heard of him, and I am, you know, French . . . from *Paris*." She
added, "My friends in Paris tell me that your doctoral work is
going to be published soon in Paris by the Centre de Recherches
d'Urbanisme and in English by the International Federation for
Housing and Planning at The Hague. Is that right?"

She had connections.

"So you can do this, I know. *Très facilement*."

The way she said "Paris" sounded like a whisper and a promise.
I could see the Tuileries. I could smell my old apartment on the rue
Dauphine.

She then said in a steady, confident tone, "We don't exploit our
speakers. How does a thousand dollars for the lectures sound to you?"

To me it sounded too good to be true. The five evenings in
Houston would provide more money than my teaching assistantship for the entire year.

In the few days that passed before I called back, I had no trouble finding out about Dominique de Menil and her husband, Jean

(John in his Anglicized form). I must have been the only person on earth—certainly the only person anywhere near the art world—who didn't know who they were. Jean had long been a trustee of the Museum of Modern Art. Dominique was a daughter of a French banking family and the founders of Schlumberger, the powerful international oil drilling and service company established in Paris, now headquartered in Houston.

Dominique and Jean had distinguished themselves as mavericks in the world of modern art. Together they were bold, knowledgeable collectors, and Dominique was a dedicated educator and scholar. As adventurous buyers with a French connection, they had acquired, piece by piece, the most distinguished private collection of Magritte's paintings in the world. They had also assembled a widely admired assortment of works by other great nineteenth- and early-twentieth-century French titans—notably Picasso, Matisse, Braque, and Redon.

I had no idea what I meant when I repeated to my taxi driver the instructions Dominique de Menil had sent to me: "We're going to the Marine Air Terminal, LaGuardia Airport." He flipped the meter flag and took off. The doorman standing at the art deco terminal portal pointed me to a slim silver aircraft waiting on the tarmac. After a brief handshake just inside the cabin door, Dominique insisted that I call her by her first name. "Bienvenu," she said.

The only noncommercial plane I'd been in previously was a U.S. Navy DC-3 cargo transport. When I was living in New Orleans from 1960 to 1963, as an alternative to being drafted, I completed my compulsory military service by serving in the Louisiana Air National Guard. After a rigorous, sweltering six weeks of basic training at Lackland Air Force Base, in San Antonio, I participated each summer in two-week-long maneuvers at Gulfport, Mississippi, as well as monthly weekend service at Alvin Callender Field, the military installation just outside of New Orleans. In those days, at least on the swampy outskirts of New Orleans, anyone could hop military flights from the naval air station without orders, so long as you flew in uniform. My mission on the plane hops, as a member of the Air National Guard, had been to visit a longtime friend, Gretchen Shartle, who lived in Houston.

The de Menil house was Bauhaus-inspired, designed by Philip Johnson. From the outside, the travertine-and-glass building looked like Mies van der Rohe's 1929 Barcelona Pavilion, only expanded and spread out in wings.

Jean de Menil must have heard the car crunch along the drive. He opened the door. After hugging Dominique affectionately, he said, "Ah, *enfin*," extending his hand to me. I felt his warm grasp and saw a man dressed in gray slacks and dark turtleneck. He was my size and about my weight, shorter than Dominique. A glossy silver-gray fringe of hair encircled his nearly bald head, framing a calm, composed face. He, like his wife, had an accessible, amicable smile.

Each evening after my lecture, Jean and Dominique arranged to be at home with me for dinner. Growing up, I'd rarely had supper at home alone with my parents.

At the beginning of our first evening, I felt shy and guarded. I had no idea what to expect from these two august strangers, who were about my parents' age, and I felt intimidated and inadequate in the presence of these art world celebrities. But I quickly found that they wanted to be personal and to know me, not put me through some qualifying preliminary. "Tell us about your parents," Jean began. "Since they live only a few hours away in New Orleans, perhaps we know them."

I told him. There was no overlap, and I didn't expect there would be, other than the fact that my mother had volunteered from time to time to work in the gift shop of the New Orleans Museum of Art.

We talked easily. The conversation ranged all over the map— art; history; the South; politics; France; the differences among New York, Houston, and New Orleans; their careers; my aspirations. I could feel my body relax and my mind engage.

Before my first lecture, I got to the designated classroom half an hour early. I wanted to see how big the room was and to be certain that I'd have two slide projectors, since my presentation depended upon paired comparisons. I wanted to be sure that there was a bulb in the lectern lamp. I wanted to test the image clarity, given Houston's intense late-afternoon sun. I needed to make sure that my carousels fit into the school's projectors and that both functioned properly. Were the windows covered? Was there an amplifying system built into the speaker's platform? I was nervous.

I also felt cautious. At Pratt Institute I'd learned the truth of Murphy's law—that if anything can go wrong, it will. Pratt was overcrowded and underfunded, and the students were restless. This was 1967, after all. I'd become accustomed to broken projectors, projection screens that would not descend, missing lecterns, and agitated students.

I could have showed up one minute before my lecture. Everything was perfect. The room, a raked amphitheater, looked as if it held 300, maybe 350 people, with excellent sight lines from every seat. The equipment was new, state-of-the-art. The room was fitted out with window shades that I could lower electronically from the stage. Built-in, paired controls on the lectern allowed me to change slides. No need to interrupt the flow to say to a projectionist, "Next slide, please."

A custodian dressed in a dark blue cotton uniform, with at least twenty keys dangling from a shiny chrome ring fastened to his belt loop, met me and said, "You must be Professor Wolf?"

Professor Wolf. I'd never been called that before. "Yes," I answered.

"Do you need anything?"

"No, thank you; this is perfect." And it was.

With considerable trepidation, I began my first public lecture series. "I want to talk about urbanism," I began, "a word and a concept invented only in the early twentieth century." I went on to explain that the urbanist "views the city in a way no one ever had previously—simultaneously from points of view of circulation, hygiene, social welfare, economics, and aesthetics." I felt the audience lean forward. This concept of a new way of seeing and understanding a city appealed to residents of one grappling with its own sprawling growth: no zoning, an intrusive highway system, increasing air pollution, and disintegration all around the core of downtown. "More than any other individual, it was Eugène Hénard who brought this avant-garde notion of urbanism to progressive France and helped publicize it internationally," I said in closing my general remarks. "His mark resides with us, unheralded, all over the world."

My introduction finished, I felt the tension subside. I was sailing. My voice became strong. My lecture notes were illuminated on the lectern, but I didn't need them. I was having fun.

Halfway through dinner one evening, Dominique asked, "Why did you give up being a cotton broker in the South to become an art historian in the East?"

I looked at her. My face must have looked blank at best. "That's a huge question."

"Jean and I have been wondering about this since you left last week. Jean gave up banking, you know, and our children have switched careers. One son has left a good business in Houston to try filmmaking in New York."

As I sat there trying to collect my thoughts, I felt more deeply than ever that Dominique and Jean were genuinely interested in me.

I didn't have much experience talking about myself. I started out shyly. "I followed my instinct." They didn't respond—they were listening. Even that was a new experience. I looked down at my plate. I took a sip of wine. This was a long story, one I still didn't understand very well.

"It wasn't a quick or easy decision," I continued. "I had a difficult time leaving the French Quarter, my girlfriend, my parents, and, in the deepest sort of way, my life in New Orleans.

"Ultimately," I continued, "I did get up the courage to leave. To take what felt to me like a huge gamble."

As I spoke, Jean and Dominique nodded their heads almost imperceptibly, the way people do when they are absorbing and understanding (and even approving) all at once. They seemed to know what was behind these vague remarks. I went on: "There was no logic I could rely on. For the first time in my life I decided to follow my instincts, regardless of my parents' disapproval. To close my eyes and leap."

"Yes. That is sometimes the only way," Jean, the consummate risk-taker, murmured, as if to himself. As he did so, I thought, This is exactly what my father, having lived through the Depression and always in his hometown, could not understand and could not approve of—this way of making a life-altering decision.

"Dominique," Jean said, at breakfast on my third visit, turning toward his wife's end of the built-in breakfast table, "does Peter know about the symposium and the supper?"

"Didn't I tell you about that?" Dominique asked, looking at me sheepishly.

"I don't know what you and Jean are talking about," I said. "So I don't think so."

"It's been planned for months. You're part of it. I must have warned you."

"She forgets things," Jean said. "She's so busy."

"The symposium takes place the evening after your last class." She gave me such a restrained, quizzical smile that I knew instantly this amazing concurrence was no coincidence. "We want you to speak at it—a short talk about Eugène Hénard and his early-twentieth-century ideas about designing modern cities. It will be a private scoop of your MoMA show for our patrons. Do you mind? Jean has already cleared this with Arthur, in case you're worried about his approval."

Again, she had all the loopholes plugged in advance. "I don't mind," I replied, "so long as the Modern has no objection."

"Half an hour is enough," she admonished. I felt relief.

My clever hostess hesitated a split second, then announced, "The main speaker will be Buckminster Fuller."

I was stunned. How could I possibly interest, even for a few minutes, an audience that had come to hear the imaginative, loquacious, brilliant Mr. Fuller, one of my heroes?

As my final class ended and the auditorium filled for the symposium, I could feel my stomach tighten. I wondered if I'd forget everything I wanted to say. Then, before I could stop worrying, Dominique was beside me, talking to the audience and introducing me. As she sat down, her smile said: Don't worry. Go for it. Have fun.

I was thrilled to be introducing for the first time to an invited public audience in America—indeed, to a blue-chip gathering— Hénard's visionary ideas, which would set the stage for Mr. Fuller, a master of contemporary experimental thinking. Now I understood Dominique's reasoning.

Toward the end of my presentation, I displayed and explained Hénard's most futuristic suggestion: a below-street series of tunnels designed to connect city buildings to an underground freight, trash, and fuel service network. The roofs of these same buildings would support small helipads for personal transport. I intended this to provide a foreground for Mr. Fuller.

Fuller, a genuine visionary and a pioneer environmentalist, showed slides of his own inventions. In remarkably rapid staccato remarks, he explained the spare structural systems of his futuristic 4-D Dymaxion House and his aerodynamically and mechanically sophisticated Dymaxion automobile. He reminded everyone of the widespread acceptance of his geodesic dome structures beginning with World War II, due mainly to their lightness of material and the reduced time and energy used in their manufacture. At the end, he flashed on the screen a model of midtown Manhattan. The entire width of the city from the Hudson to the East River was covered by one immense, transparent, elliptical, air-conditioned dome. The structure would be two miles in diameter. The bold theoretical image elicited a gasp from his audience, experienced as they were with auto exhaust and daily pollution warnings. I wondered how he would ventilate an enclosed midtown Manhattan.

When we arrived back at the de Menil house, we found it set up for a formal dinner that could have been mistaken for a state occasion at the American embassy in Paris. The invitees were prominent collectors, university trustees, and Houston business titans.

At the end of dinner, nearly midnight, Dominique stood and rapped gently with her spoon on the shaft of her water glass. Looking down on Fuller's close-cropped head, she asked in her low, musty voice, "Mr. Fuller, or Bucky, as I know the whole world calls you, would you be willing to speak to us again for a few minutes? You have been inspiring. I know we'd all like to hear some final remarks from you." Fuller hesitated a moment. He looked up at Dominique looming over him. As she folded back into her chair, he rose. He stood there with the candlelight flickering off his bulky lenses. He stood there longer than anyone expected, looking beyond the table at the artwork amid sumptuous surroundings. He seemed lost in a reverie.

The place went very quiet.

"Thank you, Mrs. de Menil. Thank you, Jean de Menil," he began. "Looking around your magnificent house, I am reminded of my childhood—one little piece of it. I think that's what I'd like to tell you about at this late hour.

"One rainy Saturday afternoon when I was ten years old, my grandmother showed me some toys stored in her attic," he began. "Lined up against the back wall under the eaves, I saw a set of twelve magnificent gold-leaf dining chairs covered in red velvet. 'Grandmother,' I asked, 'What are those chairs? I've never seen them before.'"

Then Fuller waited. I imagine he was deciding how far to go with his train of thought.

"She told me this," he went on. "'I'm only the custodian of these chairs. They were my mother's. They will belong to someone else someday. We are guardians, we don't really own anything.'"

Around the table there was not a sound. No one moved. I thought I could see chests tighten. For the first and only time in weeks of knowing her, I saw Dominique's normally composed and serene face go taut. In the dim candlelight her pale skin faded to bleached vellum.

"Jean and Dominique," Fuller then said, "this is what I am thinking about right now."

The next morning as I was packing for the last time, sad to be leaving, I heard a knock on the door, a very gentle knock.

When I opened the door, there was Jean standing before me, with Dominique just behind him. They were each smiling a happy, shy, sheepish smile—ones I couldn't read.

"Come in," I said. "I'm just finishing packing." I noticed that Dominique's long, slender arms were clasped behind her back, as if she were doing a stretch exercise.

"We've enjoyed your visit," Jean started. "Especially our breakfasts alone and the late-evening talks over cognac."

"Me, too," I said. "It's been wonderful to get to know you."

"Your class was a hit," said Dominique. "Everyone told me how much they enjoyed the fresh, unusual, contrarian things you said about planning and urban design."

"I had such a good time here," I answered. "The time we spent together and getting to know you means a lot to me. I want to thank you for everything."

At that point Dominique stepped up next to Jean. Her left arm came forward. I saw the outline of an object concealed beneath heavy brown wrapping paper, the thickness and size of a framed piece of art, around two and a half feet square. I looked at her hand extended toward me and felt a moment of dizziness.

"Open it now," she said. "We'll have Isabelle rewrap it. This is our personal thank-you gift."

I could not speak. I barely moved. Dominique then placed the package on my bed, unstuck the masking tape holding the end fold, peeled back the paper, and stepped away. On my bed in a sturdy maple frame I saw a stunning Magritte collage: an empty theater stage edged by mauve curtains with delicate doves flying away from a musical score filling an otherwise empty page.

When I looked up, I saw them watching me with a mixture of gravity and emotion. I could barely see their moist eyes through my tears.

"We want you to be this picture's custodian," Dominique whispered. "Fly with this dove, sing with this score. You have made the stage come alive for us these past weeks."

In the midst of their extraordinary generosity I could only stare at their smiling, yet solemn faces. The room blurred. Then, with an impulse I'd rarely felt in the presence of my own parents, I stepped forward and hugged each of them long and hard. I was speechless. They understood.

"We'll be on the front steps to say good-bye," Jean said, closing the door quietly behind them.

Epilogue

———

Dedication Weekend

In April 2004, I was in New Orleans, at Temple Sinai, for the funeral of my uncle Jimmy Wolf, Dad's architect brother. Afterward, with cousins Debby and Wendy Wolf and Lois and Peter Mayerson, and my sister and brother-in-law, we walked through Audubon Park, named after the celebrated artist and naturalist John James Audubon, who lived and worked in New Orleans part-time for nine years starting in 1821. I said to Gail, "Now Uncle Jimmy is gone—the last our father's siblings, the last of that Wolf bloodline. It makes me sad that you and Harvey are the only immediate family members of our generation living in New Orleans. And you're here just half-time and thinking of leaving altogether."

I was thinking as well, So many contemporary notable and talented people from other New Orleans Jewish families now chose not to live here. Nick Lemann and Walter Isaacson came to mind. Lemann had been recently ensconced in New York as dean of the Columbia School of Journalism, and was well-known as an author and staff writer for the *New Yorker*. Isaacson had forged a dazzling writer's and intellectual's career from his base in Washington, D.C., and had been recently in the news when appointed president and CEO of the Aspen Institute.

And I knew that descendants of many of the notable generous Jewish civic families that had been friends of my great-grandparents, of my grandparents, of my parents and of my own, were no longer represented or in some cases even remembered.

"It's the violent crime, poor schools, inept government, and corruption," responded Harvey, ever the rational litigator. "Those are the realities. I know you don't like to hear it, but the future here is dicey."

"I left forty years ago," I said, "and keep thinking about coming back. Each time I visit, I fantasize about living here again. I've even looked at real estate in the Quarter again."

"Would you risk a big investment here now?" Harvey asked.

"Our people made major contributions to the life of this city, yet we've almost disappeared," I said, avoiding his direct question. "Our family helped found Temple Sinai and were major contributors to Touro Infirmary, built the biggest sugar business in the South and a retail empire. Yet today the names Wolf, Godchaux, and Weis are scarcely recognized here."

"Well," he replied, "that's how things go. It's a shame, I agree." My brother-in-law and I had become fast friends over the years; we could talk with candor.

"Part of me never left, and I want to honor the family—we're practically history here: lost, gone, forgotten." All of us began to discuss this fact, and wondered how it had happened so rapidly. "I would like to do something permanent," I said.

As we continued to walk, I saw, a hundred yards farther along, perched on a rise at the edge of the sinuous lagoon that runs through Audubon Park, a beautifully proportioned, small, round pavilion. It had a green, overhanging roof supported by eight square white columns arranged in a circle. This elegant structure appealed to me; more than that, it beckoned.

I felt a certain magic in its form and site. It was like a modest temple sitting on a gentle hill. The park's lagoon curved around it, giving the pavilion a water view in three directions. Across the water, through a heavy screen of oak and water azalea, the golf course and open park space were ablaze, lit by the afternoon sun. Just beyond the site was the spot at the edge of the lagoon where Gail and I had fed the swans on Sunday mornings as children.

Up close, it was apparent that the hillock was in poor shape, its slopes nearly bare. Gullies cut deep into its contours. Although the round roof could shed water in all directions, no gutter channeled the heavy rains into a dry well. The concrete floor was cracked, the built-in benches dilapidated. The white paint on the rafters was peeling, and some of the columns sagged. Many of them sported graffiti. Judging from the scrawled dates, the little building had not been cleaned in years.

I loved the location. It stood near the formal gateway to Audubon Park. Tulane University was visible across St. Charles Avenue, as were the streetcars rumbling along the avenue's neutral ground. Fifty yards away was a well-equipped, well-used playground (complete with restrooms), where I imagined my grandchildren swinging and sliding, playing amid other children who lived in New Orleans. The site was prominent and visible and in the heart of a neighborhood where most of our family had lived for generations.

This beautiful, iconic structure, in a perfect location, spoke of New Orleans and the past. To me, it said my family; it said my city. How appropriate it would be, I was thinking, to set our own family roots in this lovely 385-acre park, purchased by the city for the site of the World Cotton Centennial in 1884, and then in 1886 dedicated as Audubon Park. In 1897 John Charles Olmsted, who was sequentially the nephew, stepson, and then business partner of the world-celebrated landscape architect Frederick Law Olmsted, began his design of the park's romantic landscape. At that time, most of the members of our family lived within a few blocks of the property.

"Let's adopt this pavilion, if the park authorities will allow us to," I said. Gail and Harvey looked at me as if I'd lost my reason.

"It's waterfront property with sunset views," I teased. "The best real estate in town." We walked on.

I couldn't get that little building out of my mind. None of my cousins were interested. But Gail volunteered to contact the Audubon Nature Institute about adopting it as a family memorial. Our idea and contribution were accepted, and the work proceeded. Then Katrina struck, fortunately not doing much damage to our little pavilion. But everything stopped for a while as New Orleans struggled to begin again.

* * *

In March 2006, seven months after Hurricane Katrina, I met my thirty-five-year-old son, Phelan, in New Orleans for the dedication ceremony. Alexis, my daughter, was ill and couldn't join us. She and I were both deeply disappointed. By this time each of my children had two of their own—ranging in age from two to five. My grandchildren, each a healthy, delightful gift to my life, consisted of Austin, India, Emory, and Elias, three wonderful boys and a charming, beguiling little girl.

When I got to the Avis rental car office, where we had agreed to meet, I found my son crumpled on a rust-colored couch opposite the sales counter. His hair was matted, his face damp, his skin tone yellowish. "Rough flight?" I asked, as I hugged and kissed him.

"No, Dad. I'm feeling sick, but I didn't want to miss the ceremony."

"What's wrong?"

"Maybe something I picked up from the kids, or maybe just my Addison's. I've got all my meds, but if I can't keep my pills down, I'll have to go to the hospital."

I was alarmed, then impressed; he'd made a heroic effort to be here.

This was the first time ever I would spend the night in a hotel in New Orleans. Before mother died seven years before, at the age of eighty-eight, I'd always stayed with her; after that, I'd stayed in my sister's guest room. But Gail's house was overflowing because of this special dedication weekend.

For decades, the Pontchartrain had been the grandest luxury hotel in uptown New Orleans. I thought Phelan and Lexie would enjoy a nightcap in the Bayou Bar, just as I had during the years I worked for Dad in the cotton business. I also imagined them riding the St. Charles Avenue streetcar "up" to Gail's house or "down" to the French Quarter, free of the constraints of our shared rental car. Given the number of people who still had not returned to New Orleans, I assumed that the hotel might be short-staffed. When I made our reservations from New York, the voice on the phone had been gracious and welcoming.

Descending the expressway exit ramp, we saw for the first time post-Katrina New Orleans close up. The great oaks lining St. Charles Avenue appeared denuded. The once-stately trees glowed eerily, like ghosts, their remaining leaves coated with silvery spray and their branches shorn at arbitrary angles. Overhead electric lines were broken and dangling. The streetcars were no longer running. The neutral ground was a debris dump.

When we pulled up to the hotel's entrance, we found the canopy torn, the space beneath unlit. I parked the car, and we carried our suitcases into the lobby.

In the old days, marble-topped tables supported urns filled with seasonal flower arrangements; these lined the walls of the wide entrance hall, alternating with high-backed, upholstered chairs. A series of gilded wall sconces and crystal chandeliers created a muted glow, enriched by the vibrant oranges, blues, and reds of Oriental carpets.

The scene we encountered was altogether different. The ornately carved wooden chairs were occupied by exhausted burly men in soiled jeans, sweat-drenched shirts, and muddy boots. One chair held a heavyset woman wearing a loose-fitting tent of a dress, nursing a baby. Instead of flowers, the marble tabletops were heaped with empty KFC and McDonald's containers.

An unshaven, dazed-looking young man in an open-collared shirt stood behind the front desk. I assumed he was a college student, as Tulane had just reopened, thanks to the heroic efforts of Scott Cowen, its dynamic president, while most of the other schools and colleges in town were still closed. Two very tired-looking men with FEMA stenciled in large letters on the backs of their black short-sleeved shirts stood at the counter drinking Dixie beer and swapping hometown tales. Looking at me as if I'd dropped from outer space, the young man said, "I'm sorry, but we have no records. The reservation system hasn't been working since the storm. We never know who's coming, who's staying, or who's leaving."

"But we need a place to stay."

"That's no problem. We have rooms tonight."

He slid a registration card across the counter to each of us. "I'm the only staff in the hotel," he said. "You'll have to take your bags and find your rooms."

"What about the car?" I asked. "We'll be here several nights. Do you have parking?"

"Sure," he said, without a trace of a smile, "at any curb you can find."

I looked at Phelan, and he looked at me. The town had only half its police force and the reports of vandalism had been lurid. I was thinking the worst.

I left Phelan on the eighth floor and proceeded up one more flight to my room. Neither the elevator nor the corridor had been cleaned in weeks. Everywhere there were bottle caps, soiled food wrappers, crushed soda cans, and empty beer bottles.

On the way back down, I checked on Phelan. "I can't make it to Gail's," he said. "Go ahead. I'll be fine."

"Call if you need anything. I'm ten minutes away. I'll say hello and bring you back some soup."

I let myself into Gail and Harvey's house with the front-door key I'd had for years. Their house smelled fresh and looked clean, though the den still had a temporary cover over its damaged ceiling. Like everyone else in New Orleans, they'd been without electricity for weeks after the storm, and they'd had no choice but to seal and later fumigate their refrigerator and freezer. For months, the streets of New Orleans had been lined with unsalvageable, discarded appliances, their doors taped shut to keep the rats out and the reeking food in. This scene was repeated in many neighborhoods.

Just as I began to explain Phelan's absence and report on the sad condition of the famed and once-elegant Pontchartrain, the phone rang. "Dad," a plaintive voice said, "come back. I need to go to the hospital."

Phelan was waiting at the curb. I sped toward the nearest hospital, Touro Infirmary. By now, I was frightened. We were in a crippled city, and my son was in trouble. One of my great-great-grandfathers had helped found this hospital. My grandfather, father, and sister had served on its board. My grandmother had had her mastectomy done there, my father's futile cancer surgery had been performed there, and I'd been born there. I realized I hadn't thought to call ahead to see if it was open. I knew that Charity and Memorial, the other nearby hospitals, had not reopened. When I saw the lit-up EMERGENCY ENTRANCE sign, I relaxed. As we registered, police arrived every few minutes with handcuffed prisoners, some bleeding from pistol shots. The city's awful crime statistics flashed through my mind. Other people walked in on their own, clearly ill or wounded. Intake was orderly, conducted by volunteers.

A nurse helped Phelan stretch out on a gurney in the large, open emergency treatment area, and pulled a curtain to separate him from an emaciated, elderly woman lying on an adjacent trolley.

Within minutes, a doctor came by to interview Phelan and check his vital signs. Dr. Margaret-Ann Sullivan had short blond hair, tired green eyes, and looked about thirty-five. I told her we'd just arrived from New York. "You're lucky," she said. "Only one other emergency room is open, and all the other hospitals in Orleans Parish are still closed." She ordered intravenous steroid and saline supplements to restore the cortisone, hydrocortisone, and Florinef levels that Phelan could no longer maintain.

All of the nurses I spoke with were men. They were volunteers from northern Louisiana, Arkansas, and Texas. Not a single member of the regular nursing staff seemed to be on duty; most had not come back to the city.

While the doctor was ministering to my son, I asked, "Are you from New Orleans?"

"No," she said. "I'm from Santa Fe. Came here to help out and haven't been home for five weeks." I could see that she was functioning despite work overload and sleep deprivation.

Later, Dr. Sullivan said, "I'm admitting your son overnight. He should be able to leave the hospital tomorrow afternoon."

The next morning, after breakfast, I drove to a nine-thirty board meeting of the Franklin Realty Company, a small real estate holding company, and the only network still binding together the shadowy remains of the once-powerful Godchaux-Weis-Wolf clan. Its family-only stockholders had long been dispersed far and wide across the United States, most now with small fractional interests passed down through the generations. Each of the other six members of the board still lived in New Orleans and represented the last vestiges of the various family branches. I held the Carrie Godchaux–Albert Wolf seat. Leon Godchaux II, my first cousin once removed, was chairman. The secretary was a cousin, Joe Friend, Julius Weis's great-grandson, who was about my age. I was pleased to serve, as it was an excuse to stay in touch with my extended family and to visit New Orleans twice a year.

Before the meeting got under way, I asked my young cousin

Christopher Roos how he was faring. "Our house was completely demolished," he said. "Everything's gone. But we're staying and we're going to rebuild."

Martha Trautman Culpepper, another cousin, a few years older than Chris, was sitting next to him. "Not us," she said. "We're leaving, even though our condo wasn't damaged. We're selling and moving to Austin."

"Why?" I asked.

She looked at me, her dark eyes moist, near tears. "We're leaving," she said, "because I cry at every stop sign."

Uncle Leon gave his chair's report. Franklin's properties had sustained nominal damage, with just one emergency: a huge oak had fallen across a small shopping center roof. Finding a contractor to repair the damage had been difficult. To satisfy the only bid we could obtain, we authorized what amounted to three times the pre-storm cost for a couple of days' work. We approved the usual fifty-cents-per-share dividend and—affirming our faith in the future of New Orleans—discussed a potential warehouse acquisition. On a motion to adjourn, we dispersed.

I headed for Galatoire's to meet my longtime friend Marty Feldman, a federal judge. I walked in at eleven forty-five, which happened to be the same time my father and I would meet my grandfather in the 1960s to "beat the lunch crowd."

Marty was seated at what had been my grandfather's favorite table. John, now our regular family waiter, still alive and well after the storm, stood near the door. Even in his tuxedo and crisp white shirt, though, he looked tired and downcast. "Mr. Peter," he said, "I'm glad to see you back in town. We've been open only a few weeks, and some things aren't right yet. The judge is over there waiting for you."

"Have you been okay?"

"We got lucky," he said. "We left two days before the storm and went over to my cousin's in Ville Platte, out in northwest Louisiana. We came back a week after the water ran out. My house wasn't too bad."

"I'm glad to hear that."

I followed him to the table.

"Welcome back, guy," Marty said. "This weekend has got to be a great occasion for the family."

We started talking about New Orleans. I couldn't imagine any other subject. I looked up after a few minutes. At twelve thirty, Galatoire's wasn't even half full. I'd never seen it so empty at that time of day.

"What's going on?" I asked. "There's nobody here."

"You should see the other restaurants," Marty said. "I don't know which ones downtown will make it."

"It's been nearly seven months. I thought things were improving."

"Maybe a little. A lot of repairs are under way uptown. Where there was high ground, the stores and restaurants are jammed, but there are few tourists. Tulane reopened with a reduced staff and only sixty percent of its students. More than half the residents haven't returned. I don't know how many ever will, since things are so much better for evacuees—especially poorer people—who went to Atlanta and Houston and Dallas. Baton Rouge has doubled in population. There's hardly a doctor left here. With the lawyers scattered all over the place and our computer servers still down, none of us can hold trials."

John came by and asked if we wanted the menu. "What's good?" we asked in unison.

"We got the best crabmeat, speckled trout, and shrimp I've seen in thirty years," he said. "Since the storm, with most of the fishing boats turned over in the marsh and the captains and crews spread God knows where, the seafood's come back, plentiful."

I ordered my favorite dish, stuffed eggplant. It was the best I'd ever had, with two times the normal chunks of sweet lump back-fin crabmeat.

Marty and I discussed how in New Orleans and its surrounding parishes, more than 275,000 houses had been destroyed. Eighty percent of New Orleans had been inundated by 30 billion gallons of brackish, fetid water. Many houses were still full of a muck composed of soil, industrial and household solvents, gasoline, oil, and backed-up sewage. Mold and mildew crawled across every surface. This was by far the largest domestic disaster to strike an American city, and it was still being handled ineptly and indifferently by every level of government. The enormity of the destruction and the scale of the tragedy were too vast to be captured by even the most skilled photographer or journalist.

The high ground, only 20 percent of New Orleans, was basically spared. All along the Mississippi's crescent, property within the "sliver by the river" (as it came to be called, post-Katrina) escaped serious water damage. The "sliver"—the higher land created by eons of alluvial flooding, which had occurred before the Mississippi River levees were built in stages from the early nineteenth century into the 1920s—is a half mile to a mile wide on the east bank, the city of New Orleans side. Though only five to ten feet higher than the surrounding land, that was enough to shed water into "the bowl," as most of the rest of the metropolitan area, including Metairie, came to be known.

The original Spanish, French, Cajun, Creole, and Anglo settlers had wisely built on higher ground near the river. As a consequence, the neighborhoods comprising the French Quarter, most of the central business district, the warehouse district, the Garden District, and the "salt-and-pepper" racially mixed neighborhoods of uptown New Orleans looked much as they had for generations. Real estate prices on the relatively elevated land had escalated more than 25 percent, and rental costs for habitable space had soared up to 50 percent.

After a long tour of the city with Harvey and Gail, the chasm closed between abstract statistics and reality. I now knew what the numbers looked like, smelled like, felt like. We walked through devastated neighborhood after neighborhood. We saw boats up-ended on streets way inland and school buses upside down. We went through the front yards of vast stretches of abandoned, rot-ting, mold-filled houses. We stood at the levee breach, now a con-struction site, where the Industrial Canal had punched into the city. We walked through debris of timber, glass, roof tiles, boat masts, and wrecked hulls, which had once been the Buck Town boat basin at the edge of Lake Pontchartrain. We drove and walked and smelled vast stretches of rubble and abandoned, hollow, shattered dwellings that had recently been the modest Ninth Ward residential neighborhood. We stood at the spot where the Seventeenth Street Canal had given way, a jagged break that flooded our neighbor-hood in Metairie.

Katrina also precipitated an exodus of Jews, along with everyone else. From a pre-storm Jewish population of about ten thousand, 25 percent had departed, leaving the New Orleans Jewish community one of the smallest in any major American city. Some were com-ing back and some new Jewish families were being attracted; but overall this was another loss, another gone away. Though we could not know it at the time, in less than a decade the print version of the hallowed, historic *Times-Picayune*, the city's only remaining daily newspaper, which had distinguished itself for exemplary journalism during the storm, would itself begin to fade away, cut back to three issues a week.

After this upsetting and unforgettable experience, I settled into my room at the hotel to try to recover. Once there, I remembered I wanted to congratulate Bud Trillin on his elegiac paean to the mem-ory of his wife, Alice, just published in the *New Yorker* as "Alice, Off the Page." Alice had died of cancer, the night of the attack on the World Trade Center. The piece was the most difficult Bud had ever tackled; we'd discussed it on a recent trip together to Ecuador. He was at home when I called. "It's your most intimate piece," I said.

"The toughest," he answered. "How'd you like the picture?"

Since the photo of the two of them walking together was the most romantic picture of a just-married couple I'd ever seen, I told him just that.

"I know," he said.

After the call, I started thinking about my long friendship with Bud and Gerry Jonas, and with Henry Geldzahler, who was now dead. Henry, who became nationally known as "the Pope of Pop," had crammed a celebrated career into a brief lifetime. He was appointed the first director of the Visual Arts program of the National Endowment for the Arts, and had served as cultural affairs commissioner of New York City, and eventually curator of the Department of Twentieth Century Art at the Metropolitan Museum of Art. Gerry had become a successful freelance writer of amazing diversity and a fine poet. He'd also published important nonfiction books of his own, and was frequently engaged by Acoustiguide to prepare the narrative for important art exhibitions around the country. Bud had become a celebrated author of books, poetry, and *New Yorker* pieces.

I thought about many other friends and talented people I knew and enjoyed spending time with in New York. My life, I mused, would have been entirely different if I'd stayed in New Orleans. It was impossible to project just how, but I did know that, were I a New Orleans resident, I'd be dealing with anguish and doubt and fear and mistrust about the future, on top of even greater anger at the public agencies that had failed to deliver timely or adequate assistance to so many. I wondered, too, if I would have ever written books or become a land-use expert, or created an investment management business while serving as a trustee on the boards of a number of interesting arts institutions.

I pictured my little shingled cottage out on Long Island, in East Hampton—my hundred-year-old retreat with its carriage house that reminded me of my place on Burgundy Street and a boathouse that made me think of Pass Christian whenever I spent time in it. When I purchased the property in 1976, the buildings were falling-down wrecks, the local economy at a standstill, and the area considered (as it had been since the eighteenth century) too far from the village. I'd jumped at the chance once I saw this long neglected, intact near-ruin of an assemblage of historic structures—surely a gesture impelled by my long-lost property in the French Quarter.

I had renovated the buildings, preserving their original character. Georgica, as we called it (because my land is adjacent to Georgica Pond and on the edge of the neighborhood within East Hampton village known as Georgica), was now our family gathering place. My children and grandchildren looked for mushrooms, inspected lichen and moss, spied fox and deer in the surrounding woods, and delighted at the occasional box turtle lumbering across the lawn. From the small dock, we trapped minnows and crabbed for blue claws in August. We sailed and canoed and kayaked. I'd made a paradise for my family that reminded me of my life at Pass Christian.

I recalled Sandra's and my wedding day, which seemed a lifetime ago. She and I had been married eighteen years. Since divorcing, we'd remained friendly, attending children's birthdays and celebrating Christmas together with them.

As I lay in bed, suspended between New York and New Orleans, an irony I'd come to understand struck again. In my father's eyes, I'd left New Orleans as a bohemian dilettante. From my children's perspective, I was a hard-driving entrepreneur—a lot like Dad—but with a bent for art and architecture, and a committed intimacy with them.

I could discern other influences from my New Orleans family, too. The artisan interests of my grandmother and my grandfather's passion for making watercolors showed up in my own enthusiasm for drawing and amateur watercoloring. The board memberships in New

York and community-planning services to East Hampton echoed the ideals my great-aunt Ida; and my graduate art history education and professional writing reflected the lifelong work of my uncle Jimmy.

* * *

Dedication day, March 25, 2006, was as clear and beautiful as the day had been of Uncle Jimmy's memorial service. Audubon Park was relatively intact, and the refurbished pavilion glowed. The Audubon Nature Institute restoration team had done a magnificent job.

Local and out-of-town family members invited for the occasion, about twenty in all, gathered in and around the little building for the afternoon ceremony. I was sorry my daughter Alexis couldn't be part of this very special family memorial event.

Laurie Conkerton, the Audubon Institute representative, said, "The Audubon Institute is delighted to have been given the privilege of collaborating on this project." She continued, "Because the renovation work came in under budget, the surplus contributed to our ability to purchase a small bucket truck. We never dreamed at the time how essential it would become."

This was a surprise to Gail and to me. We were delighted to learn that our gift had also helped with the post-Katrina cleanup and Audubon Park's restoration.

When Laurie finished, I stepped forward to say a few prepared words, then surprised myself by continuing, in a personal ramble that I'd not thought about in advance: "Our family was founded by two devout young Jews from Europe over a hundred and fifty years ago. We flourished into a large clan. Now we are no longer concentrated in New Orleans or in any single location. In fact, we are no longer even primarily Jewish. Yet New Orleans is our home, the place the family began. Gail and I planned this memorial before Katrina. We wanted to leave some tracks in the sand. This was before we knew that so many families from all over the city would be dispersed and perhaps never return. We mourn for everyone who has been uprooted; and we celebrate the Wolf, Godchaux, and Weis contributions to New Orleans."

After the ribbon cutting, everyone gathered around the bronze dedication plaque embedded in the newly finished concrete floor of the pavilion. Phelan had designed the circular image, sixteen inches in diameter, which depicted a massive oak tree like the one I used to swing under at the end of Brockenbraugh Court, and like the ones that graced Audobon Park. At the roots, raised letters spelled out ancestral family names. Each person present at the dedication was married to or a direct descendant of one of those founders. Embedded within the upper branches and leaves were names—Hawkins, Lewis, Wolf, Nykamp—Gail's descendants and mine. The text in the center said:

> In memory of
> The Wolf Family.
> To generations past and in
> hope that future generations
> enjoy Audubon Park as
> much as we do.
> Gail and Harvey Lewis
> Peter M. Wolf

I had found a modest way to memorialize our past and to anchor it, as cultures had done forever, in a symbolic structure on sacred ground. I felt suffused by an inner calm and deep satisfaction.

At the same time, I felt a surge of loss, but not loss alone. This dedication weekend had somehow liberated me from needing either to romanticize our history or to rebel against my past. Forty years after I'd gone away from New Orleans, my ravaged home had given me new energy and hope.

"Let's go, Dad," Phelan whispered, snapping me out of my reverie as I stared at the little bronze emblem. "We're all headed to Gail and Harvey's for supper."

Acknowledgments

I am grateful to a collection of individuals who helped in a variety of essential ways.

To Christopher Lehmann-Haupt, who believed in this book from the beginning. I am deeply indebted for his courageous championing of the manuscript and for his skillful and perceptive editing. Christopher's probing queries forced me to reconsider, cut, review, and sometimes rewrite in places I'd never have noticed needed more work. To his wider view of the potential in this work than I originally imagined, I owe a much-improved book.

To Delphinium Books founders Cecile Engel and Lori Milken, who are committed to publishing original voices, to recognizing excellence in writing, and to bringing that work to public attention, I am honored to have this manuscript published by them.

To Tom Wallace for his enthusiasm for this project from early days, his follow-up labor on its behalf, his advice about structure of the work, as well as his detailed comments from both France and New York. Tom has created a distinguished career as both an editor and an agent. I count myself fortunate to have appealed to his experienced judgment.

To Jerrilynn Dodds for her ongoing passion for this project. During early drafts, as she read and critiqued the manuscript, Jerri offered imaginative suggestions (particularly for the Paris chapter) and valuable critical evaluation.

To Ann Holcomb for her many hours of thoughtful labor, and her remarkable patience and skill in the initial editing of a much longer, very early version of this book. Ann challenged me to think more clearly as the work began to evolve.

To Gerald Jonas for editorial advice and constructive criticism all along the way, and as an invaluable source of inspiring confidence.

To Bud Trillin for years of fun together and his gracious Foreword.

To William Zinsser, one of the great storytellers and stellar narrative writers, for his own writings; his inspiring teaching about writing, which has been so helpful to me; and his advocacy of this project.

To Gail and Harvey Lewis for careful reading, fact-checking, family-emotional-situation reality checks, and rewrite suggestions, particularly with the chapters related to New Orleans.

To Sue Shapiro and members of her writers group for their critiques of and enthusiasm for first drafts of several short stories that became the basis of this memoir.

In the protected confines of our writers' workshop, to Marilyn Berkman, Patrick Burhenne, Lance Contrucci, Judy D'Mello, Janet Gilman, Ruth Gruber, Gerald Jonas, Roz Lacks, Sylvie Reice, and Doris Vallejo for both general and detailed critiques in deeply appreciated fearless discussion.

To Sara Bradford, development coordinator at the Audubon Nature Institute in New Orleans, my gratitude for assistance with both documentary and visual research.

To Ellen R. Feldman and Tom Pitoniak, whose detailed copyediting, fact-checking, and insightful comments helped to create a more accurate and more readable book.

To Joseph Olshan, whose editorial suggestions expanded the reach and deepened certain themes in this memoir.

To Carl Lennertz, for his much-appreciated expert assistance and advice with marketing and publicity.

To Greg Mortimer for his skilled design and patience throughout this process.

To Wendy Wolf and Hugh van Dusen, who with tireless good

humor over too many years explained to me the arcane ways of the publishing industry so that my impatience might be contained.

To Cornelia Foss for her generous gift of the author's photograph on the jacket.

Close friends and family members who read specific chapters or helped with memory checks, documentation, advice, and editorial suggestions to whom I'm indebted include Betsy Stirratt Aubrey, Peggy Polikoff Bradt, David Calleo, Alessandra Cantey, Henry S. F. Cooper Jr., Louise and Malcolm Elsoffer, Martin L. C. Feldman, Stephen Friedlaender, Joseph E. Friend, Nancy Lewis Hawkins, Catherine C. Kahn, Herman S. Kohlmeyer Jr., Aniik Libby, Kathleen Lingo, Peter Mayerson, Harry New III, Stephen Parks, Sarah Peter, Stephen Sontheimer, Jean Strouse, Calvin M. Trillin, and Catherine Cornay Wolf.

Published and unpublished work of many sorts aided my recall and added to what I'd never known. Special gratitude is extended to Irwin Lachoff and Catherine C. Kahn for their concise review of New Orleans Jewish religious civic and cultural heritage, published in 2005 as *Images of America: The Jewish Community of New Orleans.* For an impassioned, scientific account of what really happened in Hurricane Katrina and its immediate aftermath, there is no better source than *The Storm*, published in 2006 by Ivor van Heerden and Mike Bryan.

Index